Sarah Goodwin graduated from Bath Spa with an MA in Creative Writing. She now lives in rural Hertfordshire with her family. *The 13th Girl* is her second novel.

Also by Sarah Goodwin:

Stranded

THE 13th GIRL

SARAH GOODWIN

avon.

Published by AVON
A division of HarperCollins*Publishers* Ltd
1 London Bridge Street
London SE1 9GF

www.harpercollins.co.uk

HarperCollins*Publishers*
1st Floor, Watermarque Building, Ringsend Road
Dublin 4, Ireland

A Paperback Original 2022

1

First published in Great Britain by HarperCollins*Publishers* 2022

A catalogue copy of this book is available from the British Library.

ISBN: 978-0-00-846739-5

Typeset in Sabon LT Std by Palimpsest Book Production Limited,
Falkirk, Stirlingshire

Printed and Bound in the UK using
100% Renewable Electricity at CPI Group (UK) Ltd

MIX
Paper from
responsible sources
FSC™ C007454

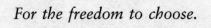

For the freedom to choose.

Prologue

I *was hiding under a droopy tree so Millie and the others wouldn't see me. I knew she didn't want me at her birthday party. The whole class had been invited but I still felt like I shouldn't be there. Like no one wanted me there.*

Everyone started playing 'It' but after a bit, I noticed no one was chasing me. I stood still and Penny didn't tag me. She just ran past like I wasn't there. So I stopped playing and went off by myself in the park. They had the whole park booked for the party so there was no one else around. It was weird to see it so empty.

The others went off on a treasure hunt for fairy figures hidden in the trees and bushes. I wanted to find one. I'd actually seen one earlier under a rosebush and it was very pretty, all covered in glitter.

When the others came too close to my hiding spot I moved on to the pond to look for ducks or that ugly swan, all grey and losing its feathers. But the pond was flat and quiet. Not even one of those black moorhens was hopping through the reeds. I kicked a stone into the water and wished I could have stayed home to watch The Moomins.

'Are you feeding the ducks?'

1

I looked up and there was a lady standing behind me. She didn't look like one of the mums at the party. She didn't look like any mum I'd ever seen. She was wearing a funny, colourful skirt that dipped up and down at the bottom. Her hair was all plaited and twisted and covered in little beads and charms and things. She looks like one of the fairy figures. She even had glitter on her eyelids.

I shook my head, too shy to say anything.

She smiled at me, blue eyes sparkling. 'No ducks out today? I saw a nest actually, with ducklings in it. Do you want to see?'

I nodded and she reached for my hand. Her nails were painted pink and she had on lots of shiny rings. Big and sparkly like the plastic jewellery above the magazines in the corner shop, but real. She walked me around to the other side of the pond, where the ground was wet and the reeds were tall. There was no path. I started to worry about my shoes getting ruined.

'Over there.' She kneeled and pointed at the rushes. 'Can you see?'

I leaned forward, trying not to fall in. I couldn't see anything and was about to tell her so when she fished a bar of chocolate out of her pocket and handed it to me.

'You didn't look like you were having much fun back there. Are you with the birthday party?'

I nodded, opening the chocolate, suddenly aware of how hungry I'd gotten whilst hiding. She glanced back the way we'd come, frowning.

'Do you want to come and do something fun with me instead?' she asked.

I felt a bit uneasy. I'd get in trouble if I wasn't ready when Mum came to get me. 'Mum said to stay in the park so she can find me on her way back from work.'

'Do you want to stay at the park?'

2

I wasn't used to being asked what I wanted, so I just answered without thinking.

'Not really.'

'That's not very fair then, is it? You being stuck here when you don't want to be. Does your mum make you do a lot of things you don't want to do? Mine always did. It was always "go to school", "pull up your socks", "get to bed" or "go down the shop" with her.'

I nodded, laughing at the funny voice she did, which sounded just like my mum when she was in a mood.

'Now though, I don't have to listen to her. I can do what I want and I live in a house with no rules and no bedtime and as much chocolate as I want. Do you want to see it?'

This time I nodded right away. She took my hand and led me off through the trees.

Chapter One

As soon as I got in from the shops I stowed my bag and hurried to the kitchen. There was, reassuringly, no smell of burning.

I'd only realised once I put the beef joint in that I hadn't replaced the wine I bought to go with it. Marshal said it wasn't the right kind and I wanted to impress, make it look like I knew what I was doing. I hadn't managed to find any goose fat for the roast potatoes either, which was why I just slogged all the way to the town centre to get it from Waitrose. I would have managed with sunflower oil, but Marshal looked so disappointed when I suggested that.

The idea to host Sunday lunch was Marshal's. A surprise for me, he'd said. He'd visited Crossley Court – his ancestral home – last weekend and returned having invited his parents. We never had Sunday lunch, or at least, not a roast. It was normally our day for food shopping and having eggs on toast afterwards. I'd never cooked a full-on roast before. Certainly not for his parents. They were lovely to me but his dad was still an MP and his mother, Enid, a columnist for some posh magazine which you basically had to have a peerage to subscribe to. They had a professional chef on staff at Crossley. I barely had a C in Food Technology.

'Please can we go out?' I asked Marshal when he broke the news.

'But they really want to see what we've done with the house. I thought you'd want to show it off. Aren't you proud of it?'

'I do and I am. It's just . . . I don't want them to be disappointed.'

'Why would they be disappointed to spend an afternoon with their charming daughter-in-law? You're family,' Marshal said, kissing me on the forehead. 'Anyway, I'll be here so you know just how to get it right.'

To him, it was a family lunch. To me it was the first family get-together in our new home, with his parents, who just happened to be insanely wealthy and featured weekly in several national papers.

So I was already nervous and then Marshal waited until last night to drop the bombshell that he had to play golf on Sunday morning. It was a networking thing with one of his colleagues on the council and someone from a building firm. I did ask if he could cancel it but he pulled a face and asked if that was really what I wanted. He also casually asked what I had planned for dessert, which I didn't know was expected. He said he might be able to go out of his way and pick something up.

I started preparing the potatoes, checking the three separate recipes I'd printed out for all the tips and tricks they had to offer. The smell of the roasting beef was making me nauseous, so much so that I had to open a window. It was strange. I liked my steaks rare, even blue if I could find somewhere that would serve it. Marshal liked to joke every time that the waiter should 'just wipe its backside and put it on a plate, still mooing'. The sight and smell of meat never bothered me. Yet now I was struggling not to retch, struggling and failing.

I made it to the cloakroom just in time. Afterwards, I rested my sweaty face against the cool tile of the wall. Fuck's sake. Today of all days. When I could manage it I stood up and opened the medicine cabinet, rinsed my mouth and took a seasickness pill in case it helped. The smell of beef was still wafting through the house, turning my stomach.

My eyes landed on the box of tampons as I replaced the pills. I froze. No. No, that could not be it. I pulled out my phone in a panic and checked my calendar app. The little red paintbrush sticker didn't appear on the current month. I scrolled back, counted forwards.

I hadn't had a period in over a month. Even though, two weeks ago, I ended my pack of the pill and took the placebos. I was meant to get it then but there had only been some spotting. I just went on to the next pack, thinking it was a light one. How could I have let it slip my mind? I just forgot about it in favour of obsessing over recipes and gravy hacks.

I looked into my own frightened eyes, reflected back at me from the medicine cabinet. Marshal and I hadn't really talked about kids. Not since he casually mentioned on our honeymoon that I could stop taking the pill and I laughed and said it was a bit soon. So I just kept taking it, thinking maybe one day . . .

I dreaded it coming up again to be honest. He was the kind of sweet, simple guy who just assumed everyone wanted to get married and start a family, which I did, totally. I just wanted to wait for a while. Until . . . well, until it felt right. Until I was ready.

To be honest, I still didn't think I deserved him or the life we had together. Not after what I'd come from. Not when I was hiding it all from him. My past, my family history.

It had been a moment of weakness, letting Marshal into my life. I met him at a fundraising fair for the hospital. I was a volunteer from the back office and he was there to shake hands and give a speech. I bumped into him, spilled his wine all over me, and was apologising when he asked me out for dinner after the event. I was too surprised to say no. He was interesting to talk to, considerate and sweet. But it was the way he left space for me that had me agreeing to a second date. He let me offer to pay for my meal, didn't try to dissuade me from taking the bus home. He asked if he could kiss me goodnight. He was careful and respectful and I wanted more than anything to spend more time in his gentle company.

Somehow it got out of hand. I never meant to get serious but suddenly I couldn't imagine losing him, being alone again. So we got married. Even after I found out he was one of *those* Townsends. Even after I realised what a risk I was taking, making myself so visible, so vulnerable as to need another person so much.

I grabbed my handbag and hurried to the corner shop. With two pregnancy tests in my coat pocket, I came back and shut myself in the cloakroom. After using both I sat and waited for the results, spraying eau de toilette to cover the smell of roast beef that was still making my stomach churn.

Marriage was one thing. I managed to convince myself that I was safe with Marshal. That, even if I was in too deep now to tell him about my past, we could still be together. I could still make him happy. I worked so hard at it, reading his moods, his needs, soothing his temper and making him laugh when he was stressed.

But a child? How could I create a whole new person, just to lie to them? How could I be a good mother when I never knew one? If I was being honest with myself, I never even knew how to be a kid. So how could I possibly raise one? The thought of heaping my issues on an innocent baby, the fear that looking at them might remind me more clearly of things I wanted to forget, scared the shit out of me. How could I make an innocent child live with that?

I checked the tests, hoping against hope for a negative. One was inconclusive, the other positive. I looked down at the little symbol, feeling so much that I couldn't tell what my reaction really was. Fear? Guilt? Horror? Need? Heartbreak? Love? It was all whirling too fast to tell.

What was I going to do? What could I do? The weight of every lie and half-truth I'd told was pressing down on me. There was no way out. No way through. I couldn't tell Marshal about any of my worries without first admitting that I'd lied to him, without telling him about the mess my childhood had been.

I began to cry, hating myself – for not being happy, for not seeing this coming, for lying because I was too scared of losing the only good person I ever knew, the only person who would ever love me.

The front door opened and I heard Marshal's golf bag trundling along the hall.

'Lucy? You'll never believe . . . Luce?'

He must have wandered into the empty kitchen. I heard him go to the lounge, then call up the stairs.

'Luce? Where are you?'

'In here,' I called, wishing he would have just stayed away for a few more minutes. I needed time to think and I couldn't be the Lucy I needed to be with him there. The real me. With him I wanted to be the normal Lucy, a wife pregnant with her first baby. Happy and without even the tiniest doubt in her mind.

'You all right?' he asked through the door. 'Do you need anything?'

'No. Just a bit under the weather, but I'm OK now.' I shoved the two tests into a box and into my pocket, then pressed some wet tissue to my eyes to get rid of the puffiness. I opened the door and smiled.

'How was golf?'

'Bloody boring – because, you know, it was golf – but productive. I'm so sorry I couldn't be here to help, but I did drive by the patisserie on the hill to buy something for dessert.'

'You're a lifesaver,' I said. 'Bear with me, I've got roasties to put on. I hurried to the kitchen where my spuds had gone past parboiled and were now just plain mushy. Only an hour ago that had been the biggest issue on my mind.

'Luce?' I heard Marshal come in behind me.

'Mmm? Bugger!' I snatched my hand back from the hot water splashing out of the colander and sucked the burn. I heard him sigh. He hated it when I swore. I turned around and froze, spotting the box in Marshal's hand. The one from the second test, which I forgot to pick up off the floor.

'Are you . . .' his ears were pink and he was gesturing at my stomach.

I wanted to say no. I wanted more time to think before I had to start acting the part. I wanted to run away, to hide. I didn't want to look in his eyes and see how much he wanted this.

Trapped, I nodded.

'Oh my God!' He crossed the kitchen and squeezed me into a hug. 'That's amazing news! Did you just find out?'

'Yes, just now,' I said, struggling to find the words. He didn't seem to notice my difficulty.

'Mum and Dad are going to be so pleased!' He checked his watch. 'If I run out now we can surprise them with champagne!'

He bounded off to get his car keys and then came rushing back and kissed me on the cheek.

'You are incredible. You know that?'

10

I forced a smile and he kissed me again before hurrying out to the hall. I heard the front door shut behind him and sagged against the kitchen counter.

Now what the hell was I going to do?

Chapter Two

Enid and Marshal Senior arrived exactly on time. I could have done with longer to prepare myself, but to be honest, I was never going to be ready to tell them about the pregnancy. I wasn't even ready for the pregnancy. Not that it mattered, it was happening either way.

Marshal got the door whilst I hurriedly finished setting the table. We were actually using the dining table for once, instead of the breakfast bar or the living room. I had to find the linen tablecloth and napkin set we were given as a wedding present.

Marshal Senior came in first, booming out a greeting and opening his arms to beckon me in for a kiss on the cheek. I went over, even though I hated being kissed by anyone I wasn't in a relationship with. Especially Marshal's dad, whose strong aftershave always triggered my allergies. But I didn't want to be rude. His dad took me by the shoulder and looked me over.

'You look very pink in the cheeks, Lucy. I hope you've not gone to too much trouble for us?'

'Not at all,' I said, trying to come up with something to say about the food or the wine but unable to think of anything. 'I'll be dishing up soon,' I finished, feeling stupid.

'Glad to hear it. We've been looking forward to this all week, haven't we?' he said to Enid, who was unwinding her silk scarf and draping it on Marshal's hands along with her blazer.

'Oh yes,' she said, coming over and taking my hand to squeeze. 'I love what you've done with the house. So . . . welcoming.'

I took the pause personally. It felt pointed, even though Marshal had made as many decorating decisions as I did. He picked the green for the walls and the wood finish in the hall, whilst I chose the cabinets and surfaces. Well, I picked the ones he said he liked. Still, I felt like I was the one being judged for the overall effect. Something about that 'welcoming' said 'unrefined' or even 'common', to me at least. Marshal didn't seem to notice, or if he did, he wasn't bothered by it.

'Come and have a seat. We'll have some wine before lunch,' he said, ushering them towards the table. I noticed Enid looking doubtfully at the IKEA cushion. She wasn't trying to be unkind, she just noticed things like that. It was her job to assess decor and fashion. Remembering this I glanced down and realised I was wearing mismatched, fluffy socks over my tights. I meant to put heels on before they arrived. Shit.

Marshal brought over the champagne and opened the bottle, pouring a glass for everyone, though he hesitated over mine. He picked his glass up but didn't sit down. His dad looked to him expectantly.

'Are you making an announcement?' he asked, in his usual loud and slightly amused tone. 'Are we in the company of a future mayoral candidate?'

'Not quite,' Marshal said, clearly having fun with the mystery. I felt like jumping up to clap my hand over his mouth. Anything to stop this from going any further.

13

'Lucy and I have an announcement, though it's early days. We've just found out that she's pregnant!'

Enid turned to me, delight all over her normally composed expression. Marshal's dad leaped up and hugged his son.

'Well done!' He pulled back and punched him on the arm like they were rugby teammates. 'About time!'

'How far along are you?' Enid asked.

'Oh . . . I'm not sure. A few weeks,' I said. 'Early days yet.'

'You can never start planning too soon,' she said, taking out a designer leather notebook and silver fountain pen. 'There's the pregnancy announcement, finding the right maternity hospital, then the christening. We'll have to get his name put down for school.'

'I don't think we know which schools we'd pick yet,' I said, half-laughing uncomfortably, 'and we don't know the sex. It could be a girl.'

Although I hoped not. It would be too much like history repeating itself.

'Townsends' firstborn are always sons,' Enid insisted.

'He'll be going to King Edward's of course. Like his father and his grandfather,' Marshal Senior boomed, interrupting her.

I let them carry on. I suppose I should have felt indignant at being sidelined but in reality, I felt relieved. It was almost as if it wasn't my baby at all, but theirs. I wouldn't have to be part of anything that came after simply having it. Though of course as soon as I found myself thinking that I felt guilty. What was the matter with me?

In the time since taking the test and Marshal finding out, I decided I had to try and get on board with what was happening. I could do this for Marshal, even if it scared me. I would do it. I just had to push through until everything became perfect. It would be eventually, I was sure of it.

Lunch was almost a success. The beef was cooked through,

14

not rare, and quite tough, but no one said anything about it. Though I noticed Marshal going back for a third pour of gravy to try and lubricate it. The spuds were kind of greasy, but Marshal's dad had a double helping. Everyone had champagne and talked and I just picked at my food and was happy to listen.

When it was time for them to leave, Enid hugged me and promised to take care of the announcement. I wasn't even sure where they were going to announce the pregnancy. The local paper? Her magazine? Some kind of Facebook group for the gentry? I just thanked her and let Marshal's dad kiss my cheek again on his way out.

Once they were gone Marshal loaded the dishwasher, still talking about which preschools might be a good fit. I kept humming in agreement as I cleared the tableware away and put leftovers into plastic boxes. After a longer period of silence I looked up and found him watching me.

'What?' I asked, smiling.

'Nothing . . . just, you seem a bit . . . distracted. Like you weren't listening.'

'Oh, sorry. I was just thinking about work tomorrow.'

'Excited to tell Ellie?'

I nodded. Though I wasn't sure Ellie would be hugely interested. She was my only work friend but she was only just leaving her university years behind, still looking for her real purpose, her goals. If anything she'd probably understand my horror over the apparent ineffectiveness of the pill. I still wasn't sure how it had failed to work. Maybe I forgot to take it one day, though I was usually pretty religious with it. Same time, every day.

That afternoon Marshal had emails to respond to. He got so many messages from locals about the most inane things. Sometimes when he told me about them I wanted to respond myself and ask them to get a life. Who cares if someone was turning a local pub into a B&B? It wasn't their business. But Marshal's unending patience and charm was what I loved about him. He always managed to win them over to his way of thinking, no matter how long it took.

I occupied myself in my art room. I'd been neglecting my painting since moving in with Marshal. It was quite ironic really. When I was a struggling student with two jobs I painted all the time, as if I might have a breakdown if I stopped. Now I was living in a gorgeous house with a man I loved, stable, secure, yet I could hardly keep myself focused on a project long enough to put pencil to paper. I was too busy decorating, trying to learn to cook, spending evenings in with Marshal on the sofa, going shopping or out for dinner. He wanted to spend every minute he could with me.

The art room was a compromise when I moved in. I didn't want to ditch my old stuff and Marshal didn't want the house looking untidy. So it all went into the spare room. I only really went in there when Marshal was working and I had some time to myself.

Even if I wasn't actually doing anything artistic I liked spending time in my art room. It was a little sanctuary with all my things in it: the easel I dug out of a skip whilst at uni, the big desk splattered with paint, my boxes of expensive pastels, watercolours and oil paints. I'd saved for months to afford some of them. My canvases hung on the walls, thirteen of them from largest to smallest. I liked to emulate illuminated fairy tales: beasts prowling at the edges of the canvas, mermaids lurking in the deep lakes, dragons hoarding their gold coins and jewel beads, towers of the purest ivory with princesses outlined in real gold and princes cradled in their arms daubed with poppy-bright blood.

I looked at them now, holding a glass of wine in one hand. The only glass I would allow myself, hoping it would take the edge off my frayed nerves. Not that a splash of red wine

16

could hope to block out what I was feeling. My emotions were all over the place; anxiety, fear, resentment, self-loathing, panic, anger. I couldn't seem to even them out or even understand where some were coming from.

Part of me wanted to look back, examine the years I'd spent with my own mother. That was where all this was coming from, I was sure. I wanted to understand, to fix whatever was broken in me so I could be the mother I was meant to be, but at the same time I kept pulling back. It was like trying to sink a needle into my own fingertip. As much as I psyched myself up to do it, my body's protective instincts wouldn't let me follow through.

I wondered if Carmen, my latest therapist, could help me break through that block. She was an expert in childhood trauma. She'd given me some good advice in the past few months.

'The mind won't give until it's ready,' Carmen had said in one of our sessions. 'You can't force it to reveal its secrets, the choice isn't up to you.'

I'd nodded along, but inside I felt unsettled. I wanted to ask if the reverse could be true; for me to be desperate for those things to remain hidden, but for my mind to reveal them anyway.

If I had it my way, I'd never learn what it was my mind was protecting me from.

Chapter Three

In my dreams I returned to the manor.

In the weeks after finding out I was pregnant, it seemed I couldn't stay away. My mind kept poking away at the sore spot in my memory, keeping it raw and painful.

Each dream was the same. It was deep winter, the night everything went wrong. Snow covered the ground and weighed down the trees, frosting the redbrick building like a Christmas cake. With ivy crawling up the side and lights shining in the leaded windows, it could have been a picture on a greetings card. Only the smell of smoke in the air broke the peaceful illusion. It was not the throaty waft of wood smoke but a toxic black stream reeking of melted plastic, vinyl and polystyrene. The light was not a lamp, but a flickering, hungry flame.

I was standing barefoot in the snow. How had I come to be there, so far from the house without shoes? Looking down I saw that I was wearing only a cotton gown. A nightdress?

The manor seemed so large that it blotted out the surrounding hills. I was a child looking up at it. Heat flowed from it like a physical force. It pushed me back, yet kept me rooted to the spot. I could hear each sound magnified, the ice and snow sizzling into the fire, the screaming.

Glass burst overhead and the sounds grew even louder. I had my hands over my ears, scrunched my eyes shut, but I couldn't keep myself from seeing. I was outside my younger self, stepping back. Remembering that moment from a thousand bad dreams. The arms at the window clawing at the frame, the black shape plummeting to the ground like a comet and hissing into the snow. The blood.

Through the cries and shrieks of those in the fire I could hear something else, sirens on the wind. People coming. I felt both the relief of my adult self, and a former childish fear of outsiders, invaders.

I looked at the manor and it seemed to sag, the roof bending inwards. It was all I'd ever known, burning right in front of me.

The world was ending.

I woke with a start, cold sweat sticking the sheets to my skin. My mouth was dry, filled with the nightmare of smoke and ashes. I stayed completely still, controlling my breathing, feeling as if I was being watched, that post-nightmare, monster-in-the-room feeling. I told myself it was just a dream. A half-imagined memory of another time that couldn't hurt me anymore. I hadn't been that girl for a long time.

Marshal was already awake and out of bed. His side of the king-size mattress cool, the white sheets pushed back. I could hear him downstairs and sighed. I was meant to be up already, making the coffee. Marshal had trouble with the machine. I could hear him banging around, trying to slot the components together. Then the hissing and spitting of the fresh brew. The sound like icicles plunging into a fire.

I pushed the thought away and was about to roll out of

bed when the door opened a crack. Marshal's head appeared in the gap, the scent of coffee wafting in around him.

'Luce? Are you awake?'

'Yes,' I said, sitting up.

'I think I got the machine going. Sorry if it's mud that comes out though.'

'It'll be fine,' I assured him.

The rest of his rugby-ready body came around the door. He looked so strange crammed into a suit. Like a boy wearing his dad's clothes. No matter how many times I saw him in one it didn't get less surprising to me. Even at our wedding it made me want to laugh. Marshal belonged in a polo shirt and jeans. It was his natural state.

He came to sit on the edge of the bed. I was desperate for a coffee. Decaf naturally. Everything was decaf now, or non-alcoholic, enriched with folic acid and calcium. I had no idea what folic acid even was. Marshal probably did. He'd thrown himself into baby preparation like a little kid trying to convince their parents they were ready for the responsibility of a pet. He had all the books, a car seat on the way, vitamins and safety gadgets already cluttering the kitchen. I tried to find it sweet, but sometimes I felt irritation creeping in. Usually when he pointed out that what I was about to eat or drink was bad for the baby, or asking if I wanted to still be burning the baby weight off when they were starting school.

'What time are you due in?' he asked.

'Not till ten.'

'Lucky. I've got a meeting in . . . half an hour.' He sighed. 'I'm not even a hundred percent sure what it's meant to be about. Something to do with parking.'

'That's what you always guess.'

'Because it's always about parking. This wretched town doesn't have enough. We could pave over the entire waterfront – hell, the Avon – and Susan Smedley from St Philip's would

20

still be up my arse about having to walk four feet too far to Argos.'

I laughed. Marshal – a member of Bristol City Council – seemed to spend most of his time wishing he wasn't. He only went for it because his dad wanted him to. It was supposed to be a 'stepping stone' to greater things in politics. Marshal often called it a 'slippery slope' into boredom-induced alcoholism.

I, on the other hand, worked in the back office of the largest hospital in Bristol. It was the first fulltime job I'd landed after dropping out of university midway through my art degree and, honestly, I think of the two of us I enjoyed my work more. Marshal loved that I worked there; it was apparently 'good optics' to be in the public sector, whatever that meant. Though since the wedding he had asked once or twice if I really wanted to keep working there. He was earning such good money compared to me after all. He was already hinting that after the baby was born I'd probably want to be at home, managing things.

I liked my job because it was quiet and dull. Most of my time was spent filing out of date personnel records on my own in a tiny annexe. I got through three audiobooks a week, on average. It was meditative, simple. The idea was just to have something to pay the bills whilst I carried on painting. Not that I'd been doing much of that since moving in with Marshal.

It was hard to know why I'd gradually stopped going into the art room. I lacked focus, couldn't finish projects or get concrete sketches down. There were also all the social commitments with Marshal and his family – parties, charity events, the wedding of a minor royal who happened to be a third cousin. They all took a lot of preparation and worry and I didn't want to stain my nails with paint, get charcoal on my clothes or go around smelling of turps, which Marshal said gave him a headache so bad that even after two showers he still wouldn't so much as hug me.

But, if I was being honest with myself, those were excuses. I didn't want to paint because my work was where I could let my emotions take hold of me, and since meeting Marshal, I was afraid to let that happen, afraid of what might bubble to the surface from the past.

'What are you thinking about?' Marshal asked, stroking my hair.

'Just . . . thinking I should use the art room more, or I'll get out of practice.'

'Oh . . .' He pulled back a little and I instantly felt like I'd said something wrong.

'What?'

'I wanted to talk about this later but, well, I thought you'd have already thought about it to be honest.'

'Thought about . . .'

Marshal shook his head in amusement, smiling slightly. 'Where the baby's going to sleep?'

'Oh,' I said. I felt suddenly very stupid that this hadn't occurred to me already. Obviously the baby would need their own room and we only had the one spare, my room. Even though I'd not been using it much, the idea of it suddenly not being there at all made me feel a bit shaken, as if Marshal just suggested I move out entirely.

'I thought it made sense. Like you said, you haven't been using it much and it's the only spare space we have,' Marshal said. 'Plus, you know, you're going to have much less time to use it once the baby's born.'

'Yeah, I get that. It makes sense,' I said, trying to sound enthusiastic. 'Maybe I can keep some of the stuff in there for when I have a bit of time, or paint with the baby,' I said, thinking that I could park the baby bouncer or whatever in the room whilst I did some painting.

Marshal chuckled. 'If you have a spare second I expect you'll want to sleep or have a shower. But we can get some crayons and poster paints. Kids like that stuff, right? I'm worried about the other stuff not being safe, you know.'

'Right,' I said, thinking of my drawers and drawers of gouache and oil paints. Babies can't be around things like that, toxic paint and turpentine. What was I thinking? When was I going to start thinking of the baby first, like Marshal? When was I going to start feeling anything other than a creeping resentment and low-grade panic?

'Still on for dinner at Crossley this weekend?' Marshal asked.

'Absolutely,' I said, managing a smile to cover my anxious thoughts. 'But please remind me to iron my dress. When I forgot last time your mother looked so put out.'

'I will. Mum's looking forward to it, planned a whole menu to celebrate properly.'

He probably didn't intend to hurt me, but he did. As if my efforts on the weekend we'd revealed our news had been somehow not up to scratch. I'd not seen his parents since then. It had been more than a month now I thought about it. Time was slipping by so quickly.

'Better head off.' He leaned in and kissed me. 'Don't work too hard.'

'You too,' I said.

Once he'd bounded off to the car I went and fetched a coffee to calm myself. I couldn't help wishing it was the real thing, not decaf. Marshal had given up caffeine too, so I wouldn't be tempted. I'd tried to talk him out of it. One of us needed to be awake after all.

Already feeling guilty I wondered if I could grab a cheeky Starbucks on the way to work. I wasn't even that pregnant yet. One macchiato wasn't going to give the thing webbed feet. It didn't even have feet yet. Besides, a double dose of caffeine would help part the fogginess in my brain, chase away that last hint of anxiety brought on by the dream.

That dream was the worst memento I had of that time in my life. It wasn't even a true memory. It was just a nightmare probably inspired by the things my social worker had told me. She'd spoken about the fire, how they'd found me outside all by myself. It was like a fairy tale, the girl in the snow and the tower that burned.

Aside from that dream I had little recollection of anything that came before. Not in concrete, real memories anyway. My real, continuous memories began at age seven. After my rescue. My social worker always said it was probably for the best, that some things were best left behind. Though she never said what things those might be.

When I finally got up to get ready I stared at myself in the en-suite mirror. It was my own little bathroom, where I could have all my 'girl stuff' out. Though most of it was stuff Enid had bought for me or recommended to Marshal – hair products, straighteners, a wax warmer and makeup in neutrals. My days of bohemian, unshaven legs were behind me now, as were the bold eye looks I'd experimented with in uni.

Tacked up on the mirror were the affirmations I was working on for my therapist, Carmen.

'I am past the past,' I said, glaring into my own grey eyes. 'I am not my trauma. I am a warrior and a survivor.' I didn't look much like a warrior in my rosebud speckled pyjama set, another gift from Enid.

As usual, the final phrase 'I am blessed and favoured' stuck in my throat. It bothered me, made me feel sick and twisty inside. I had no idea why. After a few moments of looking at it I unstuck it from the mirror, crumpled it and threw it into the toilet.

I hadn't told Carmen about the new worries, about the baby. I hadn't told anyone I was pregnant yet, aside from Marshal and his family. I'd have to say something at work; they'd probably ask why I was cancelling my leave. I had two weeks booked off for next month. Marshal and I were planning a trip to Amsterdam, to see the Van Gogh Museum, then to Prague for the Mucha Museum before heading to Paris. Now Marshal was too worried about me flying, though I'd googled it and it was apparently safe. Still, I supposed he was right about all the stress and walking taking a toll. I looked to him for how to behave about the baby, trying to mirror his concerns as my own so he wouldn't know how deficient I was in motherly love.

I was, however, unhappy about missing the trip. It would have been my first time abroad. I was never able to afford it before, and we had to cancel our honeymoon last minute because Marshal was needed at work over some kind of community protest. We went to Cornwall in the end, which was lovely, but my heart was set on the Louvre. I'd been longing to go for years, ever since I saw pictures of it at school. Not just there, but the museums in Germany, Spain, India, Transylvania and Russia. I wanted to see the art there, soak up their fairy tales and folk stories. I was hungry for new memories, new people and places. Marshal laughed when I told him that, called me his little nomad. It was true, I'd lived all over the country, bounced from foster home to foster home. But it had made me shiver to hear it from his lips. It made me sound like my mother, rootless and free-wheeling, an outsider to normal life.

I ran the straighteners over my hair. When I left it curly Marshal said I looked like Little Orphan Annie. Between the freckles and my height I still got IDed at twenty-seven. It was hideously embarrassing, especially when out with

Marshal. He was only a few years older but people looked at him like he was a child snatcher. I'd started trying to dress older to make us look the same age, wearing clothes recommended by Enid instead of my previous wardrobe of holey jumpers in bright colours and jeans with patches and paint on them. With straightened hair, a pair of earrings and my work blouse on I looked more adult-like, though it was the dark circles under my eyes that really sold it. The nightmares had been chipping away at my rest for weeks now.

I walked into town as always, letting the familiar sights erase any lingering memories of the manor. When I stopped for my illicit coffee I chickened out, ordered decaf. I also threw the receipt away at the counter; the last thing I wanted was Marshal finding that. He'd only assume I'd been breaking the rules and get upset. Then I zoned out, only called back to reality by someone touching my arm.

'You were miles away,' Ellie laughed. 'Anywhere nice?'

'Nicer than a Monday morning here,' I said.

'Got that right,' she said, rolling her eyes. 'I swear we were here five minutes ago.'

Ellie had joined the admin team six months ago in HR, but she filled in all over the hospital as needed. She was just out of university but was an older student who'd taken a gap year both before and after her course, so we were similar in age. Yet very different. She had no filter and a schoolgirl sense of humour, but was very sensitive. I'd found her crying in the toilets after being chewed out by one of the ironclad bitches who served as secretaries to the consultants. She quickly became my best work friend. In truth, my best friend, period. The people I'd known from uni were into late nights in pubs, having earnest conversations about post-modernism and smoking joints. Marshal didn't like me walking through Bristol at night and smelling of weed was not acceptable as a council member's wife. So meeting up with them was a bit complicated. Outside of work I only really met Marshal's friends and their wives or girlfriends. They were nothing like Ellie. Although I had to pretend with everyone, I felt most like myself with her.

We had a laugh together about her ex-boyfriends, sent memes back and forth on Instagram. She understood what it was like to not fit in and I loved her stories about South America, where she lived for a year. Though I suspected these stories were highly embellished. She also told me all about her shitty stepmother and how she was more or less black-balled from going home. I told her about growing up in care. We shared more things than work friends usually do. It was nice.

She was as usual layered in jewellery from Urban Outfitters, a jumble of earrings on her lobes. Over the same kind of plain black trousers I was wearing she had on a floaty paisley blouse. Through it I could see one of her tattoos, a Celtic knot on her arm. I envied her the ability to look so cool and comfortable in her skin. Beside her I still looked like a kid wearing her gran's blouse.

I waited whilst she ordered a green tea and a brownie and then we walked together up the road towards the admin block. It was as ugly and unairconditioned as every other ancient part of the hospital no patient would ever see. At least in records I was spared the pigeons that lived in the HR roof. Ellie wasn't so lucky.

'Fancy bunking off for a coffee later?' she asked. It was sort of a Friday tradition, sneaking off to the café at the back of the hospital for half an hour. We'd not done it on a Monday before though.

'You sure?' I asked.

'Yeah, I've got a bastard of a hangover and I'll need perking up. Say around three?'

'Sure,' I said, not wanting to be so terminally uncool as to worry about getting caught.

'Ace. I'm going to miss you when you're off travelling,' she said, pulling a face. 'I'll have to save up all my gossip for when you're back.'

'Oh.' I bit my lip and shook my head. 'We're not going now. I'm um . . .' I gestured to my stomach.

'Oh my God!' Ellie's eyes widened and she grabbed my free hand, squeezing. 'How many weeks? Why'd you not say! But,' her excitement dimmed, like a bulb slowly dying, 'you were really excited about that trip. You could still go, right? Isn't art and stuff meant to make your baby smarter? Or is that just music?'

I laughed. 'I don't see how it could benefit from me looking at paintings. But, no, it's too stressful doing all that travel, and besides it was an expensive trip. We're using the money to kit out the nursery.'

'Oh,' Ellie said, then brightened again. 'Bet you'll do a great job on that. You could do a mural! What about something like that painting you gave me – Little Red Riding Hood and the great big wolf.'

'I could do,' I said, knowing that if I did it would have to be toned down considerably. There were several wolves in Ellie's painting, all with long fangs and wild, luminous eyes. Little Red herself was very small indeed, like a rosebud surrounded by all that darkness. It was one of the last paintings I actually finished.

'I'm late. Let's chat about it over coffee, OK?' I said.

'Cool. I can tell you all about my new side hustle,' she said with a grin. 'Reckon if all goes well I can quit this place in a month.'

'Side hustle?' I felt a stab of alarm at the thought of losing her.

'Might finally get me away from the old cows in the office.

Not that it's too bad this morning. I'm covering reception. But still, hopefully soon I won't need this place at all. Been going a few months but it's finally paying off.' She squeezed my shoulders and air kissed me. 'Congrats again! Laters!'

We parted ways and I let myself into the annexe with my fob. It was a little-used side door that shared an alley with the mortuary. Faster than going in through the main entrance. Inside was gloomy and smelled of damp. Half the fluorescents were blown or hardly giving off light. The cleaners rarely came to this part of the HR complex and the silent space smelled of burning dust, long-stored paper and instant coffee.

I dumped my bag on my little desk with its ancient PC and surveyed my to-do list. I'd written it on Friday in an optimistic attempt to get a head start on the week. Just looking at it made me feel tired. I already wanted another coffee and I'd barely finished my first.

With my phone in my pocket I went to the archive room and started to sort last week's files into alphabetical order. We had around two hundred files a week – people leaving or moving to new jobs, retirings, firings and staff moving to other trusts. All of the files chugged through the criminally outdated analogue filing system, all the way down to me.

I popped on an audiobook and got on with it. I'd only been sorting for around twenty minutes when my phone rang, interrupting the soporific narration. It was Ellie.

'Bit early for our coffee break,' I said, on picking up.

'Luce, what's your maiden name?' Ellie asked.

'Is this another "what character are you" quiz? Because I don't watch half of these shows you know,' I joked.

'No. It's something strange in the local paper.'

I felt my insides clench. 'What kind of weird?'

'Well, it says they've managed to trace a load of people from this weirdo group to jobs in the public sector and how it's a scandal that they're, you know, in local government and the NHS. And it says Lucy Armitage and this hospital so I thought, wouldn't it be weird if that . . .'

'That's me,' I said, my voice coming out all weird and raspy. 'Ellie, I'm Lucy Armitage, or I was.'

'Oh,' she said. 'Well, that's . . . wow, I didn't think it would actually be you. I just thought it would be funny if I called you and . . . shit, Lucy.'

'Which paper?'

'*Herald*.'

'Hold on.' I put her on speaker then googled my maiden name and *The Herald*. The story came up, followed by links to local message boards and news blogs. Then I saw a national newspaper headline which made my chest go tight. Followed by another and another.

MP Daughter-in-Law's Cult Secret

Townsend Family in Commune Fire Scandal

Controversial MP Caught Out by Cult Allegations

MP's Connection to Sex Cult Leader Carlisle Riordan

Those two words dropped through me like stones. Carlisle. Riordan. How long had it been since I last thought of that name? Not since I was seven years old. Yet it had the power to hold me still, paralysed by its strange magic. A magic I didn't fully understand.

'Lucy?' Ellie prompted. 'What's going on?'

'How did they find out about me?' I whispered.

'Luce, what're they saying? What's happening?'

'I can't talk now. I . . . I need to leave . . . to find Marshal. Can you tell Marjorie? Just tell her something. I don't know.'

Ellie rallied. 'I'll tell her you're sick . . . but she'll probably find out if it's in the news.'

I'd cross that bridge when I had to. 'Thanks. I'm sorry I can't explain right now.'

'You can call me later, or text, whatever. Just to let me know you're OK.'

'Thanks, Ellie . . . I will.'

I hung up and shoved the phone in my pocket but it began to ring again right away. This time it was Marshal. My heart flipped when I saw the name come up and I declined automatically. He had to have seen or heard about this, just as Ellie had. What was I going to say?

How the hell did they find out about me?

Chapter Four

I almost ran the last hundred metres to the front door. I didn't stop to breathe and hardly paused to think since declining Marshal's call and bolting from the admin block. Too afraid of being recognised to take the bus, I walked home with my hood up. On the way I sent him a text to say where I was going, to say I would talk there and that I was sorry. I didn't want him going to the hospital looking for me. I turned my phone off, so I had no idea if he was still trying to get hold of me.

I noticed several strange cars parked haphazardly that weren't in the street that morning. As I glanced at them the side door of a van opened and two men with cameras leapt out. Several more came from cars across the road. I searched frantically for my keys and nearly screamed when the front door opened suddenly and Marshal grabbed my arm, dragging me inside. He closed the door behind me and I heard disgruntled voices and more car doors opening. The press had arrived.

Marshal stood in the hallway, tie askew, pink-cheeked and flustered. Lines of stress were clear on his forehead and around his mouth. It pained me to have put them there. I thought of his father and winced. The MP with a former cult member as a daughter-in-law. What was he going to say to that? How many lives did I ruin in one day?

'Lucy, what the fuck is going on?' Marshal asked, still holding my arm tightly. 'I got a call from Dad and he said your picture was online, that the papers are reporting on you. They're saying you were in this . . . sect, as a child. Is that true?'

I nodded, unable to speak for a moment.

'Why didn't you say anything?' Marshal asked, jerking my arm towards him. 'How could you not . . . did you just not trust me or was this some kind of . . . plan, or—'

'No!' It burst out of me, I was so horrified by what he was suggesting. 'No, I never planned any of this. I just didn't know how to tell you. We met and then things moved so fast . . . it just got out of hand. I should have told you, before.'

'Yes, you should have! Jesus, I've been going out of my mind ever since you refused to take my call. Please never do that again,' Marshal exclaimed, finally releasing my arm and throwing his hands up. His suit jacket rucked up and I saw sweat patches on his shirt. He must've been beside himself at the news, stressed out of his mind. Guilt crawled in my stomach.

'Why didn't you tell me?' he asked. 'What have I ever done to make you think you couldn't tell me? We live together, we're married. I trust you. So, why do you not trust me?'

'I just . . . I thought it would change things, if you knew. That you might not be able to see me the same way if you knew about my past,' I said.

'This is the reason you were taken away, wasn't it?' he said. 'Why you were in care.'

I nodded. I'd told him that much, that I was put into foster care at seven and from then on had no contact with anyone from the past. That my family and even family friends were either dead or estranged, which was the truth. I hid the name change from him, even when we got married. To him I had always been Lucy Armitage. Not Lucia Green.

How did the press find me after that change? Perhaps they had someone go through the records, illegally riffling through my paperwork to see who Lucia Green became. It was all out there, a paper trail leading right to me. The legal name change and the social workers' file on me. Why wasn't I more careful? Why didn't the social workers try harder to hide the truth? Probably because they thought no danger could come to me since the fire effectively wiped the cult from existence. They never imagined that the press could be just as dangerous.

I didn't want to lie to Marshal. But I didn't want to lose him either. He was perfect, everything I'd ever dreamed of – kind, considerate, loving. When I told him I grew up in care he just accepted it and gave the subject a wide berth. He assumed, correctly, that it was too painful to talk about.

Meeting Marshal changed my life for the better. Not just in terms of his care and his support, but he also gave me the home I never had before. He was the first person to see me, to love me, and now I'd destroyed his trust in me.

'When I was taken into care,' I began, 'it was because I was rescued from the manor, where the commune was. There was a fire and . . . everyone there died.'

'Is that when your mother . . .'

I swallowed. 'She died in the fire.'

'Jesus. Why didn't you tell me?'

'I couldn't . . . I didn't know how. I still don't.'

He rubbed his hands over his face and sighed. I was hurting him, still.

'I wanted to get through it all, leave it behind,' I said. 'I didn't mean to let it get this far, to lie . . .'

'But you did.'

'I did. I'm sorry.'

'So, what do you remember? What else do I need to know?' Marshal asked bluntly, his eyes shuttered against me. I felt sick.

'I don't remember a lot of it, just . . . moments really.' I didn't want to mention the nightmare and where it came from. The screaming people, trapped by the fire. 'I was only five, I think, when we moved to the manor. I remember bits from before, when we lived in London, just little things. But, after that, there's things I should remember, from when I was older. But I don't,' I said, struggling to stop myself rambling.

'So your mum . . . joined up with them when you were a kid? Why?' Marshal asked, sounding interested despite himself.

I shook my head. 'My mum was a member of Luna Vitae from before I was born. She used to tell me the story of how she found them, over and over. As for why . . . she said she was lonely, pregnant. She was looking for friends.'

Marshal's forehead creased. 'Luna . . . in the paper they said it was called Riordanism?'

My mouth was dry. I desperately wanted to gulp down some water and sit, collect myself. I felt flustered, interrogated.

'That was the name of the man in charge there. Riordan. Carlisle Riordan. But my mother called it Luna Vitae. I don't know why, or what it means. Moon . . . something.'

'Did you not look them up, find out about . . .' He trailed off and sighed in irritation when I shook my head.

'I didn't want to know. There are records out there I suppose, news stuff. I thought about looking into it when I was a teenager but I was already struggling with what I could remember. I didn't want to know anything else. I didn't want to look back.' I sighed and brought my hand up to press my throbbing forehead. There was a pounding in my temples, like a wall being knocked down by a sledge-hammer.

Marshal looked exhausted, annoyed and hurt, but he sighed, clearly trying to rise above it. 'You should rest. Do you need anything? Is the baby all right?'

'I'm OK. I just need some water.' He was already heading for the kitchen. I stood there – guilt like a stone in my belly – and heard the fridge open. He returned with a chilled glass bottle. I took it and went into the living room, taking a seat on the wide velvet sofa. Behind it the heavy curtains were drawn. At least no camera lenses could peek through. We could still hear them out there though.

'How did the papers find you?' Marshal asked. 'They said on the news you were called Lucretia or . . .'

'Lucia,' I said, the word like bile in my mouth. 'I was. They changed it when I was taken into care. But it's all on file somewhere. I even had to give it when I did my criminal record check for the hospital. I don't know if it's legal, but if they went looking for my old name, they could easily find the documentation of the change.'

The phone in the hall began to ring. 'That's probably Dad. I said I'd call him with an update. We need to manage this . . . mess.'

Another sharp sting of guilt. 'I'm sorry for not saying anything sooner. I wanted to but I was scared and then we'd been together for too long and . . . I couldn't bring myself to tell you.'

'Well . . . we can't change things now, can we? We'll just have to get through this.' He reached for the phone with a bitter shake of his head. 'I'll take it in my office.'

I listened as he padded over the Victorian tile and closed the door to his study. The distant murmuring of the phone call was eclipsed by the sounds from outside. The photographers and press people, how did they find our address so quickly? I let out a sigh. It wasn't exactly a state secret. If they could get to my records to check my name, they could find us. How had I been so stupid? Why did it never cross my mind that someone might go digging for a story? I suppose I thought if I didn't remember, no one else would either, that no one would care because I wasn't important. Stupid. By marrying Marshal I gave them a reason to care. Without him, I was nobody, beneath their interest.

I clenched my hands around the cold bottle of water. What kind of grief was Marshal getting from his father? How would this affect his career? I was so focused on protecting myself I didn't think of him. What kind of a wife was I to hide such huge parts of myself from him? Carmen had told me many times that she could help me tell Marshal about my past, but I'd always been firm. I wasn't willing to open up that box of horrors, not when I didn't know myself what was lurking at the bottom.

What awful things might someone else tell Marshal, tell the world? How could I prevent that if I didn't know the truth about my own past?

I didn't remember much of my time with Luna Vitae, aka 'Riordanism' or 'the Red Manor Cult'. What I had could not be called memories as such. It was like a flipbook of photographs, my mind's eye snapping away like a Polaroid camera. Me running in the woods. Snap. Swimming in a lake. Snap. Dressed in white in the snow. Snap. Stringing glass beads. Snap. Watching incense sticks burn by the window. Snap.

The clearest memories weren't even mine. They weren't even real, just images that formed from the telling and retelling of my mother's rebirth. It was the only memory I really had of her voice, telling that story. The story of Selene and her awakening as a daughter of Luna Vitae. It was her favourite. I heard it more than most children heard the tale of Goldilocks or the Little Red Hen.

Back then her name was Carrie. Carrie Green. She said it like the name belonged to someone else. To me she was always Selene, or Mum. She was born in the late sixties. It might have disappointed her to have missed out on that decade of hippy freedom and ended up an adult in the eighties instead.

The only thing she told me about her childhood – or the only thing I could remember – was that she spent it 'kowtowing to Christ' in Ireland. As a child I thought this weird word had something to do with actual cows. I imagined her having to feed and milk them as part of some sacred duty. I knew her family had been strict. I grew up seeing scars on her back every time she undressed. I remember them more vividly than her face. What had caused them? A belt? A cane?

Her old faith had apparently inspired her to name me for a saint, Saint Lucia. The Latin name for Saint Lucy. Not a terribly lucky name. She'd been blinded and martyred. I was born on her feast day, the thirteenth of December. Friday the Thirteenth. My birth certificate had probably burned up in the manor, but I told my social worker the exact day, as my mother had told it to me.

My mother moved to London to get a job and escape her family. She was quite successful. She must have been quite well off to own her own home in the capital at that age. Even if it wasn't terribly large or well done up. But she never said anything good about London, only that people there were slaves to money, like her dad was to the priests in his church. Even if the women she worked with could buy whatever they wanted, they weren't free. Men were still in control.

She never mentioned any man by name and spoke as if I had no father but had appeared by a miracle, just like Mary's child. I think when I was very young I believed she was my one and only parent. Now I considered myself an orphan. If

I had a father, he did not exist to me, and so he was as good as dead.

Then, the revelation. The beginning of my mother's true life, her true self. She spoke of it reverently. Over time the tale become embroidered and expanded, illuminated and ornamented like the pages of a fairy-tale book. She began the day knowing her life was about to change, though obviously she could have known no such thing. She was on leave to have me and going to yoga lessons to help keep fit. Away from the offices she'd worked so hard in, she had no friends and no purpose. Then at a yoga group she met Celeste McCormack. Her own personal goddess. The magical fairy godmother who changed her whole world.

I suppose she was lonely. I couldn't remember anyone ever visiting us who wasn't Celeste or one of her lookalikes. If my mother had any friends prior to joining Luna Vitae, they weren't around by the time I was old enough to remember their faces. Celeste was everywhere though. I remembered her almost better than my own mother.

Marshal returned to the living room looking more boyish than ever. His thick blonde hair was ruffled from brushing his fingers through it and he had the air of a scolded schoolboy. His father had that effect on him. At dinners with him I felt I was being interviewed for Oxford University, or sentenced by a judge.

'Dad thinks it would be best if we got a statement together, sooner rather than later. The less time the press has to make hay out of this the better.'

It was one of his father's phrases, slightly old-fashioned, down to earth and trustworthy. From Marshal it sounded almost funny, like a bad impression.

'Is that really necessary?' I asked, panicked. 'I mean . . . I know I owe your parents an explanation, but surely all this', I gestured to the drawn curtains, the photographers and press behind them, 'will fade away. Tomorrow's chip paper. All that.'

Marshal looked irritated. 'The thing is . . . Dad's not exactly loved by the press right now. He got a lot of attention online about . . . well, he's expressed some views that got taken wildly out of context and so they'll use any excuse to have another go at him. There's already a hashtag demanding his resignation.'

'But this isn't his fault, it's mine,' I said.

'I know, but they're saying he covered this up, maybe used some of his influence to keep it a secret, further my career. Between that and the other stuff . . .'

'What stuff? What did he say?'

Marshal flushed furiously. 'He made a case for stricter background checks for certain jobs. Talked about, you know, people coming from other countries, hiding their pasts, their criminal records, taking jobs in schools, hospitals . . .' he cleared his throat. 'Of course people jumped up calling him a racist. But it wasn't about race at all. It was about knowing where these people were coming from and if they could be trusted around children, but now . . .'

'Now everyone knows his daughter-in-law lied about her past, and was in a cult.'

Marshal nodded, unable to meet my eyes.

'But I was seven. It wasn't . . . I didn't choose to be there.'

'I know. And that's what we'll be telling everyone. But . . . unfortunately, just because something isn't true doesn't mean it can't gain traction online and take on a life of its own. Especially given that people have already made up their minds to hate Dad, no matter what he does.'

I felt so ashamed of myself that I didn't know where to look. Meeting Marshal's eyes was impossible.

'Does he know how they got hold of my name?' I asked, when I could bear the silence no longer.

'Like they get hold of anything, dug it out of the rubbish. Vultures. That or they paid someone for it. There's always someone willing to be bought,' he said angrily. I'd never seen him so worked up before. 'If he didn't want this to go away quickly, Dad would probably sue the lot of them. Tabloid bastards.'

'Should I change before we go?' I asked, feeling cowed by his anger. I was still in my plain work clothes, not exactly Crossley-ready.

'They're bringing in a team, a stylist.'

'Is that really necessary?' I asked, stunned.

'It's an image thing. Don't worry too much about it,' Marshal said, shrugging as if it was no big deal, which to him it probably wasn't. 'Dad wants everything just so, the right impression, the perfect presentation, you know how he gets.'

I did. Our wedding had been the event of the season after all, out at Crossley Court. Perfect couture, elegant decor. It even snowed. It was Enid's project. I think she'd had the wedding planned for years. I was the last piece of the puzzle. She wasn't pushy of course. She just knew so much more than me about the right way to do things. And I wanted to do things the right way, for Marshal.

Marshal went to change into a fresh suit and tie. Whilst waiting in the hall for him I got a text from Ellie asking how I was. A few minutes later came an email alert from Marjorie, my manager. It was the standard sickness absence email, explaining procedure. At the bottom she added 'Let me know if you require assistance'. For Marjorie that was almost a declaration of undying love. She wasn't known to be expressive or soft in any way. She once told a colleague in floods of tears over her divorce to 'buck her ideas up'.

I was worried about getting back out of the house. The paparazzi, or whatever the term was for them, were still clogging the front walk.

41

Still waiting on Marshal I opened YouTube on my phone and searched for 'Riordanism'. The television news had already picked up the story. The news item came up right away, posted by nearly every major outlet. Clips and longer versions already cropping up on vlog channels. A lot of people had rehashed Marshal Senior's previous gaffes. The criminal-record stuff was only part of it. He had a long career with plenty of opportunities to piss off a lot of people – environmentalists, climate change deniers, feminists, traditionalists, secularists *and* conservative Christians. If there was an issue, he managed to upset those on both sides of it at some point. And I just threw a bucket of fresh chum into the water.

I clicked the top link and watched the news presenter introduce the story. Then several pictures came up, all of them apparently survivors of Riordanism. I only recognised myself. They gave my old name and my married one underneath. The others were older women, some with greying hair. They had either left the cult before the fire, or were from smaller communes away from the manor which had fallen apart without a leader.

The pictures were replaced by others and I saw someone I vaguely remembered. A woman the age my mother would have been, had she lived. She had waist-length hair hennaed red and thick black eyeliner all the way around her pale grey eyes. I knew her. She was one of my mother's friends. What was her name? Penelope? No. Phoebe. A wave of red hair, tinkling bangles and laughter. The scent of wax and coffee. She'd been teaching me something, guiding my hand as she showed me. I played the moment over and over. She showed me . . . how to draw a five-pointed star. To draw it without taking my crayon off the page. I remembered the thick red lines left by the crayon. The way the paper pushed down to the plush carpet underneath, crinkling.

I blinked. Phoebe's picture was whisked away and mine

was shown again, replacing them all. The presenter appeared in front of the picture, taken from the trust website. I was tending a cake stall at the fundraiser, smiling, a fabric rose in my hair. That was the night I met Marshal, the night my life started to change.

'The revelation that MP Marshal Townsend's daughter-in-law was one such cult member has caused outrage amongst many, who have taken this as evidence of a cover-up. Some insinuations are being made about Townsend's own religious affiliations, given his strident opposition to the creation of more church schools, only two years ago. What this means for him in the days to come is uncertain, but it is clear that answers are being demanded, both by his fellow party members and the public.'

I sighed. Yes, answers were definitely being demanded. But I had few to give. I got the feeling, however, that I wouldn't have a choice. The truth was out there now. People had a taste for it and they weren't going to leave me alone in a hurry.

Chapter Five

We braved the cameras outside to get to a car sent by Marshal Senior. Behind the tinted windows I relaxed slightly into the leather interior. Crossley had gates. We'd be fine once we got there. I found myself craving a coffee to keep my mind sharp. Though if anything the caffeine would have made me even more jittery than I already was.

Enid met us in the foyer at Crossley. The large house was outside of Bristol overlooking the Georgian splendour of Bath and its surrounding villages. Ringed by trees and parkland. Inside it was slightly gloomy, to preserve the antique furniture, art and wallpaper. Crossley had the kind of silence only metre-thick sandstone and distance from major roads could buy. The whisper of footsteps on expensive carpet and the sigh of doors kept oiled by staff and money were the exact sounds I associated with privacy. Despite its imposing appearance, I felt calmer there than I had all day. That was until I saw the camera equipment being wheeled around in one of the drawing rooms.

'We're doing a statement here, now?' I asked, utterly terrified. I thought it'd take until tomorrow at least to prepare me.

'Of course. Did Marshal not tell you?' Enid asked. She shot him a despairing look and shook her head, sending her pearls chattering. 'Well, you must see that we need to get ahead of this as soon as possible. It's had quite the airing in the press already.'

'I'm sorry. I didn't mean to—'

She took my hand in her own. It was cool and powdery, more ring than flesh. 'Nothing to be done about it now but weather the storm. But I do hope you've been honest with my son now. We don't want any more surprises, do we?' she said, hand tightening around mine.

'No,' I said, feeling my blouse stick to the nervous sweat on my back. 'No more surprises.'

She released me and accepted a kiss on the cheek from Marshal, then rushed off to corral the stylist. Over her shoulder she instructed Marshal to take me upstairs to the rosewood suite. I'd been to Crossley only a handful of times, and then only in the dining room or the room I changed in for the wedding. Marshal's parents spent more time in London, where they had a luxurious flat close to Parliament. I'd been there more often, to stay after shopping trips with Enid or theatre evenings and restaurant dinners. Comparatively it was a cosy home away from home, though just as secure, with a password-protected garage and front desk security. Marshal Senior had been threatened more than once by more than one group.

'Here we are,' Marshal said, flinging open a door off a corridor lined with dense carpet and stuffed pheasants.

The room was panelled, presumably in rosewood. A four-poster bed draped in soft pink curtains faced the large windows. Settees and couches were arranged in front of the glass, looking down on the lawns below. However, the room was dominated by a marble statue, larger than life, of a woman. She was in a corner, almost a foot taller than me.

Her sightless, white-stone eyes were luminous in the shadows. Her silent judgement reminded me of Enid, something I instantly felt guilty for thinking.

The door opened soundlessly and a young woman in a spotless pair of white jeans and an effortless off-the-shoulder jumper came in. Behind her came two other women in dark outfits, carrying garment bags.

'Mrs Townsend, I'm Poppy and these are the options we've prepared for you,' the stylist said smoothly. Her lackeys unzipped the bags, displaying crisp outfits all featuring high-necked blouses and demure skirts. I suddenly felt very scruffy.

'I'll leave you ladies to it,' Marshal said, giving my hand a squeeze tighter than Enid's and shutting the door behind him.

I surrendered to Poppy and her suggestions. The sooner I got this over with, the better. Whilst one of the women applied makeup and the other tended to my hair, Enid returned with a man in a suit. This was the image consultant retained by her husband, the one who helped get him a photo with a bishop to smooth over the whole 'church school' issue. He was dressed slickly, with a flashy watch and well-styled hair. Slightly older than he was trying to present, with the tell-tale stiffness around the forehead and eyes. Just like Enid, he worshipped at the altar of Botox. With an iPad in hand he went over the statement with me.

'This is the prepared statement which has been approved by myself and Mr Townsend,' he said, meaning Marshal's father. 'We had some party input as well. It's in everyone's interest to correct any assumptions being made as quickly and as decisively as possible.'

The idea that my past had been discussed by other MPs made me instantly nervous.

'At the end we're opening the floor to some questions, as

our focus is the spirit of transparency and prioritising the actions of the press in this matter. It works in our favour to be seen as willing to put all our cards on the table,' he said.

I nodded, earning myself a yank on the hair from the stylist working on me. I winced as the teeth of her comb bit into my scalp.

It was past midday by this point and my stomach was gurgling. The consultant shot me a look. I'd had a banana for breakfast hours ago and desperately needed both caffeine and calories, but I didn't dare ask for anything to eat or drink. I didn't want to be any more of an inconvenience than I already was.

Then the moment I'd been dreading since our arrival came. I was escorted to the press room as if to my execution. It was about a thousand times more intimidating than walking down the same hallway to my wedding. Such a weird echo of that day, when I was so happy and thought I knew what my future would be.

The journalists were sitting on carved chairs from the dining room. The actual conference was held in the drawing room beneath the portraits and gilded heraldry on the ceiling. The message of the room was clear: this family has history, pedigree and money for lots and lots of solicitors. I only hoped it would work. If Marshal's father really didn't want to go the lawsuit route, the threat of it was all we had, all I had.

A bookstand from the library stood in front of the enormous fireplace. A tablet was on it already and I took my place by it, swiping the screen to find the statement ready to go. Marshal stood beside me and his parents took position behind the two of us. Enid placed her hand on my shoulder, briefly squeezing. I glanced back at her – hoping for a bit of reassurance – but she only gave me a steely look. She wanted this over with as much as I did, clearly. But she also didn't want me to fuck up more than I already had. My skin prickled with shame. Whatever relationship I had with my mother-in-law was dead in the water now.

Around the room TV cameras had been set up. Photographers were in place as well, some at the rear of the room, others closer. The chairs were full of journalists. They shifted their Dictaphones and notebooks in their laps, eagerly awaiting the start of the conference. Members of my father-in-law's security staff were spaced out around the edge of the room, almost in the shadows. I took a deep breath. I could do this. I would do this and then the worst of it would be over. Things could start to get back to normal.

'Good afternoon,' I began, glancing up as the consultant recommended. 'Eye contact. Smile, but not too much. Smile *bravely.*' It was gross but he had a point. He was the professional after all, trying to clean up my mess. Cameras flashed intermittently as I continued.

'Today it was made public knowledge that, as a child, I was rescued from the Red Manor Cult. This was not something I expected to be shared without my knowledge or consent. Whilst those close to me', here Marshal took my hand, 'have always known of my difficult past, it is not something I wish to advertise.'

It was a daring deception and I felt all my guilt again over lying to Marshal.

'I am deeply disappointed in the way this has been handled by the press, that I was not consulted or contacted prior to the release of my personal information. I am a private citizen, and using me in an attempt to embarrass my father-in-law, or to create a false narrative, shows a reprehensible disregard for unbiased journalism. This episode speaks to a culture of victim exploitation, and an overall disrespect for survivors of trauma. In the interest of setting the record straight, I will now answer questions about that time, in so far as I am able, given my young age at the time of these horrific events,' I said, too quickly, wishing whoever had written the speech had made it sound less haughty.

I paused and looked up, waiting for that first question. Hands flew up and several people leaped from their seats. It reminded me bizarrely of primary school. The overly eager kids just dying to get the teacher's attention, to be picked to give an answer, their arms almost wrenching from their sockets. Sitting at the back, struggling to keep up, I'd hated them all, just as I hated them now.

'Mrs Townsend, what can you tell us about your time with the cult?'

'I remember very little. As I said, I was seven at the time of my rescue. I do not recall being involved in any religious activities.'

'Can you describe the events leading up to your rescue?'

'There was a fire at the manor,' I said, trying to make my face as blank as possible. 'When the smoke attracted outside attention the authorities came and discovered me, outside in the snow. All the occupants died in the blaze, including my mother.' I kept my replies as dry as possible. The consultant had been very clear. 'They're looking for scandal, for blood, don't give it to them.'

'Are you in contact with any other former members of the cult who were not present at the time of the fire?'

'No. I've had no contact with anyone since the night my mother died.'

'What is your current religious affiliation?' chirped a woman in the back.

'Church of England,' I replied, though in truth I wasn't baptised and only went to church with Marshal's family, for Easter and Christmas. Still, I did go. That counted, surely?

I looked over the sea of faces and waited for another question, feeling for the first time like I was handling this

OK. I could survive this. Then I could make it up to Marshal, somehow.

When the next question came though, I felt it land, hard, against my chest, like a stone or a bullet.

'Mrs Townsend, what do you have to say regarding the fact that your mother, Carrie Ann Green, was a suspect in the disappearances of at least three girls, all under the age of five?'

The room went silent aside from the mechanical lip-smack of cameras as they lapped up the tension. The lights blinded me as flashes rebounded around the room. The supposedly safe and controlled environment, rich in history and authority, seemed to fade away, leaving me unprotected, alone.

The man who asked the question stood at the back of the room. He was balding, wearing a khaki jacket and carrying a large camera. He was looking at me as though he didn't just crack my world apart, as if this was just another day for him, another job to be done.

'Do you have any knowledge about the whereabouts of the three girls, or the numerous others who were thought to have been abducted by members of the Red Manor Cult?' he said, unwavering. As if, like me, he had rehearsed his lines. 'What about the prostitution ring reputedly headed by Carlisle Riordan? Was your mother a participant?'

His words came so quickly yet so clearly. I heard them from a great distance. My vision blurred and I felt sick and dizzy, low blood sugar and shock combining as I leaned heavily on the bookstand.

'What . . .' I said, my voice barely above a whisper.

I was thrust aside as Marshal's father took my place, nearly pushing me over. I staggered into Marshal's arms and he caught me, fingers digging into my arms. With a ham-like fist in a death grip on the bookstand, Marshal Senior leaned into the microphone.

'This press conference is over.'

I was swept from the drawing room between my husband and father-in-law so fast that my feet barely touched the ground. Behind me came the clamouring of voices, questions, insults and shouts as the press were forced back by staff. Over all of it came the man's voice, ringing like that of a priest, thundering from a pulpit.

'Do you have anything to say against the accusation that she participated in the ritual murder of those girls?'

Then the heavy door closed, cutting off the sound like the entrance to a tomb.

Chapter Six

I watched the new women from London arrive from the roof. I'd found one of the windows that actually opened. Most were painted shut. But this one I could climb out of onto the ledge right by the little wall that went around the outside. It was a good place to hide from Lona when she came looking for someone to clean or help carry stuff from the cars.

Lona was the only person that bothered with us kids. Everyone else let us do whatever we wanted, never called us in for meals or bed. We took food from the kitchen if we wanted it and slept where we could find space. If we wanted clean clothes we had to wash them, or take clean ones from someone else. Toys were fair game too. No one told us we couldn't have something or shouted about the electric bill. When the electric went we had candles and there was singing and dancing and laughing all the time.

Lona was the one who'd picked me up from the flat that the woman in the park took me to. I'd not learned her name right away though. Then she was just the horrible woman who didn't say much.

At the flat I played with a cat called Monty. I had juice

and chocolate and then fell asleep. When I woke up Lona was carrying me to a car. She was a great big woman, strong and not like a fairy at all.

'Where are we going?' I asked.

'Home,' was all she said.

I thought she was taking me to my home, which was stupid because how was she supposed to know where I lived? But I was too exhausted to think. I slept again in the back of the car and when I woke up it was light again and we were parked in a forest. Lona was shaking my leg, telling me to get up.

'Is this . . . London?' I asked, because I'd never been outside London. Not even with the school. But it didn't feel like that's where we were. It was too quiet and it smelled all green and muddy.

'No,' she said, but didn't say where it was. 'Come on.'

I wasn't awake enough before to have a bad feeling, but now I did. The blonde lady, Astraea, was nice. This lady wasn't nice at all. She was like a teacher, bossing me around. I didn't know where I was, but I wanted to go home.

Lona stopped a few steps away and turned back, annoyed. 'Come on, I said!'

'I want to go home,' I said and didn't move.

She looked at me for a moment, then pointed the other way to where she wanted to go. 'All right then, off you go.'

I turned and looked back at the woods. The car was parked on some mud and a thin, winding road went off back into the trees. It was very dark under the trees. How far was London? I couldn't hear any people or cars, just the wind in the branches. I never heard it so loud before. Even in the park. It was scary, like the trees were moving all around, getting ready to swallow me up.

I turned back and Lona was gone, walking up the path. I ran after her. I didn't want to be alone in the woods. She didn't say anything, even though we walked for a very long time. My legs were aching and I badly needed the toilet but I didn't dare say so. After all the walking we finally saw a big house off in the distance.

'Is that where you live?' I asked, because we seemed to be walking towards it.

'That's home,' Lona said.

We walked all the way down to the house and she took me inside. I wasn't scared exactly. Mum had only said to watch out for bad men, and there weren't any men there and all the women in the house smiled as they passed us. But I wanted my mum. I wanted to know what was going on and when I could go home. I knew I was going to be in trouble when I got back.

I soon found out that I was already at home. The house, the manor, was home now. That was what Celeste told me when Lona took me to her. Celeste was in charge, like our headmistress at school. Only pretty and nice, not scary. She put her hand on my head and said I was one of her sisters now. Just like Lona, just like all the women in the house. She said I was very special and lucky to have found them, because now I could be free of all the evils in the world. I was going to be the first of Luna's new daughters. I didn't know who Luna was then. I thought she was another lady I was going to meet. But she's the moon. The goddess.

When I asked about my mum, Celeste sighed and said that one day she might find us too. But until then, I must be patient.

So, I was on the roof – hiding in case Lona was looking for kids to clean – and being patient. But none of the new women was my mum. I was starting to get annoyed with her. Why wasn't she finding us? I found Celeste and I was just a kid. It wasn't hard. But she was probably busy with work or trying to fix the washing machine, or – a tiny part of me whispered – she was happier without having to take care of me. Lona said that a few days before, when I ran into her on the landing and she dropped her cup of tea.

'Your mother's lucky to be shot of you,' she snarled, then made me clean up the mess.

I hated Lona even more after that.

Trying to ignore thoughts of Lona, I watched the new women. Some of them had kids, one was a girl about my age with red hair. She was clinging to a woman's skirt, tripping her up. The woman looked annoyed, but carried on as if the girl wasn't there. They looked alike. I guessed she was the girl's mum. I wanted my mum even more then.

Women started to come out of the manor to meet the new people, who put their binbags and plastic baskets of stuff down to hug the manor women. Someone had put a record on and thrown open the windows. I could smell incense and cigarettes, both regular like Mum had and the funny ones everyone smoked at the manor.

Lona had managed to find some kids to help out, I was glad I'd managed to hide. One girl was carrying a tray of plastic cups of wine around. She had one of the special bottles as well, the small ones with a dropper that Celeste brought out for parties. I watched her put drops in the wine carefully, her tongue between her teeth.

The women drank and linked arms for a group hug which turned into a sort of long dance, arm in arm, circling up to the house. Everyone was laughing and tripping over boxes and bags. Someone knocked into the tray girl and she spilled wine on herself and the ground. No one shouted or told her off. They didn't even seem to notice as she threw the tray away and licked wine off her arms.

The last woman to join was the one with the little girl. She took a step but almost tripped, weighed down. For the first time she looked down and said something to her, then tugged her skirt away, waving towards the garden, the pond, anywhere else. They all went up into the house and the girl sat down on the dusty ground and cried. Around her the wine girl and a few others picked up bags and boxes and started dragging them into the manor. They would be taking them upstairs to the attic.

I watched her cry for a while. She was there long enough for women to start coming outside again to build a bonfire at the bottom of the garden. They walked around her, talking to each other. One of them danced around her and screamed. They did that sometimes. It was called 'primal' and it was like a tantrum but for adults. They acted like kids a lot, sitting in circles singing or telling stories, painting the walls, making daisy chains and bead necklaces or just lying in the grass watching clouds.

Eventually the girl went quiet, got up and wandered into the garden behind the house. The women came out and lit the bonfire and I watched it burn, wishing my mum was there. I hated that girl for crying when she was so lucky. She had her mum at the manor.

'Hello?'

I jumped, twisted round and saw the red-haired girl at the window. She crawled out after me and sat looking down at the fire.

'This is my spot,' I said, annoyed that I hadn't heard her. She must have come in through the garden and up the stairs.

'Oh. Can I sit here?'

'You're too little.'

'I'm five and a half,' she argued.

I was younger, but she was shorter than me and skinnier. I could push her back in the window if I wanted. But just then she took a chocolate bar out of her pocket.

'Want some?'

I took half and we sat and ate. After a bit I asked where she and her mum had come from.

'London. But I'm not meant to call her Mum. She's Selene here. We're sisters now. Like she and Phoebe are sisters.'

'Where in London?'

She didn't know.

'Do you know where your school was?' *I asked, thinking it might be mine.*

'Don't go to school. Selene knows Celeste really well and she said that school never made them happy so why would it make me happy? Did your mum send you to school?'

'Yeah.'

'Where is she?'

'London. She's not one of them.' *I pointed down at the* women. 'She's from outside.'

'You're lucky then,' *she said.* 'That they found you without your mum being with Celeste. Celeste says kids are lucky to be here, because we won't have to suffer like our mums did. She says we're the easiest to save.'

I hadn't thought of it like that. Maybe I was lucky that out of all the girls in London, I was chosen by the woman in the park. Otherwise I'd be in the flat right now, cold and doing homework and waiting for Mum to come home from work to make dinner. All by myself.

'And I'm lucky because now you're my sister,' *she said.* 'I'm Lucia.'

'Jasy,' *I said, the new name still a weird shape in my mouth.*

'Come on, I'll show you where there's space for a bed.'

Chapter Seven

The next few hours were torture. Swept away from the press I was returned to the rosewood suite and left there, alone, whilst everyone else convened to discuss the latest bombshell, or rather series of bombshells. The accusations that my mother was a kidnapper, murderer and prostitute.

Even Marshal deserted me without a word, like he was too ashamed to even look at me. I couldn't blame him. My mother was accused of multiple terrible crimes on national television and in front of journalists from every major paper. It was a disaster.

I'd been so focused on my own secrets I hadn't worried about hers. What did I really know about my mother, beyond the fact that she took me to the manor? Nothing. Hardly any memories at all. I'd assumed that the fire was the worst of it. I was wrong, blindsided, and had just made things a thousand times worse for Marshal and his family.

Now I looked like an idiot. Worse still, Marshal and his father looked like idiots, like people with something to hide. My ignorance implicated them in some kind of dodgy cover-up. Humiliation and shock turned me hot and cold as I paced the room. Peeping through the velvet drapery I saw press vans heading to the gates, where they stopped and formed a circle, like hungry dogs waiting to be thrown a steak.

After struggling out of the stupid frilly blouse and skirt, I wiped the makeup from my face. With the clothes left in a pile, I put my own things back on. The mirror over the elaborate dresser showed a blotchy-faced woman with a ridiculous chignon already frizzing out. I yanked out hair grips and furiously raked my fingers through my hair. I felt so stupid, so naive.

I let every chance to find out about the manor and Luna Vitae pass me by and this was the result. I was so focused on keeping one secret that I didn't look for any more. Now everything I didn't know was being used against me and the man I loved.

Was it true? Did my mother kidnap and kill girls my age and younger, whilst I lived with her completely unaware? Were the children who died in the fire being held against their will? I put my face in my hands. Did my mother help to cause their deaths?

Did my mother prostitute herself for the cult? Is that what Luna Vitae was about? But because of who? I remembered Celeste being my mother's guru, but if she'd been in charge why did Carlisle's name cause such a strong reaction in me? Were they in it together? Did the prostitution have anything to do with the missing children? I felt sick. Surely I'd remember if I witnessed anything like that.

I closed my eyes and tried to force a memory to the surface. Any memory. Did I see anything, hear anything about this? I couldn't recall anything. Yet the name 'Carlisle Riordan' filled me with a dread I couldn't begin to understand. Far worse than the name of Celeste. Who was in control of that place? Of my mother?

My mother, the accused kidnapper and prostitute, implicated in child sacrifice.

How could I not know what went on? Why was I never told? Why had I never asked? All my life I was convinced that I knew as much as I ever wanted to about the past. What else did I need to know? To carry with me? My mother was suckered into a cult, then it fell apart in one awful night. She lost her life. That, I had told myself, was all there was to it.

I imagined things, sure. I was aware of other cults and weird fringe groups in films and sometimes on the news. But most of that was made up for shock value. I naively thought that I would remember anything like the awful true stories – the sex trafficking, paedophilia, drugs, torture and murder. No, ours was just some stupid hippy commune, I convinced myself. My mother was feckless and irresponsible, leaving me unschooled and neglected, but that was all. The fire was the worst thing to come of it. What more was there to know or care about? It was all over, gone. I thought that was the only thing that could hurt me.

I was wrong.

I could hear shouting from a room nearby, mostly muffled by the thick walls and elaborate panelling. I heard Enid's voice rise up, piercing through.

'Why you had to marry that silly little girl . . .'

I flinched. It wasn't just this. It seemed like she never liked me, only tolerated me. Something else I took at face value. I felt like such an idiot. Though it wasn't as if I could blame her. She never signed up for this, for me.

I imagined Marshal's father was doing anything he could to stop the interview going out. Fat lot of good that would do. This was explosive and he had to know it. There was no way any channel or newspaper would give up the chance to show an MP's daughter-in-law confronted with her mother's murder accusations. Particularly if that MP was already unpopular across the board.

Taking out my phone I did something I should have done years before. I googled my mother's name. It didn't seem important before. I knew everything I needed to know about her, or so I thought. It would have only added to my nightmares. By the time Google was even a thing I'd pushed my thoughts down so deep that I could hardly remember her. I didn't want to dredge her up.

I scrolled through the results. Carrie Green was a common enough name that the page was clogged with other people, other lives. Nothing about murder or kidnap. It wasn't until I included 'Luna Vitae' that she came up. There were several old newspaper stories about the manor and the fire. She was listed as a casualty. Nothing else mentioned her. Had the journalist made it up? I felt a brief glimmer of hope.

I tried her name with 'kidnap' and 'murder', then substituted 'Selene' for 'Carrie' in case they used her unofficial name. Finally, I searched for 'kidnap' and 'Luna Vitae'. As the screen filled with results I choked on a lungful of air.

Cult Suspected in Child Abduction

Where Are Our Kids? Parents Left in the Dark by 'Moon Cult'

Seven Children Still Missing In Sex Cult Scandal

Ten Tried in Cult Fraud Allegations

Cult Prostitution Ring Busted

None of this was what I remembered. Of course, I remembered basically nothing but surely if this had been going on I would know. If I had been part of something so disturbing it couldn't just slip out of my memory. Could it?

I already knew the answer to that. I'd forgotten so much, aside from the fire, and even that I mostly repressed. What were a few slivers of happy summer memories? Certainly not proof of a good life, a happy life.

What if there were other things, stuff my mother was doing, buried so deeply not even Carmen could winkle them out? According to the internet there had even been trials, though for fraud not murder. Still, a crime linked to the commune. What happened and who was prosecuted? What fraud were they talking about?

The door opened and I stuffed the phone into my pocket. I had no idea what prompted the action. Perhaps shame or the instinct to hide my past from Marshal. He came in alone and looking extremely tired. I was glad for a second before I felt the judgement of his father's absence.

'Well . . . this is a mess,' he said, sighing and peeling off his suit jacket. The sweat patches were back and his neck was red from humiliation. He looked like a schoolboy who was given triple detention for the rest of the year. I desperately wanted him to look at me, to just look me in the eye. But he didn't.

'I'm so, so sorry. I had no idea he was going to say that. I didn't know anything about it, I promise—'

'Obviously,' Marshal said, cutting me off. I felt myself go red, feeling scolded.

He came across the room and put his arms around me, trying to soothe away the harshness of his words. 'No one thinks you did this on purpose. No one's blaming you, OK? It's them, the bloody vultures, crawling out of the woodwork.'

I managed a snuffled laugh at the ludicrously mixed metaphor. Still, I knew his words were mostly empty, even if he believed them. Maybe he still loved me, forgave me, but his family didn't. I couldn't even say that I was surprised. I certainly didn't blame them. I was every bit as deserving of their hatred as my mother was.

'Dad's not sure what we're going to do about all this just yet,' Marshal said, smoothing my hair. 'No one found any of this stuff about your mum during the search for the conference, though obviously that was a bit of a rush job. I

62

wish we'd known she was using another name then. If you'd told us that . . . but anyway, he thinks that bloke, the journalist, likely has a police informant. Going to try and get to the bottom of it. She might have been a person of interest but given that she died, she was never charged. We can put that out there.'

I felt hopeless. 'What do we do now?' I asked.

'Best course of action for now . . . he thinks you should take some time away from work and keep a low profile, at home. He thinks it would be the best thing for you, and the baby, and I agree. Eventually this will die down.'

Shame bubbled up again. I had barely thought of the baby since that morning. God, how would our child live with this over their head?

Another thought occurred to me. Was the baby the only reason Marshal wasn't on the phone to a divorce lawyer right now? I told myself not to be so stupid. He would never even think of doing that. But maybe his father would. I couldn't stand the thought.

It was clear that I was being relegated to the sidelines. I was being grounded. Having caused my father-in-law an enormous amount of embarrassment and political disgrace in less than twelve hours, it was to be expected. I only hoped that was where it would end. Even if I deserved to lose Marshal, I knew I wouldn't be able to stand it. Where would I go? I was nothing without him.

'He's sending security back with us to clear off the front walk,' he said. 'Let's just get home and think about all this in the morning.'

Marshal shepherded me out of the room and back downstairs to the car that had brought us. Neither of his parents were around to say goodbye. I was glad. I doubted I could have faced either of them. I felt lower than low, a complete disgrace.

Still, a tiny bit of hope remained. Maybe Marshal was right. How long could this really go on for? His father had weathered many political storms. Besides, Luna Vitae was old news; most people my age had no idea what it was. It might just fizzle out of the news cycle, replaced by something more serious or more sensational. Perhaps, in the morning, things would look different.

With that optimism in mind, I managed to delude myself enough to get to sleep that night. Even the nightmares couldn't compete with my complete exhaustion. But when the phone woke me and I heard Marshal swearing outside the bedroom, his fist thumping against the wall, I knew it was not going to be so easy. My stomach felt filled with concrete and nausea made me shudder, bitterness on my tongue.

Morning sickness on top of everything else. Wonderful.

That day was, if anything, worse than before. The news had a new photo in the morning cycle, a blurry bit of nineties CCTV showing a woman leading one of the abducted girls to a car near a park. The woman had blonde hair and was only seen from the back, but there was already speculation that she was 'the mother of MP Marshal Townsend's daughter-in-law'. The little girl was just a blur on camera but she looked very small, maybe four or even younger. She was taken from a birthday party in the park. I googled it. The mother who organised it said she only looked away for a moment, then the girl, Anne, was gone. Where was she now? I couldn't stop looking at the picture, trying to force myself to remember anything, anything at all, about her or my mother. Nothing came. Was she at the manor? Did she die in the fire?

Marshal worked from home, emerging from his office for coffee or paracetamol. He looked strained and exhausted, but waved off any attempt to help. I felt so useless, shut out of the mess I made, watching him struggle.

I could at least ring Marjorie and explain that I needed some time off. She agreed almost before the words were out of my mouth. Clearly the trust was getting some of the negative attention being showered over me and Marshal's family. She gave me several weeks and told me to take care of myself. It didn't seem like the time to tell her about the baby, though she might well have been ecstatic. Maternity leave would be a great excuse to get rid of me for a while.

Whilst Marshal took call after call and rattled off emails in his office, I hid upstairs. I texted Ellie to let her know I was at least physically OK. Even if my stress levels were through the roof. The press was back on the doorstep. More of them this time. I could hear them talking and occasionally calling out, trying to provoke one of us into opening the door. It wasn't going to happen. Still, hearing it was driving me up the wall.

Upstairs I forced myself to watch the news, which was showing my picture and the CCTV image again. This time they led with the kidnapping allegations and the prostitution ring. Apparently shortly after the fire, police managed to pull off a sting and arrested quite a few Luna Vitae members from the small communes. The charges at the time were solicitation and fraud, mostly in cheques and credit cards the women had stolen from their customers. Some of them were high profile – a judge, several police officials, even MPs. There was speculation that the real aim of the prostitution was to gather blackmail material to protect the communes, to help them gain influence and perhaps even to bury the investigations into the missing children.

This all came up because someone was writing a book about Luna Vitae. Their research was enough to turn up the names of surviving members – some of whom were charged with crimes and others who'd simply left the communes. Clearly somewhere along the line someone decided there was a story in it and tracked those names to public sector jobs. The cult had tried to blackmail and rob men in those jobs before. What if they were now infiltrating the same offices?

It was rubbish obviously. Luna Vitae was gone, had been gone for years. But it was still a story they could sell. So that didn't matter.

They had the author of the book on the news. He was middle-aged, skinny, wearing a brown suit in either an ironic nod to the seventies, or out of sheer lack of care for changing fashions. His dense beard and thick glasses gave him the look of an academic from one of my school's old science videos. I could imagine him in a tweed jacket, talking about covalent bonds to a group of suitably diverse kids.

'Doctor Ketler, what is it that inspired you to write this book?' the news presenter asked. 'And did you expect this kind of reaction based on the research you turned up?'

'Douglas, please, and no, I didn't expect anything like the stir the book has already caused. I wanted to write about the Red Manor Cult because it's gone rather undocumented in comparison to other cults at the time. As an organisation, it was fairly small scale in terms of numbers, with the majority of the activity and devotees being at the manor itself. There were satellite communes elsewhere but the manor is where most of the members ended up. It was where the big decisions were made, where you'd find the inner circle, if you will. When the fire wiped it out, the cult disbanded. It was active for less than a decade.'

This was the man who ruined my life? What if he was still digging? He had my whole life in his hands. I hated him for seeming so likeable, so casual. Did he not care what he was doing to me? To everyone else he was shining a spotlight on? I turned the news off and put my face in my hands. What was I going to do?

I forced myself to sit back and take a long, shuddery

breath. I had to keep it together. Marshal had enough to worry about without me going to pieces on top of everything else.

I was about to go down and ask if he wanted a cup of tea when my phone pinged. It was a message request through Facebook. I had a few of these since the news ran their story about me. Mostly they were hammering the landline with calls, but a few journalists and bloggers messaged me personally. I flicked the notification balloon, intent on deleting it. Then I noticed the picture.

She had the same hennaed hair and thickly outlined eyes I noticed when I saw her photo on the news. The Facebook message said her name was Bernadette Stokes but I knew her as Phoebe. My mother's friend.

The message said simply: 'We need to meet.'

Chapter Eight

I was four when our home became a Luna Vitae commune. I remembered bits of it, the way a child remembers change. One day it was just the two of us, then three, then four. Phoebe was the first. The only one I could remember clearly, because she stayed with us the longest. The rest moved in and out, on and up, a faceless blur of women.

One day my mother came home from one of her meditation workshops with two women. One I knew. Celeste was Mum's best friend, always coming around. She gave me chocolates and called me 'Lovely Lucia'. She wore so many tinkling silver bangles she was like a little orchestra. I was obsessed with them and with her candy-coloured eyeshadow – blue and lilac and pink – all the way around her eyes in a teardrop shape. Celeste had waist-length black hair and pale, pale skin, just like Snow White in my picture books. She was like a princess.

The other woman had red hair which looked dry and crackly, like the coconut mat in the bathroom. She smelled of patchouli oil and cigarettes, just like Mum's room.

'This is Phoebe,' Mum said, stepping over my discarded

dolls and taking a cigarette from the packet on the fireplace. 'She's going to be living with us.'

'Why?' I asked, because I was four and it was my favourite word. Why why why, all day every day.

Mum looked to Celeste. She did that a lot. She also dressed quite a lot like her. In the old photos in her albums Mum wore neat skirts and blouses, tights and high heels. She had permed hair and a fat black handbag on a chain. That was before I was born. I never saw her in anything other than long dresses or peasant skirts. Just like Celeste. Aside from her hair, which was a cloud of messy blonde curls, they could have been twins.

'Lucia, do you like being on your own?' Celeste asked.

'Not really,' I said. I remember being alone a lot, whilst Mum was meeting Celeste or other women. Sometimes she was gone at night too.

'No one does. It's lonely, isn't it? But that's how most people live. Isn't that strange? It doesn't seem natural, does it? Wouldn't you like to have a sister with you instead? Someone to play with, to talk to?'

I nodded, because being on my own wasn't fun. I got scared sometimes and I couldn't turn the heater on by myself or make spaghetti on toast.

'Well, that's why Phoebe's here. She's Selene's new sister, and my sister and yours too. And maybe soon you'll have other sisters staying here as well.'

I looked at Mum, who I was meant to call Selene but kept forgetting. Phoebe reached into the pocket of her cotton skirt and offered me a Sherbet Dip Dab. I ran over and hugged her around the waist.

Having a sister sounded great.

'Absolutely not.'

Marshal paced around the living room for the fiftieth time.

It was late by this point and after such a bad night's sleep I was fighting to keep my eyes open. I forced back a yawn, knowing he would be upset if he thought I wasn't paying attention. I was craving coffee. Inwardly I cursed myself for not bringing this up in the morning. Phoebe's message had caught me off guard though, and I went to Marshal. He was now freaking out.

'You cannot seriously want to meet this woman,' he said, making a pit stop by the drinks tray on the side table to freshen his glass of whisky. He knocked it back and resumed his pacing. 'You don't even know who she is.'

'I do . . . sort of. She lived with my mother in London.'

'As what?' Marshal looked disgusted and I felt a stab of annoyance. What was he imagining?

'As a sister. Mum's house was where some of the women lived, before the move to the manor. It's hard to remember faces, with all the coming and going. But Phoebe was there the longest.'

'How many other people did you live with?' he said, looking even more disgusted now. 'This sounds like a . . . flop house.'

'I'm not sure how many,' I said, ignoring the second half of his comment. 'A few. I can't really remember. This was all before we moved to the manor. I'm not sure if they came with us then or if they just stopped with us for a bit before moving on somewhere else. But Phoebe did come with us. I want to know why she left before the fire. She could tell us what it was like there. What my mother was like.'

I couldn't remember anyone's names or really recall them being around. The people who faded away or suddenly disappeared I assumed went back to their old lives or off on some new trip. I suddenly recalled a whole pile of abandoned treasure – a shoebox stuffed with glass, wood and plastic jewellery, loose crystals, odd tarot cards and I Ching coins.

70

Things I found after people left, things they forgot or ditched. The scent of that box, patchouli and sage, dust and joss stick ash, enveloped me. Things left behind by those passing through. I collected them and then lost them somewhere. Perhaps they burned in the fire. I winced, imagining the kind of heat that melted metal and plastic, imagining what that could do to a person.

Marshal snapped me back to earth, letting out a groan and setting his glass down heavily.

'I forgot. I said I'd give up drinking with you and look at me. You should have said something.'

'It's been a stressful few days,' I said, with a flush of guilt as I eyed his glass enviously. The flood of new memories unsettled me and I desperately wanted even just a small glass of wine to soothe my nerves. But we decided I wasn't to chance even the amount supposedly allowed in the books. We wanted to do things right.

'I'll get some water. Do you want anything?'

'I'm fine.'

He came back with a carafe and two glasses anyway. Thoughtful to a fault. Whilst he drank his glass down I pulled myself together. The truth was I wanted to see Phoebe. I had to know if what that journalist said about my mother was true. For the first time in my life I wanted to remember more about my childhood. I tried to ignore the part of me that was telling me I didn't want to remember. The more I knew, the more I could help Marshal and his father to get ahead of the scandal. I'd also know what to keep from them at all costs, what other time bombs might be about to blow up in my face.

'I think we need to see her,' I said, after a long silence. 'She was my mother's friend, she might be able to tell us something important before the press gets hold of it.'

'Like what?' Marshal said, suspiciously. 'Is there something else you haven't told me? Because you promised, Lucy. You said you've been honest.'

I curled my toes inside my slipper socks. 'I don't know if there's something else. That's the point,' I said, feeling rattled. 'Look, she got away from the cult just like me. She's probably perfectly safe; you can even be here or have security at the door.'

'She can't come here, not with the press watching the house.'

'All right, so we arrange to meet somewhere out of the way. A remote village pub or a service station. I need to see her, Marshal. She might have answers that can help me. Help us. She might know about my mother and these awful accusations.'

He sighed and I knew he was thinking about his dad and how they needed all the information they could get. He was an open book like that. Not a great trait for a politician. Like his inability to lie convincingly. I could always tell when he was hiding something. It was, ironically, something that drew me to him. Hypocritical of me really, given I was hiding things from him. Maybe that's why I valued honesty in others. I knew how much it cost.

'I'll have to discuss it with Dad,' he muttered. 'But . . . this is a big risk, Lucy. I'm not happy about it.'

'I know. I'll make it work, I promise. And I will make this up to you. I know all this is . . . I'm so grateful that you're still here.'

He seemed satisfied and went to make the call.

I could only hope that his dad would be desperate enough to seize any opportunity to untangle the embarrassing situation I landed him in. Whilst Marshal went to argue my case over the phone, I tried to distract myself and stop stressing so much. My jaw ached from clenching it and my heart kept fluttering; the anxiety was eating away at me.

More than anything, I wanted to sit down and paint something. The ritual of pencil sharpening, sketching, mixing my colours and carefully shading was the perfect way to get the pain and fear out. It always had been. Absorbing myself in what I was doing, living in the colours and shapes as I created them, focusing my mind down to a point on the page – it was a way to forget and let go. In the early days of our relationship, I often got carried away and arrived late for dates with Marshal. He was always so nice about it though. And I made it up to him.

I could always find peace in those moments of fierce concentration. Only now I couldn't, because it would feel like a betrayal to spend time painting whilst Marshal was soldiering on downstairs. So, instead of distracting myself with drawing, I looked through Phoebe's Facebook page some more.

Most of it was private but some pictures had clearly been profile pics at some point. Looking through them I saw her on a black sand beach, in the woods somewhere with a pagoda and on a street with German or Dutch signs. She looked happy, relaxed and successful. No sign of anyone else in the pictures. I wondered if she was married, if she had a family. I felt jealous of her life, which, from the pictures I could see, took her all over the world. She saw all the things I wanted to see. I touched my belly and wondered if I'd ever get to travel so far now. People with children did, I knew that. But I didn't think it would be the same. I couldn't sit and sketch for hours on end, uninterrupted, or take off on a whim. Children needed stability, care, food, rest. Their needs had to come first. A good mother put those needs first. Mine did not.

That became clear when I was taken into care and put into school. I was years behind, unable to read, write or tell the time. I remember how they had to shave my head because the hair was too matted to comb out. No one ever made me brush it or washed it for me.

I wanted more than anything to understand what happened to Phoebe, to my mother. Why were they part of Luna Vitae? What did it offer them? Why did my mother apparently neglect me so much? Why did Phoebe leave the manor and why did my mother stay until the last, terrible night?

Small memories were returning to me, as if some kind of wall had been chipped away. Just little things: the feel of glass beads in my hands, the smell of incense, the tinkle of bells, my hand reaching up to paint crooked stars on woodchip wallpaper. They intrigued me but frightened me too. I already had to carry the memory of the fire around with me; what if I discovered something worse?

Though what could be worse than that?

With my arms wrapped around myself I thought again of the journalist's accusations. What if I'd seen something back then? What if I interrupted or overheard something the adults were hiding from me? Did I want to know? No. But I had to find out. I had to know the truth. Could I handle it if it was as bad as I feared? There was no way to know. I had to find out. I had to know if there was anything I could do to clear my name and fix the damage I did to Marshal's life.

Besides, there were others who needed to know what happened at the manor. I saw the news articles, the interviews and dated photographs of gap-toothed girls. Girls who'd been missing for two decades, like the girl at the birthday party. Her mother was still out there, waiting. She deserved to know, one way or the other, what happened to her child. It wouldn't come close to making amends. It wouldn't even begin to fix the damage, but it was something. I had to do something.

If I found a way to exorcise those nightmares, maybe I

could face up to the future, to my own child. More than anything I wanted to be the wife Marshal deserved, the mother our baby needed. I had to fix things, for Marshal, for the parents of those children and for the baby.

I just had no idea where to start. Maybe Phoebe would be my first step.

Chapter Nine

It took four days to arrange the meeting with Phoebe. Marshal insisted we meet at an out-of-the-way café in a tiny village over an hour's drive from home. By the time the meeting came I was a nervous wreck. Those were some of the longest days of my life.

For four days I was unable to go outside, even into the garden. There were photographers taking pictures over the back gate, waiting on the front walk, tapping on the windows. I felt like an animal in a zoo. The story had a life of its own now, with internet conspiracies popping up about my father-in-law and his ties to 'satanic organisations'. It was madness.

Far from losing interest, the story seemed to gain new traction every day. Whilst it wasn't headline news on the TV anymore, other MPs were being asked about it every day, even if they only came on to talk about the congestion charge or house prices. It trickled into opinion shows and daytime TV gossip panels. Enid's magazine was being dissected for 'occult ties' and 'satanic dog whistles'.

The tabloids and social media were in a frenzy. Whether because they really believed the story or just because they thought it was a great joke, I couldn't tell. It was awful all the same. Pictures cropped up of some candles in the garden, the kind used to keep bugs away, along with an ugly, goat-footed faun statue that was there when we moved in. Speculation that these were 'ritual paraphernalia' got #MPofHell trending on Twitter, briefly replacing #TownsendResign. There were people saying they could see a pentagram marked out on our lawn.

The hospital was also getting a lot of attention. Rumours that I had access to the children's wards had sprung up. A supposed 'former nurse' saw me going there and leaving with vials of blood. Children 'went missing' from the ward afterwards. It didn't matter that this was pure rubbish from a deleted account. The screenshots spread like a plague. The hospital refuted the claims but that only made things worse. The more they dismissed the outlandish rumours, the further they spread.

It all left me feeling drained and on edge constantly. I couldn't sleep, couldn't stop myself from looking online and seeing all the awful things people were saying about me, about Marshal and his family. All of it my fault. My heart was constantly fluttering from anxiety and the morning sickness only became worse. I couldn't keep anything down except water and plain crackers.

Marshal worked from home and I often heard shouting or the thuds of thrown things from his office. He was under a lot of stress and I was almost glad that he rarely came out. It was miserable, but I knew I deserved it. I lied about my past and hid it all from Marshal. Just like I was keeping my fears about the baby a secret. I deserved all the bile in the papers and online. But Marshal didn't and neither did his family. It piled guilt on top of guilt. I was ruining their lives and damaging the reputation of the hospital as well.

I was glad when the day of the meeting came around. We left the house very early, via a car provided by Marshal's father. Ours would stay on the driveway as a decoy. It felt very cloak-and-dagger to be spirited away behind tinted glass in the small hours. Marshal was with me of course, reminding me throughout the drive to 'be prepared' and 'take nothing for granted'. He was clearly anxious over the whole thing. For me curiosity overwhelmed fear, at least until we reached the little café and went inside.

It had only just opened. There were five little tables, each with a chintzy cloth and a lace doily. The whole place smelled like toast, tea and talcum powder. Only one table was occupied. Phoebe, aka Bernadette, was waiting for us. She looked uncomfortable with her surroundings and I didn't entirely blame her. The place was rundown and not particularly clean. Dusty china dolls and teddy bears glared down at us from shelves and the plastic floor tiles were sticky underfoot.

Phoebe looked pale; her hair was undyed now and fully grey. Dressed head to toe in black, with black-framed glasses, she was totally different to how I vaguely remembered her, different even from the woman I'd seen on Facebook. No more florals or floaty hippy skirts. No more silver and gemstone jewellery or love beads. Maybe that was the point.

She stood up as we approached. I saw how tall she was and how thin. Her mouth was puckered and her eyes were sharp, moving quickly around the place. She reached for my hand then held herself back as if she was nervous or unwilling to touch me.

'Lucia. Lucy, sorry. You look . . . incredible,' she said, her voice soft and rasping as a cat's tongue, telling of decades of smoking. 'Let me look at you. So much like your mother.'

I flushed, uncomfortable under her gaze. 'Thanks. You look um . . . very well too.'

'Ha!' she said ruefully. 'I suppose I do, considering. This

past week hasn't been easy. I suspect we have that in common.'

Marshal sniffed pointedly and I remembered him, flushing with guilt. 'This is Marshal, my husband.'

'Pleased to meet you,' Phoebe said, glancing at him for a moment before returning the weight of her stare to me. 'You've done so well for yourself. I'm glad. Selene – Carrie, I should say, would have been proud of you.'

'Thank you,' I said, feeling a little uncomfortable. I had never concerned myself with whether or not my mother would have approved of my choices. In fact I spent most of my life asking myself what I imagined she would do then doing the opposite.

As soon as we sat down the aged owner came over and took our drink orders then left us to it. If she recognised me, even with my hair under a hood and wearing Marshal's reading glasses, she gave no sign.

'It sounded quite urgent when you asked to meet,' Marshal prompted, after a few moments of silence. Clearly he wanted to get to the point right away.

'I'm sorry if I worried you,' Phoebe said to me, as if he hadn't spoken. 'I just . . . with everything that's happened the past week, I had to see you, before I lost you again. You see, I have something for you.' She hauled an overstuffed black leather tote onto the table and started to dig through it.

I exchanged a glance with Marshal as she unloaded a packet of wet wipes, several seemingly new lipsticks and a knot of charging cables, headphones and costume jewellery. Eventually she turned up a black cardboard jewellery box. It was scuffed and white at the corners. When she opened it, the cotton wool inside was shrunken and yellowed. A smell of stale cigarettes and patchouli wafted up. It reminded me strongly of my childhood, of Mum.

'This was your mother's,' Phoebe said, peeling apart the layers of cotton wool and holding up a large pendant. It was silver. A thick, reasonably modern setting. On it four moonstones were set as compass points with opals in between. A carved moon face was the focus at the centre. The placidly smiling moon looked like it was made of ivory or bone. With slyly half-closed eyes, it was hard to tell if the moon was intended to be sleeping or peering from beneath heavy lids.

'Do you remember it?' she asked.

I opened my mouth automatically to say no. But there was something familiar about it.

'Sort of,' I said. 'But . . . it's different to how I remember it.'

'She did go through a fair few,' Phoebe said. 'Celeste had them made especially by a jeweller in London. They were sent away for when someone went up a rank or a new woman joined. Everyone was jealous of the more ornate ones, the more expensive. It's meant to be the face of Luna herself.' She sniffed derisively. 'We worshipped her, the great moon goddess. I saw this face everywhere at the manor.'

'What's it made of?' I asked, feeling a stir of recognition the longer I looked at the little face.

'The lesser ranks had bone in the centre. Yak bone I think it was. Celeste, her consort and her handmaidens wore ivory. Antique ivory, re-carved in Luna's likeness.'

Her consort. I noticed that she was yet to say Carlisle's name, but she had to be talking about him. She made it sound like Celeste was the leader of the cult. That was something I'd been curious about. I had such a strong reaction to Carlisle's name, yet I could only really remember Celeste. She was the one who recruited my mother. She visited us and brought Phoebe to us. Where did Carlisle come into it? Or was he always the mastermind and Celeste the bait to attract women who were wary of men?

'What about these?' I reached out and caressed the pale

80

moonstones. I didn't want to scare Phoebe off by asking about Carlisle directly.

The old woman came with our drinks orders and I saw her eying the pendant with interest. Although it held only semi-precious stones, it was a large piece of silver. If the face really was antique ivory it had to be worth several hundred pounds at least. I was touched that Phoebe saved it for me for so long.

'One for each rank, from initiate up to handmaiden.'

'So Mum was . . .'

'Handmaid to the high priestess, the highest position, other than priestess, obviously, or her consort. Celeste designed your mother's pendant herself, with opals to heal the discordant energy of her past.' Phoebe pursed her lips. 'Amazing to think I used to believe in that stuff.'

'How did you end up with her necklace?' I asked.

A blush painted her crêpey cheeks. 'I stole it. I was ashamed of that for years, but I try not to be, not anymore. You probably don't remember how it was back then, when things started to fall apart. By the time I realised how badly I needed to escape I had nothing. No money of my own, no car, there wasn't even a phone line. We gave everything to Celeste when we joined, to fund the commune. Though I suspect she was pocketing most of it, with the amount she spent on couture and parties in London. So I stole some things: jewellery, a chalice, this gilded knife that turned out not to be worth anything . . . and your mum's pendant. It was worth so much more than mine. Then when I heard about the fire and how she died . . . I just couldn't sell it. She would have wanted you to have it. It was her prized possession.'

'What do you mean, things "fell apart"?'

This was what I wanted to know since learning of the accusations against my mother. I believed it was the fire that

81

ruined everything. But Phoebe was making me aware that there was something before that. I had to know what.

'Oh . . . well, things had been changing for a while. New dictates, new rules and practices and . . . by then it wasn't really Luna Vitae at all. At least not how I knew it. It became something . . . darker,' Phoebe said, not looking at me.

She still wasn't saying his name but I could feel it just under the surface. It was the only name she wasn't saying. The one with power.

'Darker as in . . . on the news they mentioned prostitution, kidnapping . . . murder. Is any of that true?' I asked.

'Perhaps we'd better not . . .' Marshal began, glancing around for the owner in case she was listening. Phoebe cut him off.

'I don't know about a lot of it. There were children who were brought to us. Girls. I wasn't sure where they came from. Celeste called it fostering. She said we were raising a new generation, a new kind of woman who wouldn't be second class. But there were also . . . secrets in the inner circle. I wasn't part of that. But I did know about the uh . . . business. It was how we made money for the manor, for Him.'

'Carlisle?' I said.

She nodded but didn't say anything else. I was dying to know. Did she mean that they all worked as prostitutes? Even my mother? Why? Was that not at odds with the feminine power that Celeste preached? Why would they retreat from the outside world only to return for that? If the 'peace and love goddess power' seemed naive, the idea of them making money through prostitution was almost the polar opposite – greedy and cynical. Like someone else's idea entirely.

I looked at Phoebe. How much did she know about the missing children and the fraud charges? Did she have no idea or was she just protecting herself? I wanted to know but I sensed that she wouldn't give it up. Her face was set and unreadable.

'How did you get away?' I asked instead.

'It was chaos on that last day. Preparations were underway and no one was where they would ordinarily be. I just stuffed what I'd taken into someone's old handbag and went into the woods. It took ages to hike back to civilisation. I was too scared to go on the road in case someone realised I was gone and came looking for me.' She sighed, a network of crinkles around her eyes telling of stress and worry. 'I was scared of a lot of things by then,' she said, then trailed off.

'Preparations for . . . what?' I asked.

She couldn't meet my eye. 'There was a . . . special ritual planned for that night. A secret, only for the highest members to know. They did that sort of thing a few times, shutting us out, keeping us away. I didn't really know what it was all about. Just that the rest of us were to stay in the attic dormitory and not interfere.'

The highest members such as my mother, with her impressive pendant and title. So she was involved. And everyone else was in the attic when the fire started. My stomach rebelled and the sight of the greasy cup of tea in front of me almost made me retch.

'Why not involve you?' I asked, trying to keep my nausea under control.

'There were . . . fractures by then,' Phoebe said. 'Different ideas about what we should be doing or not doing. About the direction Luna Vitae was going in since Celeste's disappearance.'

I looked up, startled. 'What do you mean, "disappearance"? She wasn't there that night, the night of the fire?'

Phoebe looked surprised. 'She disappeared before then.

Quite a while before. That's why things changed. When he took over.'

'Carlisle Riordan,' I said, and saw a flicker in her eyes. Something almost like fear, or reverence. So, they weren't co-leaders then. There was Celeste and then Carlisle. Only I couldn't remember him or what he did. Why was that?

'That's when all the problems began. It became so secretive. I knew I had to leave. He made so many changes. I don't think any of us realised at first how much or how fast things were changing—' She cut herself off, biting her lip nervously.

'What sort of things?' I asked, desperate to know, but she shook her head.

'Nothing I want to burden you with. Besides, I wasn't privy to all the decisions being made above me. He had his entourage just like Celeste. They carried out his wishes. Your mother mentioned rituals once but she never told me what happened in them.'

'What kind of rituals?' Marshal said, making me jump. I almost forgot he was there, watching Phoebe in stony silence, like she was someone else's grubby child and he didn't want her making a mess.

'I don't know,' she said, looking only at me. 'Only that some of the others, like me, who weren't in the know about everything . . . they were afraid. Afraid of something they heard or saw. The rumours started going around and quite a few of us wanted to leave. It was only the lack of cash or a car, or remembering how good things had once been, that kept people there.'

'That sounds awful,' I said quietly, wondering at the same time how she could have left me, left other children, behind when she ran away, knowing there was a reason to be afraid.

'I didn't feel safe for a long time, but when the trials and all that were over I could finally breathe again. I found myself a job by then and got back on my feet.'

'Trials? I read something about those. Was it fraud or this prostitution racket?' Marshal interrupted again. I could see he was making Phoebe uneasy but she answered anyway.

'Both. There were some small communes in cities. Houses with five or six people in them. Small operations like your mother's house. Those members survived the fire. They'd supported the manor even before Carlisle took over. Mostly with credit card fraud and theft. All part of Celeste's belief that consumerism was patriarchal and to be flouted. It wasn't until after she disappeared that Carlisle introduced other avenues of income – the prostitution, the blackmail. He convinced us that it was a revolt against our prudish society, a way to claim back our sexual liberty.' Her cheeks turned pink and she looked away.

Marshal made a scoffing sound under his breath. I wanted to hit him. Could he not see how upset Phoebe was? How embarrassed? I could see how easily one idea turned into another. How Celeste's idea of casting off patriarchy and misogyny was twisted around until it was 'liberating' to use prostitution to make money *for* a man.

Phoebe seemed to read this from my face. 'At the time I was convinced we were blazing a new and more enlightened trail. A lot of us were younger, had run away from home, been disowned or punished for having relationships that were considered inappropriate. We wanted to leave that behind, to be free of all the stigma. But . . . he had us go too far in the other direction. In the end nothing was taboo.'

She broke off to sip her tea. I wanted to ask what other taboos they ignored or broke. But she began to speak again, ignoring what she just said.

'In the aftermath of the fire there was a lot of news coverage and pressure to bring surviving members to justice for their crimes. So the charges of fraud and running brothels were brought. A few members were put away but most drifted off. Like me they went back to normal life, tried to forget.'

'And what about the kidnapping?' Marshal put in. 'Murder. That's what Lucy's mother's been accused of, killing children.'

Phoebe ignored him but didn't meet my eye. She only shook her head. 'The leadership, the inner circle, died in the fire. Like I said, Celeste claimed we were rescuing unwanted children, taking them in. If it was kidnapping, and if there really was murder at Luna Vitae, it would have been the inner circle who knew. Celeste or Carlisle and their most devoted followers.'

She didn't say 'like your mother' but I heard it just the same. Phoebe took a breath and looked up, eyes pleading behind her glasses. 'I did try to track you down to see if you were all right, but no one knew where you were.'

'They changed my name when I went into foster care,' I said. Marshal squeezed my hand comfortingly, which only made me feel worse. I didn't deserve his support.

'When I saw you on the news I knew it was little Lucia all grown up. I can't believe I found you on Facebook after all this time.' Phoebe smiled and covered my hand where it still rested on the pendant.

'Thank you for saving this for me,' I said politely. I was slightly irritated that she sent me such a dire message over a necklace, however ornate and meaningful it was to my mother. She gave me some information as well but not what I wanted most: proof of my mother's innocence. Phoebe seemed to pick up on my restlessness and withdrew her hand.

'I wanted to see you for more than just the necklace. To warn you,' she said.

Marshal sat up straighter. 'Warn us about what?'

'About Luna Vitae, or what's left of it,' Phoebe said.

A chill went through me. 'I thought . . . you said anyone who remained after the fire was locked up or left it all behind.'

'I thought that was the case, but recently . . . I feel as if I am being watched. As if someone out there is taking an interest in me. I've been doing some watching of my own and I'm seeing some worrying activity, almost like . . . they aren't gone. I keep thinking about Celeste, about where she disappeared to. What she's been doing all these years. I feel like I'm being followed, like they're interested in me again. Now that you have been exposed as one of us, I fear they may be taking an interest in you too.'

'You think the cult is still active, that they're . . . after me?' I said, my voice sounding strained even though I tried to sound calm. 'Why?'

'It may be a vestige of the cult itself, or someone with an agenda tied to it somehow. Perhaps it's Celeste coming back to revive it. I don't know. As for why, I believe you were very important to someone at the manor, my dear. Very important indeed.'

'How can you possibly know that?' Marshal snapped.

Phoebe fixed him with a bright, birdlike stare. 'Because she survived.'

Chapter Ten

I was looking for Lucia when I saw the man.

I stopped right there in the hallway looking at him. There were no men at the manor. Some boys, mostly little ones who ran around naked with snotty faces, pooing in the bushes outside because we never had nappies. But no older boys and no men.

It never really seemed weird to me. My old home had no men and Mum never said much about my dad. He left us, that was all there was to it. Her friends were all mums. At school and weekend club I saw mums. Only three of the teachers at school were men and they taught upper years.

This man didn't look like one of those teachers. He had a longish dark beard and his hair was down to his shoulders. He was wearing a necklace like the one Celeste gave out to the women – a moon face and glittering stones. I wanted one so badly but I wasn't old enough. His was one of the nicest with lots of gems.

His clothes were like everyone else's, washed out and loose. A white shirt and jeans with boots on. I looked at the boots, great big leather ones with heavy buckles. No one wore shoes inside the manor. It wasn't a rule. Celeste didn't do rules. But she didn't wear shoes, so her handmaids didn't and everyone else did what they did. My shoes were too small anyway and I couldn't find another pair. I went barefoot everywhere. In the wet I wore wellies which were too big and left blood blisters on my heels.

He saw me looking at his boots and smiled, like he knew something I didn't. Then he reached towards me and took the joint from behind my ear. I found it already rolled and left on a table. I was planning on sharing it with Lucia in our den out in the woods. He put it between his lips and held out his other hand.

I knew what he wanted and handed over my matches. He lit the joint and shook the match out, then put the packet in his pocket, dropping the used one on the floor. He crushed it under his boot, smearing black dust on the rug. He sucked in a lungful of smoke and looked up at the ceiling, ignoring me. I started to pass him, thinking he was done with me. He held out an arm and took my shoulder, stopping me.

He didn't say anything but let out a long smoky breath and then handed the joint to me. His fingers tapped on the back of my neck for a moment. Then he walked off.

I turned and watched him go. As he got to the stairs he took a rolled joint from his pocket and held a plastic lighter to it. He hummed to himself as he climbed the stairs, smoking.

I ran out to the camp to tell Lucia about him. She was already sitting on a rock on the ground by our fire hole. She had flapjacks from the kitchen and a tin of condensed milk to make into toffee. Only I didn't have matches for the fire anymore. I described the man to her and she scrunched up her nose.

'That's Carlisle. He's Celeste's boyfriend. Selene talks about him sometimes. He came to our house once.'

'I didn't know she had a boyfriend.' None of the other women did, not really. A few didn't have their kids with them, but they came to visit with their dads. They never came up to the manor though, just waited at the road for the women to go down there. From the way most of the women talked they didn't rate boyfriends much. They only wanted to be around Celeste and listen to her talk, in real life or on the tapes she started to make and send to other women who weren't ready to join us yet.

Lucia nodded. 'She does but he lives somewhere else. I think in her old house. Selene said something about him doing the business stuff for them. But maybe he's moving here now that Celeste's here all the time.'

I nodded. It felt like the day Lucia had arrived. Like it was the beginning or end of something. The day things started being different or stopped being the same. That sounds like the same thing, but it isn't. Wishing things had stayed the same was nothing like wishing they were different.

All afternoon I kept thinking about meeting him, about how he took my joint and didn't give the matches back, how he wore his boots indoors. He seemed . . . special. The way Celeste was special but not exactly. She was special because she brought us together, we were all there for her. But Carlisle didn't do that and he still felt magical somehow.

If Lona or anyone else took my things, I'd have grabbed them back and run off, or told Lucia about it so we could come up with a revenge plan. Like when we stole all of Lona's underwear and rubbed it on some old fibreglass in the shed to make it itchy. But I gave my matches to him and he hadn't even asked, even after he took the joint.

I didn't tell Lucia about the joint or the matches, or the way he grabbed my shoulder. I didn't tell anyone but I wasn't sure why. It felt like something secret that made me special, the way Selene's talks with Celeste made her special. Celeste's *boyfriend spoke to me. It was almost as good as getting my own necklace. It made me feel important and I didn't want anyone to take that away. Maybe it was because of how Selene was getting so close to Celeste, which made Lucia special too, even more than she was already because she had a mum and I didn't. Even if hers was always busy with Celeste and we hardly ever saw her.*

I watched for Carlisle after that. I almost couldn't help it. My eyes found him without me thinking about it. Every time we were in the same room I had to look at him, the way all the women looked at Celeste. Only now they looked for him too.

Every time I saw him he was talking to a different woman. He leaned in to listen, one hand on their shoulder. Other times he took a cigarette from their hand or a glass of wine. He'd smoke or sip and look in their eyes. It was like they didn't notice he was doing it, just like when I gave him my matches without thinking about it.

I wanted him to look at me again. They did too. I could tell because they started bringing him things – drinks, cakes, cigarettes, joints, clothes to replace his old ones, handmade soap and candles. They were always outside his and Celeste's room with plates and cups and armfuls of stuff.

I saw Celeste look at him too. Before she spoke, instead of looking up at the ceiling or at the murals of Luna, she looked at Carlisle. When he wasn't talking to the others he was at her side, his arm around her. She curled into him, stroked his arm, let him talk whilst she listened.

When he walked through rooms every woman turned to watch him. Like they were sunflowers and he was the sun.

Chapter Eleven

Somehow the following week was even worse.

The reputable papers were back with a thoroughly researched history of the cult. Not quite the bloodthirsty accusations and fake images of the internet mob, but no less damning. Pictures from the trials surfaced, women with blazing eyes and set shoulders being manoeuvred into the court. Pictures from the raids of these 'satellite communes' showing the brothels they had become – the used syringes, dishevelled beds, discarded condoms, sadly wilting lingerie hanging over a dirty bath.

There were other pictures too, from before the fire, showing a man with a dense beard and wild eyes. Carlisle Riordan, the man whose name made me shudder. It was the first time I came across a picture of him; Celeste was a socialite, he was a bit more camera shy. People were trying to find out where he came from but the papers were getting nowhere. Carlisle Riordan was a fake name, obviously, but not a legally changed one. He had more privacy than I did. The man who led the cult after Celeste vanished, who disappeared into the fire with everyone else. In one of the few pictures of him, my mother was at his side, smiling. On one site it was captioned 'The Devil's Right Hand?'.

Celeste was in lots of pictures, dressed in designer clothes and wearing expensive jewellery. Phoebe might have been onto something with her claim that she was funding herself rather than the commune. But where did she go and why give up her whole empire to a man when it was built on women? What was Carlisle planning that even Phoebe, who knew only scraps of information, fled with almost nothing to her name?

The other pictures were worse. Blue-eyed little children in bright, hand-knitted jumpers or school uniforms with blaring captions reading 'Still missing'. An entire double-page spread on what the general public 'needed to know' about the 'sinister cult' that hid in the Welsh countryside.

Come Monday morning the phone calls were almost nonstop. We had the ringer off but the messages piled up. Only now they were accompanied by letters and random visitors. Someone somewhere was putting our address about online. Public interest was high and everyone seemed to be throwing together a documentary or a podcast about Luna Vitae. Interview requests flooded in from professionals and amateurs alike.

The public also seemed to have made up its mind that I was some combination of Little Orphan Annie and the Antichrist. Aside from the interview requests clogging up the phone and my email inbox, there were the ranting, poorly spelled emails and letters from my new 'fans' and haters alike.

You hav ebeen through so much. Please let me know
of anything you need or if you want a place to stay and
are ever in the Lake Distict. You remind me so much of
my daughter and it is such a terrible thing for you to

have lost your mother like that. Come and visit and I will tke you to my church to be blessed. Christ will take your sins onto himself and your soul will be safe with him.

From the sounds of it, Deborah from the Lake District was in a sort of cult herself. I had never been comfortable with anyone who professed to have the one and only 'light', 'way' or 'saviour'. Even politics gave me a slight chill when people got too into it. The do or die, my way or no way, 'my God can do no wrong' aspect cut a little close to something darker lurking in my mind.

If the notes from my well-wishers were a little off-putting, the hateful ones were even more so. I could just about tolerate all that sincerity and Christ-the-redeemer stuff. The letters and emails from furious members of the public were just frightening – blotchy, bold capitals, threats of rape and murder, graphic and laden with a kind of unhinged glee. It was like receiving letters from dozens of serial killers.

On Wednesday a particularly nasty one came through the door. Marshal was trying to get our post rerouted and screened elsewhere, but wasn't having much luck. His dad was too busy putting out political fires to be worried about a little thing like our sanity and safety.

Marshal was in his office and I decided not to bother him with another lot of post. After all, the letters were for me not him. I would open them, put aside any that warranted further action and shred the rest. I galvanised myself, determined to laugh at the frothing hatred. My resolve lasted until I opened the third letter.

At first glance I took it for red ink, but then the smell wafted up. That awful smell of blood left to congeal. It looked like it had been written with a finger, leaving lumps of dried blood. When I noticed what looked like hairs matted into the sticky smears I retched and threw the thing away.

It was a visceral reaction. Of course if anyone implied that one kind of blood was more disgusting than another, I would scoff. I considered myself a feminist. Not as good of a feminist as I should have been – I did still read glossy magazines and spend too much on lipstick – but the idea that periods were somehow unclean was something that never stuck in my mind. I always assumed this was to do with my mother, something she drilled into me as a child. She was, after all, part of a sisterhood of goddess worshippers. Periods were practically their piece of the one true cross.

It was, however, difficult not to turn away from the letter and dash to the sink to scrub my hands. For one thing, I was still experiencing morning sickness. For another, it was one thing to know that my period was a natural thing and nothing to be ashamed of, and quite another to envisage someone using theirs as an inkwell to daub out a threat. If it was a threat. Though it was hard to misconstrue the word 'Heretic' written in letters several inches tall, in blood.

'Marshal!' I called, unwilling to pick the thing up and take it to him or go anywhere near it. The smell, like the roasting beef from so many weeks ago, was making me sick to my stomach.

Marshal came into the living room, looking annoyed that I'd disturbed him. I only pointed at the letter and he looked down at it, face changing from annoyance to disgust. I hurried to wash my hands, scrubbing up my arms with palmfuls of anti-bac soap. When I returned, Marshal was back in his office and on the phone. He left the door open and I heard him insisting he needed to speak to his father immediately.

Too stunned to do much else I sat down and looked at the letter on the floor. It had the feel of a dangerous, invasive insect that might sting or burrow if I took my eyes off it.

When Marshal finally came out of the office he was red

in the face and looked incredibly stressed. He poured himself a measure of whisky from the bottle on the drinks tray and downed it in one. I didn't mention that he had sworn off alcohol, even though he wanted me to remind him.

After a long silence he sighed and sat down. 'I've spoken to Dad and he thinks it would be best if you went away for a while. I agree.'

His words were almost as shocking as the arrival of the bloody message. Sent away. Like some naughty child being packed off to boarding school, or a disgraced woman sent to a nunnery?

'What do you mean, "away"?'

'I mean it's pretty obvious that you being here isn't the best thing right now. You should be somewhere where you and the baby aren't at risk,' he said. 'I've been thinking it too for the past few days but I thought things would get better. Clearly they're not.'

'You think we should move to a hotel in town or . . .' Marshal was already shaking his head.

'Not we. You.'

'On my own?' It came out too loud, my indignant voice so piercing that Marshal winced, looking annoyed. 'What will you be doing?'

'I have to work, Luce. I'm not some admin assistant. I can't just disappear and leave all my duties behind. That sends a poor message. I don't want to be known as the sort of man who vanishes in a crisis.'

I ignored the jab about my job. 'But if it's not safe here . . .'

'Dad has arranged a security detail for the house. I can stay with him and my mother. Our post will be handled by the security firm and they'll keep an eye on the house in case of break-ins or vandalism.'

'And what about me? Can't I stay at Crossley?'

'I don't think that would be for the best . . . Mum and Dad are still very upset about everything. I don't want to make that worse.'

I felt sick, the rejection making me want to cry. It was like being moved on from a foster home. I was an inconvenience, an annoyance. Marshal didn't want me around and neither did his family.

'Think of the stress this is putting on you. You need to be somewhere you can rest,' he was saying.

'Like where?'

'Mum's recommended a private cottage rental in the Peak District. She can have it set up, all the shopping laid in, all ready for you by the end of the day.'

In other words they wanted to stash me in a secluded cottage with a full fridge and all the curtains drawn until it was safe for me to come out. How long had Enid been planning this if she already had a place picked out? I felt angry and guilty at the same time. Furious that they were making decisions about me, guilty because I knew how much trouble I was causing them, how much embarrassment.

The idea of being on my own, miles and miles from anyone to talk to, made me feel slightly sick. I wasn't used to being alone. I hated it. Being alone was a punishment. Something I had a lot of in my first years in care, every time I climbed over the fence to get away from primary school, took food from the kitchen and went off on my own for the day, took something that didn't belong to me. It was all met with the same punishment. Hours alone in the 'quiet room' or on the 'naughty step' or in the 'time-out shed'. I shuddered just thinking about all that silence. Being alone with my own thoughts which all too easily turned to the fire and my nightmares.

'I can't go there all by myself,' I said, panicked.

Marshal held up his hands and I heard irritation creep

into his voice. 'Well, there aren't really that many options at the moment. It's either you go to the cottage or we go with Dad's idea and book you into a health facility that can assure discretion.'

'You mean like a rehab centre? As if there isn't enough gossip about me already!' I cried.

'Which is why I think Mum's idea is the best possible option. Think of the baby, Luce. You can't stay this stressed and expect everything to be fine. You need to be responsible.'

I ducked my head, feeling suddenly ashamed. I knew stress wasn't good for me, let alone the baby. But at the same time I wanted to shout at him that the baby wasn't the only concern, that my health and sanity mattered too. I couldn't take being on my own for weeks on end.

'It's going to stress me out being on my own,' I said, as calmly as possible. 'Besides, what if something happens and I'm all alone?'

Marshal looked for a moment like he wanted to hit something. I'd heard him punch the office wall more than once. Just looking at him I could tell he was at the end of his rope and felt even worse. He was trying his best. I was the one causing problems. Again. I should have just agreed right away, not made more issues. I was being so ungrateful and all he was trying to do was protect me. Still, the idea of being packed off on my own aggravated me. Why couldn't he see how awful it would be for me?

'So what do you suggest?' he asked through gritted teeth when I didn't offer any solution.

'I don't know!' I said, frustrated and on the edge of tears. 'I don't know what to do about this, all right? I don't have any answers. I just want you to leave me alone!'

He stared at me and I felt myself going red. I hadn't meant to shout like that. I felt even more like a naughty child than before. I felt like what I was, a burden.

'Well, if that's what you want. Fine. I'll book the cottage,' he said stiffly, clearly hurt. 'You won't have to see me at all.'

'Marshal . . . I didn't mean—'

'No.' He held up a hand. 'Don't. I think you've said enough. I'll get it arranged and then . . . maybe after some time apart we can have a reasonable discussion.'

I nodded, miserable. I'd hurt his feelings and shouted at him. After everything he did for me, after everything I put him through. Yet a tiny voice at the back of my mind said that he started the argument. He pushed me.

My phone hummed in my pocket with a text. It was the perfect excuse to rush upstairs and shut myself in our bedroom. Thankfully it was a message from Ellie asking if I needed a chat. I rang her straight away.

'Hey, how are things going?' she asked as soon as she picked up.

'Pretty terrible. I feel like I've been stuck in this house for months already. Everything just keeps getting worse.' I let out a long sigh. 'Marshal thinks I should go and hide out somewhere.'

'What? Where?' she asked, clearly astonished.

'He isn't sure yet. But it's looking like a cottage some-where or a fancy rehab centre where they keep your identity a secret.'

'Like where celebrities go?' I heard typing and realised she was probably at work. I felt bad for ringing her in the middle of the day. Time was starting to lose all meaning for me, shut up in the house.

'I hope not,' I said. 'I'm sort of trying *not* to get photo-graphed right now.' It came out sharper than I intended.

'Oh, right, sorry . . .'

'It's fine. Sorry, I'm on edge. How are things going for you?'

'Oh, they're fine.' Ellie sounded distracted and I couldn't

tell if it was because she was working or putting on a brave face.

'Come on, I'm sick of talking about me. I want to know what's going on with you.'

'All right . . . it's going to be so stupid though, compared to your thing. You know I said about my new side business?'

'Yes. What is that exactly? You never said.'

'Just a health business, you know, supplements and that. But there was this seminar week thing I wanted to go to and I just found out this woman I was meant to be splitting a hotel room with isn't going anymore. I . . . er . . . met her in the company chat and she's got to go in for eye surgery now. Anyway, now I can't afford to go.'

'That sucks. Did you have to pay for the conference already?'

'Yeah and it wasn't cheap either. I'm tapped out. And I'm having no luck selling my place to someone else so I can't get any of the cash back. Honestly I thought next week was going to be *it*, you know? That I could come back and finally tell those bitches in the admin office to shove their job . . . no offence.'

'None taken,' I said, trying not to laugh. A thought occurred to me 'Listen, whereabouts is it?'

'Caernarfon. At the Imperial Hotel. I was meant to get a room there but it's a five-star sort of job, and even the places nearby are too expensive. I'm skint and payday's not until after.'

'What if we went together?' I said.

'Like . . . you'd come hide out in Wales?' she said, sounding uncertain.

'Yes. I couldn't stay in a hotel or anything but I could get Marshal to find a cottage outside of town and you could drive in to your conference in a hire car. I'd pay for it, or at least Marshal would.' I crossed my fingers, hoping for her to say yes, hoping that Marshal would agree. I was giving him what he wanted after all.

'Well, shit. Yeah! That sounds great. As long as you don't mind?' Ellie added doubtfully. 'I've really missed you, but I don't want him thinking I'm just on the make.'

'Honestly I'd rather be with you than on my own with only pheasants and squirrels for company. Besides, with the baby and everything . . . I don't want to be alone if something happens.'

'Sure, I'll look out for you. We can have a proper girly getaway.'

I promised to email over the details once I sorted everything. If I could get Marshal to OK my plan I'd be off to Wales. Only a short drive from the manor. I always tried not to buy into the idea of divine intervention or magical thinking; still the coincidence was striking. Perhaps I could get some answers and a bit of time to poke around without being followed. More than anything I just wanted space to think, and remember.

Chapter Twelve

I tried not to be offended by the speed with which Marshal arranged everything. My constant morning sickness was also joined by sore breasts and an ache in my back, so I wasn't in the best mood anyway. Still, his tight-lipped efficiency made me feel as though I was being punished, as if each expense, each new arrangement, was a burden he blamed me for.

I knew it was probably all my guilty conscience getting the best of me. He wasn't keen to be rid of me, I told myself. It was just his concern that made him get it all organised, and money was no object. He was worried about the baby, and for me. Still, a little corner of my mind felt guiltier and yet more irritated every time he broke out the credit card to push through a short-notice reservation or express-deliver shopping. I felt like he was still angry about our argument, waiting for me to apologise. Even though I already did so many times.

It was getting harder and harder for me to share space with Marshal without feeling guilty over one thing or another. Either it was the raw territory of the argument, the lies I told him, or the presence of the baby. The way he couldn't hug me without putting one hand on my belly, patting me like the bonnet of a new car. Every time he mentioned what would be best for the baby I wanted to shake him to get him to listen to *me*, to what I needed. The selfishness of my thoughts appalled me. It was his child. Of course he cared about it. But still I felt this rift between us. He never failed to acknowledge the baby and I was desperate to forget about it.

Finally the time to leave came. Marshal arranged a rented car under the name of one of his dad's trusted employees. It was parked in an out-of-the-way car park where I could switch from our car to the new one without being seen. It was necessary to avoid the photographers but it made me feel like a criminal. Marshal kissed me and made sure I had the credit card and his emergency numbers. Somehow they managed to get me a new joint card with a different name on it. I didn't ask how. When I drove away, guilt still gnawed at my stomach. I was leaving Marshal to deal with my mess after all.

To distract myself I turned the radio up loud, and after picking Ellie up from her flat my first stop was for coffee. Ellie went to get them whilst I hid in the car. We were still too close to Bristol for me to feel safe. It had been a grim few weeks and I was glad to feel the caffeine in my veins. Though after gulping down my latte I had something else to feel guilty about. It also brought on my heartburn.

Ellie was her usual bright self, singing along to the radio. She also asked a lot of questions, but nothing about my mother or the accusations, for which I was grateful.

'So, how's Marshal coping?' she asked as we shot down the almost deserted predawn motorway.

'About as well as can be expected. I think it really shocked him. Obviously, I wish I'd told him sooner but . . . I just didn't know how. It's not exactly something I had much of a roadmap for. Carmen tried to help but she didn't really seem to know how to broach it either.'

'That's your therapist?'

'Yeah. I've been seeing her for a little while now. Before then I did all the NHS CBT stuff, which didn't help. Then when I was in care it was this social worker I had to talk to.' I shuddered in mock horror. 'Linda. Loony Linda, the other kids used to call her.'

'Yikes. Not what you want from a therapist-type.'

'Not really. She was all right I suppose, just a bit earnest. Loved making dolls and teddies talk and thought everything could be fixed with some jelly babies and a cuddle.' To be fair, I always enjoyed the attention. I don't suppose I had much one-to-one care in a commune. Not if Phoebe was right about the hierarchy. It seems like everyone was focused on Celeste, not on mundane things like childcare and education. My first memories of school were struggling to read and needing special help in every subject, except for art.

'Did you tell her about all this?' Ellie asked, bringing me back to the present.

'I've been too scattered to try and talk about it. Not exactly the best time to go in and see her anyway. Not with the people still camping outside.' I paused for a moment, then said, as offhandedly as possible, 'I've been getting some weird letters as well.'

'What, like . . . hate mail?' Ellie's eyes were wide when I glanced over.

'Sort of. Some "come to Christ" stuff and some that call me a murderer or a devil worshipper who eats babies,' I said, with a little laugh. It came out a bit forced and I regretted it immediately. 'But there was one that was a bit . . . well, it's the reason I'm taking this trip. It spooked Marshal.' And me.

'What did it say?' Ellie asked, sipping at her coffee. She

was sitting up straight, listening to every word. I felt a tiny bit pleased to have her attention after so many days of being ignored at home, spoken about and moved around like a piece of furniture that didn't quite fit in.

'It called me a heretic. That was it. Just that one word,' I said. I didn't say about the blood. The last thing I wanted to do was scare her after she agreed to come with me.

'A heretic? What does that even mean? More spawn of the devil stuff? I saw some memes about it. They put horns on your father-in-law,' she snickered.

'Maybe. I mean, Luna Vitae was definitely alternative, radical even, not exactly church approved. But . . . just that one word. It felt different to all the outraged letters. Like it was more personal.'

'You don't think it was someone who still believes in all that stuff, do you?' Ellie asked. 'They said on the news that everyone was either in prison, dropped the cult stuff or ended up dead. There's no one left.'

'I know. It was just weird,' I said, and hurriedly changed the topic by pointing out a flock of sheep.

The fact was, I had wondered exactly the same thing as Ellie. Since Phoebe had warned me about the possibility I tried to put it out of my mind, but it kept coming back to the surface. I didn't understand though why anyone in the cult would still care about me. Surely as a child I wasn't really part of what went on.

From what I gathered of Luna Vitae since looking it up online, their beliefs weren't fanatical. No hard and fast rules or doctrines to follow. They were about empowering women, withdrawing from the world of men and living without the responsibilities they had elsewhere – being employees, daughters, wives and mothers. They did what they wanted, when they wanted, and did not believe in shame or obligation. It was softcore feminism and hippy peace and love. Hardly the

105

kind of thing that suggested blood feuds and long-lasting vendettas.

So why did I suddenly feel so worried that someone out there might think I was a traitor, a backslider, a heretic? Why could I not shake the feeling that I did not want to find out just what Luna Vitae did with heretics?

'Are you all right?' Ellie asked. 'You look miles away.'

'Yeah, I'm fine. Feeling a bit sick.'

'Here, have this.'

She took out a blister pack of fat, square chews and popped two out. She held them out. I glanced down at them briefly.

'What are they, Tums?'

'Natural sickness remedy. Ginger pastilles.'

I took them, popped them into my mouth and chewed. They tasted pretty good actually. Ginger and honey. After a few moments I felt my minor nausea subside.

'Where did you get them from? I should stock up,' I said.

'Oh, I can give you some packs. I've got loads. It's my side hustle. Nutrisoul. They make so many yummy remedies. I actually brought some along.' She produced a small brown bottle with a purple label from her handbag. 'Lavender and tonka drops, for stress.' She wafted them at me. 'They smell lush. Couple of those in your bath and your worries will melt away,' she said happily.

I had my doubts that it would help. But they did smell lovely. At least I wasn't feeling sick anymore.

We arrived at the cottage around noon. It was a little drystone thing with two storeys and a slate roof. A glazed tile outside said 'Tri ar ddeg'. Marshal said he chose it for the garden and the rainfall shower. I suspected it was more to do with the tall fence around it and where it was situated. We had to go down a tiny, unmarked lane for miles to get to it. There was no through road and grass grew

106

in the centre of the lane. 'Out of the way' didn't do it justice.

After parking up and dragging our bags inside I saw that someone had been by. There was fresh fruit in a bowl on the tiled kitchen island and a basket with bread and a fruit-cake on the scrubbed table. The fridge was fully stocked and there was a scent of fresh ironing in the air. A stack of parcels had been brought in and piled in the lounge. These would be the things Marshal ordered and had sent there for me – maternity clothes, back-supporting cushions, books on pregnancy and multivitamins. I wasn't in a hurry to look through them.

The two bedrooms were up a creaky pine staircase. One double and a single separated by a bathroom. Ellie took the single. I dumped my bag in the double room and looked out the gingham-curtained window. Green and brown fields stretched away. I couldn't even see the main road from where we were, though I knew it was out there, somewhere.

I had the urge to draw those undulating lines of hedges and ploughed fields. The colours were muted by the grey sky but it made the whole scene look beautifully tragic, like something out of a period drama. Of course I had nothing with me to draw with, let along paint. I didn't want to aggravate Marshal by packing supplies and he was there the whole time I was filling my suitcase. Maybe I could get something in town or have Ellie get it for me. Just a cheap set of paints and a good stock of watercolour paper. Whilst I still had time to paint.

I promised Marshal I'd call once we got there but I couldn't get reception on my phone. The welcome book I found in the kitchen said I'd only get signal at the crossroads, back up the lane. Wonderful. There was, however, a landline and though it was a bit muffled and I could hear clicks and beeps on the line, I managed to get through.

'We made it,' I said, trying to sound light-hearted.

'Your connection's terrible, sounds like dial-up in the background,' Marshal said. 'How's the cottage?' He sounded stiff, like he hadn't yet forgiven me for my outburst.

'Oh, it's . . . lovely,' I said, trying to placate him. 'Thank you for choosing such a nice one. How's everything on your end?'

He warmed a little. 'About the same, though I'm over at Crossley now. There were some journos at the gate. Bit inconvenient but we managed.'

I wanted to apologise, but it would have been my thousandth one and I was getting tired of falling all over myself trying to make things right. Instead I told an inane story about the horse lorry we got stuck behind for several miles. He laughed dutifully.

'Well,' he said once I lapsed into silence. 'I'll let you go.'

I said goodbye but it felt all wrong and stiff, like I was talking to a former colleague, not my husband. I felt depressed after putting the phone down. I almost wished there wasn't a landline to use. I shook off the thought and went to find Ellie.

After we fully explored the house and found the usual collection of old paperbacks and DVDs that haunt holiday cottages, I was fairly exhausted. Whilst Ellie brought down her Nutrisoul bag I stashed the parcels, unopened, in the under-stairs cupboard and crashed out on the sofa. There was Wi-Fi, just about, and I started looking for local takeaways. No such luck.

We made the best of it. Although quite luxurious the cottage was draughty and Ellie had a go at lighting a fire in the log burner. It smoked a bit but thankfully warmed the place up. After wrestling with the fancy range I was able to cook some frozen pizzas and we shared some of the 'welcome basket' wine. I savoured my half glass whilst Ellie showed me her products excitedly. She had something for everything – hair growth, high blood pressure, depression, exhaustion, iron deficiency, psoriasis and infertility.

'Not that you need that one,' she laughed, putting aside the little blue glass bottle. 'But there are supplements for pregnancy. Not all those chemical ones either. Proper naturally sourced ingredients with a FIE-20 rating.'

'What's that?'

'First Index Element,' Ellie reeled off. 'It's how Nutrisoul ensure their products are the best. They developed their own ranking system. Twenty means it comes directly from a natural source. It's the highest you can get. It goes down to minus twenty and that's what's in those capsules you get from the supermarkets, all those polluted fish oils and overly processed chalk dust.'

I'd never seen her so excited about anything before. I had to hand it to her, the remedies looked beautiful. All green and blue glass dropper bottles, purple and aqua packets of pastilles and amber glass pump bottles of lotion. All in a case lined with green velvet. I was glad for her. She'd not had a good time working in admin. If this was her way out it had my vote.

By the time we ate and watched a random film on the large TV, I was barely keeping my eyes open. Ellie wanted to get a good night's sleep for her first day at the conference and said a hasty goodnight whilst hunting for a night cream in her bag. I took myself upstairs and slid into the unfamiliar sheets. Of course once I was lying down in the dark my mind refused to let me sleep. I lay there for ages, even after Ellie had stopped moving around and presumably dropped off.

I watched the shadows in the room. They were new and different and I kept anxiously checking them for movement. I felt like a child looking for monsters. According to the wall clock over the door, which I could just about see in the dark, it was just gone one in the morning. I couldn't will myself to sleep though.

Suddenly, white light flooded in through the window. I jerked against the mattress then made myself lie very still, holding my breath. I strained my ears. The outside security light clicked off. I let myself relax, bit by bit. Probably a rabbit or a badger or something. I'd not heard anyone walking on the gravel outside.

Still, I watched the shadows, terrified that the door might creak open. That I was being watched.

Chapter Thirteen

The next morning Ellie was fresh-faced and chipper. I felt like an old woman, shuffling around in my slippers, desperate for a coffee. Although the kitchen was stocked up there was only decaf. Clearly Marshal provided a list but the wine somehow slipped through. Something I hoped he never found out about.

After breakfast I drove us into Caernarfon and dropped Ellie off at the Imperial Hotel. It was a square building plastered a buttermilk colour, with faux pillars outside. There were already a lot of women milling around outside. Most of them were dressed like Ellie in bohemian floaty tops, though some were clearly fitness pros, in leggings and jumpers which hung off their shoulders. The amount of glowing skin and shiny hair on show made me feel older and more exhausted than I was already. There was a sign outside the hotel showing that this was not a one-off event. They had dates every month until the New Year.

'See you later,' Ellie trilled, already letting herself out. 'I'll try and bag you some samples.'

With that she was off and I was left to entertain myself for the day. My first stop was to find a supermarket where

I could get some forbidden treats like proper coffee. I had on my disguise again: a hood over my red hair, a pair of cheap reading glasses on my nose. It wasn't strictly necessary but it made me feel less conspicuous, less worried that someone would recognise me. The horrible letters were bad enough; I didn't relish the idea of a face-to-face confrontation.

After finding no art supplies in the supermarket and not knowing where the nearest shopping centre was, I told myself I'd look it up later. Instead I got myself a takeaway latte and set my satnav to take me to the manor. Excitement and apprehension dogged me the whole way there. I was afraid I wouldn't find the answers I needed, and afraid that I would.

The manor was situated in the countryside away from Caernarfon, between the village of Llanberis and Snowdon itself. Hidden away in the National Park, the site was never redeveloped. I had to go back several decades to even find it on a map. It was as though someone tried to erase its location. I supposed to keep the public away. It seemed like everyone was pretending it didn't exist. Just like I had been doing for twenty years. I wasn't sure how much of it would even be left standing.

When I rounded a bend and saw the turning for the manor I felt a wave of emotion so strong that tears sprang to my eyes. I recognised it. The way you might recognise a picture from a book you read when you were little. Smaller, not as striking, but underneath the same lines and shapes. I turned off and drove down the winding track until I approached a metal gate.

There was a knot in my throat as I got out and opened the gate so I could drive up the track. I felt closer to my past than ever before, as if I could almost smell it. At the same time I felt anxiety creeping in. What if there were journalists or bloggers taking pictures or recording at the

112

manor or the site where it had been? What if I was headed right for them? Still, it wasn't enough to make me turn back. I don't think anything could have done that by then. I was too close to leave it behind again.

After driving a short way I found a clearing where someone had spread gravel a very long time ago. There wasn't a lot of it and mostly it was hidden by weeds and leaf mould. The manor site was only accessible on foot from there. I knew that much from comparing old and new maps. An overgrown path led away to elders, nettle banks and huge rocks.

As I made my way along the track I tried to remember what it was like to walk it as a child. Though no full memories came, I could imagine it well enough. The women, my mother, me. Like a nomadic tribe moving on with children, bedding, clothes and kitchen stuff in tow. I did remember the car, which smelled like dogs and cigarettes. God knows where they bought it from. It was the first car I'd ever been in. Based on what Phoebe said it must have belonged to the commune from the moment we arrived, like everything else we took there.

I wove my way through the trees for over an hour. By the time I crested a small hill and saw a bridge below, I was happy to see any sign of civilisation. It was a wooden foot-bridge with chicken wire to provide grip, but it had come apart in places. Beneath it was a two-metre drop into a gully where a stream frothed over rocks. A long time ago, someone carved or rather scratched directions onto the pillar on one side. It was a crude representation of the moon face from my mother's pendant, which I had in my pocket. An arrow pointed over the bridge.

I knew I was close. After a bit more struggle, this time up a flinty hill, I came to a point where the land suddenly plunged down. It formed a rocky hill straight down to a clump of old oaks. I could see from there that the manor did not burn to the ground as I'd always imagined. The roof poked over the trees. It was clear that no journalist would be waiting for me in there. Not unless they had a ladder. Just through the first trees, there was a tall fence. The hefty kind put up around demolished buildings in Bristol to be smothered in spray paint and posters. I couldn't see any kind of gate from that distance. Something told me there wouldn't be one. The manor was cordoned off, like the crime scene it was.

At least it was downhill all the way, though dark clouds were gathering overhead. I was in for a very wet walk unless I hurried. As I reached the bottom of the slope and came around the side of the screen of trees, I began to fully appreciate the size of the hoardings all around the place. Easily one and a half times my height. The posts for them were sunk into the ground. No chance of squeezing underneath, or so I thought.

I was circling the fence, trying to find a gate or a handy stump to help me climb over, when I almost twisted my ankle in a large hole. It was deep and went right into the sandy soil under some trees. A badger sett. The little hill there was riddled with holes and the dirt around the bottom of the hoardings was loose, falling away into the tunnels. I went looking around and found a sturdy stick to poke and thrash at the weeds and crumbling soil with. In the end I was left with roughly a foot of space at the widest part of the gap.

Overhead thunder rolled threateningly. I had to get a roof between me and the oncoming downpour. I didn't fancy the long trek back to the car in soaking clothes. I got down on my hands and knees and, mindful of my stomach, slid under the fence on my back.

After kicking and pulling my way through, I got up and knocked the sand and dirt off my clothes. Around me the weeds were tall and undisturbed. I doubted anyone had been past the fence in years. There had been no reason to, I supposed. The cult ceased to be interesting to anyone long ago. Even now the press was more concerned with staking out Crossley and our house than hiking out into the countryside to find a ruin.

I turned around and caught my breath as I got my first proper look at the manor.

It was not as I'd seen it in my dreams. For a start it was smaller, which made sense. My memories of it were those of a small child and exaggerated by years and nightmares until the place was miles wide and many storeys tall. In reality it was a large house. Nothing more or less. Not multi-winged or turreted. It could perhaps have been subdivided into several small terraced cottages. It had only three floors, one of which was the attic, with gabled windows in the roof.

The redbrick walls were charred on the upper floors and partly obscured by ivy, elders and greenish slime from a broken gutter. The slate roof was cracked open on top like a boiled egg. Beams jutted towards the sky like blackened bones. The windows were mostly glassless holes. A mouldering curtain flapped at one of them.

Mindful of broken glass, rusted metal or anything else that might be lurking in the overgrown grass, I picked my way towards the building. It was probably my imagination getting the best of me but the area inside the hoarding seemed somehow more silent and still than the fields outside it. Almost as if the place was waiting for me, holding its breath.

The ground around the manor was rutted where old tyre tracks had been worn away further by rain. I remembered the fire engines, the police and ambulances. They had to come over the fields, by tractor trails, their lights whirling. I looked off to the side and noticed several shapes covered in ivy and half sunk in brambles. Small buildings I couldn't remember at all. Wary of the crumbling manor I started my search in those outbuildings. There were three, two brick and one made of irregular stones. Perhaps these were once stables or sheds.

I went into the larger of the two brick buildings first. The air smelled damp and of things slowly rotting in the dark. I didn't bring a torch and, cursing my own stupidity, had to use my phone to light my way. On one wall peeling paint showed where a mural had once been. I could still see a bit of it – stars and a full moon. Most of it was painted over in red. A rusted tin of paint was on the floor as if the job was abandoned. There was furniture in there too – odd dining chairs and coffee tables, wood pallets with slabs of foam on top. People slept there at some point. Perhaps it was where visitors to the commune were allowed to stay. If any of the manor residents slept there they would have avoided the fire. Yet, as far as I knew, there were no survivors other than myself. Why were these sheds empty that night?

I remembered then what Phoebe said. They were told to stay in the attic rooms, away from whatever ritual Carlisle and his loyalists were planning. Did that order extend to those sleeping in these outbuildings? If so, why? Was it just bad luck that placed them directly in the path of the fire?

A sudden sound above me made me leap back, certain the roof was about to come down. But it was just some swallows that nested in the beams flitting around. The roof looked reasonably solid, though some light shone through where the odd slate was skewed.

As I looked around I quickly realised that everything was simply left behind. Clothing, bedding, the odd toy or book. I guessed that the disarray was caused by a police search following the fire. Anything of use as evidence was likely locked away somewhere, leaving only the drossy remnants of day-to-day life behind to rot. So much stuff.

I found out from an archived newspaper story that the manor itself belonged to a woman called Jean McBride. After joining Luna Vitae she changed her name to Arianrhod and gave the manor to Celeste. A place to build one huge commune far from prying eyes. She and Celeste seemed close if the pictures online were anything to go by. A pair of glittering goddesses, arm in arm at parties and events. She must have been at least equal to my mother in terms of position. I wondered what happened to her when Celeste vanished. Maybe she went with her, or died in the fire like the rest of them.

I guessed the manor technically belonged to someone, somewhere. Maybe even to Celeste herself. Yet it was just left. Perhaps it was too large and expensive to restore. Perhaps, if some other McBride now owned the place, they just wanted to forget it existed.

The second brick building was similarly laid out: makeshift beds, some clothes, holey sheets tacked up for privacy. Candles were clustered on the little windowsills. Wax dribbles still clung to the red tiles there and ran all down the brick walls. There was no sign that there had ever been electricity or water laid on, though in the corner there was a wood stove, rusted up and full of cobwebs.

The last building was the one with rough stone walls, set a way back from the others. The roof was made of slate, but the door to it was not a wooden shed door, but a hefty metal thing. It looked like the kind of place you'd store expensive tools to keep them from getting stolen. Fortunately the door was broken open. The metal was warped as if great force was used to get in. Did the police do that? I eased open the creaky door and peered into the gloom.

Inside were metal animal stalls. They reminded me of the pig pens I saw at the city farm on a school trip, but these were rusty and the straw on the floor was old and damp, turned to mulch. The walls were plastered, but there were no windows, no signs of candles either. It was odd that a group so concerned with freedom and hippy living would have raised animals in the dark, locked behind a metal door.

I shone the light of my phone around and jumped. On the wall opposite the stalls was another mural, but this one did not show the familiar moon. The entire wall was painted in furious slashes of bright red gloss paint. It reflected the light like fresh blood. Primary yellow was slathered on as well, forming a single, giant circle. Around it were black rays, spiralling out. At the centre of the circle was a face: wide-open eyes with red irises and deep, dark pupils; a mouth like an open wound, with a cavernous black throat. Beneath it, in precise white letters, were the words 'Hail the Divine Sun and Know Peace'.

My insides lurched. I dropped my phone, hands suddenly numb. Scrabbling for it, tears sprang to my eyes and I found myself shaking uncontrollably. Yet when I looked up and saw the mural again, I couldn't understand my own fierce reaction. It was just a laughing sun on a badly painted wall. The paint was just that, not blood, but old paint flaking. Its eyes were not searing pits, just dots daubed on the plaster.

With my phone in my hand and my heart in my throat, I edged away from it. Why did it seem so huge, so frightening? It was just a mural, like the moon painting. But still my flesh crept to look at it. For that moment I saw it with my child's eyes, before I could reason it out, and my response was pure terror.

I was about to leave, shuddering, when something else caught my eye. A shape in the shadows of a stall. I jumped, thinking it was a person. Then common sense took hold and I realised it was a wood frame. I went closer and saw that was wrong as well.

It was a set of wooden stocks held shut with an iron ring

and padlock. The post they were on had sunk deep into the ground where a slab was torn up.

I checked the next stall, then the next. All but the one nearest the door had stocks in them. Though there was a hole in the first stall, where they might have been before. A line of stocks. Stocks that pointed straight towards the sun mural, with its laughing mouth and blood-red eyes.

Chapter Fourteen

It was summer and Lucia and I were swimming at the lake. It wasn't too far from the manor but far enough that we stayed all day, with a bag of apples and stale cakes from the kitchen. We didn't come back until it was getting dark and too cold to swim. Dragging the wet towels behind us on the ground and wincing when our bare feet landed on thistles and sharp stones.

It was fun. I hadn't been seeing Lucia as much since her mum got them their own room on Celeste's floor. We didn't sleep next to each other anymore, whispering when we couldn't sleep. Selene was around more during the day too. Before that she only saw us if we passed around the house. She petted Lucia on the head like a stray cat she hadn't seen for a few days. Now, though, Selene was one of Celeste's favourites so she was always by her side, taking Lucia with her to serve wine or just sit next to her.

'Want to swim tomorrow?' I asked, not wanting to go in the house and split up to our own floors.

Lucia nodded, but then drooped. 'Can't. Full moon.'

The full moon was a big night at the manor, but not usually for us kids. The women had their special circle out in the garden, with singing, wine and chanting, but we were normally left out of it. Only now Selene was a handmaiden, so she'd be doing a ritual with Celeste, which meant she'd have Lucia there to show off. Mostly for Carlisle.

Carlisle spoke more often now, in the circle on full moons or in the main hall when everyone was there in the evening. I saw him when slipping through to get outside or when playing chase in the dark. He'd stand up with Celeste at his feet and talk about how special it was to be a mother, to bring life into the world and pass on the teachings of Luna Vitae, how mothers were the future. Celeste would stoke her big belly and smile up at him, nodding, and he'd put a hand on her head. Given all the talk about mothers, the women who had kids and wanted to impress him now took them to rituals or to listen to the talks at night. To show they were special too, like Celeste. They could be beside Carlisle and have him look at them too.

'Don't go to circle then. Or come swimming and we'll come back before then,' I said.

Lucia thought about it, then nodded. 'OK. If we're back before night.'

We went upstairs then and I said night on my way up to the attic.

The next morning we met outside. Lucia had the towels which were still damp. I had a bag with oat biscuits and half a packet of raisins. We had a stick fight on the way to the lake and when we got there we played pirates on the little island in the middle. When we got hungry we lit a fire to get warm and eat round. Lucia looked into it and chewed her lip.

'Carlisle's been in our room,' she said, like she was dying to say it for ages.

I stopped with a biscuit halfway to my mouth. The rooms on Celeste's floor were the only places we weren't allowed

121

to just walk in. They were private places for her and her handmaids to be with Luna. It wasn't a rule, not really, but it was something we all knew. I thought about Carlisle's boots, which he still wore every day, indoors. He was special.

'What for?' I asked. Because he spoke to Selene enough in the manor anyway, now that Celeste was in her room more, resting.

'Sex,' Lucia said, squashing raisins into a ball.

I wrinkled my nose. We knew about sex stuff. The women talked about it and had it too, in the attic room, alone or together. Sometimes when their men visited you'd spot them in the woods. It was funny but gross, like when the little kids pooed in the main hall. Celeste was going to have a baby because she had sex with Carlisle. I accidentally saw Carlisle having sex with other people a few times. Not in the attic or the woods, but in the old bunker under the house. With the rusty pipes and the dead, cold air. No one went down there, unless you really wanted to hide from someone. It's where I hid after Lona found out about the fibreglass in her underwear. And a few times since when we did other stuff to her.

'Do you think Celeste knows?' I asked, because I never heard of him going to someone's room before, or even to the attic. It was something we weren't meant to mention, like the boots, like how he was a man but still at the manor.

'She was there too,' Lucia said. 'He said he wants her baby to have a brother or sister. So my . . . I mean, Selene, she's got to have a baby too. Only . . .'

'Only what?'

'She said she can't, ages ago,' Lucia said, looking into the fire. 'She had a lot of wine and she told me that when I was born they said it did something and she can't have another baby. She was happy about it, I think. Because she doesn't have to worry. Only now she does want one.'

122

'Did she not tell him?' I asked. It was so weird, thinking about someone not telling the truth, especially to Carlisle. Everyone wanted his attention. That meant being open. We were all open all the time. Even about things that could get us in trouble, like the tricks we played on Lona or the things we took. We never hid anything, except ourselves, when Lona was after us.

'I don't think so,' Lucia said. 'Maybe . . . maybe it's fixed now.'

'Maybe Luna fixed it, like she made Arianrhod stop being so sad all the time.' That was why she gave us the manor, or rather gave it to Celeste. Celeste helped Luna to heal Arianrhod and make her happy after her husband died.

Lucia nodded and then didn't say anything else about it. We finished eating and went to play with the sticks from the fire, putting them in the water to make them hiss.

It got dark, darker than it had been the day before. It must have been later. We were building a new bit of our camp and didn't notice. By the time we got back to the manor the moon was up and shining with no clouds, so it was easier to see, but very, very cold. Especially for us in our damp t-shirts and knickers.

From the front of the manor we could hear the full-moon circle. Their chant was going up and down, louder and softer. 'Luna, hear our joyful SONG, in service we find freeDOM. To serve you is to serve ourSELVES. To love you is to love our WORLD.' Along with the shaking of bells, there was clapping and the rumble of hand drums.

I was listening to the familiar song, looking up at the moon and wishing, like I did every month, for my mum to come to us, when someone pushed me. I went staggering to one side as Selene rushed past me and grabbed Lucia by the arm.

'Where have you been?' she snapped, shaking Lucia. 'Do

123

you have ANY idea how much you have embarrassed me tonight?'

Lucia looked frozen. I'd never seen Selene yell or grab her before. Selene never really touched her at all. None of the women shouted or hurt us. Not even Lona. When she got angry she just hissed like a snake and got you by the shirt to take you to the pantry and shut you in for a while. But Selene was twisting Lucia's arm so much it looked like it would snap. I looked around for someone to help, and saw Carlisle.

He was on the steps in front of the manor, in the dark under the porch. I could only see him by the tiny glow from his cigarette. He watched but didn't say anything.

Selene was still ranting at Lucia about how she'd embarrassed her, ruined the full moon, thankless, thoughtless. After everything she'd done, everything she'd given. She was ashamed of her, disgusted, wished she never kept her. Next time she'd have a good child, a better daughter. I felt sick, scared. Lucia was crying, her arm pulled up and looking like it was about to pop off.

'Stop it!' I jumped at Selene and she didn't have time to stop me. I pushed her and she let go of Lucia, who fell down, crying. Selene swung around and slapped me across the face. I tasted blood.

The three of us stood there. The chanting carried on. Smoke went up from Carlisle's cigarette. He didn't move.

'You can't have another baby,' Lucia said. She was whispering, but it was so quiet out there I could hear it like she was right next to me. Selene heard. Carlisle heard. I knew because he straightened up, the glow by his face getting brighter as he breathed in.

'Carlisle,' Selene said, and it sounded like she was about to cry then. 'Carlisle, wait. Please. I can. Of course I can.'

She didn't look back at us. She chased after him as he

turned away. After a second her words cut off in a short, sharp slap. The door opened and I saw Carlisle had her by the neck, pushing her inside. Then the manor door slammed shut, leaving us in the dark.

I turned back to Lucia. She was already on her feet. We were used to it. Picking ourselves up, wiping our own cuts.

'You upset him,' I said.

'I didn't mean to.'

I felt bad then. Selene lied to Carlisle. Lied to be special, when she already had everything else – a room, Celeste, her special necklace. And Lucia had all that too, and a mum. I didn't have anything. Only that one time Carlisle looked at me and it was just us. No woman at the manor ever looked at me like that, not even Lona when she was angry with me. She looked at me like I could be any of the kids there. She hated us all the same.

I wanted him to see me again. To know I wouldn't make him angry or upset him. I was good, better than Selene, than Lucia. I had a joint hidden upstairs, to make him happy. I ran towards the manor to fetch it and take it to him, leaving Lucia outside in the cold, where she belonged.

Chapter Fifteen

Unable to spend one more moment in the presence of the mural, I made a quick getaway. I only felt secure once I hiked all the way back to the clearing and shut myself in my car. Once there I felt stupid and annoyed with myself. I'd walked all the way out there and then fled at the first sign of something moderately spooky. Yes, the stocks were a shock, but it wasn't like they were dangerous. Just things. They couldn't hurt me.

The weather had turned bad as I was walking back. Rain now sheeted over the windshield. I cranked the heater up to keep the glass from fogging over. Between the long walk there and back, plus the time I spent poking around, it was already late afternoon. I had to get back and collect Ellie. As I put on my seatbelt I told myself firmly that tomorrow I'd come back, get a grip and take on the manor itself.

On my way to pick Ellie up I stopped at a retail park and went into a bargain store. I bought a torch, a large pack of batteries and, on impulse, a cigarette lighter. There were some candles left, stuck on ledges about the place. Maybe some more light would keep me from panicking again.

Ellie was somehow packed with energy after a day at the conference. She had indeed bagged many samples, all in little plastic bottles and foil packets. She went through all of them on the drive home, describing their health and beauty benefits. She only stopped talking about the purity of their natural ingredients long enough to tell me what she wanted from McDonald's for dinner.

I didn't tell her where I'd been all day. When she paused long enough to ask I just said something vague about Netflix and let her carry on her lecture about kale and raspberry leaf tea. I didn't want her to worry about me getting freaked out or being off on my own. Mostly I didn't want to talk about what I found.

Whilst Ellie took her food into the living room I said I had a headache and went upstairs. As she set about vlogging for her Instagram followers, I tried to find more information on what I saw at the manor.

Nothing came up about the 'divine sun' that I saw in the stone building. I supposed that the police investigation after the fire was confidential, but it was surprising that seemingly no one else had gone out there to snap pictures, not even a solitary urban explorer. The more I thought about it though, it made sense. The place was quite out of the way, not easily accessible for bored teenagers, or anyone else who spent their time in abandoned buildings. That and the fact that it partially burned down probably put people off, made them think there'd be nothing to find.

Perhaps like me, the world was content to ignore the very existence of the manor. It had been two decades after all. Every day some new headline papered over the horror of the previous one.

I sighed, feeling a real headache starting up behind my eyes. I was getting them more and more since I got pregnant. Perhaps it was related to that or the stress. What was definitely the pregnancy were the fierce aches in my joints. After that hike I felt like my bones were coming apart.

Frustrated and uncomfortable, I wondered if I could get some answers about the stocks and mural from Phoebe. Although I didn't have her number, she was on Facebook and had already messaged me. Only I had no idea what I wanted to ask. Beyond 'Hey, what's the deal with the creepy stocks and the sun mural?' I wasn't even sure she'd tell me. She didn't seem to want to admit any involvement and would probably run a mile if I started asking questions about things she'd rather keep hidden. Besides, what if someone hacked my Facebook account for information? I didn't want anyone to come up to the manor, snooping around. Not while I was there.

I had to find more out before I started asking questions. I had to have a reasonable grasp on what the truth was before I opened myself up to half-truths and outright lies.

'Lucy?' Ellie tapped on my door. 'Are you all right?'

'Yeah, come in.'

She popped her head around the door, still carrying her strawberry milkshake. 'Headache still bothering you?'

'Yes,' I said, truthfully, as it was now spreading throughout my skull. 'Let me guess. You have something for it?'

She grinned and held up a minute glass bottle. 'Got me. This is the Relieve blend. It's for headaches. You rub it on your temples.'

I took the bottle and obediently rubbed some of the pungent oil onto my temples. The smell was very strong and made me feel a bit sick, but the rubbing helped ease some of the tension. I'd have to ask if she had anything for muscle aches, or the acne that was popping up on my cheeks and chest. Delightful. I let her hoover up my mostly untouched meal whilst I chewed a ginger pastille for the nausea.

'I wish you could come along to the sessions. It was so much fun. I think you'd really enjoy the distraction,' she said.

'It sounds great,' I said. Though to be honest the idea of spending seven hours in one room hearing about the benefits of Nutrisoul sounded less like fun and more like work, or torture.

'It is! I mean, I have a chat going with some of the other reps but meeting everyone in person is so much better. It's like the polar opposite of working in that stupid office . . . no offence.'

'None taken. There are a couple of battleaxes there. I'm glad I get to work on my own most of the time.'

'You think you'll go back, after this and the baby?'

I'd been trying not to think about it actually. Although I didn't mind my job I wasn't sure I could face going back now that everyone there knew about me. That was if the hospital would even have me back after all the negative press they were getting. Marshal was dropping some hints even before all this that I'd probably be glad to get to pack it in and stay at home with the baby. Seeing me hesitate, Ellie put her hand on my arm.

'Hey, it's OK. Maybe you could come work with me? We'd be such a great team and it'd be just like before. Only better because we won't be stuck in the office. We can work anywhere, even from home with the baby next to you.'

'Thanks, that sounds nice,' I said, grateful for her support, even if it wasn't something I was keen to commit to. I liked being in an office. It gave me time alone, away from Marshal, to be myself. As fun as Ellie made it seem, I didn't want to branch out into anything too weird and different. I couldn't imagine staying home with the baby. Not when I could hardly think about it being born without being paralysed by the fear that I'd end up like my mother, neglecting the child I

129

never wanted. The more I found out about my mother the more worried I became that I was looking at my own future.

'I'm going to go try out some of the stuff I got today. Want to join?' Ellie asked.

'I'm pretty tired. Probably just going to have a bath and turn in. My back is killing me.'

'Oh, try out those drops!'

She bounded off and I gathered my things for a bath. Although shower gel was provided, there were no bottles of bubbles for the bath. I used the drops instead. At least they smelled nice. I popped on a book review podcast and lounged, trying to let go of the worries that kept surfacing.

Annoyingly, despite the lovely scent, the drops didn't help me get to sleep. I lay awake listening to the wind working itself into a howling rage outside. From the sounds of things there was a storm brewing, and we were right in the middle of it. I kept thinking about the eyes of the sun mural. Those deep dark pits. I felt like they were tattooed inside my own eyes, staring back at me every time I closed them. Why did that thing scare me so much? I had no recollection of seeing it before.

I was about to give up on sleep and go make myself a decaf tea, when the security light came on outside. The thin curtains did little to block it out. I glanced at my phone: it was thirteen minutes past one. I listened for the crunch of gravel or a sound from whatever countryside creature was hunting around out there. Nothing. Maybe it was a fox or a badger being stealthy.

Carefully I eased out of bed and crept to the window to spy on it, hoping not to scare it away. I peeked out around the edge of the curtains. Nothing in the driveway or the front garden. Not so much as a rabbit. Though perhaps the light had made it bolt. It cast jagged shadows from the rosebushes as they thrashed in the wind. Maybe that set the light off. It seemed far too sensitive, especially for such a remote area.

I'd just turned from the window when the car alarm went off. I flinched back and felt my heart pound against my ribs. Through the curtain I could see the lights on the car flashing. What set that off if there was nothing out there? Unless whatever or whoever it was hid behind the car.

I stood there, frozen, until I heard Ellie's footsteps come thudding down the corridor.

'Lucy? Are you up? The car alarm's going off.'

I opened the door and found her there in her pyjamas and a baggy jumper. Her hair was sticking up and her cheeks were very pink. There was a dense blue cream dotted all over her face. At any other time I might have found this hilarious; now though I found myself too afraid to speak.

'Are the keys downstairs?'

I nodded.

'You're freaking me out,' Ellie said, eyes round. 'Is there someone out there?'

'I don't know,' I said. The 'I' was lost, almost a squeak.

'I'll go turn the alarm off,' Ellie announced, but didn't move.

I seized hold of what courage I could muster and refused to let go. I'd already been scared of nothing once that day. I wasn't about to make a fool of myself twice. Firmly, I put my arm through Ellie's and the pair of us crept downstairs.

The keys were on a hook by the door. I grabbed them and jabbed the button to silence the alarm. With it shut off I could hear the wind flinging fistfuls of rain at the windows, leaves and sticks skittering outside. With Ellie just behind me I went to the front window and looked out. As I did so the security light went off again, making me jump.

'Do you see anything?' Ellie whispered.

'There's a big twig on the car. Must have blown down from somewhere and set the alarm off,' I said, peering into the dark. I could just see the stick across the windshield. It must have triggered the security light as well. Though that came on before the alarm did. I felt a shiver travel down my back. Enough. There was nothing to be scared of. No one knew where I was and even if they did, they wouldn't hang around throwing sticks onto my car. *Unless they wanted to set off the alarm and scare you*, a little voice whispered.

'Lucy?' Ellie asked in a tiny voice.

'Mmm?'

'Can I sleep in your room?'

I nodded. It wasn't even to reassure her. I was scared too.

It was just as well Ellie slept in my bed. She had to drag me out of it come morning. Two sleepless nights at the cottage, plus however many more since the news broadcast, had me sleeping like the dead. I peeled my eyes open and instantly wanted to burrow back under the covers. My whole body ached and every movement made it protest with a thousand new pains.

'Wakey wakey!' Ellie beamed, putting down a steaming cup of instant coffee and one of the muffins I bought. 'We've got to get going soon or I'll miss the affirmation circle.'

I had no idea what that was, nor did I wish to. I only wanted to sleep. But clearly that was not going to happen. I sat up and made a start on the coffee whilst Ellie dashed off to get ready.

When I finally dragged myself to the bathroom and looked in the mirror I winced. There were dark circles engraved under my eyes and instead of being naturally pale, I looked ill and spotty. My hair was flat, the ends frizzing around my face. I'd also managed to bite my lip as I slept.

It bled and there were little tooth-shaped bruises on it as well. Just thinking of what Marshal would say about how I looked made me want to pull my pyjama top over my head and hide. I could almost hear him. 'Do you need me to get you some new straighteners? Have you tried that cream Mum recommended? You're looking older than me for a change! Jesus, Luce, are you going to work looking like that? They'll send you straight to the mortuary.'

When Ellie bustled in to apply lipstick I sighed. Beside her I looked ten times worse.

'Anything planned for today?' she asked, once we were in the car.

'Not really. Might get a nap in,' I said.

'Help yourself to anything from my bag,' she said. 'I've got some cucumber and lemon eye masks you'd love.'

Personally the only cucumber and lemon I fancied was in a glass of something soothing, but that was off the cards. I'd have to content myself with a double espresso and a couple of ginger chews. My head ached so much it had my stomach churning.

Ellie finally seemed to realise that I wasn't feeling my best. When we got to the Imperial Hotel she touched my hand and bit her lip.

'I don't have to go. If you want I can hang out today, look after you.'

'It's fine. I'm just a bit tired,' I assured her.

'OK . . . but ring me if you need help, all right? I'll get a lift or an Uber and be right there.'

She smacked an air kiss and dived out of the car, already waving to a group of tanned goddesses with waist-length hair. Looking at them I wondered if perhaps I ought to just head to the cottage and slather myself in Nutrisoul potions. I felt like hammered shit and they looked like models. Besides, the thought of going back to that place, seeing that mural and whatever else was there, frightened me. The night's interruptions didn't help either.

'Get a grip,' I muttered to myself as I turned the car around. Scared or not, I had to know.

Chapter Sixteen

I was winding my way through the outskirts of town when my phone rang. After pulling over it stopped but it looked like Marshal had been calling. Several times, in fact. When I saw the number my stomach turned over. He was going to be so angry. The phone probably didn't ring because I was out of signal range at the cottage. I rang back and he answered almost before the first ring had finished.

'Where have you been?' were the first words out of his mouth.

'Dropping Ellie off,' I said, trying to sound innocent, though of what I wasn't sure.

'Oh, so you *are* OK then. I was worried when you didn't answer any of my calls.'

'Sorry, yes I'm OK. I was just out of signal and then I had to find somewhere to pull over before I answered. I didn't mean to worry you.'

'I was worried. I didn't hear from you at all yesterday. I thought you might spare a thought for those of us not at a country retreat.'

I bit back the part of me that wanted to point out that this whole thing was his idea. 'Sorry, I went for a walk and

I left my phone at the cottage,' I lied, feeling bad. 'I forgot to call you later on the landline,' I said, pointedly, hoping he'd remember that my mobile didn't work at the cottage. Though of course I wasn't at the cottage yesterday to pick up the landline.

'That's not working either. It's just dead. Did you make sure to hang it up properly?'

'Of course I did.' I felt instantly cold. 'It was working when we got there.'

'I wonder if it was the storm.' He sounded slightly less irritated now, more concerned. He was just worried and stressed out and I took it personally. 'There's been some coverage on the news, sixty mile an hour winds in parts of Wales. Maybe it's taken out some of the phone lines.'

'Maybe,' I said, thinking of the debris that set off the car alarm and the security light. Before taking Ellie to the hotel I had to remove a lot of sticks and leaves from the windshield.

'It looks like there's more storms coming over the next few days. Are you out at the moment? You should really stay at the cottage. If you need shopping order some in. Make sure you have enough non-perishables so you don't have to drive. I worry about those country roads.'

'I'll stock up,' I said, knowing that if I needed shopping I would go and get it. I didn't want strangers knowing where I was. What if the delivery driver recognised me and posted online? Why didn't Marshal think of that? It was like he only cared about keeping me shut up.

'So you haven't had a power cut or anything?' he asked.

'Not that I'm aware of. Though the outside security light keeps coming on at all hours. Probably just the wind or falling leaves.'

'Right . . . but the lights inside are working fine?' He

sounded like he was trying to get at something, working up to a point. That's when I realised what he was really on about.

'Marshal . . . have you been looking at my receipts?' I said, instantly realising how stupid I was to give my email to the woman on the checkout at the bargain shop. It was just automatic.

'Well, they come to our joint email,' he said. 'I check it all the time. And it seemed like you were buying some odd stuff. A torch? I was worried there was something wrong with the cottage, or am I not allowed to worry about you now?'

'You don't need to worry. I bought a torch just in case we did have a power cut. I've never been this far out in the country before and I wanted to be prepared,' I said, feeling guilty for the lie. 'If you don't want me spending money, just say.'

'I just wasn't sure about the receipt and some of the random charges on the card. That's all. It didn't seem like you. There were charges for Starbucks and McDonald's. Lucy, we did talk about the diet side of things, and . . . have you been smoking? Because there was a lighter on that receipt.'

'No!' I said, thinking quickly. 'It was for the wood burner. I should have bought matches instead but you know me, scatterbrain. I thought it'd be a good idea in case it got really cold and we needed the extra heat. It's rained so much since we got here,' I gabbled. 'And I got some food and stuff for Ellie, you know, on the way. I had decaf coffee and I didn't get any burgers or anything for me. I had some of the salads that were in the fridge.'

'OK. Well, that's fine. As long as you're eating right. There's so many women who use being pregnant to justify eating any old rubbish. I want you and the baby to be healthy. I sent some vitamins and supplements down. They should have been there when you arrived.'

'They were, and I'm fine,' I promised, feeling guiltier now about the unopened packages still under the stairs. 'How are things at home?'

He sighed. 'Not great. This thing's really got a life of its own online at the moment. There's a new hashtag, Manorgate. The red-tops are still reporting on it too, though it's slipped back a few pages. Lots of new pictures coming out though. They published one of your mother, luring one of the missing girls at a cinema.'

My insides went cold. 'You're sure it's my mum?'

'Looks just like she does in the picture with that man, Carlisle. There's been a real backlash against the police. They've had this CCTV all this time and never got anywhere with it. But mostly there's a lot of anger at . . .'

'Me,' I said dully, remembering that awful letter, the comments online.

'Well . . . at your mother, but . . . yeah, they're aiming at you too. And at Dad. There's all this speculation that he helped bury the original investigation, which is ludicrous. He wasn't even an MP back then. But there's an old picture of him with Jean McBride making the rounds.'

Arianrhod, the woman who owned the manor.

'What was he doing with her?' I asked.

'Nothing, obviously. She just happened to be at a charity event. They aren't even together, she's just in the background. But you can bet everyone's making a meal out of it all the same, especially given how she vanished from public life just like that other woman did.'

'She disappeared at the same time as Celeste?' I asked, wondering why the hell I didn't find this out online.

'Not the same time, afterwards. But it doesn't matter.

They're still giving Dad hell about it,' Marshal snapped, clearly annoyed that I didn't focus on that detail.

I felt a fresh wave of guilt crash over me. Whilst I'd been safely out of the way Marshal's family was bearing the brunt of the media backlash. I wasn't even aware of the hashtag or the new photo. I kept my searches to the history of Luna Vitae and ignored anything more recent than the mid-nineties. Twitter was a definite no-go.

'It'll be all right soon, I promise, so long as you do what's best,' Marshal said. 'I know you didn't want to go to the cottage, but we're all making sacrifices. I miss you.'

'I miss you too,' I echoed, feeling yet more guilt envelop me. I hadn't really thought about Marshal since I last called him. All my focus was on the manor, on my past. Even the baby hadn't really entered my thoughts since arriving in Wales. It wasn't even born yet and already I was neglecting it. I was following in my mother's footsteps, going after my own wants without a thought for the child being dragged along with me. Not a promising start to a future of motherhood.

Marshal rang off after making me promise to ring him every day, or email if the phone wasn't working. I said I'd find out what was going on with the landline and let him know when it was fixed. I was glad when the call was finally over and I could get on my way to the manor. I was worried that if I waited too long, I would lose my bottle and just go back to the cottage to shut myself in.

This time as I left the car and hiked towards the manor I felt more prepared. I had a rucksack which I'd borrowed from Ellie and in it was the torch, lighter and some sandwiches. Though I didn't expect to feel very hungry in that place. I also took one of the musty cagoules from the hooks beside the back door of the cottage. If it rained again I was prepared, and it looked like rain was inevitable. The sky was grey and the wind coming through the trees was strong

139

and sharp. I strode with purpose, determined to spend the day looking around the manor. No excuses.

The walk didn't seem to take as long, yet when I got there I couldn't shake a sense of unease. I kept looking at the stone outbuilding and jumping when the wind crashed branches together or moaned through the manor's broken roof. After checking out the brick buildings again with my torch I could assure myself there was nothing of importance there. Just clothes and domestic rubbish. I wanted more than that. I wanted evidence. Something to shed light on the shadowy accusations and innuendos of the press.

I was a bit wary of going into the manor; there was no way to know if it was structurally sound. The roof and most of the second floor were gone, only some jutting beams and the chimney stack remained. The ground floor, however, appeared solid, the first floor barely touched. After doing a quick circuit, peering through the windows, I couldn't see any bricks on the ground, no signs of imminent collapse. Granted I had no idea what I was looking for, but I thought it seemed safe enough.

I was around the back, looking in through a set of shattered French windows, when I was struck with déjà vu. I'd been there before. Exactly there, on the uneven red and yellow stone patio, looking in through the paned glass doors. That sense of remembrance pushed me forward. I reached through a broken pane, unlatched the door and went inside.

Although the outside of the manor was fairly plain, red brick and slate with sash windows, inside it was a true stately home. The walls of the room I found myself in were papered in lavish pink and pale green florals. Although most of the paper was speckled with mould. Overhead a chandelier chimed softly in the breeze and around me were chairs and a chaise, mouldering but clearly once expensive. It reminded me of Crossley.

In a corner was a plain pine storage unit piled with rolled-up yoga mats. The foam rubber was perished and crumbled at the edges. Candles lined the window ledges, discoloured and melted by sunlight on one side. Perhaps this was used as some kind of meditation room.

Everything was still and quiet. I could smell the mould and damp on the air, but beneath that was the throaty stink of burned things. I shuddered. Yet I was determined to find out more.

The door to the hallway was hanging on one hinge. I eased it open and began to explore, determined to find something, anything that could tell me about the life I had forgotten.

Downstairs there were two sitting rooms, a kind of study-cum-library and a kitchen. Off the kitchen was a large pantry and a dining room. The second sitting room had an ornate armchair on a wooden platform like a throne. The study had floor-to-ceiling bookshelves, but these were mostly empty aside from a stray audiotape and a crumpled pamphlet. There was fibreglass soundproofing stapled into the delicate wallpaper. Maybe they had some kind of studio for recording tapes in there. I saw all this from the doorway. The floor was littered with chunks of fallen plaster, so I didn't dare go in. Presumably the bulk of their books and tapes had been seized as evidence.

The dining room still had a large table in it, but it was against a wall. The rest of the space was taken up with wooden picnic benches and plastic camping tables, some overturned. It looked like a cafeteria, with what was probably the original mahogany trestle now the 'top' table, overlooking the rest. Odd for a commune, but then, from what Phoebe had said, Celeste put herself above her 'sisters'. The table had thirteen chairs around it, arranged like the last supper. Perhaps my mother sat there, as one of Celeste's handmaids.

On the wall behind the table was a mural. Around the edges there was still some blue but over the top the same sun had been painted. It was huge, the rays and flames shooting from it lovingly outlined in gold paint.

I left the dining room very quickly. The sun's black eyes seemed to follow me.

The kitchen was the most intact room in terms of contents. I guessed because not much of it was classed as evidence. Cheap shelving covered the walls and huge catering pans warred with bags of rotten lentils and flour for space. The smell was awful, musty and putrid. Still, I searched every drawer in the woodworm-riddled sideboard, finding only institutional cutlery and utensils. No knives though. Those had apparently been taken. I imagined them in a big tray, being tested for human blood, one by one. I shivered, thinking of the missing girls. The girl my mother was seen with. Where was she now?

The skeletal remains of drying herbs hung over the windows, their leaves curled and crisp on the draining board of the huge butler sink. I reached out and brushed the crumbling leaves to one side, their sound loud in the overwhelming silence. A scent drifted up, faint memories of rosemary and sage, bitter and green.

As I looked at them, breathed in that dusty smell, I remembered someone lifting me up to tie a bunch in place with hairy brown string. Was it my mother, or some other member of the commune? I had no idea. Turning to the tiled island in the centre of the room, I could almost hear the clatter of people at work. I could feel a soft white roll being pressed into my hand, the top gluey with icing and sprinkles. A pat on my head.

'There. Now go and play, Lucia. You're under my feet!'

I'd clenched the sticky bun in my teeth as I climbed a tree. There was another girl pelting along at my side. Who was she? A visitor or a friend? Was she one of the missing girls, maybe even the one my mother had ushered into a car?

I looked out the window and saw that there was in fact a great lightning-struck oak in the overgrown garden. I'd sat there, I was sure of it, right in the crown of thick branches. I closed my eyes and tried to send myself back there. What was I doing? Watching the garden, the adults arrayed there under the scorching sun, bending. I remembered their red skin, the hours they stayed out there, motionless in the heat. What were they doing? Surely nothing fun. A punishment maybe? I thought of the sun on the wall and shivered.

The memory disturbed me and I turned away, blinking to dispel it. The fact that I recalled anything at all, however, was a distinct change. I was onto something and I had to keep going. I had to see what else I could recover from that time. Using my torch to guide me, I returned to the hallway and approached the stairs to the first floor.

The stairs were creaky but stable. Still, I went cautiously, very aware that if I fell there was no way for me to call for help. My mobile was just as useless at the manor as it was at the cottage.

Upstairs the ceiling plaster was cracked, the paint bubbling from either the heat of the fire or two decades of rain. Huge portions of wallpaper had sloughed away and damp spread in large patches over the plaster and paper that remained. Most of the doors were swollen shut and I had to force them open. Every creak or pop of tortured wood made me hold my breath, afraid the ceiling was about to come down. Using my torch to navigate I began to feel as if I was on board a sunken ship, a ghost ship.

Despite the darkness and the fear that coursed through me, I was disappointed to find that the rooms upstairs seemed less interesting than those below. They were bedrooms, presumably larger and more spacious than the attic rooms

143

above. There were beds, indicating only one or two people shared the space. The privileged ones not obliged to share with everyone else perhaps? Was this where the 'inner circle' Phoebe spoke about lived?

It was only in the third bedroom that I found something that held my interest. It was a drawing on the wall. A pink horse with its body painted in with glitter nail polish. Beside it a curling black-marker tree sprouted golden apples, lovingly daubed in more polish.

I drew that horse.

The memory came to me vividly. I'd sat on the floor, on a ratty batik cushion, and drawn the horse whilst my mother was off somewhere. The room smelled of her cigarettes and patchouli oil, of sweat and candle smoke. The sharp pear-drop tang of the polish. With my fingers pressed to the crumbling plaster, I shut my eyes and tried to see the room as it was then, draped in coloured scarves and throws, empty glasses and overflowing ashtrays littering the floor.

This was where I lived.

The bedroom, our bedroom, was just as damp and ruined as the rest of the first floor. Piles of cloth mouldered on the wet carpet. It was hard to tell one thing from another. In one corner was my bed. A child-sized mattress on pallets. In a plastic milk crate beside it I found my treasure box, disintegrating and spilling beads and limp, wet tarot cards everywhere. There was a naked baby doll with no hair as well. I couldn't remember if it had a name.

Crouched over the crate I felt tears spring to my eyes. I couldn't help but sob, looking down at the sum total of my childhood. A bed, some beads and a naked doll. My old existence left so little behind. At seven I was still sleeping in my mother's room with barely a thing to my name. No school work because I didn't go to school. No books because I couldn't read. Ancient hand-me-down toys because we had no money. Not even a bit of paper to draw on. In a sudden burst of rage I picked up the doll and threw it across the room. It landed on my mother's bed.

I remembered then, looking from my crouched position towards the big bed. I could conjure up a memory of my mother in there. Only she wasn't alone. There were other people with her, doing things. Making sounds and stinking, squealing. All with me a few feet away in my bed, awake.

I cried harder. What had I done? Was this why I came all this way? To remember the disgusting antics of a cult that neglected and ignored me? A mother who appeared in only a handful of memories? I shut my eyes and wished more than anything that I hadn't come, that I had stayed at the cottage just as Marshal wanted. This was not helping me at all. The only thing I had seen evidence of was that I came from a bad mother and was probably going to turn out just like her.

It took a while, but eventually I had no more tears to let out. Instead I had a deep ache in my chest and sore, tacky cheeks. My nose was streaming and I sniffed, but my snivelling only made me feel ashamed. Embarrassed, I got to my feet and hiccupped, hunting in my pockets for a tissue. I took a long breath and let it go.

I looked, I saw, and now I needed to move on.

There was no point in taking anything from my former room. What was there that I wanted to hold on to? Instead I left the room and did a quick check of the others. If there was ever anything of interest there, it had long since been taken as evidence or simply stolen. Only wet rags and rotting furniture remained.

I did find what had to have been Celeste's room. There was ivy painted around the door. It was right at the back, overlooking the garden, the best room in the house and certainly the biggest. Standing at the shattered window I thought I could almost remember where the rose garden was. There was also a sort of depression in the tangle of weeds and brush that might have once been a pond with a fountain, the stone tower now toppled. I could sort of see it in my head. There were fish in it, orange and white spotted ones. I used to feed them scraps of bread.

The room itself had probably once been grand. The walls were panelled in wood and there was a chandelier overhead, listing drunkenly. The crystals spun crazy darts from my torchlight and threw them over the walls. There was a large bed with a carved frame, the mattress and bedding sodden and mouldering. I turned to leave. It was only then that I noticed the mural on the one wall that was in complete shadow, far from the window.

It was similar to the other sun murals. The central sun in burning yellow, with a leering face and a red gloss paint background. This sun, however, eclipsed a moon. The edges of her grey-white face were barely visible. The single exposed eye of the moon was cast down, eyelashes long and cow-like. On the ground, below the sun, twelve pregnant women bowed their heads, crowned in flowers, their eyes closed and their faces etched in expressions of placid contentment.

Looking at the painting, I felt strange. It was just like the first time I saw the sun mural, the day before. Part of me thought it weird and ugly, but under that was a deep terror I could not explain. It suffused my nerves and made my hands shake. What was it that was so threatening about it, that sun with its all-seeing eyes?

Already feeling stressed by my breakdown in my old room I could hardly stand to look at it. I was so unnerved I almost missed the thirteenth figure, curled beneath the sun's enormous form.

It was a girl in a white dress.

Chapter Seventeen

I stared at the painted girl for a long time.

She had bare feet under her dress and the shape of it was almost a cartoonish triangle. The flowing material standing out like a child's drawing of a gown. She was hunched with her hands on her stomach, the sun's rays coming down and cutting her off from the rest of the mural. Her hair stood out like a halo as if blown by a magical wind. Each painted lock was a different colour – black, blonde, multiple browns, auburn, ginger. I swallowed. Her face was a blank, unfinished.

My breath caught as I fought to stay calm, my heart racing. What was this? Why was it painted? Why was she dressed just as I was on the night I was rescued? Could it really be just a coincidence that I was found wandering in my white nightdress, barefoot, just like this painted girl? That dream was so fragmented, so nightmarish. Perhaps I just imagined what I was wearing. I could have seen the mural and remembered it.

I was too unnerved by the first mural to really think about why it was there. The sun and moon were related, two sides of the same coin. It didn't really trouble me before. The newspaper articles I read were fuzzy on details about the cult's belief system – goddess worship, feminism and anti-consumerism – but no mention of specific rituals or myths, nothing about a divine sun. No real mention of men at all either, though Carlisle was there.

Phoebe told me that Luna Vitae was the cult of Luna, the moon goddess. Who then was the sun meant to be? Another goddess? A god? What did it mean? I felt sick. Turning away I fumbled for the pack of ginger pastilles and chewed two. Though this sickness was less to do with pregnancy and more a product of shock.

Casting about the room I noticed a dressing table with bottles and other things scattered over it. Glad to get away from the mural, I went over to examine them. There were combs, an ashtray, cologne turned rusty in the bottle, condoms – men's things. Celeste must have shared the room with Carlisle. But where were her things?

I opened the drawers of the dressing table but found only men's shirts and underwear, coated in mould. At the back of one drawer were a few shards of brown glass. The wood there was stained a darker brown. Something had broken, leaked. Like the dressing table the nearby wardrobe was filled with only men's clothes. No sign of so much as a discarded shoe, or a picture of Celeste. Hard to believe that the police would have taken every scrap of her away, leaving so many of Carlisle's things behind. No, this looked very much like someone had packed them up. But why?

What did Phoebe say? That one day Celeste just disappeared? Yet somehow she managed to take all her things with her on the long hike away from the manor. Without being seen? More likely they were disposed of later. But she was the leader of Luna Vitae, my mother's own guiding star and the earthly shape of the goddess Luna, according to one article I saw. How did the manor residents let her go so easily, without keeping even one of her belongings as a relic?

They'd blotted out the moon murals and allowed her room to become his, Carlisle's.

Carlisle Riordan was her consort. Whilst she ran Luna Vitae he was there to help and care for her. I saw a picture of him in the newspapers online, at her side. They called him her biggest supporter, a man who believed it was women who should lead, who shunned the capitalist world of his patriarchal forefathers.

The man who assumed control after she left.

I wondered what it was like after she left. Why she did it. Whether she got bored or moved on to a new scam to make money and avoid scrutiny over the kidnapping charges. What might that have done to the women she left behind? How did Carlisle manage to keep the community together?

Thinking about all that I saw in the manor, I began to feel like there was a purposeful rebranding. Each Luna painting obscured, no reminders of Celeste anywhere, not even a photograph casually pinned to a wall. I recalled the memory that struck me: the people under the sun, the sun murals, the message on the wall about the divine sun. A new deity for a new order maybe? Not just that, but a new structure. The high table in the dining room seemed odd to have in a sisterhood, a community. Perhaps they weren't for Celeste at all. Maybe after she left the manor was no longer a commune as much as a kingdom.

'Don't be ridiculous,' I said aloud, squeezing my eyes shut. 'You're imagining things, Lucy. Letting your mind run away with you.'

The wind moaned outside and I heard timbers creak above. Still I couldn't shake the feeling that I was right. That I wasn't so much realising as remembering. I had seen this before. I had lived through the change from moon to sun, goddess to god. There was something pressing at the inside of my head, a memory too enormous and terrible to be borne. The wind cried again and I heard a loose door somewhere slam. The storm was blowing up. I had to go.

But I couldn't. Not yet. Not now.

I found myself at the base of the stairs to the second floor almost without thinking about it. They were certainly unsafe, charred and cracked like bonfire-night residue. They'd crumble beneath the slightest weight. Above where the entrance to the attic bedrooms had once been, there was only sky and air, a ragged hole eaten through by the fire. The clouds above were dense and dark, threatening rain. Wind scoured over the exposed beams and sent a shower of ash and charcoal down on me. I bent my head, shielding my eyes. An awful sense of déjà vu pressed at me from all sides. I had stood here before, fixed to this very spot.

There was something on one of the steps. A mangled chunk of brass, half covered in ashes and bonded to a melted stair rod. As I pulled it loose, ruby-red glass shards fell away, coated in black char. I hardly noticed. I was transfixed, remembering the last time I had this thing in my hands, on the night of the fire.

'Hold tightly now, Lucia,' she says, hands wrapping over mine.

The glass globe is slippery and heavy, its contents sloshing around. I poke my tongue between my teeth, concentrating hard on keeping it level. When my mother takes her hands away my arms start to ache. I concentrate harder.

'There you go. Well done,' she says, patting my head.

I smile up at her. She looks beautiful in her long robes, a gold metal circlet on her head. Recently she started wearing more makeup and it did scare me a little. Now I'm used to her heavily outlined eyes, the deep black and blue shadows painted around them like bruises. Her lips are very red and shiny. When she kisses my forehead I know she leaves a print. There's a similar one on Carlisle's cheek.

He's standing behind her, watching us. His eyes are black and glittering like beads. Mum's are the same, all the blue eaten up by the black dot in the centre, which is huge now. They've been drinking from a plastic cup of syrupy squash. Mum lifts it to my lips with a smile.

'Have a drink, Lucia. You'll feel better.'

I drink. It's sweet but tastes a bit funny. Whatever Carlisle put into it from his little dropper bottle is bitter. I cough, already feeling dizzy.

'There now.' She strokes my face. 'You're all ready. Make me proud. Prove you're worthy of being his.'

'She's perfect,' Carlisle murmurs, putting his arm around her. Mum turns to him like a sunflower, snuggling into his armpit with a smile. He is her sun. He shines like one now. Little pinpricks of lights settle on him like dust. I blink but they don't go away. It's like I'm looking through my glass prism. Rainbows scattered all over.

I giggle.

They look down at me and smile sticky smiles. Mum's lipstick is on Carlisle's mouth now. He reaches down and pats my head.

'Go on now, Lucia. It's time. Do it quickly now. We have to run.'

His hand is around my back, pushing me onward and past him. Ahead are the stairs to the upper floor. It's night and everyone else is in bed. No, not everyone. Behind me I hear rustling, hushed whispers. The other women like my mother, the special ones, are heading downstairs.

Carlisle pats my bottom, pushing me forwards.

'Go on. Prove yourself.'

I walk unsteadily towards the stairs, the oil lamp glowing in my hands.

'She's perfect,' my mum whispers, echoing Carlisle.

The glass dome explodes and liquid fire splashes over the stair carpet. It is so beautiful I can't look away, can't run, despite the screaming. Breathless I watch the rainbows shift and twirl over the roaring flames. My skin is too hot. The fire inside my blood is fuelled with sticky bitterness and lapping at the outside. I reach toward the fire where it ripples like silk ribbons in a breeze.

A hand clamps onto mine like a vice, dragging me back. Carlisle is above me, face glowing red and deep black eyes gleaming above his smeared scarlet mouth. I scream. He opens his mouth and fire shoots out. He is like a dragon, the sun king, our god.

Behind him the fire rages.

The screaming becomes a hundred voices, all harmonising in their agony.

I dropped the warped remains of the oil lamp and staggered back. Around me the house seemed to sway as the wind groaned through a thousand cracks and shattered windows. Rain had begun to fall in heavy drops, cratering the ashy floor. I hardly noticed.

One hand crept to my face, covering my mouth. Ashes and blood on my lips. The lamp had cut me. I turned and ran for the stairs back to the ground floor. Abandoning caution I scurried down them even as they creaked and wailed, the wood shifting. Around me the manor seemed alive, breathing with the force of the wind outside. When I reached the French windows they were being thrown about, fresh glass shards littering the ground. One door caught me as I tried to get out. I dropped the torch. My shoulder reverberated with pain, but I kept going.

Outside, premature darkness crept in, the storm clouds blotting out the weak sun. Rain crashed down in sheets, soaking me instantly. I was so disorientated, so filled with panic that I tore off in the wrong direction. Instead of going between the outbuildings towards the path I took to reach the manor, I mistook one brick building for the other and turned right. I only realised my mistake when I looked and found myself at the front of the house, by the front walk and what had been the lawn. Where they found me on the night of the fire. The night I set fire to innocent, sleeping people.

I cried out as the thought sank into me like a knife. My wail was drowned out by the wind. This was what I'd managed to block out, the full extent of my involvement, my guilt over being a murderer. I wasn't rescued from an accident caused by recklessness; I was part of a premeditated murder, multiple murders. I killed so many people with one action, women and children.

Too shaken to move, I stood rooted to the spot as the rain came down. Looking up at the manor, I hated myself for going there, for pushing forward when everyone else was telling me to be wary, to leave well enough alone. I touched a hand to my stomach and cried harder. How would I look my child in the eye now, knowing what I did, what my mother involved me in, knowing that I was a killer of children, that her madness ran in my blood? I thought of Marshal, waiting at home, trying to fix everything back to how it had been. It could never be the same again.

The wind pushed at me, whipping at my cagoule. I stumbled against its pressure, blinking rain and tears from my eyes. The ground seemed to tip beneath me. I felt suddenly so dizzy and tired, faint from the stress and strain of it all. I staggered forwards and a great cracking sound filled the air. I had a moment to fear that it was lightning, before the ground underneath my feet split open, and I fell into the darkness.

153

Chapter Eighteen

One morning Celeste didn't come to breakfast.

By then Carlisle had suggested we have meals cooked for us instead of sharing the kitchen or taking what we wanted when we were hungry. There were women in there all day now, baking and stewing and chopping. We ate together in the main hall. Normally, at the big table, Celeste sat in the centre with Carlisle and her handmaidens around her. Today Carlisle was in Celeste's seat. Selene was in his old place to the left. She looked pale but focused. In the seat on his other side was Arianrhod, who looked confused by Carlisle being there without Celeste.

People started to whisper as they came in and saw, but once they were all sitting down he stood up and everyone went still and silent. He held out his arms and let us sit that way for a moment, waiting.

'Celeste . . . has ascended.'

A wave went over everyone, like when the wind goes over fields, each bit of grass bending and sighing under it. I didn't know what it meant and from some people's faces they didn't either. Some women looked confused, upset, but most only looked at Carlisle and nodded.

'She has gone to Luna, to be at her side,' Carlisle said, 'to be a handmaiden herself to that great spirit. And . . . she has left me, in her stead.'

Some women jumped up at that. I saw Arianrhod was one of them. She leaped out of her chair and started pointing a finger at Carlisle, shouting. He ignored her and Selene swept behind him to push Arianrhod away. I heard a plate hit the floor and smash. People were calling out, others shushing them, wanting to listen. I looked at Carlisle as he watched them. His face was the same as it always was, but his eyes moved everywhere. Arianrhod tried to push past Selene and she slapped her across the face.

'. . . the baby!'

I turned my head as silence went across the room, aside from Arianrhod swearing and struggling with Selene. The woman who shouted blushed.

'What about the baby? Her baby?' she repeated.

Carlisle nodded, thoughtful. 'The baby. My baby', he said, 'was a sign from God.'

God? The whisper ran through the room like a mouse, quiet but quick. I'd never heard the word said like that before. My mum used to shout it. 'For God's sake! God knows why your father didn't stick around.' Even the women at the manor said it sometimes, when they talked about the world outside, the world of men and rules and shame. God. But Carlisle said it the way Celeste said 'Luna'. The way the women said 'goddess'. Like it was something special and powerful.

'Remove her so I can speak!' Carlisle suddenly roared, and two more women got up and helped Selene drag Arianrhod outside. The doors banged shut behind them, cutting off Arianrhod's angry shout of '. . . can't do this, this is my house!'

Carlisle raised his hands in the silence. 'God sent my son

to enlighten me, to enlighten all of us. But he was not of flesh. He was a spirit, a vision. He brings us the message that Luna has taken you from the world long enough. You have healed from the shame society placed on you and you have learned to be strong. Your femininity is not a weakness, a reason to retreat. It is a tool, a weapon. Now it is time to return, to enter the world as warriors, as prophets to those you left behind, to guide new souls to us, to light our way. By the sun. By God's light.'

I looked at the woman who asked about the baby. Her face was scrunched up, following his words, but still she wasn't nodding with the others. She still wasn't happy. I saw her look at the doors Selene and the others had gone through. What was the matter with her? Carlisle was telling us something very important, something that might bring my mum to the manor, guide her. It was simple. The baby was a spirit and now it was gone, like Celeste, gone somewhere good and pure and free. I wanted her to let Carlisle speak. Some other women reached up and brought her back down to her seat, shushing her as she tried to ask another question.

'We all have our part to play in this new mission,' Carlisle said. 'Today I will select three of you to prepare to go out into the world and begin the battle, to win the hearts and minds of those men who would stand in our way. Who amongst you wishes to be chosen?'

Women started leaping up, hands in the air. They jumped onto chairs and waved to him. Some were left sitting, looking at each other in confusion, but not too many. I was jumping up too, arms in the air. Carlisle had filled us all with energy. I couldn't help joining in.

He picked three women. Not old ones like Lona and Selene, but young pretty ones. I wanted to be one of them, but they were older than me. I couldn't go out there yet. But

I really wanted to. I wanted to be part of this mission, to go and see the world outside.

After breakfast when Carlisle and the rest of the hand-maidens and the three women went to his room, I found Lucia. I was Carlisle's favourite to serve and I was carrying morning tea up for him. She was sitting on the stairs to the attic, listening. From there, I knew, you could sort of hear into Celeste's room. I hadn't seen Lucia for a while. I was busy because Carlisle always asked me to serve wine at night, or clean for him, wash his clothes or bring food up for him. Since that full-moon night Lucia wasn't around much. She hid. Sometimes I saw her in the big tree outside the kitchen, or running across the garden to the woods in the early morning. Selene didn't seem to care anymore. She looked through Lucia at meals. And I was glad. Because that meant I was the special one now.

I pretended I didn't see Lucia and went into Carlisle's room with my tray of tea.

He talked to the three women for ages. I brought more tea, wine, cake. He ate and drank but they didn't. They kneeled on the floor and listened. He smoked, walked around, got louder and quieter. The room filled with smoke from joints and incense. Sometimes the women moved, like they were stretching or trying to shift so their knees weren't on the hard floor. Carlisle went to them and held their shoulders until they were still.

Finally, after I thought he was going to talk into the night, he stopped. Selene came and led them away. She took them downstairs and outside. They weren't sleeping in the attic when I went to bed. I thought maybe they were in one of the sheds outside. Normally only visitors from other houses stayed there. Because of that one time we all got bedbugs.

I also noticed that the door to Arianrhod's room on the

first floor was open, and Lona was packing up her stuff. She shut the door when she saw me looking. I guessed Arianrhod got angry and left. I didn't get why she left her stuff behind though. Not that it would be hers for very long. If you didn't watch your things at the manor, they'd be someone else's by the end of the day.

The next day we did it all again. Me fetching and carrying, Carlisle talking, the women listening. He talked about the sun, about how they had given their shame to Luna and let go of it. Now they would be tested, they would show the world that they were not ashamed of their bodies. He talked about how every other war was fought with violence, with death. But they would capture their enemies with pleasure, with love. Open their hearts with it, change them, bring them to us. He had a chant, strange words that made my heart beat faster. They were like a magic spell.

I listened to this for days. By the end of it, the women were chanting along with him. 'In servitium, voluptatem. In voluptatem, libero.'

Then Selene took those women away. The next day, three more were chosen.

They learned the teachings too and went off into the world. Then three more.

The ones who learned first left the manor sometimes and then came back. They wore beautiful clothes in bright colours and painted their faces like the pictures on album covers. Bright lips and dark shadowy eyes. They left for several days with Selene or one of the other handmaids and then came back, tired and less pretty. But they'd been outside, at war. I imagined them pushing against crowds of men who were trying to stop them speaking, shouting Carlisle's message outside churches so that the women inside would hear, so they would come to us and be free. I imagined that one day they might come back with my mum.

But the same women came and went. My mum didn't come to the manor. It wasn't working fast enough.

I wanted to go with them so badly. I could do it right. I could find my mum and convince her, because I knew all the words to the chants, all the teachings. I heard them so many times I could say them out loud to myself at night. I dreamed them. *In servitium, voluptatem. In voluptatem, libero.*

New things arrived at the manor. A big bed for Carlisle's room. A stereo system. Heaps of new CDs to replace the tapes and records. Bottles of wine and whisky in wooden crates. Paint for new murals of the sun. Carlisle wore new boots, a gold sun necklace, a leather jacket. A big safe appeared in his room and whilst I was serving I saw him filling it with bundles of money. Money he took from the outside world, our enemies. So much of it we had to be winning against them.

I loved the new music, the coloured lights that spun in the main hall at night when it played. More women wore sparkly clothes and makeup now. It wasn't just talking and wine and chanting. It was fun and bright and colourful.

There were still some women doing the full-moon rituals though. They didn't like the music, the colour, the missions outside the manor. I heard them talking one day in the kitchen when I went to get things for Carlisle. I listened at the door and heard them asking each other about Celeste, the baby, Arianrhod, the money. They called the women on the mission whores and other horrible names. They wanted things to go back to how they'd always been at the manor.

They talked about leaving, about the shed outside which was now locked all the time, except for when Selene took food and water there. I wanted to know more but they shut up when I went in to get things.

I must have looked different when I went back upstairs, because Carlisle took my shoulders and asked what had upset me. He said if I was open with him, he could make it all right again.

So I told him who I saw in the kitchen and what they said. I asked about the shed but he ignored me and said he'd take care of everything.

That night, at dinner, he got up and said he'd had a vision. There were some people there who had darkness in them, who didn't believe in the cause, in our freedom. He read out their names and everyone turned to look at the women from the kitchen. They wriggled like worms drying out on the pavement.

Carlisle stepped down from the top table and walked through the women. He looked down on the little group and he looked so sad, disappointed.

'I can help you to appreciate His glory. The power of the sun.'

Red-faced and not looking at anyone, the women got up when Selene and Lona came up to them and took their arms. They took them away to the locked shed outside. They didn't come back for two weeks. Their eyes were small and squinty in the sunlight after so long in the dark.

I made that happen. And I was glad. It was my part in the mission.

Chapter Nineteen

I woke up in agony.

When I opened my eyes rain and grit washed into them. I blinked, spluttered as I fought to swallow the water that had collected in my partly open mouth. As I tried to sit up pain blared through me. I fell flat again with a gurgling scream.

It was dark – the true, deep pitch black of a place without lights for miles and miles. Overhead a ragged circle showed me nothing but stars, struggling to get through the clouds. Night had come whilst I was unconscious. Aside from the pain I felt numb all over. I was lying in several inches of ice-cold water, soaked to the skin.

Feeling around with one hand I came across lumps of mud and shards of rusted metal. I remembered dropping the torch. Cursing myself I squinted. I tried to move my head without lifting my body.

As my eyes adjusted to the darkness I thought I saw a deeper shadow stretching away to my right. I waved my arm that way. There was an opening. On my left my fingers met bricks, a curved wall. Some kind of well?

Forcing myself to breathe I tried to find the source of the

pain. Not my belly, though I knew that didn't mean everything was OK. Even now I could be bleeding, losing the baby. I felt a surge of fear. I didn't want it to die like this because of me.

My body was twisted, the right leg not flat but wrenched upwards, caught in something. I couldn't see what, but it felt hard, thick and unyielding against my ankle. When I tried to pull against it my leg wouldn't move, but pain exploded in my ankle, then coursed through my hip and nearly knocked me out again. I screamed and it echoed up the hole.

Light. Lighter. It was in the pocket of my borrowed cagoule. I tried to roll slightly, tasting metal in my mouth as my hip bones ground together and my limp leg twisted further. Getting my numb hand into the pocket by touch took forever. I kept slipping, thinking I'd got it only to realise it was just a fold in the too-big jacket. Finally I felt the plastic lighter against my fingers and pulled it free.

With fingers like sticks I tried to strike it. Once. Twice. I started to cry. No sparks. Nothing at all. Was it too wet to work? Had it cracked and lost all its fuel into the stinking water I was stuck in? I shook it. Struck again. Nothing. Nothing. Then a small yellow flame sprang up, joyful as a flower. I cried out in surprise, like a child seeing a magic trick. My finger slipped and it went out.

I struck again and the flame sprang up.

Lighter in hand, I reached up as far as I could without pulling on my leg. When I saw my foot I moaned. It was bent sideways, caught in a metal rung that stuck out of the wall. My ankle was at an unnatural angle, my weight pulling down on the leg. I couldn't feel my toes at all. With the boot on it was hard to tell but I knew it had to be broken. How badly, though, I had no idea. From the pain in my hip I wondered if the joint had separated. I could hardly stand to move. Just getting the lighter had sapped my energy.

162

The flame clicked off and I dropped the lighter onto my chest to keep it out of the water. I let my hands rest on my stomach, feeling for any unusual spasms or obvious wounds. I couldn't feel any pressure or bruising but that didn't mean anything. This was all my fault. I'd been so careless, so selfish, and now Marshal's baby, our baby, was going to die. I was worse than my mother.

I started to cry. Then I started to panic.

No one knew where I was. I didn't tell Ellie or Marshal where I was going. When I didn't turn up to collect her, Ellie might ring me or the cottage. But my mobile was out of signal, possibly broken in my pocket. The landline at the cottage was down too according to Marshal. She'd have to get a taxi or Uber and go there before she knew I was missing. Then she might wait, thinking I was out shopping, stuck in traffic. Later, when she realised I was missing, she'd have no idea where I went.

How long was I unconscious? It was dark, but then, it had been getting dark whilst I ran. Was it early evening or the middle of the night? How long had I been missing and did anybody know yet? I started to breathe too quickly, my chest tight. What if no one came for hours and my foot got damaged too much? Would I lose it?

What if no one came at all?

I bit my tongue and forced myself to breathe slowly through my nose.

'Don't panic. Don't panic,' I muttered to myself. 'Marshal knows the commune was in Wales. He'll work out where I am once Ellie calls him. Eventually he'll work it out.'

But when? Although he knew the manor was in Wales he didn't know where. The modern maps wouldn't be able to tell him. Even if he did find it, he'd have to get someone to come looking, the police or search and rescue. Finding the clearing and the route to the manor itself in the pitch black would take longer. Did I have that much time to wait? My foot was held up so high it had to be losing blood flow. I already couldn't feel it. I couldn't even move with it stuck up there.

Overhead came a rumble and fresh rain began to fall. Within minutes it was coming down hard in icy bullets, striking my face and getting in my eyes. I turned my head to one side but then the dirty water lapped at my cheek. A new fear turned me cold inside, to match my frozen skin. What if the well, or whatever it was, filled up?

Peering at the shadowy hole in the wall I tried to see if there was a tunnel or drain that way. Would the rain water escape? Getting the lighter to stay lit in the downpour was impossible. I couldn't see that far with no light.

I tried to stay still, not move the water around. I had to see if the level was rising. When I felt it swell to my ears I gasped and tried to sit up, only to jolt my leg again and scream in agony.

Trapped, my mind whirled. If I didn't get my leg free I wouldn't be able to keep my head out of the water. Sitting up in that awkward position put pressure on my stomach muscles and was quickly exhausting me. I had to get my leg down so I could keep my head up.

Straining to stay upright, cursing myself for not having a stronger midsection, I reached for my ankle. Even the pressure of my own fingers made me bite down hard in pain. There was a hideous grinding inside my ankle, bone sliding on bone.

My lips trembled as I counted off. 'One . . . two . . . three.'

I screamed, loud and long and shrill like an animal in a trap. My brain short-circuited. With my eyes clamped shut, colours exploded across my lids from white to red to yellow and back again. Finally my slippery fingers wrenched my ankle free and my leg crashed into the water. White-hot pain

164

came instantly, as if my bones were hooked up to electrodes. The sounds coming out of me were guttural snarls and whines. Losing all control I threw up bile and nearly choked.

Only the icy rain slapping me in the face kept me conscious.

Dragging my useless leg and sobbing in agony, I pulled myself into the little opening I'd seen. I couldn't feel the back of it. It appeared that the tunnel kept going, though it must have been blocked somewhere, as the water was still rising. At least I could lean on the wall. The slick, slimy bricks held me upright as I cried, coughing and spitting bile into the murky water.

In my new upright position my head began to throb. What if I had concussion? The pain sapped my energy and my eyes kept drooping closed. I forced them open each time. Falling asleep with a concussion was bad, I knew that. I had no idea why, but I had to stay awake. Awake and ready to call for help if anyone came. Though in the belting rain my hopes weren't high.

I leaned, straining my ears over the pounding rain for the sound of voices or swish of helicopter blades. I kept thinking I heard footsteps and looking up but no faces appeared in the opening of the hole. Maybe it was sticks falling, battered by the rain, or water pouring from a broken gutter.

The water level in the hole continued to climb. It was up to my waist, with the rain still coming down. I couldn't stand up. My hip was seized up, agonising. If the rain kept coming down and water kept running off the ground I'd soon be up to my neck.

Wrapping my arms around myself for warmth I leaned my head back and screamed until I was hoarse. My voice echoed up the brick-lined shaft and seemed to bounce around in the open. Someone had to come. Someone *would* come.

It stayed dark. I had no idea how much time was passing

but the sun seemed unwilling to rise on me. I started to shiver. Each tremble sent spasms of pain through me. My leg, lying like a log in the water, had gone numb, but my back and hip still hurt. I was too exhausted to cry or scream. I was soaked, my body heavy. I just wanted to sleep.

When I stopped shivering I was almost relieved. The cold didn't even feel as bad anymore. I almost couldn't feel anything. I was barely conscious of anything but my own breath, rasping in and out, in and out. Perhaps I was dying. After what I did I deserved to die like this. I deserved far worse.

But the baby didn't.

'. . . cee!'

I blinked raindrops from my eyelashes. The rain had stopped, finally.

'Lucy!'

Instinctively I tried to shout, choked, then managed a wordless bellow.

A head appeared over the edge of the hole. I looked up, squinting. It was just a shadow. A deeper black shape against the night sky.

'Oh my God, Lucy.' The shape retreated. 'She's here! Over here!'

Returning, the shape spoke again and I realised it was Ellie, the familiar voice finally registering in my frozen brain.

'Lucy, hold on. We're going to get you out of there. Oh my God. I had no idea, when you didn't turn up . . .'

She kept talking, crying, but I was having trouble following. The words slid over and around me and my eyes were creeping closed again. I just wanted to sleep.

When I opened them there was someone climbing down the rungs into the hole. They came to a stop and carefully put their feet down into the water. I realised that the murky brown tide was up to the middle of my chest. Water ran in small waterfalls down the sides of the shaft above me, splashing into the pool.

Whoever it was had on a woolly hat and a thickly padded jacket. I let myself be moved about stiffly as buckles and straps were put around me. Only when they tried to lift me did the fog recede, replaced by blinding pain. I screamed and cried the whole way back out of the well. I hardly realised I was out until the pain shrank and I found myself on a stretcher.

Two people carried me along. I bit my lip hard as I was jostled around. The pain was unbearable and I was too exhausted to brace myself against it. How far they carried me, or in which direction, I couldn't tell. But eventually we passed through the hoarding, which was partly opened. So there was a gate after all.

Without warning the stretcher lowered and they put me into a too bright van. The white lights dazzled me and I slitted my eyes against them. Someone was piling blankets onto me. I heard strangers talking softly. Ellie appeared over me, drenched and pale.

'It'll be OK, Lucy. We're going to hospital now,' she said said. 'The ambulance is taking us straight there and you'll be OK.'

'The baby . . . my leg . . .' My lips felt like cold rubber.

She stroked my hair back from my face. Her skin felt like a brand, scalding my stiff cheek.

'It'll be OK,' she said again.

'I'm going to give you a painkiller now; you might feel a bit sleepy,' said a stranger's voice. 'Small scratch . . .'

I felt a sharp sting in my upper arm and within a few seconds I was finally able to sleep.

Chapter Twenty

I awoke to the antiseptic smell of hospitals and doctor's surgeries. Blinking, I squinted into the dim room. I was in a bed. To my left was a window with the blinds drawn, on my right a closed door with a line of white light under it. Opposite me I could see through a slightly open door to a bathroom. A vent overhead sighed warm air into the room, making the blinds sway.

Swallowing hurt my throat. My lips were dry and cracked. Glancing around I saw a plastic jug on the bedside table, beside a vase of fat pink roses. I tried to reach for it but my arm wouldn't obey me. It squirmed uselessly on the waffle-textured blanket, my fingers weighed down with plastic grips and wires. Rolling my heavy head the other way I found a television on a metal arm and a lamp attached to the wall. One chair sat in a shadowy corner, empty.

'Hello?' I croaked.

Outside there were footsteps going back and forth, clattering and scuffling. I imagined gurneys and wheelchairs going up and down the halls of the hospital. Was Ellie out there, waiting for me?

Keeping my eyes open was too great a struggle. I closed them and let sleep take me again.

When I next opened my eyes, the room was brighter and there was a woman by the bed. A doctor in a white coat. Behind her a nurse hovered expectantly, carrying a tray.

'Hello Mrs Townsend, glad to see you awake. Would you like some water?'

I nodded groggily and the nurse came forward to help me sit up. A plastic cup was brought to my lips and I drank the slightly stale-tasting water down greedily. Once the nurse had me settled on my pillows the doctor smiled and pulled the chair over to the bed.

'Where am I?' I managed, throat still raw from all the screaming I'd done.

'This is the Pinewood Clinic. We're a private hospital, near Caernarfon. I'm Doctor Mead and this is Nurse Brody.'

Doctor Mead looked very severe, her greying blonde hair pulled back into a slick ponytail, eyes narrow behind her thick-framed glasses. She reminded me of someone, maybe one of my social workers. She had the same kind of detached friendliness that set my teeth on edge. She smiled slightly as if sensing my discomfort. Nurse Brody on the other hand was plump and motherly with a heavy brow. She squeezed my hand after checking my monitor clip and left the room.

'I'm not sure how much you remember of the accident,' Doctor Mead began.

'Fell,' I said, even that one word like razors in my throat.

She nodded. 'You were found in a deep hole. From what the search and rescue team said it sounded like an access hatch had rusted through. You were scraped by the old metal and we've given you a tetanus injection as a precaution.'

'Baby?' I whispered, guilt at my own foolhardiness practically choking me.

Her voice softened from its clipped tones. 'Your pregnancy was our top concern and according to all the tests we've done, there was no damage to the foetus during the accident.'

The guilt eased, but I felt a sliver of something else, a kind of . . . disappointment. Even though in the moment I'd not wanted anything to happen to it, I couldn't help but think perhaps things would have been simpler had it just . . . vanished. Then it would never have known what a terrible person it was being born to. How was I ever going to look this child in the eye, let alone spend the rest of my life having a relationship with them, knowing what I did now?

Doctor Mead was oblivious to my crushing guilt. 'You're on quite a lot of painkillers at the moment because of your injuries. I've actually been in to see you before but . . . obviously your memory's a bit of a jumble.'

That explained why she looked familiar then. How much time had I lost? I looked down at the humpy white form of the blankets. How was my leg? I couldn't really feel anything. I supposed the painkillers were fairly heavy-duty. Just remembering the pain I'd been in made me feel shaky.

'We've had to put a cast on your leg. Your ankle was broken, you had three broken toes, a fracture in your shin and a dislocated hip. Although we did initially attempt to relocate your hip via a closed procedure, we had to resort to arthroscopic surgery in order to correct the displacement. The incisions were minimal, and scarring should also be minor.'

I swallowed. I'd had surgery. How long was I unconscious for? I imagined myself being pulled about by doctors as they tried to get my hip joint back into place. I shuddered. Something about the idea absolutely horrified me. I'd almost rather be awake.

'Once you're able you will likely have to undergo physical therapy to recover your former range of movement. We are concerned about damage to the sciatic nerve; there was a lot of swelling and how you fell potentially caused the nerve to stretch. We won't know until we're able to do some more tests. At the moment the important thing is for you to keep still, rest and recover. You had a touch of hypothermia and were quite dehydrated.'

I nodded to show I understood. Inside I was frantic. Hypothermia and dehydration, nerve damage and surgery. Was I going to be able to recover fully or was she just trying to placate me? The thought of being heavily pregnant with an injured hip and sciatic nerve damage did not sound pleasant. It sounded like agony, which my guilty heart said I deserved.

Doctor Mead was checking her watch. 'I should continue with my round, I wanted to check in on you and make sure you were aware of what had occurred. Your friend has been waiting here for you but we couldn't give her much information. I'm sure you can understand.'

I nodded again. Where was Marshal? I wanted to ask but she was already standing up and opening the door with a brisk jerk. The corridor outside was bright compared to the gloom of my room. The door closed soundlessly behind her and I let my head fall back on the pillows.

Ellie was somewhere in the hospital. She would come and see me soon. Perhaps then I could find out where Marshal was and how long I was going to be laid up here for. I hoped Ellie had called him, otherwise he'd be frantic, furious. I felt almost sick when I imagined how he might react to the news of my injury, when he found out how careless and stupid I'd been. He'd probably have me moved to that clinic his father had suggested. Leave me locked up there alone so I didn't get myself in more trouble.

More than anything I just wanted to be in my own bed in my own home. A lump of sadness settled in my stomach.

Not that home was really a restful option. Going back there would lead to only more complications. The press photographers would be ecstatic to get a snap of me being stretchered into the house. Then there was Marshal. He'd take care of me, but it would be such a burden for him. One I couldn't repay, when he had already done so much for me. I didn't think I could face him ever again. Not now that I knew I was part of a murder plot.

For a moment I was struck by the wild thought of running away. I could get up, leave the hospital and take a taxi somewhere else, anywhere else. I could run away from everything I learned about myself. From the remainder of Luna Vitae, the mother who abandoned me, the people I killed.

Only of course I couldn't leave. I was trapped in plaster and unable to even raise my own arm, completely helpless. Then there was the baby. Marshal's baby. I couldn't steal his child away from him. He'd look for me, for us, with all the influence he and his dad had between them. More than that, how could I look after the baby on my own? Wasn't that exactly what my mother tried to do? And look how that turned out. She neglected me, ignored me and in the end, used me. How would my baby grow up with a murderer taking care of it? No, this baby needed Marshal. Of the two of us, he was the good one. I was the one who was broken and screwed up. Marshal could give it everything it would need – a home, private education, holidays and opportunities. Without him I had nothing. I was nothing.

I began to cry, buried under a black cloud of all my wrongs. A terrible mother. A disloyal wife. Worthless daughter. Liar. Murderer. Inside I felt rotten, disgusting, like there was something bad in me that others must sense. No one could forgive what I did, the fire I caused, the deaths. I couldn't forgive myself.

'Luce?'

I looked up and saw Ellie in the doorway, clutching an armful of shiny magazines and a bunch of flowers. I broke down into fresh sobs at the sight of her.

'Oh, hun!' she exclaimed, dumping her things onto the chair and swooping down to hug me. I tried to pull away, knowing I didn't deserve comfort, but she held me tightly. As I cried she rocked me slightly and shushed against my hair. Eventually I calmed a little, gulping air and hiccupping. Ellie sat down on the edge of the bed.

'Has something happened to the baby?' she asked gently. I shook my head. Ellie let out a breath.

'Thank God. You gave me such a scare. What's wrong then? Did that doctor upset you? She's a right scary one.'

I laughed wetly and Ellie took my hand. 'I'm so glad you're OK. Honestly, when I saw you in that well, or whatever it was . . . I thought you were . . .' She sniffed and I noticed for the first time that her eyes were red. She'd been crying.

'I'm OK,' I croaked.

Ellie nodded, but I saw her eyes begin to gleam and moments later tears were sliding down her cheeks.

'Sorry, sorry. I know it's stupid. You're the one who got hurt. I just thought for a minute that I'd lost you forever,' she babbled.

I squeezed her hand as best I could with my uncooperative fingers. Looking her over I could see she hadn't slept. She was still in the clothes she was in when I took her to the Imperial and her eyes had large dark circles under them. Her hair was soaked through and dried flat, hanging in rat-tails. Even her lips were bruised and peeling from being bitten.

'Why were you there?' she asked. 'When you didn't pick me up I was so worried you were in an accident or something happened with the baby whilst you were stuck at the cottage. I got a lift back there and there was no sign of you. I scared

Marshal half out of his mind when I called and said I had no idea where you were. He was shouting at me and saying I was so selfish for leaving you—'

'Sorry,' I croaked, furious that Marshal did that. 'Wanted to see . . .' I said, with great effort, 'see where I lived.'

Ellie was nodding but I could see she didn't really understand. How could she? It wasn't exactly a common occurrence to want to see the cult commune where your mother died, where she used you to kill so many people. What was the plan? Did she and Carlisle want to run away together to start again? I had no idea. I wasn't sure of anything anymore.

'Marshal thought you might have gone there. He had a search and rescue team go up there and I made him tell them I was going too. I couldn't just sit at the cottage waiting for you. Then it was so dark and stormy out we could hardly see. I just sort of blundered about with this torch they gave me. Honestly if I'd seen that hole a second later I'd have gone in right on top of you.' She laughed shakily. 'It must've been so awful. Just hearing them get you out, you sounded so scared and in so much pain . . .'

Her voice trailed off and she hugged me again. I sat limply and let her, despite knowing I wasn't worthy of her care. I still wanted it, awful person that I was, I still felt comforted. I wondered what she'd say if she knew, if she'd shed any tears at all for me if I told her what I did.

Chapter Twenty-One

I was in and out for the next few days. I slept during the day, sometimes waking at night. Occasionally Ellie was there in the visitor chair, sometimes Nurse Brody appeared to check me over. I drank water, ate jelly and slowly regained some of my voice. It was still cracked and croaky but at least I could speak without pain. Ironic, as I never wanted to speak to anyone again.

My nightmares were so much clearer now. The memory of the fire was never far from my mind. The pit in my stomach only grew deeper with every thought spared for my past. Sometimes the nightmare changed; I was up at the window, floating like a ghost and watching the faces of women inside contorted in agony, begging me to open the window and let them out. I held it shut and saw their flesh bubble and blister. My mother told me she was proud of me.

I woke sweating and in pain from these nightmares, the painkillers having worn off. I would lie there and feel the throbbing and sharp pains in my limbs, too guilt-stricken to summon the nurse. I deserved the pain.

Ellie visited and brought me magazines, crossword books and Sudoku. Those were some of the hardest hours because

I could hardly look her in the eye. Whilst she talked about the stories in the magazines and tried to do puzzles with me I offered only one-word answers and wished she'd leave me alone. It seemed, though, that she was sticking around. According to her, Marshal had extended the cottage rental and she recovered the hire car from the clearing by the manor. Ellie was there to take care of me because Marshal was still in Bristol.

There was a part of me that felt hurt – betrayed even – that he hadn't come to see me. I was his wife, his pregnant wife, and I'd had a horrible accident. Surely he was meant to rush to my side and do all the things Ellie was doing; comfort and console me as I recovered. The bigger part of me was relieved. If dealing with Ellie made me feel uncomfortable and anxious, even thinking of Marshal filled me with guilt and despair. The idea of him so much as holding my hand made me want to cry. I had no idea how to begin to hide what I knew from him. How could I face him now I knew the truth about myself, that I was a murderer? The longer he stayed away, the better.

'He wants to come,' Ellie assured me as she unpacked ginger pastilles and some aromatherapy oils onto my bedside table. 'I've spoken to him a few times, but he's so worried about the press finding out where you are and stressing you out, or anyone else for that matter,' she added softly.

'Who?' I asked, opening my eyes to look at her.

Ellie's cheeks flamed. Perhaps she thought I was asleep. I was 'resting my eyes' for the past thirty minutes, hoping she'd leave.

'Well . . . he didn't want me to worry you,' she hedged.

'Ellie,' I croaked, in what I tried to make a commanding tone. 'Tell me.'

She sat down, twisting her hands together. 'There's been some kind of . . . incident at your house. Some people were staking it out – the papers have pretty much cottoned on that no one's there aside from security – but these others broke in. They didn't take anything, not that Marshal knows of, but they did . . . vandalise some stuff.'

'How? What stuff?' I asked, wondering why the hell Marshal bothered with security if they were just going to let this kind of thing happen.

'Apparently the guy watching the place that night went out for a cigarette in his car. He must've fallen asleep or something. Next morning he had to call in and tell Marshal these people had been in, through a busted window.' Ellie bit her lip and let out a sigh. 'They painted stuff on the walls. Smashed up some furniture. He says it's nothing irreplaceable. That reminds me actually.' She rummaged in her bag and produced some catalogues from a DIY store. 'Marshal said if you picked some stuff out he can have the whole place redone. Even get the nursery painted.'

She was trying to distract me. I could feel it. People had broken into our home and vandalised it? This was getting worse. Was that why Marshal didn't come to see me? Was he actually afraid now, not of the media, but of the band of crazies following the news story? I remembered the bloody heretic letter and felt sick. What were these people after, and what were they capable of? Was it Celeste, still out there somewhere? I shuddered.

'What did they paint?' I asked.

Ellie shrugged and looked at her hands.

'Ellie,' I insisted. 'I have a right to know.'

'He didn't give me the details, honestly,' she said, seeing my face. 'He just said it was creepy religious-nutter stuff. "Repent ye sinners", all that kind of thing. Like those weirdo street preachers you get down by the Galleries.' She gave a little laugh but it sounded hollow and forced. She was worried too.

177

I closed my eyes, trying not to cry. It wasn't just the press and the scandal of it anymore. People were actually mad enough to be smashing windows and sneaking into my home to make a statement. Everything felt like it was spinning out of control. No matter how hard I tried to get away from it, the craziness followed me, growing and growing like a wave, sweeping up everything and everyone in its path. First the news, the press conference bombshell, then I ran away to Wales and still people were after me. How stupid I was to think it would all go away. If I learned anything the past month it was that nothing stays buried. Eventually, somehow, someone was going to find out that I caused the fire. Then they'd never leave me alone. Would the baby even be safe with me in its life?

'Let's not go on about what some nutters are doing,' Ellie said, spreading out the catalogues. 'Come on, let's do some interior design.'

We looked at paint charts for a while. Ellie did most of the talking and I honestly had no opinions on what colour the nursery ought to be. I couldn't face imagining the baby being a real solid thing in my arms, a vulnerable thing that needed me. All I could think of was how easily I could destroy their life, how much better off they would be without me, without the burden of what I did.

Sometimes it felt as if I'd been in shock since that stick turned blue. After all, the chances of me getting pregnant were so low. I was still coming down from the whirlwind romance, taking my pill religiously. We'd not even talked about children since just after the wedding when he said I could stop taking the pill and I . . . didn't. I wasn't hiding it or anything. He knew. But that wasn't really a discussion. It was just him floating an idea in newly wedded bliss.

When I took the test and waited, thinking about what would happen if it was positive, part of me thought I'd just naturally feel a wave of joy or elation. That all my worry was on the surface and underneath I was sure. I really did want to be a mother. Only that didn't happen. If anything, the opposite happened. I suddenly became aware that I knew I couldn't be a mum, that every time I imagined it, I thought of my own mother and felt sick, terrified of following in her footsteps. That was before I knew how bad she really was, how bad I was.

If I thought confronting my past would fix things, it only showed what an idiot I was. Nothing I learned reassured me that I would be a good mother. I was more certain than ever that I came from a terrible woman who used me to do terrible things. She raised me for seven years and that had to have left a mark. I had no business being a mum.

Pain and self-hatred were my constant companions as I rested in my hospital bed. When Ellie left and it was just me and the four walls of my room, I had nothing else to think on. The only thing that made me feel worse was the knowledge that I couldn't stay in that clean, white limbo forever. Sooner or later I would have to go back, either home or to the cottage. Then I'd have to face the future – Marshal, our baby, the truth.

Doctor Mead came to see me once I was managing to stay awake during the day. She looked grim even before she told me she had bad news. I was still using a catheter and unable to walk; all I wanted was to be able to have a shower and go to the toilet. Surely things couldn't get worse?

'Mrs Townsend, I've had a look at the X-ray we did yesterday and I'm afraid I have some concerns about your back.'

I felt a surge of anxiety. It took ages for them to convince me that the X-ray wouldn't hurt the baby. My anxiety over my own failings had me trying too hard to protect the baby and it took both the nurse and Doctor Mead to assure me that one X-ray was perfectly harmless. They wheeled a portable machine into the room to take a look at my back, now that the swelling was reduced.

'It looks like several vertebrae were damaged. You may also have a ruptured disc.'

'What does that mean?' I asked, heart fluttering. 'Can I not . . . will I still be able to walk?'

'Oh yes, of course,' Doctor Mead hurriedly assured me. 'It does, however, mean we are looking at more extended bedrest and possibly a back brace once the baby is born, to help manage things.'

'Oh . . .' I said, waiting for the rest of whatever was coming.

'With that in mind . . . when I spoke to your husband previously he wanted to have you moved somewhere more comfortable, but I'm afraid your needs may mean a longer stay in hospital. Moving you unnecessarily and relying on support outside a hospital setting would be against my advice, especially given your pregnancy, which may well complicate your recovery.'

From the look on her face she clearly expected me to be upset by this news. I was, sort of. The hospital wasn't exactly a great place to rest. There was noise in the corridor and Nurse Brody bustling in and out to check on me throughout the night. Not to mention the scratchy bedding and lack of distractions aside from the four-channel television and magazines. But at least I was able to avoid speaking to Marshal since there was no phone in my room. The only phones were payphones in the hall, and I wasn't able to get out of bed to use them. Mobiles were not allowed on my floor.

'I hope that's not too distressing for you,' Doctor Mead said.

'No, I . . . I understand.'

'May I ask what those are?' she asked, indicating the bottles and packets on my bedside table.

'Oh, they're things my friend Ellie brought in,' I said. 'She has this business that sells supplements and aromatherapy stuff.'

'May I?' she asked.

I nodded and she picked up the packet of ginger pastilles, pushing up her glasses to squint at the ingredients on the back.

'Those are for morning sickness,' I said, feeling embarrassed on Ellie's behalf. After all, this was her business, and although some of the stuff was a bit out there, the pastilles at least had been helpful.

'Hmm . . . well, there doesn't seem to be anything objectionable in here. Just be sure you're checking the ingredients and researching their impact on pregnancy. Not to mention their efficacy.' Doctor Mead put the packet down and gave me a small smile, like she was amused by Ellie's potions. 'There's a lot of quackery and pseudoscience aimed at pregnancy and women's health these days.'

'Will do,' I said. Though how I was meant to look anything up without my phone or any internet I had no idea.

'You don't need to worry, Mrs Townsend. We'll take good care of you here. I know it's difficult to be parted from your family, but trust me, you want to do what's best, don't you?'

I nodded, guilt swirling in my stomach. Doctor Mead was being so nice but really she didn't need to be. I was glad not to see Marshal. It meant I had more time to think, more time to escape seeing him now that I knew the truth, that I couldn't be a mother to our baby. Doing so would only ruin our child's life.

Chapter Twenty-Two

Ellie continued to visit every day. A few weeks into my hospital stay I was together enough to realise that she must have long since used all her annual leave. When I asked her she only laughed.

'Sweets, I'm not working for those bitches anymore! After the accident I told them I was staying up here to take care of you and that they could stick their shitty job.'

'But what are you going to do?'

She indicated the litter of bottles and packets on my bedside table. 'My real job. I've made so many sales from the cottage. I can do this anywhere. Honestly it's such a great earner. You should have seen the women speak at that conference. It really lit a fire under me.'

Ellie spoke about the conference a lot. Although she missed one day due to the accident and being at the hospital with me, she went back and attended the rest. She even brought me some leaflets and booklets. I wasn't that interested but it was good she had something on the go now that she'd left her admin job.

Aside from Ellie's visits the days blended together. I slept, read, did crosswords and watched the few channels available on the TV. There wasn't much choice – two documentary channels, 24/7 gardening and reruns of old daytime mystery shows. I didn't mind. None of them showed the news, and I was glad not to see what people were saying about me on there.

Nurse Brody was attentive but not particularly talkative. She brought meals three times a day, checked my catheter and, later, when I was able to shift about without too much pain, helped with the bedpan. She was the one to administer medication and bed baths and help rearrange me in bed to keep me comfortable. Yet we never really spoke more than her giving me instructions and me obeying. It was actually kind of nice. I preferred her stoicism to Ellie's relentless positivity.

As for Marshal, he communicated via Ellie for the most part. Afraid of my location being discovered, he mostly emailed her and she printed these on the cottage's ancient inkjet and brought them in. Through Ellie I wrote messages back, on paper, which she typed and sent. I got the sense that there was a lot he wasn't saying. Whether about the house, the situation in the press or his relationship with his father, I didn't know. Underneath the few lines he wrote and I felt for him. Though he was also clearly annoyed that I hadn't followed his advice to stay in the cottage. He told me several times that he knew something bad was going to happen, and now look.

Since everything came out in the press, Ellie had been an amazing friend to me. I knew that. Although we'd known each other for a short while, mostly as work friends, she really stepped up. Coming to Wales with me, even if it was convenient for her, was a big thing. I felt guilty imagining her at the cottage all on her own. Although Marshal assured me that he was taking care of the car rental and food shopping, it still had to be tough for her. All on her own, without friends or even a working landline.

As the weeks went by I relied on Ellie more and more for news from outside. She didn't bring me papers – I think Marshal had told her not to – but she told me about anything and everything that wasn't to do with me. When I bemoaned the unkempt state of my hair it was Ellie who bought special scissors and cut it for me. It actually turned out fairly well. I wanted to pay her back, but couldn't without her having to type up my request for Marshal. As soon as I was well enough to reach the payphones I would phone him and ask him to do something to thank her properly.

My main occupation was to sit back and watch my belly grow. I felt at times like a pumpkin patch – lying still and seeing my stomach get fuller and rounder. My body still ached but at least I wasn't feeling sick all the time. It seemed impossible that I might be four months gone already. Only five months left and I still had no idea what I was going to do about Marshal and everything I was keeping from him – the fire, my mother, how scared I was that I would be a danger to our baby, no matter how much I didn't want to be.

The obvious course of action was to keep my mouth shut and carry on as if nothing was wrong. Have the baby and return to a delighted Marshal. I would apologise for ignoring him and getting myself in an accident, accept my future as a stay-at-home mother and try to keep it together. Let everything return to normal. Only I didn't think I could do that to him. Not without the guilt eating me up inside. It was getting worse, not better, and all that guilt would become resentment and anger. I wouldn't put that on a child.

I could tell him everything, including how afraid I was that I would turn into someone like my mother if I stayed with him and the baby. But that almost seemed worse. There was no getting away from it now. I wasn't certain his father would ever allow a divorce, even with all the scandal already surrounding me. Would Marshal and I be trapped together, me facing his disappointment every day? That would only create more problems, push me further towards instability and spite.

Lastly, I could say nothing and vanish. Somehow that felt like the worst thing. Not only would I be abandoning Marshal without explanation, I'd also be committing the ultimate sin as a mother, leaving my child. Something else I'd have to hide from the world and carry with me, always. The idea of losing Marshal made me feel sick. He was the only person who ever loved me. I couldn't bear the idea of destroying his trust in me. Even with everything hanging over us, I still loved him. If I left I knew I'd never love like this again. Besides, he would never let me go. I knew that.

I went through those options a hundred times a day, each time coming to the same conclusion. I could stomach none of them. Yet I still couldn't think of a way forward without choosing one of the terrible alternatives. Sooner or later I would have to make a choice.

I was fretting over it as usual when Doctor Mead came to my room with a new woman. She wasn't dressed as a nurse, but similarly, with a long plait down her back. She was wheeling an ultrasound trolley.

'Good afternoon, Mrs Townsend,' breezed Doctor Mead. 'This is Sita, our ultrasound technician. She's going to be performing your twenty-one-week scan.'

Sita beamed at me. 'Hello! You were asleep last time we met. I heard you took a bit of a tumble?'

I forced a smile. The agony of my time spent in that hole was very much still with me. I did not appreciate her attempt at sweet concern. It reminded me too much of social workers who had no idea what to say to me. Behind her, Doctor Mead slipped her hands into her pockets and hovered unobtrusively.

185

Unbothered by my silence, Sita began to set up the machine and then rolled down the blankets to apply gel to my now noticeable bump.

'Are you excited to learn the sex of your baby?' she asked.

I felt terrible. It didn't even occur to me to ask when I might find that out. It seemed like at every turn I was failing to be the kind of mother everyone expected.

'Not worried so long as it's healthy?' Sita trilled as she began to slide the wand to and fro, completely misunderstanding my helpless shrug. 'Did you want to know anyway?'

'Yes,' I said, not wanting to come off as worse than I already looked.

'Well . . . everything looks great,' she muttered, shifting the probe back and forth. On the screen, a small blob morphed and changed. It was a sort of dark patch the size of a pear. I was unconscious during my last scan and this was the first time I could see the baby developing. I expected to feel something positive – joy, recognition, love – but there was only a spike in the ever-present worry. This little thing was depending on me and I kept screwing up. I felt my eyes well up.

'Oh, bless. Here you go, lovey,' Sita said, handing me a tissue. 'Overwhelming, isn't it? You're not alone there.'

Her incorrect assumption only made things worse. She thought I was overcome with joy at the sight of my first child. Shame made my face hot. How could I ever tell anyone the reality, that I was petrified of being the worst thing in my baby's life.

'Now, let's get a good look around . . . ah, there we are,' Sita was muttering. Doctor Mead came forward slightly, leaning to see the screen better.

'Everything as expected?' she asked shortly.

'Oh, everything is right as rain.' Sita smiled. 'One happy, healthy little girl.'

'A girl,' I echoed. 'I'm having a daughter?'

'That you are,' Sita said. She looked so happy for me. Doctor Mead nodded in her tightly controlled way.

A daughter. It felt impossibly cruel. How many more ways would my life mirror my mother's? How many more signs could I be shown that this baby would know nothing but misery with me in her life?

There was a knock on the door.

'One moment,' Doctor Mead called. She turned to me. 'That'll be your visitor. Are we finished here?'

'All done,' Sita said, swabbing the mess from my stomach with a handful of thin tissues. I folded my pyjama top down and rearranged the blankets. 'Here's a little picture for you. Would you like one to send to your husband?'

I nodded and she handed over another card. 'Congratulations.'

'Thank you,' I said, sounding wooden to my own ears.

Doctor Mead ushered Sita and her trolley out and Ellie came in before the door had even swung closed.

'Everything OK?' she asked.

'Fine . . . here,' I said, holding out the scan printout. I didn't want to show it to her really. She'd only want to talk about it, coo over it, and I wasn't sure I was up to pretending any longer. I just wanted to be alone and cry.

'Oh, sweet,' she sighed. 'Do you know what it is yet?'

'A girl.'

'A little baby girl . . . Oh Luce, isn't that amazing?' She beamed. 'I didn't want to say anything and jinx it but I was so hoping you'd have a girl. I've seen so many lovely little dresses and a big cuddly unicorn whilst I was hanging around in town. I had to send a picture to Marshal. She'll love it! Maybe I had a sort of sixth sense that it was going to be a girl, eh?'

'Maybe,' I said, trying to muster a smile.

187

'What's wrong?' she asked, sitting lightly on the side of my bed. 'You look like you've just found out Santa isn't real.'

I sniffed, trying to laugh. 'It's nothing. I just feel a bit . . . stressed.'

'I know. I can't imagine what it's like not having your husband with you at a time like this,' she said, pulling a sympathetic face. 'I'll tell him though. Do you have another picture for him?'

I handed it over.

'Aww, he'll love it. He said not to post stuff but I'm sure someone here will scan it in for me. He's going to want to send you all sorts now, which reminds me . . .'

Ellie rummaged in her bag and pulled out a slightly crumpled looking pink gift bag. In the depths of her handbag I thought I saw a matching blue one. She caught my look.

'He wanted to be ready for either event,' she grinned, rolling her eyes. 'Here.'

Inside the bag was a little rosy-pink velvet jewellery box. I opened it and found a delicate gold chain with a single pale pink pearl on it. Ellie was grinning, watching me expectantly, but I was at my limit. As soon as I saw the beautiful gift Marshal had sent I burst into tears.

Hunched over, sobbing, I felt Ellie's arm's go round me.

'Aww, sweetie . . . don't worry. You'll see him soon.'

If she noticed that her words made me cry harder, she gave no sign.

Chapter Twenty-Three

After my breakdown over the necklace, Ellie treated me with even greater care, clearly thinking that I missed Marshal. She must have said something to him, as more gifts came regularly to 'cheer me up' – expensive pyjama sets, weighted blankets and eye masks, flowers, whole gift baskets of soaps and snacks. With every load of things she brought me my guilt grew. Everywhere I looked there sat a pile of reminders that Marshal loved me and that I was a monster for deceiving him.

The nightmares only got worse as my pregnancy developed. I could hardly close my eyes without seeing the fire, hearing the screams. No amount of white noise machines and essential oil diffusers could combat my dread of sleep. At night, when left to my own devices for hours upon hours, there was nothing to distract me from the memory of that oil lamp crashing down, condemning so many people to an agonising death.

One night I jerked awake, sweating cold beads, my heart racing. The room was dark, save for a line of light under the door to the hallway. As I tried to calm myself and make sense of the threatening jumbled shadows, I realised I needed the toilet. It was the latest annoying side effect of the pregnancy, I needed to go all the time now. I closed my eyes and gritted my teeth in frustration. I didn't want Nurse Brody fussing around me. I didn't want anyone anywhere near me.

I opened my eyes and looked at the door to my private bathroom, yet to be used. It wasn't that far. I'd had weeks upon weeks of rest. Surely I could get over there on my own. There was even a rail around the edge of the room I could use to support myself.

Doctor Mead's words came back to me, about the potential damage to my spine, the surgery on my hip. But I wasn't in any pain and they'd long since stopped the drip of painkillers. Surely I had to have healed by now.

I pushed back the blankets and sheets and pulled the waistband of my pyjamas back. There were two tiny marks on my hip. They might have been scratches or surface cuts. The surgery was very neat indeed. I poked the spot experimentally. No pain. The bones and joints underneath felt normal, not grating about or aching at all, though there were so many veins and stretch marks there I hardly looked like myself.

After pulling the bedding away I looked down at my legs. One was still in a cast, the other basically fine aside from some healed scratches, which still showed up pink on my pale skin. I braced myself and swivelled sideways, sitting up with my legs hanging over the edge of the bed. Still no pain, though my legs did feel weak and hard to move. I'd been lying down too long.

Encouraged, I set my good foot on the floor and, gripping the bed for support, levered myself upright. My knees wobbled and I felt dizzy. But I remained upright. My leg didn't collapse under me, though the muscles began to burn under the strain of being used.

With my bad leg and immobilised ankle off the floor I did

a small hop, reaching for the wall rail. Although my leg was shaky from lack of use, I felt OK. Nothing hurt. I was just cramped and weakened from being in bed so long. It was nice to be upright for a change, with something else to focus on other than my thoughts.

Using the rail I hopped around the edge of the room, reached the bathroom and made it to the toilet. Sitting down was a relief as my leg was starting to really ache. Still, I savoured my victory. Seeing the room from a new perspective was strange. I hadn't left the bed since waking up in it all those weeks ago. The idea of getting back into it now made me feel sad. I didn't want to lie back down and try to sleep, only to be haunted by nightmares. I wanted a distraction.

I thought of the payphones in the hallway. From what Ellie said they were literally just outside. Surely I could reach them. I didn't really want to use them, not as such. It was dark and I had no idea what time it even was. Not to mention I didn't want to have to face Marshal, even over the phone. But reaching the phones was a goal in and of itself. It was a challenge and one that would delay going back to sleep.

After washing my hands I hopped out of the bathroom and inched my way along the rail. The door was closer than the bed, I reasoned. It couldn't be that hard to get out there. Besides, if I couldn't manage there were bound to be nurses or someone around to help me back to bed. Full of confidence in my newfound mobility, I reached for the door handle and pushed.

The door didn't budge.

Frowning, I jiggled the handle and even tried pulling, though I knew the door opened outwards. Nothing happened.

The door was locked.

It didn't sink in right away. I stared at the handle, unable to understand what was going on. Why was the door to my room locked? Surely there was no reason to lock the patient in at night, even in a private room. Were they worried about someone coming and stealing from me? Or one of the press photographers finding out where I was and snapping photos whilst I was unconscious? I was still looking down at the handle when something else occurred to me.

There was no lock on my side.

No latch or keyhole. No way to unlock the door from inside.

The back of my neck prickled. I was locked in.

My good leg was starting to buckle, so I limped back to the bed and sat down, looking at the door. Why on earth was I locked in my room?

I tried to remember if I ever saw anyone unlock the door when leaving my room. Did Doctor Mead or Ellie ever use a key card or fob on some part of the handle that wasn't immediately obvious to me? No, not that I could think of. So . . . maybe the door wasn't locked during the day, only at night. Nurse Brody checked in on me at night of course, but I was at least half-asleep most of the time and she just opened the door to look in – a slash of blinding light and then darkness and the click of the latch.

I was still trying to puzzle it out when I heard the unmistakeable tap of shoes on tile. I had just enough time to haul myself into bed and pull the blankets over me before the door opened.

Through slitted eyes I saw the outline of Nurse Brody's bulky body against the light of the corridor. I held my breath as she stood there just looking at me. Then she stepped back and the door closed. Taking a few shaky breaths, I sat up. That time I did hear it because I was actually listening. Just before the door opened, the mechanical snick of a lock.

I sat still for a while, thinking. I kept hoping that if I

turned the puzzle this way and that in my mind, I would find a way that it all made sense. A perfectly reasonable explanation for why I was being locked into my room every night, and why no one ever mentioned it. But as many times as I went over it, I couldn't get it to add up. Surely the risk of me being trapped in a fire was more of a concern than wandering paparazzi? Even the thought of being trapped in a blaze made me come up in goose bumps. Though there was a small part of me that said it was what I deserved.

. I glanced over at the window, where the blinds were snapped closed. They had been that way since I arrived. Anxiety pushed me out of the bed, hobbling towards the window. I wouldn't calm down until I knew there was some way out. It was ridiculous, or so I told myself as I made my way laboriously across the room. Hospitals had fire alarms and sprinkler systems and staff trained to get even the sickest people out in an emergency. I was fine. There was probably a fire escape, like the one behind the HR building. The last thing I'd have to do was throw myself out of a window.

Still, I was relieved to finally reach the blinds and pull the cord to haul them upwards. I was so ready to see a fire escape that for a moment I couldn't register what I was actually looking at. Behind the blinds there was . . . nothing. Just a flat white rectangle of plastic. Through the milky panel I only saw the outline of bulbs to illuminate it, mimicking sunlight. I pressed my hand against the plastic, hoping to feel a chill, some kind of sign that there was a real window there, somewhere. But there was nothing.

I stood there, frozen. My entire reality was crumbling around me. For months I had been confined to my bed, watching the sun rise and set through the plastic blinds, and never had any idea that behind those blinds was . . . nothing. That the window was just as false as the idea that, had I been able to walk, I might have wandered out into the hallway.

Where in the hell was I? What was this place? I looked around the room, desperate for a hint, a clue as to where I had been for the past endless weeks. But it looked just like a hospital room, or at least how I expected a private room to look. I only ever really saw private hospitals on television.

Still, everything looked right, believable. The bed was utilitarian, the walls white and covered in oddly shaped plug points and small signs about hand washing and indicating the call button. It smelled like disinfectant and plastic. It felt like a hospital.

Even as I started to panic there was a small part of me still trying to rationalise. I was in a hospital room. They X-rayed me and gave me an ultrasound, for fuck's sake. Perhaps it was just a part of the building with an awful view of a brick wall, so they rigged up a light to make it feel more welcoming.

I knew that was bullshit but I so wanted to believe it. I didn't want to accept the reality I was being presented with. That I was trapped, with no idea where I was. Only everything else was suddenly making sense, the evidence piling up. Like the fact that there was no phone in my room, no way for me to contact anyone. If I wasn't so desperate to avoid him I might have questioned why Marshal didn't send me a tablet to email or FaceTime him. He sent enough things that he could have afforded to. Unless he had no idea where I was.

Oh, God. Were the emails from him even real? Was he out there now looking for me? Was that why the television only showed reruns? So I couldn't see the reports of my disappearance on the news? And Ellie! Oh, Ellie. She had to be in on it. There was no way she could have come by, day after day, and not known. No, she was helping whoever it was to trick me, to keep me calm and controlled and oblivious to my situation. Perhaps she was messaging Marshal pretending to be me, bringing things he sent to the cottage. He might not even know I had an accident.

Ellie, who I'd known for six months before ever thinking of going to Wales. How long had this been planned for? And by who? She was the one who let me know the press were onto me, that day the story broke. Was that just to sell the illusion that she was a trusted friend?

When I phoned her and told her about having to go away, was she frantically typing away, not at work but to someone else? Asking what she should do? How she could isolate me? It was all so convenient – Ellie with her conference problem. The perfect solution. She probably just picked an event at random.

I thought of the security light at the cottage flicking on at night. At the same time both times, just after one. Was that Ellie sneaking off to use her mobile and report on me? Or setting it off to scare me, to make me believe I wasn't safe anywhere, that I had to stay far away from Marshal and everyone else I could depend on.

I went over everything that happened since I woke up in 'hospital'. Everything Ellie told me. What stuck out was the story about the break-in at home, the vandalism. More evidence that I wasn't safe in Bristol. Was it to stop me asking to go home?

I dragged myself back to the bed, exhausted. I needed to rest but the idea of going to sleep there now that I knew I was a prisoner made me even more panicked. Instead I sat in bed and tried to think.

How did I come to be in the hospital? I fell and was rescued. I was injured. I knew that. I felt the agony of my damaged ankle and hip whilst I lay in the water hoping for help to arrive. That was real. That was an accident. Nothing made me stand on that rusted hatchway. So, that couldn't have been planned, right? It wasn't part of this, but then how did it happen to me? How did they plan all this to convince me I was in hospital?

I thought back. After the accident Ellie came with those two paramedics and I went into the ambulance, or what she said was an ambulance. They gave me something for the pain and I woke up in this room. But there was no way they could have planned for that. How could they? I suddenly felt very scared as I realised I had no way of knowing how long I'd been unconscious. They could have kept me under for days whilst they set the place up, drugging me over and over again. Was that why I felt so dreadful when I finally woke up? So thirsty and exhausted?

If they were keeping me here, that must have been their intention from the beginning. Maybe not the whole 'fake hospital' bit but some of it. They scared me into hiding, tricked me into isolating myself with Ellie. Perhaps they planned to kidnap me from the cottage eventually, but I sped up their plan by having my accident.

Phoebe's warning came to mind. Was this Luna Vitae? Celeste? But she'd have no reason to care about me, not after all this time, surely. Was it some other nutters who thought I was the Antichrist?

I had no way of knowing who was responsible or why they were doing this. I only knew that I had to get away before they got to their end goal. There was no way they planned to keep me in the dark forever. Sooner or later they would act. I didn't want to be around to find out what that meant for me, or the baby.

I lay in bed until the fake window began to glow with simulated dawn. When Nurse Brody came with my breakfast, I smiled as she put it on my bed tray, though I wanted to throw it at her. I spooned up my porridge like a good prisoner who was none the wiser. Then I put on the television and pretended to watch someone planting brassicas, whilst inside I wracked my brain, trying to work out what to do.

Chapter Twenty-Four

'We need a solution.'

I froze. For a minute I thought Carlisle was talking to me. But that was stupid. I was under his bed and there was no way he could see me. I'd gone under there to sweep up – nut shells, ends of joints and cigarettes, bottle tops, condom wrappers, condoms, fake nails and hair clips. He must have come in with someone else.

'We can't keep on like this. They'll never learn, never heal. Punishing them has brought a few round but the rest of those bitches,' he hissed, 'they will never let go of Celeste. They're too old to adapt. Ugly and fat and useless. Pretending they came here to get away from men, when no man would ever want to touch them. They're holding us back. Every moment we spend managing them or trying to change them is a moment wasted.'

'What else can we do?' It was Selene. I curled up further under the bed, not wanting her to know I was there. She was the one who reported the most to Carlisle. She handed out the punishments and organised other women to take the bad ones away to the shed or out under the sun when it was so hot you'd burn after only an hour.

'We can't let them go. They know too much. The moment we let that bitch out of her cage she'll have this manor off us and tell the world whatever she wants. There are already too many people investigating us, watching us . . . they could have infiltrated this place.' I heard Carlisle pacing and saw his boots as they passed the bed, back and forth. He was muttering and I couldn't hear him. Then he stopped, suddenly.

'That's it . . . we'll leave. Leave this place and go somewhere else. Where they can't find us, watch us. Where they can't interfere.'

'How?' Selene sounded breathless, excited. Both of us were waiting to see what he would say. I couldn't believe it. We were leaving the manor? To go where?

'I'll take care of everything,' he said, suddenly calm. 'Bring the ones we can trust to the room under the studio. The bunker.'

'And . . . Arianrhod?'

A long silence. I thought of the locked shed in the grounds.

'Have Lona take care of her. Make sure she hides her in the attic afterwards.'

I heard Selene rush out of the room. I listened, waiting for Carlisle to leave so I could get out from under the bed. I didn't want him to get angry at me. It went so quiet that I thought he'd already gone. Then I heard him whisper.

'You will be my hand in this. Our secret, to bind us together, always. You'll never be able to leave me. What destroys me will destroy you.'

This time I was sure he was talking to me. That somehow he knew I was under the bed. He had seen me, noticed me. He wanted me to help him.

But when I slid out from under the bed to meet him, he was gone. It was just me, and the painted girl on the wall.

Chapter Twenty-Five

By the time the 'sun' was fully up I could hardly believe what I knew to be true. It was so realistic, the way the yellow light peeped under the blinds. I almost began to wonder if it had been some new kind of nightmare, especially when Ellie arrived, full of chitchat as usual. It all felt so normal. Like I really was just a patient in a hospital and not a prisoner.

'Hey,' she beamed, spreading glossy magazines out and unloading some more puzzle books on top. 'Awful weather outside.'

Her hair was in fact windswept and a bit wet as if sprinkled with rain.

'Looks bright out,' I managed, watching as her eyes darted to the window and she forced a smile.

'Yeah . . . must have been a quick shower,' she said hurriedly.

Not a nightmare then. Despite myself I hoped that Ellie wasn't in on it, but she knew. She knew and she helped to do this to me.

'How are things at the cottage?' I asked, watching her closely.

'Oh, same old. Boring without you there,' she said, relaxing into the chair. 'Probably a good thing you're staying here though. It's been a bit chilly upstairs away from the fire. Not that you'd be able to manage the stairs.' She winced. 'How's the leg, any more news?'

'Doctor Mead said it's taking a while to heal. Something about pregnancy affecting bone density. The baby's sucking up all the calcium. Probably also why my teeth hurt.'

'Guess we'll have to get you plenty of milkshakes.' Ellie grinned. 'Shall I smuggle you in a Happy Meal too?'

I felt like crying. She was just like normal. It was almost like she knew I'd been craving that exact thing. 'You could try it. They're keen on clean food here though.'

'Well, they've got to keep you healthy, haven't they?' Ellie said seriously.

If she was lying – which she had to be, coming to see me every day and claiming I was in a hospital – then it was as easy as breathing for her. She lied so smoothly I couldn't tell what she meant and what she didn't. Was she really worried for my health and that of the baby? I had a sudden awful thought. Was this all about the baby? Did they want to get their hands on it? Suddenly the sonograms and the healthy food made sense. It wasn't me they wanted, was it? It was the baby. Oh, God.

'What?' Ellie asked, clearly noticing the look on my face.
'Nothing.'

'You just looked a bit funny. Are you feeling all right?' she pressed.

I couldn't help but push back. 'It's a bit stuffy . . . can you open the window?'

She didn't even wrinkle her brow. 'We're really high up. I don't think they open. Health and safety, you know.' She rolled her eyes then sprang up and twisted a dial near the door. 'There, I'll crank the aircon for you.'

'Thanks,' I said, managing a smile. Oh, she was good. I wanted to shout at her, jump up and slap her and force her to tell me where I was. I felt the strain of staying still go through me as I fought to remain calm. I had to keep them believing that I was ignorant of what was going on. If they had their guard up there was no way I'd get out.

I'd given it some thought and I had a plan. A terrible one. But it was all I had. I just needed them to leave me alone for five seconds.

'Any word from Marshal?' I asked.

'He was happy to get the scan. I think he's probably decking the nursery out with stuff as we speak.'

'I thought he'd be too stressed out to worry about all that, especially after the break-in.'

'Oh, they've fixed the place up now. He told me. I think the security company had to stump up for some of it in the end. It was their guy who let it happen. But I sent over all the paint colours you picked and it's all finished. Lots more guards on the job now. No one's going to break in again.'

Was it all bullshit? Was she lying right to my face and keeping Marshal in the dark? Or was he in on it too? I suddenly wondered. The refurbished, guarded house sounded like a prison. Was that where this was leading? I tried to put Marshal into the jigsaw of events that led to me being trapped in the 'hospital'. He wanted me to go away somewhere, but he didn't choose Wales, I did. I picked it because of Ellie. But then maybe they were working together. He was the stick, Ellie the carrot. They were driving me onwards whilst I followed like a stupid little lamb. Were Marshal's parents involved? Was it their money that created this place?

I forced my whirling thoughts to a stop. I had to be logical. What if Marshal was innocent; was he not worried that I didn't call him at all? Then I remembered the cut-off landline and inwardly groaned. No signal and no landline at the cottage meant no calls. Ellie was probably emailing him and pretending to be me. I thought desperately. If he was innocent, just being kept in the dark, could I use that to my advantage and raise the alarm somehow?

'Ellie,' I said slowly, still frantically pulling together my thoughts. 'Can you email Marshal and ask him to send down my stuffed toy, the one I won at school when I was little?'

It was my one and only childhood toy. Growing up in care most of the toys were communal, or, if bought for birthdays, they ended up broken or stolen by jealous kids. At thirteen I won a scavenger hunt put on by the school. It was a great day. Working out the clues made me feel oh-so-clever. But the best part was the prize, a larger than life-sized Jemima Puddle-Duck soft toy. I was too old for it but I didn't care. As soon as I got her home, I had a carer lock her up in a drawer. She was mine, and only I got to play with her.

'Aww, that's sweet. You want it for the baby?' Ellie asked.

'It's just a comfort thing. Childish, I know,' I said. 'If you could just ask him to post my Eeyore down, I'd be so grateful.'

'Will do,' she beamed.

I mentally crossed my fingers. Marshal knew the story of my duck. I told him when he showed me his room at Crossley with all its dusty teddies. Jemima sat on top of the alarm clock on my side of the bed. I could only hope his confusion would make him start asking questions. His dad was an MP. If he sparked a hunt for me I would be found. I had to be.

Of course if Marshal was in on it, I'd have just tipped him off that I knew. But I had to try something, anything. If my terrible escape plan failed, it could be my only hope. *Our* only hope, because no matter what, I had to keep the baby away from these people.

Ellie chattered on for a bit and got me to do a crossword with her. There was no clock in the room but she stayed for ages. I wanted her to leave so I could put my plan into action, but she wasn't in any hurry. I was starting to worry that she'd only leave once it got dark. The door would be locked then. I was sure it was open during the day. The only time I heard a lock retracting was when Nurse Brody brought my breakfast.

'Right, I hate to leave you, but I do need to go and get some bits for dinner,' Ellie finally said. 'Get some rest and I'll see you tomorrow, kay?'

'Sure.' I smiled, thinking that the only way she'd be seeing me again was if something went very wrong. 'You'll remember to email Marshal, right?'

'Course I will. He's probably sent me six messages whilst I've been here, asking me how you are and what's going on with the baby. He's a bigger worrier than my nana.'

I smiled and watched her get her things together. With a final wave, she left and let the door click closed behind her. I forced myself to count to fifty to be sure she wasn't going to come back for something then eased myself out of bed.

Using the chair for support I hopped across the floor and reached for the wall rail. With my fingers around it I moved as quietly as possible towards the door. In my other hand I had two ginger pastilles, wrapped in their wax paper. Holding my breath, I depressed the handle slowly, ever so slowly, wincing as it rattled slightly.

This was the moment I'd know for sure if I was fucked or not.

I applied a small amount of pressure and pulled. For a second I thought it was firmly shut but then the heavy door began to move. I inched it open and chanced a peek into the corridor.

There wasn't much to see. It was long and white, the

walls a rough, grainy concrete. The floor was probably the same under its dark grey linoleum. It definitely wasn't a hospital, that was for sure. There were no signs anywhere and the walls weren't plastered; the lights overhead were bare bulbs. It looked more like part of a multistorey car park.

Afraid to waste too much time, I found the gap in the doorframe where the latch would lock with the turn of a key. One after the other, I pressed the wrapped chews into the gap. I had no idea if it would work, but my hope was that the door would just about latch, but that the lock wouldn't engage. I could only hope that whoever was in charge of shutting me in for the night wouldn't notice the difference.

I was breathing quickly as I slowly inched the door closed. It looked normal from my side at least. Being on my feet, or rather my foot, for so long was very draining. I could manage a hobble using the exposed toes and the ball of my foot that poked out of the cast, but it wasn't exactly quick. If I met anyone outside I'd have little chance of running. I'd have to hope no one came.

Sitting on the bed I cast about for anything useful. I had no shoes, not even slippers. It had never occurred to me that I might need them, bedbound as I'd been. I would have to go barefoot. I also had no real clothes, only pyjamas, not even a dressing gown or anything to keep me warm. If I escaped and found myself in the middle of a town, this was less of an issue, but walking any distance in the freezing night could be problematic.

A weapon of some kind would have been great, but I had nothing. The cutlery that came with my meals was plastic, cheap and flimsy. I didn't have so much as a pair of nail scissors. Looking across the room I thought for a while of trying to unscrew a bar from the towel rail to use as a club, but I couldn't risk it being seen before I had a chance to escape.

They did a great job at keeping me powerless. I had no phone, no money or ID, nothing to fight back with and nothing to wear. If I got away it would be in the pyjamas I stood up in, barefoot and penniless with no idea where I was.

But I would be out, we would be out, and that was all that mattered.

I could hardly keep my nerves in check to eat dinner when it arrived. Nurse Brody brought the tray, then left without a word. I held my breath the entire time, afraid she would suddenly start jerking the door handle, feeling something wasn't right, but she didn't, not even when she came to collect the tray and help me with the bedpan before lights out. As she left I heard the clunk of the lock turning. Squeezing my eyes shut, I hoped with all I had that my plan had worked.

Lying stiffly in bed I forced myself to wait until I didn't hear footsteps for a count of two hundred. It was well and truly dark in my room, not that this meant anything. The only light came from under the door. I swallowed, sat up and froze.

After all my preparations, my frantic planning, I was too scared to move. No matter how frightening it was to know I was a prisoner, I felt that it would be so much worse to go out there and run into one of my captors. I had this sense that if they knew I was aware of what was happening, the gloves would be well and truly off, and they would attack.

I took a shallow breath, then another, and another. I had to do this. Whatever these people wanted from me and my baby, I didn't want to give it. I had to get away.

Trembling, I got up and hobbled to the door. My skin was like ice, my heart a tight knot in my chest. I felt almost on the edge of tears as I gripped the door handle and eased it down. If it didn't work, if I was still locked in . . .

The door swung open a crack and I peered out into the empty hallway.

The easy part was over. Now I had to escape.

Chapter Twenty-Six

I carefully closed the door behind me and crept along the corridor. As I saw in my quick peek, it was basically feature-less. At both ends, double doors with reinforced chequered glass partitioned the corridor. In my section there were three doors aside from the one to my room. I doubted they actually led to an exit.

I went right, down the corridor. It was a random choice. I had no way of knowing which way to go. Limping along, my feet quickly became numb from the freezing floor. There was a slight dampness to the air, a chill creeping in. The place felt unfinished, with its lack of heat and the bare bulbs hanging overhead. I wondered where I could be.

At the end of the corridor I kept close to the door and peered through the edge of the window. There was no one on the other side. The hallway didn't continue but ended in a dimly lit concrete stairwell. I tried the door and wasn't surprised to find it open. There was no visible lock on it.

The stairwell was even danker than the hallway. The walls were stained in places where the stair railings had rusted, leaving long beards of red down the wall. I leaned on the cold rail and looked upwards, then down. Nothing to be seen above except a single bulb. Below there were shadows and caged sconces, flickering.

Which way went out and which further in? I chewed my lip, already exhausted from hobbling up the corridor. I glanced fearfully through the door and found the hallway still empty. Struck by the sudden fear that there might be cameras, I scanned the corners of the stairwell but couldn't see anything except spider webs.

Heading down was the best bet. I had to reach the ground floor to get out. I set my foot at the edge of the step and prepared to start limping down, then stopped. Going down was the right way to get out of a building, but what if my windowless room was underground? I stood frozen. If I made the wrong choice I'd be screwing any chance at escape.

A bang suddenly echoed through the stairwell. A door slamming shut, then footsteps tapping on the concrete steps. I backed away from the edge, scared someone might see me. Turning my head this way and that, I tried to work out where the sound was coming from.

Above me. Someone was coming down the stairs, right towards me.

I grabbed the rail and started limping down the steps as quickly as I could. With each one, the angle drove the rough edge of my cast into my foot, but I hardly cared. I had to get away, get down the steps before someone saw me.

The echoing footsteps chased me as I dragged myself along. Out of breath, air sawing in and out of my lungs, legs shaking, I blundered onwards. The stairwell became darker as I left the overhead lights behind. Only the dirty glass domes on the wall lit the way, caged in with metal and spider webs.

Then my cast glanced off a slick patch and my leg shot out from under me. I pitched forwards, waving my arms, then swung back and collapsed, landing hard, my tailbone taking the shock of the concrete. Stunned, I sat there panting, arm wrapped protectively around my swollen middle. It took a moment for me to register that the footsteps were no longer coming after me. There was only the beating of blood in my ears and my rasping breath.

Using the railing I hauled myself back to my feet. My legs were trembling, just like the rest of me. Where was I now? Closer to safety or further than I'd ever been? I wanted to cry. The stress and intense fear were shredding my nerves.

Gritting my teeth I forced myself to take slow breaths until the tightness in my chest eased slightly. I had to keep my head if I wanted to stand any chance. I had to control myself. The hand on my belly stayed there, reminding me that I wasn't alone. I had to get away to keep both of us from being held captive.

With one hand in a death grip on the railing, I started down the steps again, passing padlocked metal doors like the kind on electrical substation buildings.

Two turns around the steps later I arrived in a square space under the stairwell – a dead end. I looked around in numb disbelief. At the bottom of the stairwell there were only concrete walls and metal boxes, padlocked shut. Stencilled letters marked these out as fuse boxes and shut-off valves. Clearly some kind of utility area. No way out aside from a hatch in the floor, also padlocked.

I leaned back against the cold wall and looked up to where the naked bulb at the top of the stairwell hung like a distant star. The way out was back there, and I was further away from it than ever. I would have to make the whole exhausting climb up again.

It was harder going up. I had to drag myself up each step using the railing as a crutch. As my muscles burned and my legs shook, I told myself that at least I had not been found. At least something came of me going in completely the wrong direction. I had to remind myself or lose hope altogether.

At last I reached the door I'd come through originally. I hopped past it then ducked and pressed myself to the wall. Through the window, I glimpsed the bulky shape of Nurse Brody standing at an open door; my open door.

I seized the rail and began to climb as quickly as I could. Behind me I heard a wordless shout of alarm. Then the door being slammed. Within a few seconds as I hauled myself upwards, an alarm began to sound. I had no time to worry about where it was coming from. The implication was clear: they knew I was out and they were coming.

A few flights up and I reached a door. If I had even a second to think how close I'd been to it before, I might have wept. Instead I tore it open and found myself in another corridor. It was more of the same – concrete and bare bulbs. Only at the other end there wasn't another school-style double door, but a hefty metal one. It looked like one on a submarine: rounded-edged and with a crank wheel on the inside. The way out?

I was already limping towards it, dragging my bad leg behind me. There was almost no hope that it was unlocked. It looked like it could withstand a bomb blast. It was not just going to open for me. But I had to try. I had nothing else. Frustrated tears blurred my vision as I struggled towards it.

The door behind me banged open and I glanced back. Nurse Brody was coming at me like a bulldog, another woman behind her, one I didn't know. I turned back, still staggering towards the door. I wasn't going to make it. A scream bubbled up as I realised I was going to be caught.

They reached me and grabbed my arms, dragging me back. Nurse Brody's hands were like clamps under their plumpness, digging into my flesh as if trying to get at the bone. The other woman wasn't as strong but her long nails scratched me as I flung myself around, trying to get free. I screamed

210

as loudly as I could until a beefy hand slammed over my mouth, driving my teeth into my lip. I choked on bloody spit as Nurse Brody got her arms around me and the other woman picked up my legs. They half dragged, half carried me back towards the stairs. I thrashed around, trying to kick with my good leg.

The doors crashed open at the other end of the hallway and Doctor Mead appeared, wearing a dark red pyjama set, no sign of her slick hair and glasses disguise.

'What the fuck is going on?' she demanded. 'You,' she pointed at Nurse Brody, 'how did you let this happen?'

'I locked the door,' Nurse Brody spat. 'I know I did.'

'Locked my arse,' Doctor Mead said. 'Diana, fetch a sedative from the supply room.'

The strange woman let my legs drop, leaving Nurse Brody to restrain me around the shoulders, one hand still on my mouth. She ran away, glancing back and giving me a glimpse of her sallow, rat-like face and wild witch's hair. The door banged shut at her back.

'Get her on the floor,' Doctor Mead snapped.

Nurse Brody lowered me. I was still flinging myself around, though growing weaker and unable to breathe around her meaty hand. Doctor Mead came closer and easily pinned my legs against the floor. I snapped at the fingers against my lips, biting until Nurse Brody snatched her hand away.

'Bitch!' She slapped me, raised her hand to do so again, then froze as Doctor Mead seized her wrist in a death grip.

'Watch yourself, Lona,' Doctor Mead said, her voice soft but full of the promise of violence, like a dog's growl. 'You are not irreplaceable.'

Nurse Brody's face shut down, a mask dropping into place. I never saw Doctor Mead like this before. Her usually confident but professional manner was gone, replaced by a crackling ferocity. Her eyes seemed to snap with power, boring

211

into Nurse Brody's until she was forced to look away. Then Doctor Mead turned those eyes on me.

'As for you. Stop this struggling before you do yourself some damage. Do you honestly think you can escape now?' She had the cold condescension of a teacher addressing an idiot pupil. I felt my insides turn cold, but even as they did, I realised she was more familiar now than she had ever been. And she was right. Even if I could get away from Nurse Brody – or Lona, whatever she was called – where would I go? I couldn't run. People were awake and alert now. I had no way of escaping.

Her eyes blazed in triumph to see me slump, all the fight going out of me. The doors rattled and Diana came hurrying back, a capped syringe in hand. She scurried over and handed it to Doctor Mead.

'No! I'll go back, please don't—' I renewed my efforts to escape but it did me no good. The needle stung the flesh of my hip and I began to feel drowsy almost at once.

Doctor Mead leaned over me as my vision blurred. As I lost focus, it was as if two decades of time fell from her face. Those same wildly sparkling eyes and haughty brows. The mouth pursed impatiently. I'd seen it before but I didn't realise why it felt so familiar to me.

'Mum . . .' My lips formed the word, but no sound escaped me and the overhead light whirled away, leaving me in blackness.

Chapter Twenty-Seven

I woke for a second time from a drugged sleep in the now familiar bed. My mouth was dry as paper and it took a while for me to convince my sticky eyelids to open. The smell of antiseptic and clean sheets was familiar, but was now joined by that of sawdust and glue fumes. I blinked and looked around. It was indeed my old room. Only now it looked very different.

All the 'gifts' from Marshal had been cleared away, leaving the place bare. The false window was removed, leaving only a depression in the wall and a plug socket. Likewise the television was gone. The visitor chair was still there but was now bolted to the floor, like my bedside table. The call button and other hospital props had been removed. The door to the hallway now had a hole cut into it at the bottom. There was a sliding metal hatch installed. There was also now a keyhole on my side of the door, I guessed so that once someone came in, it could be locked again immediately.

The door to the bathroom was closed with a freshly installed bolt and padlock drilled into the wall. The padlock was undone, however, and from inside I heard movement. Someone was in there.

I took all this in, rolling my heavy head on the stiff pillows. It looked like what it was now: a cell. Nothing in there left loose or open for me to utilise. Even the wall rails were removed, leaving holes in the plaster. Frustrated tears trickled from the corners of my eyes and I reached to wipe them, only to have my hand stop short.

Looking down I saw why. Attached to the metal bedframe were the kind of restraints I only saw in horror films, used to secure the criminally insane. Leather straps held both my ankles down, allowing only an inch or so of movement. My arms were on longer ones, able to reach maybe halfway up my chest. I jerked my arm but the strap didn't give an inch. It was buckled tightly. Although lined in foam, I could feel the weight of them dragging at my limbs, now that I was fully awake.

I heard running water, then the bathroom door opened and Nurse Brody came out. The sight of her filled me with equal parts rage and fear. Rage because she hit me and helped bring me back here, fear because of how helpless I was and how much hatred her eyes held for me. They were black as pits, burning like coals. How did I ever think she was 'motherly'?

As she took a step towards me, the collar of her scrub top slipped down and I saw the skin beneath. Around her neck there were red welts and blisters. I glanced down and saw the same ones on her wrists. I knew immediately where they had to have come from. I remembered the stocks in that outbuilding well enough. Clearly the same kind of punishment was going on wherever I was now. She was punished for her part in my attempted escape.

If there was any doubt that I was being held by the remnants of Luna Vitae, it fled my mind. It was only then that I remembered being subdued by Doctor Mead, finally placing her face as my mother's. My mother who I thought had died in the fire she had me start.

'Princess Lucia's awake,' Nurse Brody said mockingly. 'Alert the press.'

'What . . . do you want from me?' I said, voice coming out hoarse.

As an answer she came forward and placed her hand on my belly, pressing too hard. I winced and she laughed.

'His child. The only thing you have to offer. Once you bring it into the world, we'll be done with you.'

So I was right. They did just want the baby.

'Why Marshal's baby? How is he involved in this?'

She shook her head as if I was talking nonsense. 'Not that idiot. Carlisle. Carlisle's heir.'

She said his name like it brought her pleasure. As if it were a holy thing or a magic spell. A god, a lover and a miracle all rolled into one. It made the hair on the back of my neck prickle.

'Lona, that's your name, right?' I said, heart racing as I realised how insane she was, how much anger and resentment was coursing in her veins.

'It's not yours to use,' she snapped.

'OK . . .' I licked my dry lips. 'But there's been some kind of . . . I'm not pregnant with Carlisle's baby. It's my husband's. I haven't seen Carlisle since I was seven, when the manor burned down. Is he . . . here?' The idea was terrifying. But if my mother was here, surely he was too.

I watched her – hoping to see my words landing, to see reality creep in, pushing the delusion aside – but she only stared at me as if I was the mad one. As if I was speaking another language entirely or gibbering like an idiot.

'You will never understand,' she said imperiously. 'You were never one of us. You don't deserve this honour.'

She stalked towards the door and unlocked it with a key hanging at her hip.

'Wait!' I cried, voice cracking.

Lona turned back to glare at me.

'I want to see her,' I said. 'I want to see my mother.'

She only curled her lip and shut the door behind her.

I collapsed back against the pillows, already feeling the need to sleep again tugging at my eyelids. Whatever they sedated me with was powerful stuff. That or I completely exhausted myself with my futile escape attempt. Either way, I forced myself to stay awake. I had to try and make sense of the insanity that surrounded me.

Nurse Brody, who was probably not even a real nurse, thought that my child was Carlisle's heir. But how could he be the father of my child? There was no way. Marshal was the only man who could have gotten me pregnant. So what was she on about?

Perhaps it was just insanity. But then why was it targeted at me specifically if any pregnant woman would do? There had to be more to it. Was it to do with my mother? In the hallway it seemed that she was in control of everything. Perhaps she was running things for him, still one of Carlisle's favourites. Was that why they wanted my baby, because it was descended from her, through me? Perhaps she wanted me to give him the child she was too old to have?

Or – and here I felt physically sick – was 'Lona' telling the truth? My child really was related to Carlisle. That meant either Marshal was his relative, or, worse, I had somehow been inseminated. Artificially. Perhaps drugged and attacked in my own home, which meant Marshal was in on it. How did they find me? How did she do it?

The idea was insane. But no less so than what was already happening to me. All because of my mother. Selene.

I never thought I'd see her again. Until I went to the manor and realised she had helped to cause the fire, I thought she was just some misguided hippy, never meant to be a mother.

216

But now I knew the kind of evil she was. Obviously she escaped with Carlisle. They murdered the others, but why? To cover their tracks, fake their deaths? Perhaps to destroy the last traces of what Luna Vitae had been under Celeste and pave the way for a new philosophy. One with Carlisle at the centre, rather than sisterhood. And they implicated me in the crime, maybe hoping I would die, or as a way to keep me quiet if I ever tried to fight back.

How could my mother take part in destroying the manor? Everything I could find about that place and everything I remembered about her and her history made it seem like the answer to her prayers. A place where she didn't have to be ashamed of being an unwed mother, or compete against a sexist corporate structure for success. No priests, no misogyny thundering from a pulpit. How could she give that all up for one man?

How could she give up her own daughter? And what did that mean for my child?

I was filled with so many emotions. On the surface, anger, hatred, disgust. She was the one doing this to me, keeping me here. She left me for all those years in care, alone. Did she know I was alive that entire time? Did she just not care? Or was I expected to die with the others? Perhaps that was why she used me to start the fire. She just wanted rid of me. She never wanted to be my mother.

Only now, she wanted my daughter. Knowing now that she was behind what was happening to me, possibly working for Celeste or Carlisle, I knew I had to do whatever I could to get my baby away from her. My mother destroyed my life, made me a murderer, and I was not going to give her a chance to do it all over again to someone else. I would do whatever it took to get away from these people.

The door opened and I looked up, expecting to find my

mother there. Instead my eyes landed on Ellie and a swell of rage crested in my gut.

'Get. Out.'

She didn't listen, just shut the door behind her and locked it. When she turned back I got my first proper look at her. I expected the same kind of transformation in her that I saw in Lona – a slipping of the mask. But she still looked almost like Ellie, only exhausted and tearstained. There were dark circles under her eyes and her mouth was a miserable slash on her unmade-up face. Her hair was limp as if in need of washing and she was without her usual collection of jewellery and bohemian wardrobe. She was wearing a plain khaki t-shirt and jeans.

Was this the 'real' Ellie? If Ellie was even her name. Was all of it – her friendship, her appearance, even her interests – put on to lure me in? To make me believe she actually cared about me? Yet she looked upset, like she was worried about me. But I was too angry and afraid to let that get to me. She was the reason I was there. She was the bait on their hook.

'I'm to watch you,' she said, not looking at me, but making her way to the chair. She sat down stiffly.

'Like fuck you are. I never want to see you again.'

She flinched but said nothing, pressing her lips together. I realised I had no way of making her leave. I had no way of getting out of bed even, let alone getting some privacy. With a growing despair I realised that Lona had locked the bathroom door when she came out. Apparently someone had to watch me at all times now, and look after my needs whilst I was restrained.

I looked at Ellie and found her watching me, though she quickly looked away. It was clear she saw the weight of my situation hit home. She sighed and rested her hands on her knees as if bracing herself.

'How are you feeling?' she asked, in a small voice.

If I could have leaped out of the bed I would have slapped her. I could feel cords standing out on my neck from wanting to do just that. I settled for shouting.

'How the fuck do you think I feel!? You lied to me, for months, keeping me a prisoner so you can steal my baby, because you insane bitches think I got knocked up by a man I haven't seen for twenty years! How do you expect me to feel? Radiant with joy?' I took a deep breath, ready to lay into her further; after all she was just Ellie, not my mother or a terrifying hulk like Lona. I could shout at her all I wanted, let it all out. Only she suddenly burst into tears, covering her face with her hands.

I stopped short, mouth open and tirade stuck on my tongue. My skin burned with outrage and fear and the need to take somebody, anybody, to pieces. Ellie sobbed, shoulders shaking.

'How dare you,' I said, in a low voice which made me cringe because it sounded almost exactly like my mother's when she spoke to Lona. 'How dare you sit there and feel sorry for yourself when you are the entire reason I'm here. Take your fucking crocodile tears to someone who gives a shit.'

Ellie shook her head, mumbling something.

'What?' I snapped.

'I'm not the reason,' she said, lifting her teary eyes to mine. 'I had no say in this . . . and you're wrong. We don't think he *knocked you up*.' She screwed up her face in disgust. 'Carlisle . . . is dead. This child, it's his because he chose you. Chose you to be the mother of his divine child. You're all we have left.'

'What do you mean?' I asked, hardly able to breathe. It felt like a fist formed around my heart, choking off the blood, the life in me. Carlisle was dead?

'He chose you,' Ellie repeated, fresh tears spilling as she announced this injustice. 'Don't you remember?'

I didn't, couldn't find any memory in me that matched what she was saying.

So she told me.

Chapter Twenty-Eight

*I was standing on a chair whilst Diana fussed with a
length of old sari material. She was trying to turn it into
a skirt using a handful of pins. I'd been stuck a few times
already. Over her head I saw myself in the mirror on the wall.
I didn't look like me. I looked like a fairy, like a princess.*

*My eyes were outlined in black and my lips sticky and
red with lipstick. My hair was braided into loads of little
plaits, all pinned up in swirls and patterns on my scalp. Over
the plaits and all over my skin, there were little sparkles
from the glitter paint Diana dabbed on to me.*

*I breathed in and felt the pins pinch me. The incense in
the room stung my eyes. Diana took a step back and looked
me over, frowning.*

*'Hardly worth bothering,' Lona said from behind her,
holding the pins and a pot of gold paint. 'She's too plain to
be chosen.'*

*I looked at her and saw how much she hated me. Maybe
because she was ugly and not thin and pretty enough to be
a handmaid like Selene, like Diana. Even if Diana had missing
teeth and wild eyes that never stopped moving.*

Diana took the paint and drew a sun on my bare chest, the rays coming up to my neck.

Satisfied, she helped me down from the chair and pressed my cheeks in one hand. I opened my mouth and she put a pill on my tongue. I swallowed the dry tablet and followed it with a sticky slurp of juice into which she'd counted out drops from a brown bottle.

The door opened and Selene came in, leading Lucia. With her red hair piled up on her head and her body plastered in gold makeup, she looked like a shiny metal statue. Even her lips were painted gold. Like me she was naked to the waist, a black sun marked on her chest. I tried to smile at her because in that moment I forgot that we weren't friends anymore. But my face was already feeling numb. Her eyes were rolling like marbles in her head. I remembered that Selene had made me take a cup of special juice to her earlier, so she wouldn't run off before the ritual.

'You gave her too much,' Lona snapped. 'She's dribbling.'

Selene shook Lucia and she wobbled on her feet, unblinking.

'It'll be fine,' she said defiantly, pushing her towards the door.

Diana pushed me out after them.

Together we, the two golden girls, were led down the stairs. Other girls were too, each led by a woman. Each acting as their handmaidens. We were queens for the day.

We stumbled down to the foyer and into Carlisle's study where he normally recorded his tapes and dictated letters for the other women, who didn't live with us yet. There was a great hole in the floor, dark and wide like a mouth into the earth. It led down to the secret hiding place. One of the girls cried out when she saw it. I heard a smack and then the sound cut off.

One by one the women sent us into the hole and down

222

the dark corridor until we were all in the secret room, which had been filled with candles. Tiny flames flickered as one in glass jars and old candelabras.

In the centre of the room, masked in gold, was the Divine Sun. His body was covered in oil, reflecting the candles until he looked like he was made of light – gold and shining. It made me shiver. He was not a man. He was a god.

'Be at rest.'

Diana pushed me to the floor. I was crouching with only the sari between me and the cold concrete. She bowed beside me.

'In servitium voluptatem,' the Sun God said.

'In voluptatem libero,' the women chorused, like a moan from every part of the room.

'We begin. Bring forth the first to be tested.'

A girl with streaming black eyes was thrust forward by her woman. She stumbled, nearly fell, but the Sun God grabbed her and kept her upright. I couldn't see what was happening but I heard her cry out, watched as she backed away.

I knew without seeing that she had failed the testing. Whatever the testing was.

'Be at rest,' the Sun God said to the girl, like shooing a dog.

Another girl went to be tested. Another. Another.

None of them passed. The cries of disappointment continued. One girl fell down on her way to him and couldn't get back up. Another one went to be sick in a corner whilst her woman pulled her hair, furious.

It was my turn.

I went to him and saw what was on the table by him. A knife. Long and sharp. Already bloody. He picked it up and held it, blade upwards.

'This is your test,' he whispered. 'My power can keep you

223

from feeling pain. If you believe. You must believe completely to be worthy.'

I believed. He grabbed my hand and pulled it across the blade. It cut deeply and, even though I had faith, even though he was my god, I cried out in pain. The knife bit into me and blood dripped onto the floor.

'Be at rest, Jasy,' he said, shaking blood off the knife. 'Now is not your time.'

I staggered back, crying, knowing I had failed him, failed the test. Back on the floor by Diana, my hand bled onto the concrete and throbbed with pain.

I wanted to lie down, to sleep, to be sick. The candle room was no longer beautiful to me. It was spinning, the air thick and hot. My teeth felt like they were crawling around in my mouth. I could feel the air in my lungs curling around itself. I knew I was going to be sick.

More girls were taken up. The tenth, eleventh, twelfth . . .

Then I heard the women cry out in joy.

I looked up and he was holding a hand up high. Blood dripped down his arm and the arm of the girl. She looked up, not crying, not screaming, but just watching the blood drip onto her face from the cut on her hand.

'Lucia has passed the test!'

'Lucia will be the vessel!'

Chapter Twenty-Nine

I looked up from my clenched fists and found Ellie staring at me.

'That's what all this is about? The fact I was too drugged up to feel a psycho cutting me?'

Ellie shook her head. 'You don't understand. You were the only one who passed. So you're the only one who can have his child. It's what he decreed.'

'This is insane.' I let out a breath and tried to control my pounding heart. The awfulness of what she just told me was eclipsed only by the sick fact that I had no memory of it, that something like that happened to me and I just . . . blocked it out. Maybe the drugs helped with that too.

'You knew me, then?' I said, trying to find a way in. To talk Ellie round. 'We were . . . friends? So not everyone died in the fire?'

She nodded. 'The faithful were spared. We were like sisters when we were younger. But . . . things got in the way. I was jealous of Selene, of you for being her daughter. I let that poison me against you. But when the fire happened . . . when I thought you died with the others, I was devastated. When they told me you were still alive, sent me to watch over you, I was so happy. And you were a good friend to me still, even though you didn't know who I was. I think you felt it, though, how close we used to be.'

'What do you mean, they sent you? How did you people find me?'

'I didn't know they were looking until they found you. But lots of handmaids were out there searching. It was Carmen who found you. Well, you found her. They were all getting jobs in hospitals, social work offices, even the HMRC. Checking records. But Carmen set herself up as a therapy specialist and you just walked in and told her who you were. Like it was meant to be.' She looked so happy, it made me feel sick.

'A *cult* specialist,' I said, stressing the word, trying to get through to her. 'Because that's what this is. That's what you're in.'

She shook her head, looking disappointed. 'No, that's what they say we are. Because we don't conform to their rules, their standards of what a woman should be. Because we're free, so they have to try and control us, discredit us. But soon we'll have Carlisle's heir with us and we'll be stronger than ever.'

I wasn't going to get through to her that way. I could feel it. The bombshell that Carmen betrayed me, that she was part of this, made me want to scream. But I had to try something. Ellie was around my age. She thought she was my friend. She had been my friend, or at least I had thought so. If there was anyone I could get through to, it was her.

'This is not his baby,' I said, trying to force her to see the truth. 'You know that. You know it's not possible for him to have a baby when he's dead.'

She only shook her head pityingly. 'You were chosen to be the mother of his child. You're this child's mother; that makes the baby his chosen one. Can't you see that?'

226

'That's insane. How can you . . . if you remember what he did, what that "test" was, how can you sit there and pretend he's some kind of god? He drugged a bunch of children and tried to make us hurt ourselves. He was a sadisti—'

Ellie was on me before I could finish, dealing a stinging slap across my face. She stood back, both of us stunned by her sudden violence.

'Without him we were lost,' she said, her eyes huge and wet with tears. Desperation filled them and something else . . . fear. Fear of being wrong, of being truly lost. 'Celeste left us, then Carlisle. We had nothing. But now we have this child. God is returning to us.'

My face stung and I didn't want to speak, didn't want to do anything that might provoke her again. I just sat there scared of what she'd do next.

'He chose you for a reason, Lucia. When the time is right, you will give us his heir.'

With that she took her seat, pulled out her phone and put in earbuds. Calm and collected, as if she hadn't just hit me for speaking against Carlisle.

With him dead, it sounded like Ellie was directionless. Desperate. They needed someone to follow and, for some reason, my mother wasn't cutting it. She was giving the orders, arranging things, but she wasn't their god. Just a priest, using borrowed power.

I turned away as much as I was able, given the bonds. There was no hope of escape now. I blew my one chance. I could only wait and hope that since it seemed Marshal was not part of this insane plot, he would realise something was wrong, and come to rescue me.

If he even knew I was missing at all.

After the first day in my new confinement, Ellie did not return. Whether she was busy doing something else for the cult or just wanted to avoid me, I had no idea. I was watched every day by Lona instead. She parked herself in the visitor chair and stayed there all day, only rising to use the toilet or collect the meals that were slid under the locked door. These were the same as before, though I was scared that she'd try and feed me them as if I were a child. Instead she elongated the strap on my arm so I could feed myself, then tightened it again afterwards, usually more brutally than necessary. I think it was the only perk of her new role as a jailer. The ability to flaunt her power over me.

I wondered if I knew her as a child. If she had some grudge against me or if she just hated me because of some rivalry with my mother. After all it was Selene who punished her for allowing me to escape.

To keep busy she sewed and sometimes knitted. It turned my stomach to hear the click of needles as she worked on baby blankets, tiny socks and jumpers. There was a glow about her as if she was the pregnant one. Hope and joy and gleeful expectancy poured from her like honey.

I hated her.

I had no doubt she knew what she was doing, sitting there and gloating over their plans for my body, my baby. She stamped her ownership on me with every touch. The way she touched me to manoeuvre me for the bedpan or wash me. She never missed a chance to finger my belly as if already planning for the moment she'd be able to root around inside it. The idea of her holding a defenceless baby made me want to vomit.

When I was able to shut her presence out, all I could think of was what Ellie told me. How I was chosen. The thought was a sickening one. He chose me as the mother of his child when I was barely seven years old. To be raised and kept for him, like a prized piglet. The thought of him looking at me that way when I was a child myself sickened me. I was glad he was dead, however that happened.

The more I thought about it, the idea that Ellie was somehow jealous of me seemed more and more monstrous. What happened to her, to us, to get her mind so twisted? Was that what I'd been destined for? Did the fire and my escape really save me from being devoted to a sociopath? I wondered if, had he not died, he'd have chosen other girls as well. What kind of twisted family had he been planning?

My mother allowed that to happen to me. She had groomed me for it. She manipulated me into murder, left me to die, forgot me for years. Now I was completely under her control again.

She didn't come to see me. She'd neglected me, let me believe she was dead; now she kidnapped me to steal my child and she couldn't even face me. Didn't I deserve that? To confront her now, after everything? Was I really of so little value to her that she didn't think me worth talking to? Did she even see me as a person, let alone her own daughter?

My days and nights were much the same. Lona watched me during the day, then Diana came at night. They took shifts and just sat there whilst I did my best to ignore them. Diana, for her part, put on headphones and chewed her jagged nails. Sometimes she rocked in her seat. She reminded me of some of the addicts living rough around Bristol, edgy and twitching, unable to stay focused on anything, eyes darting. I considered for a time that she might be the key to my escape, but with the straps holding me down, I couldn't so much as get a foot on the floor. Even if I could overpower Diana or trick her, there was no way to get myself off the bed and out the door. No way to run with the cast on my leg. I doubted I even still needed it. It was just another way to hold me back, weaken me, like a ball and chain around my ankle.

I lost track of the days but my body kept time. My belly rose and I felt the baby inside move and shift. I felt so power-less lying there with no way to protect her from what was coming. Once she was born I knew they'd have no use for me. They wanted her, not me. I would be an inconvenience, hard to keep under control, hard to hide. Perhaps even now my face was in the newspapers as Marshal looked for me.

I convinced myself that they'd kill me and dump me somewhere after the birth, if the birth itself didn't kill me. I highly doubted my mother actually earned the title of doctor, that anyone involved in this was qualified at all. Without a hospital and trained help, I could quite possibly die whilst giving birth. I knew that lying down for weeks and months on end wasn't increasing my odds. I was getting weaker and weaker, wasting away despite the carefully put together meals and piles of vitamin pills being doled out every day.

Perhaps that was my only way out: deteriorate so much that I could force them to take me to some kind of hospital. They wanted the baby alive after all. If I became ill they'd have to get help, or at least disrupt the routine I was trapped in. It was a desperate plan but the only one I had. I wasn't even sure what I hoped to achieve with it. But I set out to do it anyway. I had to do something, even if it only gave me the slimmest chance of getting myself and the baby away from them.

I stopped eating. When the food came under the door and Lona dumped it onto the tray attached to my bed, I ignored it. Of course she noticed right away.

'Eat,' she snapped.

I said nothing, just stared straight ahead. Inside, my heart was hammering but I tried not to let it show. I expected her to try and force the food into my mouth, maybe hit me again, but she didn't. With a tightly pursed mouth she took the tray and left it on my bedside table. It sat there for hours, into the night, just out of reach. I knew what she was doing. It was a punishment. To make me go hungry but be able to see the food I rejected. A tactic to break me.

It was a mistake on her part. She gave me something to fight against. The expectation that I would snap hung over me. I could look at that tray and remind myself that if I gave in, begged Diana or Lona and her hateful eyes to bring it over, they would win. So I refused to break.

It went on for days. I wouldn't eat, only drank water, until they took that from me too. I was put on a drip for hydration so I couldn't fill my belly with water.

In the end it wasn't food or water that broke me, it was the baby. And Ellie.

She came one day instead of Lona. I saw her come in but didn't move my head or acknowledge her. I was so tired. Too tired to do anything but lie there. When she kneeled down, taking my hand in hers, I couldn't so much as twitch my fingers away.

'Oh Luce . . .' she said quietly, then sniffed. I realised she was crying. 'What are you doing to yourself, eh? To the baby?'

I closed my eyes, but I couldn't shut her out. I knew this was bad for me, for the baby. But it was all I could do to try and get us both out of there. I had to do something.

'I'm sorry about before. For snapping like that. I know you don't understand. You were taken away from us. Even when I was jealous of you, we were still sisters. Sisters fight but we still love each other, don't we? I was so happy when Selene told me I was going to see you again.'

I tried to find a hint of dishonesty in her words. But she sounded completely sincere. Like she really was my best friend, my sister, who only ever wanted what was best for me. I couldn't fight that with anger and spite. I couldn't fight it at all.

'If you carry on like this, you're going to die. The baby will die,' she said, voice twisting with emotion, cracking apart. 'Please don't. I couldn't bear it. You're my best friend. You were always my best friend.'

I didn't even have the energy to be angry at her. There was just a knot in my chest. Tears started to leak from my eyelids. She was deluded. But she was the only person who shed a tear for me since I tried to starve myself. My mother didn't so much as put her head around the door to check on me.

And she was right. In trying to save myself, the baby, I would end up killing us both. It wasn't working and I had to admit that and start taking care of myself again, taking care of the baby. But I also had to try and make Ellie see where this was heading, with or without my attempts at starvation.

'They're going to kill me,' I whispered, cracking my eyes open.

Ellie, eyes red and wet, shook her head. 'They won't. You're the vessel. The divine mother . . .'

'I'm surplus to requirements,' I rasped. 'As soon as this baby is out, they won't need me.'

'No,' she said, more forcefully. 'You're important – special. He chose you! You'll be honoured, just as soon as you come around.'

I tried to whisper, but my lips stuck together and no sound came out.

'What?' she said, craning her neck, her ear almost against my cracked lips.

'They'll never . . . let me go,' I managed. 'She's using me. Like before. Then she'll throw me away.'

Whilst Ellie sat there in dismay, I looked at her. Was she like me? Her mother dragging her along into Luna Vitae and its madness? Or was she like the others, whose pictures I saw online? Those faded, out-of-date pictures of missing children, clasped in the wrinkled hands of the parents who had almost given up hope of seeing them again.

'Ellie,' I rasped.

She seemed not to hear me.

'Ellie . . . where is your mother?'

'She . . . she never came. Never found us.'

I swallowed. 'You were taken from her, weren't you? And they lied to you, said she'd come but she didn't.'

'They didn't lie. She just never found us.'

'They kidnapped you, Ellie. Just like they're going to kidnap my daughter.'

'I . . .' She looked stricken, some kind of blockage holding back her words as her mouth moved soundlessly. I thought for a moment she was about to be sick. When she bolted from the room I wasn't surprised. I felt only bone-deep exhaustion and a sickening horror so familiar it was almost a part of me. This place was built on it. Horror and secrets, and death.

When Lona came in a few moments later, face like a gargoyle, stony and furious, I indicated the container by my bed. It was empty. I'd drunk down the shake she brought me and I could feel it in my stomach, heavy and reassuring. My body hungrily scooped up the energy and nutrients to feed my aching muscles and muddled mind.

Lona looked at me long and hard. Then picked up the container and left for a moment, returning with another shake and a bottle of water. I sipped obediently, slowly, so as not to be sick. When she gave me a vitamin tablet I took that too. Although her face didn't change, I sensed triumph in the set of her shoulders. She had won. I had lost.

But it was worth it, knowing that now the baby would be OK. At least for now.

The truth was, I had no idea what to hope for anymore.

Escape was impossible. Arguing was pointless. Appealing to their sense of morality doubly so. My mother had gifted me to a madman. She could and would do anything she wanted with me, even kill me. I knew that. Trying to outsmart someone so focused, so determined, was pointless. They would never let me leave my room – not even in an emergency – because it was not part of their plan and therefore the idea could not even be entertained.

Their insane plot required secrecy, so secrecy it would have. Even if it meant me dying and the baby with me. Because it wasn't about the baby. It was and had always been about Him. Carlisle, who was no longer a man. He was an entire religion, and I couldn't fight that.

Not alone.

Chapter Thirty

Ellie didn't return the next day or indeed for the next few weeks. It seemed that once again I scared her off. Though at least this time I saw a chink in her armour of blind devotion. She wasn't angry at me, she was afraid that I might be right. That gave me a tiny amount of hope. It was all I had.

I saw only Lona and Diana, who didn't speak to me or do more than bring my meals over, fetch water and administer the bedpan. I got a damp cloth and toothbrush to use in the mornings, and a packet of baby wipes for after using the pan, but that was it. My scalp itched and I longed for a shower. With each passing day I felt more and more like some kind of animal, fattened for slaughter.

I thought about Ellie a lot. I remembered how she cut my hair for me. Did she really care about me or was it all an act? She looked so scared as she dashed away. She remembered a life outside this place. A family. I was right. I knew I was. She was taken like the children I saw on the news.

In my more hopeful moments, I managed to convince myself that she had a realisation about everything they were doing, that she escaped and went straight to Marshal. That was why I didn't see her. It was a stupid fantasy but the only comfort I had. Ellie had been with Luna Vitae since she was a small child. One conversation with me wouldn't be enough to sway her to my side. Still, I dreamed that it was, and when I couldn't do that, I hoped she would come back to see me again.

The only break in the new routine came when the door banged open and the ultrasound scanner was wheeled in. Accompanying it was Sita. Just her, no sign of my mother. I expected her to be different. 'Nurse Brody' had, after all, abandoned her fake professionalism and revealed her spiteful nature. Surely it was time for Sita the friendly ultrasound technician to do the same. Yet as she breezed into the room she beamed at me as she did when we first met.

'Hello again, Mrs Townsend – or Lucia? Can I call you Lucia?'

I was too stunned to respond, but she carried on as if I'd greeted her like an old friend.

'Shall we see how things are progressing? Hmm? I expect you're keen to have this all over with now, aren't you?' She gave a tinkling laugh and I could feel how forced it was.

She burbled on as she turned down the blankets and lifted my pyjama top. I just lay there, limp and unhelpful. I didn't want her to touch me, to look at my exposed belly. But I had no choice. I couldn't make her stop any more than I could make Lona unstrap me.

Sita smeared gel on my skin and started sliding the probe around. She at least seemed to know what she was doing. Was she really an ultrasound technician, as she claimed, or something else? A paramedic, maybe? A nurse? Did she know anything about delivering babies? I wanted to ask but I was afraid to make a sound, in case the illusion broke and she lashed out, just like the rest of them.

'Oh, wow, you're doing very nicely,' she murmured, sliding

236

the probe back and forth. She had the screen turned away from me and I couldn't see the baby, but she and Lona both leaned closer to look at it.

'Isn't it wonderful?' Sita breathed, and even Lona looked a little misty-eyed, stroking the screen with her cruel, pinching fingers.

'Can I see?' I asked, when I could stand it no longer.

Sita jumped as if she'd forgotten I was there. She glanced at Lona, who shook her head slightly. I felt a jagged wrench of anger. What more could she possibly take from me? She already had my freedom, my dignity and the use of my body. Now I couldn't even look at a bloody monitor without her permission.

'She's not your boss,' I snapped at Sita. 'My mother is. So unless she tells you I can't see, you have no reason not to just show me,' I said, feeling desperate tears prickle my eyes.

Lona's cheeks went red, but Sita actually seemed to think on this for a second. Then, slowly, she turned the screen so I could see the image on it.

Unlike the last scan I was awake for, this time there was no little black blob. The baby had a face now. In profile I could see the curve of her skull down to a little bump of a nose. I saw blurs and shadows that might have been arms and legs. I felt a sense of relief that she was still there, alive. Though she wasn't any safer in that place than I was.

'How . . . how far along am I?' I asked.

'Eight months,' Sita said, with so much gentleness it nearly made me burst into tears.

Eight months. I'd been locked away in my room for months and months, and still no one found me. Worse, I was nearing the end of my pregnancy, almost ready to give birth. Out of time and with no options. Unable to bear the care in Sita's face I bent my head and sobbed. I couldn't even raise my hands to cover my face.

'I said it was a bad idea,' I heard Lona say pitilessly. 'Now look at what I have to deal with.'

I hated her more than ever, more than I thought it possible to hate anyone. I wanted to grab her, shake her, crack her head against the walls and scream in her face. A bubble of hysterical laugher welled in me, and I snorted through my tears.

'Mad,' Lona said, 'that's what she is.'

I laughed again. Here they were, keeping me tied to a bed, locked up so they could steal the baby they thought belonged to a dead man. And I was the mad one. I couldn't stop laughing.

Lona's hand caught me across the face and I bit my tongue. The laugher died in my throat. Tears dripped from my chin and my nose was streaming with snot. She was glaring at me with such viciousness and disgust that I honestly thought she would strangle me then and there. Would she be the one to kill me after I had the baby? Would I have time to catch my breath before her thick fingers closed around my throat?

I glanced again at the screen. The baby's image hung there, a still capture. I had to do something to save her from this but I had no idea what. Once I was gone she'd have no one. Perhaps if I could just get myself a stay of execution, I could find a way to escape with her after the birth. But how? What did I have to offer?

Sita was packing up her things and wheeling the cart out. Lona looked set to return to her knitting. I swallowed down the last of what pride I had left.

'Wait,' I called after Sita. She put her head back around the doorframe, surprised.

'I want . . . I want to see my mother,' I said.

Lona snorted. 'She has more important things to do. Who do you think you are?'

I pulled myself up as well as I could against the flat pillows and glared at her. I was going for imperious but I'd settle for deluded, anything to get them to do what I wanted.

'I'm the mother of Carlisle's heir . . . and I have a message for her. From him.'

My words hung in the air and for a moment I dared to hope. I dared to believe that it would work. Then Lona laughed, a disbelieving caw, and I felt my insides shrivel.

'Go,' she said to Sita. 'If she carries on I'll use this.'

From inside a pocket of the nurse's uniform, which she still wore religiously, she produced a capped syringe. The idea of being unconscious and at Lona's mercy filled me with dread. Sita stood there a moment, biting her lip, then nodded and hurried away. I heard the door lock behind her. Lona waved the syringe at me before settling down and picking the half-finished knitting up.

I sat there as if turned to stone. All hope had gone out of me. I had nothing left to try, no cards left to play. It was clear from Lona's attitude and my mother's indifference that I was worth less than nothing to these people. They wanted the baby. I was just packaging.

With Lona's whistling tormenting me I lay down and turned my face away. With my eyes tightly closed, I tried to shut her out and just breathe. I wanted to sleep. At least in sleep there was freedom.

I was just wondering if it would be worth the risk of lashing out at Lona just to get sedated when I heard the door being unlocked. I turned over and found myself looking at my mother.

She had given up the 'Doctor Mead' disguise now. Her hair was loose with one side sporting a braid. Instead of a white coat and blouse, she had on a long linen dress in pale blue, with many bronze-coloured beads on it. Around her neck was a necklace, similar to the pendant Phoebe had

239

given me all those months ago. Though this one was not a moon face, but a sun in beaten gold surrounded by red gems.

Lona leaped to her feet. For a wild moment I thought she was going to salute. Instead she looked at me once and then stepped between us.

'Selene . . . this is a surprise. I didn't know you were going to visit.'

'I wasn't,' my mother said, in that soft yet disdainful way she spoke the last time I saw her. 'Sita came to speak with me.'

'Oh . . .'

'Yes, *oh*. Tell me, Lona, at what point did you gain the authority to decide what I do and do not need to know about?'

'I only thought . . . she was being hysterical. Mad. I didn't think you would want to be bothered by her ravings.'

'The reason I have the honour of this', my mother said, lifting the pendant so that the red stones glittered, 'is because I am the one who thinks. You are the one who follows. Do I need to remind you of that already?'

Lona flinched and I saw a flush creep up her neck, where the welts and sores had since healed. She was punished for my escape attempt. It didn't look like she relished the idea of repeating the experience. Clearly she had no love for my mother. I'd interpreted correctly.

'Now go and find something useful to do. I believe Bendis and Mani need help bringing in the latest delivery.'

Lona charged out the door without a backwards glance. I knew, however, that she would be back. I felt a shiver go through me at the thought of what that might mean. Then the door closed and I was alone with my mother. Suddenly, I wished Lona had stayed.

She looked at me with her head tilted, eyes narrowed,

then she strode to the chair and sat down. I watched as she tossed Lona's knitting to the floor with a look of disgust.

'Well, Lucia, you wanted my attention. Now you have it. What was it you wanted to say?'

Looking at her I could see that she didn't believe for one moment that I had some kind of message from Carlisle. Sita may have, or she was just afraid to keep anything from my mother. Lona didn't believe me either, but she believed in Carlisle, in his heir. I saw that on her face when she looked at the sonogram. In my mother's face I saw quiet amusement, and something else. A disquieting awareness. A sanity I had not expected. I'd thought only of getting her into the room with me, of speaking to her. Seeing her there, I had so much I wanted to ask. For a moment I was speechless. What finally came out was a question I didn't even know I wanted to ask.

'Did you ever believe in this? Any of this?' I asked.

She looked at me for a moment as if I was a stranger, which I suppose to her I was. She hadn't seen me or spoken to me since I was seven years old. Even before that I had so few memories of her that she must have hardly been there at all.

'I believed in Celeste,' she said. 'I believed in leaving the whole filthy rotten world behind and embracing something new, something that wasn't the church or corporate bondage. A sisterhood. Freedom. Sex,' she said, as if daring me to react. 'A place without judgement, where I wasn't called names or looked down on for having a child without a husband, for not sacrificing everything to get ahead in a man's world. That, I believed in.'

'You seem to have done all right for yourself. Gotten ahead,' I said. 'And you only had to sacrifice innocent children, your *sisters* and your daughter.' I could feel all the anger and pain of her neglect, her betrayal, oozing up my throat. I wanted to hurt her but she remained stubbornly blank.

'I wouldn't expect you to understand, not yet.' She looked at my swollen belly as though it was an alien thing. 'To be free, you have to have power. Power to hold the world at bay. To have power, you have to cut ties. Be strong.'

I thought of the priests and the corporate bosses she'd run from. Afraid of them, hating their power over her life. Maybe she'd had enough of being controlled, preached to. Being a handmaiden. Maybe this wasn't just about fleeing the lash of her dad's belt. It was about getting a taste of its power for herself.

'Well, so long as you were OK. Fuck everyone else, right?' I said. 'Is this why Celeste left you all? Because she knew the kind of monsters she'd created? Women willing to trade their own children once there was a man to impress.'

My mother looked down and I thought I saw a shadow of regret cross her face. Then she was back. The mask of cool calm back in place.

'Celeste didn't leave. She died.'

'That's not what—'

'What Phoebe told you. That's because she doesn't know,' my mother said, interrupting me.

'How do you know I spoke to her?'

'Because just like she wants to know what we're up to, we like to keep an eye on her, including her online activity. I know she contacted you to arrange a meeting. And I knew that you, being the kind of curious girl you always were, would go.'

I swallowed. How far did her reach extend? How long had she been watching me? Not just through Carmen but at work, online. Was I ever free of her at all?

'Phoebe was never one of Celeste's favourites. Never a

handmaiden,' my mother continued. 'She wasn't in on quite a lot of the activity at the top of the order. Only a few of us knew what was going on with Celeste and Carlisle. The arguments they'd have. Despite everything she preached, Celeste was quite traditional when it came to her relationships, limited. Didn't like it when he slept with other women. No matter what she said about freedom, about breaking out of patriarchal morality and anti-consumerism, she was the one raking it in, living like our queen. She had the money and the man, and she wasn't ever going to share. Even if Carlisle wanted more than just what she could give. It only got worse when she got pregnant.'

'Celeste had a baby?' I was floored.

'She nearly did. There were complications. She miscarried in the night. Carlisle came to get me. Blood all over the place and her in the middle of it like a mannequin.' My mother chewed her lip. 'She was dead when I got there. Blood loss. Carlisle was beside himself, losing Celeste and his child. He wanted his own dynasty and that was his firstborn. Looking back, I think it knocked a screw or two loose. He was never the same after that. But even in the midst of all that he knew that Luna Vitae had to be protected. No police, no investigations and scandal. Above all, no one could know that Celeste died. She was too important to simply die. Knowing she was so mundane would have sent everyone scattering, looking for something new to blot out the pain.'

'You covered up her death,' I said.

My mother only shrugged as if we were talking about a misplaced library book. 'We buried her at the manor. Carlisle said it's what she would have wanted. Only he and one or two handmaidens knew the truth. Maybe that bitch friend of hers suspected, but we kept her quiet to hang on to the manor, at least until things changed and she needed to be dealt with.'

The disappearance of Jean McBride suddenly made sense to me. If they wanted the manor, they'd have to get rid of the person who had a claim on it once Celeste was gone. I wondered if poor Arianrhod was buried in the grounds like Celeste, or if they just locked her up with the others and let her burn.

'It was the mystery that kept it all alive,' Selene was saying. 'If she'd just been dead to them, everything would have come crashing down. When Celeste vanished she became ethereal, a true goddess.'

'I didn't see a lot of goddess worship going on at the manor,' I said. 'Just those hideous sun murals. That was him, wasn't it? Carlisle.'

'He was so fierce,' my mother said, seemingly off in her own little world. 'Through him we became fierce too, fearless and bold, strong. Celeste taught us to hide, to subvert and escape. He showed us how to live, how to take what we wanted.'

'And how to kidnap children for him, how to prostitute yourself for him?' I demanded.

Her eyes met mine. I searched them for any hint of shame or regret. Some acknowledgement of what she did, what she allowed him to do. But there was a shutter there. A blankness that said nothing could shock her, and nothing could reach her. She'd already seen it all.

'There was no better way to get back at those stupid men. The same ones who'd jeer at unwed mothers and turn out their pregnant daughters whilst they sent their mistresses to the abortion clinic. They would fling cash at us for sex. We used them, robbed them, even drugged some of them, sent pictures to their wives. They didn't get to escape the consequences anymore. We were the ones who melted away into the night. We got what we wanted, and they had to live with it.'

'And the children?' I said, seeing a spark of madness hidden deep inside her cool demeanour. 'What did you do with them? Are they all like Ellie? Brainwashed?'

She laughed. 'Who's really brainwashed here? We freed Jasy from a world that didn't care about her, where she would always be second best. We gave her a home where she was never hungry or lonely or looked down on. We gave her equality. You are the one who has been brainwashed. I've seen Carmen's notes. I know how unhappy you are with that overbearing cretin you married.'

So Marshal definitely wasn't involved. I thought I'd feel more relief but instead I was . . . ashamed, embarrassed by her assessment of my life and the realisation that she wasn't entirely wrong. I had been unhappy, stressed by the effort of keeping up appearances for Marshal. I told Carmen that I found him taxing, hard to please, a bit strict with me. Because he cared so much.

'Why are you doing this to me?' I asked, on the edge of tears. 'Why couldn't you just leave me alone?'

'Because he chose you. Out of thirteen girls. You were the one. The last one. And it's actually perfect. Not only are you his chosen mother, you are my daughter.'

'Why us? Why not one of you?'

For the first time, she looked angry. 'You destroyed any chance I had of having another child. Not that I was keen to repeat the experience. But for him I would have. But after Celeste . . . she was too old to be pregnant, that's why it went wrong, he said. She wasn't pure enough to carry a child. None of us were. By then we'd been with Luna Vitae for years, we were . . . past our prime.' She hissed the last three words and I saw then how much hatred for Carlisle was simmering under the surface, however much she had loved him, feared or even worshipped him. That time was gone, just like he was. Now he was just another man who deceived her and let her down.

245

'He needed someone innocent, someone we could raise to be the perfect vessel,' she said, recovering herself. 'Someone who would never leave him, not in life or death.'

'And you believed that? Or did you just want to give him whatever he wanted? Keep him happy so he'd notice you?'

If I was hoping for a rise, I was disappointed. The mask was back. She only tipped her head as if considering my question.

'That was my role then. I was part of his order and that was how we lived. It was our only rule. *In servitium, voluptatem. In voluptatem, libero.*' She smiled, lips peeling back from vulpine teeth. 'In service, pleasure. In pleasure, freedom.'

Service to a monster. There was no point, I realised, in asking her why she did it. She gave me the only explanation she ever would. The only one she needed. She did it to please him. That was all it took for her to offer me up as a sacrifice: his desire.

'What's your role now then?' I asked instead. 'Carlisle is dead. He doesn't want anything anymore.'

'When we lost him . . . there was nothing. Then I realised everyone was looking at me.' She smiled, as if remembering the happiest moment of her life. After all that time, she was the one in the spotlight, holding the keys to her own kingdom.

'And since then, I have been building something, something far greater than Celeste or Carlisle ever could have.' She removed a small glass bottle from her pocket and placed it on the tray attached to my bed. It was one of the bottles Ellie had toted around with her. The ones from her Nutrisoul kit. But I'd assumed all that was just a ruse to get me to Wales, for an event she picked at random.

'What does that have to do with any of this?' I asked.

'It's my baby,' she said, stroking the smooth glass. 'The legitimate arm of Luna Vitae. We needed to walk away from how we used to do things, begin anew. I invented Nutrisoul.

It wasn't long before we had the money to build a hidden space where no investigator or authority could reach us, which', she gestured around us, 'we have since expanded, as you saw.'

'And what does any of that have to do with me?'

'If I had my way, you'd never have seen me again,' my mother said, harshness creeping back into her tone. 'After all, it was your fault Carlisle died in that fire. You couldn't do the simplest thing for me. Though I suppose in the end it worked out for the best.'

'He died . . . in the fire?' I was stunned. Since realising they planned the fire, I assumed they escaped together and he died afterwards. God knows what kinds of drugs they were into. He could have dropped at any time. But did he really die that night?

'How is it my fault if he didn't escape the fire he planned?' I asked, confused. 'He made me start it. You both did. You had to have a way out.'

She laughed then, surprising me. A bitter, angry sound as if she couldn't believe her own child was so dense, so useless.

'We did have a plan, one you ruined, like you ruin everything. All you had to do was throw a lamp. The one thing I ever asked of you. But no, you just stood there like a stoned idiot. Couldn't do anything for me, could you? You wouldn't even give it back to him so he could finish the job. He had to wrestle it off you, and it must've been covered in oil . . .'

'He dropped the lamp,' I whispered, more to myself than to her. 'It wasn't me . . .'

'If you just did your duty, the three of us could have run. We would have been far away by the time anyone came to investigate. All those spineless, unworthy bitches would have burned up, our secrets safely turned to ash. The rest of us, his chosen, would have been free. It was all planned. But then you couldn't do it. He dropped the lamp right at his

247

feet. The fire just . . . ate him up. I had to run before it took me as well. Gather everyone, escape. Then it was a new era. My era, as his most loyal lover. His heir.'

There was a fire in her eyes as if he still burned there. An obsession that bordered on madness. It terrified and mesmerised me. A combination of devotion and loathing, hatred and love. She adored him and he used her, betrayed her. So she became him, taking everything he had built for herself.

That was when it clicked. Lona's begrudging kowtowing, Ellie's devotion to Nutrisoul, too intense to be faked, my mother's fierce pride, and me . . . tied to a bed. Two heirs to Carlisle's mad kingdom: my mother and my child. Nutrisoul and Luna Vitae. The new and the old.

'You're losing them,' I said softly. 'They followed him, and they were so lost they followed you, for a while. But it was never you they wanted . . . it was him. You can't make your money off them without giving them something to worship. Not a product, a god.'

'And that's what we're going to give them,' she said, stroking my knee. 'With his child on my side, there will be no more infighting. I can give them a messiah to believe in and it will keep them happy, working for me. They can have their delusions, their rituals and superstitions. I will be the one with the money, the empire, the power. Just like Celeste, like Carlisle. CEO and grand-high-priestess. With nothing to hold me back.'

I saw then that I had never been a child to her. Just another obstacle to her greatness. A setback. A hurdle. She now had a use for me. I felt my fury die and in its place there was only agonising loss and the desperate need of a child to be loved. I had wanted, so badly, for her to care about me. And that was never going to happen.

'I will not let you use me anymore,' I said. 'Or my child.'

'This is the only thing I want from you,' she said, standing

248

up and making her way to the door. 'I gave you life. Now you owe me one in return.'

The door closed and she left me with only her words to cling to. Her words and the terrible knowledge that she told me everything because she knew I wouldn't live to tell anyone.

Chapter Thirty-One

After she left, I watched the door my mother had gone through. I felt so confused and hurt, angry, desperate and guilty. I felt afraid for myself and my child, who was going to fall into that madwoman's 'care'. She was not my mother. She never was. She was Selene. Selfish, remote Selene, chasing after her goddess and god, dragging me along through the dirt. I always thought that my life would have been better if I had parents like everyone else. Now I realised that I was lucky she left me alone for so long.

I didn't matter to her, except when she needed to use me to win Carlisle's affection, or to keep control of her cynical little business. That was what I had to work with. It was Selene who held all the power. If I was useful to her she wouldn't get rid of me. If I wasn't . . . well, then Celeste wouldn't be the only one in an unmarked grave.

I could see now, though, how the whole trap had been set up. How they traced me by using Carmen as bait, then planted Ellie in my life to watch and wait for me. Perhaps they planned to just snatch the baby once she was born. Ellie would come by with a present and then vanish out the door with my daughter in her arms. Never to be seen again.

The sudden press attention must have complicated everything. It threw me into the spotlight where I could not be touched. That was why they scared me so much with their letters. To get me away from home and keep me there. They had so many Nutrisoul events one was bound to be coming up. The perfect excuse to pack me off somewhere with Ellie.

But how could they have known I would get pregnant? Or did they just assume that since I married Marshal, we would inevitably have children? If my birth control hadn't failed they might have waited years. Unless . . . no, there was no way they planned that as well. Marshal wasn't involved, Selene practically said it. The only person who could have tampered with my pill was Ellie, but I never left her alone with them for long enough, surely. They were in my bag and I always had it on me, even took it to the bathroom out of habit. Marshal was always going on about how expensive my phone was and worried about it getting stolen. No, she couldn't have been through my bag.

So why did I feel like I was tricked, trapped? Worse, why did I feel like I'd known all along, from the minute that test turned positive, before any thought of Luna Vitae had entered my mind? I didn't want to think about it, didn't want to know.

But I couldn't shut it all out. I thought of what Selene said about Marshal. About my unhappiness. Carmen made notes about me and gave them to Selene. Notes where she put together what I was too afraid to say. That I was unhappy, that Marshal – sweet, thoughtful, always there – was smothering me, controlling me.

Every decision I made was questioned and adjusted for his input. I felt like I owed him for every thoughtful gesture, every kindness. A feeling he only encouraged with his silences and hurt looks if I did anything without his say-so.

The way he didn't want to come near me if he could smell turps. If I even set foot in the art room, he pushed me away, like he wanted to train me out of my hobby with constant negativity. How he suggested the shared email account, shared credit card and bank accounts. How he didn't like me going out alone or doing anything that didn't involve him. The comments that sounded harmless but left me feeling self-conscious about myself. 'You look so much better with your hair straight, Luce' or 'Are you sure you'll be comfortable in that? It's looking a bit snug lately.'

Looking back, I remembered how he scoffed at the wine I bought for Sunday lunch with his parents. The way he threw the whole bottle in the bin and told me he'd have to go and get something now. If only I'd asked, it would have saved him time. I felt so bad for inconveniencing him – so bad that I walked all the way into town the next day to get a different bottle, one he'd like, whilst he was out playing golf.

Then there was the redecoration of the house. He picked everything. Even when he handed the decision off to me, I had to choose what he wanted. The one time I bought something on a whim, just a cute utensil pot I'd seen in a shop window, he hated it. And only two days later I'd come home to find he'd knocked it over and broken it. An accident, he said. God, how stupid had I been not to see it? I glued it back together with some strong glue I found in his office, only it dried a bit yellow and looked awful. So in the end I threw it away anyway. That was when he started locking his office when he wasn't in there.

I'd changed since we started going out. My hair, my clothes, the people I socialised with, how often I drew or painted. Trying to cut bits of myself off so I could fit into Marshal's life. Getting up early to make him coffee every day, antici-pating his wants and apologising endlessly when I got it wrong. A sudden chill between us made me desperate to please, wanting his affection back.

Every day brought a tiny erosion of who I was and what I wanted, until I found myself pregnant and agreeing that my art room should be packed away, wondering how things had changed, how I had changed so much that I hardly recognised myself.

As delusional as she was, Selene saw what I did not see. Marshal was just as manipulative as Carlisle, as she was. I changed myself to fit his life, his family. Just as she conformed to the rules of the cult. So, the big question was: if the cult didn't doctor my pills, had he? Was my pregnancy really an accident, or just one more decision he took out of my hands?

I didn't want to believe it. I wanted it to feel insane to even think it. But I couldn't shake the thought. I couldn't quite make myself believe it was all in my head. All the things Marshal asked of me because he wanted 'what was best' – but for who? Was it really for me that he forbade going out at night, meeting my old friends, having a second bit of cake at our wedding, wearing clothes for someone my own age? Was that in my best interest? Or was it for him?

I swore to myself that when I got out of that place – when, not if – I would confront him. I would not trade one kind of prison for another.

Lona didn't return to watch over me that night. Diana didn't come either. I thought perhaps Lona was undergoing punishment for keeping things from Selene, in whatever passed for the punishment room of this place. That didn't explain Diana's absence. Maybe Selene was giving me time to stew over what she told me. A new tactic for manipulation. Maybe she was just annoyed that I managed to influence Sita and didn't want to give me another chance at getting to one of her followers.

Whatever the reason, it gave me a lot of silence in which to stew.

I thought of Phoebe, sitting at that chintzy table, telling me her tale of escape from Luna Vitae. I'd felt so sorry for her, so grateful that she thought to save something for me, to think of me at all. Yet she must have known about the choosing, or at least that something was going on involving us girls. Ellie said the thirteen of us had been paraded through the house, each with a woman escorting us. It wasn't a secret. Perhaps Phoebe was even there.

She only left right before the fire. She must have been in on some of it. But she didn't tell anyone or go for help. If she did the commune might have been raided right away. The 'final ritual' of the fire never would have happened, and everyone would have been caught. If Phoebe reported them, or even told me anything about the cult's latest activities, the connection to Nutrisoul, I wouldn't have been stuck in the situation I was in now.

I fought back tears and looked down, then saw the little glass bottle still on the bed tray. I froze. Did Selene forget it or was this some kind of test or manipulation?

Still, it gave me something, something I could use. For what, I had no idea. But having something, anything, at my disposal was better than nothing.

Stretching my restraints as far as possible I reached for the bottle. It was just slightly out of reach. Was that the point of it, to torment me? I reached until my wrists ached and the straps pinched white lines into my skin. Still the bottle sat a few millimetres away.

I slumped back. This was infuriating. If it was a test, I didn't want to participate. I'd had enough. Yet . . . there was nothing else to focus on. Nothing else to do. Either I struggled or sat with the knowledge that everything and everyone around me was fake.

With a jerk I brought my knees up, bumping the tray. The bottle jumped on the hard surface and slid further away from me. With my teeth gritted against a frustrated growl, I raised my knees again. This time I tried to bump the furthest edge of the tray. The bottle shuddered, then tipped over and rolled towards me.

I reached out and snatched it up. It was full, a small weight in my hand. The label on the front said 'Energy Drops'. The glass was cold and amber coloured. I ran my fingers over it, thinking.

If I could break it somehow, I could use it as a weapon. Though a pretty terrible one. It was a tiny bottle, not exactly what you'd glass someone with. But maybe I could use it to cut my restraints and get free if I found a way to break it without leaving evidence behind.

The bottle was full, which was the first problem. I unscrewed the cap and got a waft of some kind of essential oils. It wasn't too strong, but if I broke the bottle and it went everywhere, someone would surely notice. I'd have to try and empty it.

There was a plastic dropper cap on the bottle. Bending my head down and jerking my arm as far up as possible, I was able to get my mouth around the top. It tasted vile. I was, however, able to prise it off with my teeth. I spat the little plastic dropper onto the bedclothes and used my other hand to hide it under the mattress.

I sniffed the bottle. I obviously couldn't empty it in the bathroom. It was locked and I was restrained. I could pour it on the floor but the smell would be a giveaway and I couldn't bank on it drying before someone came to check on me. That left me with two unappealing options.

There were no ingredients printed on the bottle. I assumed it was just oil but had no idea what kind or if there was anything else in there to preserve it. Was it meant for consumption or application? Drinking it would get rid of it effectively, but what if it poisoned me? Worse, what if it made me sick and someone realised what I did?

Option number two was safer. It was unpleasant, but the only thing I could do. With a sigh I resigned myself to it. Working around my restraints I awkwardly shifted the blankets and sheets that covered me and emptied the bottle onto the mattress. The scent of the oil rose up as the colourless liquid spread and I quickly tapped out the last of it and put the blankets back. Then, with a fresh wave of anger over the indignity of my situation, I peed the bed.

It was the only thing I could think of to hide the smell and sight of the spilled oil. That didn't make it pleasant or make me feel much better about waiting in a wet bed for someone to come check on me. Still, I had the empty bottle and that was worth it.

With the bottle wrapped in a corner of sheet, I raised it up and rapped it hard on the tray. It made a loud noise but the thick amber glass didn't break. I sat waiting to see if someone would come. No one did. I tried again, this time aiming for the metal rod that held the tray up. Another loud crack. No luck breaking the glass.

This time when I stopped to listen, I heard footsteps in the corridor. Faint but growing louder and accompanied by a weird rumbling sound. A trolley or gurney? Were they coming to take me somewhere else? Somewhere worse? Heart in my throat, I raised the bottle as high as my restraints allowed and cracked it on the edge of the tray like an egg.

The bottle cracked in half, small shards loose inside the sheet. I carefully put the two halves into the breast pocket of my pyjamas, forcing my body forwards so I could reach, then turned the shards out in the gap between the bed and the small table.

I'd barely righted myself when the door opened and Lona's

face appeared. She looked around the room and then pinned me with her narrowed eyes. Opening the door a little wider, she stuck her head in. Behind her I could see what the rumbling sound had been: a wheeled bucket with a mop in it. She had her hand squeezed tightly around the handle, like she wished it was my neck.

'Don't think you can get one over on me again,' she hissed, clearly not wanting to be heard by anyone hanging around in the corridor.

My heart beat heavily under the broken glass in my pocket. I was certain that she would see the small lump there.

'I thought you might want to know I saw your husband today.'

My heart jolted. Marshal? He was . . . here? Despite everything I'd been thinking about him, I was still excited. He was the only person who might be able to get me out of there. Lona's gloating eyes searched my face, soaking up my reaction.

'On the news. He's looking for you. They filmed right outside that cottage you were staying at with Jasy. I wonder if he'll be on again when they find your body.'

I went cold. Even after all my speculation, to have it confirmed that they planned to kill me shook me to my core.

'Not that they'll ever find you. I'll be sure to take you somewhere he'll never think to look – bury you nice and deep.' She smiled and I saw that she was looking forward to my death. Actually impatient for the moment to come. 'The sooner you pop the baby out, the better,' she went on. 'You'd better hope it's not overdue or I'll have to help you along.'

With that she swung the door shut and locked it. I heard the rumble of the bucket as she moved it along.

I thought of Marshal at the cottage, so close to where I disappeared and yet he might as well still be in Bristol. Lona was right, he'd never find me. I didn't even know where I was myself. How could anyone else begin to find me? After they loaded me into that van they might have gone anywhere. For all I knew I went through the Channel Tunnel and was currently somewhere in Europe.

The idea that my one hope of rescue was Marshal – who might well have tricked me into getting pregnant – made me feel ill. There was no one out there I could trust. No one I could turn to. Everyone wanted something from me, wanted to use me. I had to try and save myself, and my baby, from everyone. Not just the cult but Marshal too if he'd done what I suspected. No one else was going to save us.

When the footsteps and dragging of the bucket faded away I took one of the glass shards out of my pocket. It was small and keeping hold of it was quite difficult. I carefully manoeuvred my arm and got the shard into position against the restraint. If I could cut through the bottom part it wouldn't be obvious to anyone coming into the room.

It was hard going. The leather restraints were thick and strong. The glass was very much not the right tool to go about cutting them with. I could see a pale line where the sharp edge was scoring the leather, but it didn't seem to want to do much more than that. I kept at it. After all, time was the one thing I had in that room all alone. I got into a rhythm with the glass – scratch scratch scratch on the leather. My wrist began to ache. The glass piece slithered about in my sweaty fingers. I rested for a few moments then carried on.

Slowly, my fragile hope began to wane and die. The glass wasn't doing anything against the thick leather of the cuff. It was only getting blunter and more useless. Even if I could get out of the restraints, where could I go? The door was locked. Perhaps I could grab someone, put the glass to their neck and force them to let me out, but they'd just set the fire alarm off again and people would come running. Looking down at my distended belly, I knew that even if I could escape, I'd not be able to run far. Even without the weight of the baby, my legs were wasted from lying in bed for so long. The cast still weighed on me. I didn't even know the way out.

I stopped cutting and put the now dull piece of glass back in my pocket. After giving the cuff a few half-hearted tugs I had to admit to myself that I wasn't getting out of it. There was no way I could escape the room I was locked in. I'd have to wait until they let their guard down. *If* they let their guard down. I'd have to be ready.

Lying in the dark I realised that a piece of glass wasn't going to save me. I had to be more cunning. Like Selene. She was cynical. A practised manipulator. A businesswoman. Out of all the people I saw, she was the least enthralled by the mystical rubbish behind the cult.

Perhaps that was the key. I could try and talk her round by making my survival the most practical option. I'd have to show I could be trusted to push her agenda, to mother the child she wanted so badly, and lie to her that she was blessed by Carlisle, his true heir.

If I wanted to live, I'd have to slot back into the role I'd been rescued from two decades before – the mother of Carlisle's heir.

Chapter Thirty-Two

Unfortunately, for my plan to work, I needed to speak to Selene again, which Lona seemed dead set against. Her punishment did not endear me to her and when she checked on me and found the bed in need of changing, she looked like she'd happily suffocate me with the wet sheets.

Diana still came to watch me at night, but I doubted she'd be able to get Selene to come and see me. For starters, she had her headphones on and ignored me when I tried to speak to her. For another, I got the impression that Diana was even lower in the pecking order than Lona. I couldn't see Selene making much time for her or anything she had to say.

That left Sita or Ellie, neither of whom returned to see me. I waited, hoping with each shift change that one of them would appear to watch me. I was disappointed every time Lona or Diana appeared. More than that, I was afraid. I'd already had my eight-month scan. That was just over thirty-four weeks, and it had been a fortnight since then by my reckoning. My due date was meant to be at forty weeks, the thirteenth of January. So I had only around four weeks left to convince my mother not to have me killed. Less, if the baby came early, which I prayed she wouldn't.

As more time went past and Lona's warnings of 'helping me along' preyed on my mind, I grew more and more desperate. Who was to say they wouldn't induce me to get it all over with? After all, they'd waited so long already, perhaps Selene would get impatient, or her hand would be forced by mutinous true believers.

To keep myself sane, I started trying to exercise my legs, getting ready for any opportunity that might come my way. Under the blankets, inside the infernal cast, I flexed my muscles. When Diana closed her eyes or nodded off in her chair at night, I lifted my legs against the restraints. With eyes burning with the need to sleep, I raised and lowered each leg, over and over again, trying desperately to keep the muscles from wasting any more than they already had.

In the end I was so desperate I tried asking Lona. Begging was probably a more accurate word for it. I said I needed to speak to my mother and that if she didn't come I'd stop eating again. Lona only smiled and left the room. Shortly afterwards she returned with a length of tubing and a funnel.

'I'm to use these if you try that trick again,' she said.

I think she was actually disappointed when I obediently ate my steamed fish, rice and broccoli. It gave me no enjoyment to take that vicious pleasure from her though. I still wasn't any closer to seeing my mother.

Time wore on and every twinge in my belly made me sweat with anxiety. Each time the baby turned over or shifted I closed my eyes and prayed that this wasn't it, that I wasn't about to go into labour. When things settled down and no contractions came, I began to breathe again. Not this time. I was safe this time. But soon. It would be soon, and once my baby was out of me, I'd have no way to protect her or myself.

The reality that I was going to give birth in a few short weeks took up most of my thoughts. I worried constantly.

Not just about what would happen to me after the baby was born, but about the birth itself. If I thought I'd be spared first-time-mum jitters, or that they'd be lost under the greater fear, I was mistaken. Before being shut up in my room, I didn't read a single baby book or attend a prenatal class. I felt incredibly alone and unprepared, with no idea what labour was going to be like, or if I'd be able to get through it.

I still wasn't sure if there was anyone with medical training to help me. Sita clearly knew something about ultrasounds but was she trained in any other way? Was Lona a nurse or was that all just an act? What if something went wrong? What if the baby was in a weird position or I bled too much? Would they just leave me to die? I could almost see it: me in a room full of candles, the baby screaming in Lona's arms as she was carried away, bundled in an embroidered blanket. The room emptying as their voices faded, leaving me in a pool of blood as my heart slowed, beat by beat.

Was that what happened to Celeste? Selene said she miscarried and there was nothing they could do to save her. But was that true? Did Carlisle just let her die right in front of him once he realised his baby was gone and that she was no longer useful to him? Did my mother watch? Was she part of it? If she could do that once, she could do it again.

It was enough to make me try the glass again. I used the second half, which was still sharp. It made very little difference but the action was almost meditative. Sawing at the leather strap kept me focused, calmer. Though not in any way relaxed. I felt like a prisoner on death row, scratching lines into the wall and waiting for the inevitable summons to the gas chamber.

In my lowest moments I thought of using the glass on myself. Perhaps if I was found bleeding and on the brink of death, they might have to get help. I already tried that with my hunger strike but perhaps with a serious injury they'd be forced to act. Only the thought that I might hurt the baby, or that they might simply cut her from me and let me die, stopped me. I did not want either of us to die. I wanted us to get out.

I was dozing when I heard the door to my room open. It was dark and I assumed the sound was Diana slipping out for a cigarette. She did it occasionally, usually in the dead of night and only if I pretended to sleep. It wasn't until a hand went over my mouth that I jerked into full wakefulness.

It was Ellie. She was standing over me, one hand on my mouth, the other raised with a finger to her lips. I swivelled my eyes and saw Diana on her chair in the corner, fast asleep, her headphones still on. Slowly Ellie withdrew her hand and crouched by the bed.

'She shouldn't wake up,' she whispered. 'I spiked her vodka with painkillers.'

'Why?' I asked, hardly daring to hope.

'I wanted . . . I want to talk to you,' Ellie said.

My stomach twisted. So she didn't come to free me. Just to talk. I tried to keep my disappointment and frustration hidden. Ellie drugged someone and snuck in to see me. That was something.

'What about?'

'I remember my mum,' she said. 'I remember being scared when I first got here and . . . wanting to go home. And thinking about the choosing. The way things were then . . . I started to think maybe I should have been scared then too. That it wasn't right.'

She went silent and I looked at her properly, my eyes adjusting to the darkness. Ellie's eyes were huge in the dark, afraid and shining with tears. Her hair was frizzy and unkempt and there was a dark line around her neck.

'They put you in the stocks?' I asked.

She rubbed at her neck and nodded. 'For leaving you unattended. Lona was pissed she had to take over. She was meant to be going into . . .' She broke off and I realised she was about to say the name of a town.

'Ellie, please tell me where I am.'

Before I even finished she was shaking her head. 'I can't. You know that. I shouldn't even be here,' she said, looking at the door anxiously.

'But you are. You came anyway. You know what Carlisle did was wrong, that this is wrong too.'

'I just wanted to see you. No one tells me anything about how you are. I know it's not really my business anymore, now you're here, but I care. I know you don't believe me but I wasn't pretending. I do care about you . . . sometimes I wish you never got pregnant. Then we could have just kept on as we were. I liked seeing you every day. It was even worth that awful job, living away from everyone else. Just to be friends. But once all this is over with, we can be better than friends, we'll be sisters again. You'll understand us better and it can all go back to how it was before the accident.'

I looked at her incredulously, then realised she still didn't believe they'd kill me. I told her what I feared before, but she brushed it aside as hysterics. She had no idea what Selene had in store for me, what Lona said to my face. She was even further down the pyramid than Diana. She probably didn't know about the fire either, that it was intentional, that Carlisle had ordered it.

'Ellie . . . we won't be friends because they're going to kill me.'

'That's not true,' she said. 'How can you still think that?'

'Because it's true. Lona told me she would take me away and bury me. Think about it,' I pleaded. 'Selene wants this baby. But once it's born she isn't going to need me. I'm not one of you and she knows that. She knows there'd be no point in me hanging around, trying to escape, putting you all at risk. And she can't just let me go. I know what you all look like. I know your names.'

Ellie started shaking her head as I spoke. Slowly at first, then faster and more frenzied, as if my words were bees she wanted to bat away.

'No!' she said, so loudly that my eyes darted to Diana, who only twitched and slept on. 'No, that's ridiculous. We don't kill people. We help people. Lucy, do you think I'd hurt anyone?'

'I don't think it's up to you,' I said, as gently as I could. 'And . . . Ellie, the fire? It wasn't an *accident*. It wasn't whatever they told you. It was all him. Carlisle. His idea, his plan, to get rid of people who didn't support him. He was the one who made the people who weren't true believers sleep in the attic that night. He tried to make me set the fire so he could escape with his followers. To escape the investigation into the brothels and the kidnappings. I think he wanted me to do it to keep his hands clean, in case we got caught, or just as another way to tie us together, to control me. Only it went wrong and he died. And I got away.'

'That's crazy,' Ellie said, shrinking away from me. 'It *was* an accident. Our sisters died. We lost everything. How can you . . .' She looked away as if just the sight of me made her sick, but behind her eyes I saw something dawning. She knew something and it was rising to the surface, no matter how hard she tried to push it back down. 'How can you lie like this? What is wrong with you? I knew you'd been out there, in the system, corrupted, but . . .'

'I'm not lying. Ellie, look at me.' She wouldn't and I sighed. 'Ellie . . . you remember the testing. You told me what he had us do. He had us hurt ourselves on his say-so. Because

265

if we would do that, we'd do anything for him. It was only my bad luck that I was so drugged up I didn't flinch. He was a sick, disgusting predator.'

Ellie's brow furrowed. 'You're wrong. You're just . . . negative, corrupted. All we've done with Nutrisoul, changing people's lives, giving them an income and access to life-changing products, and you think we're a bunch of murderers? What happened to you, to Lucia?'

'I was rescued from this!' I hissed. 'I was taken in and I went to school and had a life away from all this – from Carlisle and Selene. I can see them for what they are, what they did to us.'

'Your mother loves you,' Ellie said. 'She went through all this just to find you and bring you home, to protect you and your child from the corruption of the society that took you away. If you hadn't come out here, digging up the past, you wouldn't have been hurt. We'd be at the cottage, together like sisters.'

'My mother', I said, biting out each word, 'never wanted me. She hated being a mother so much she went running into Celeste's arms, and then she ignored me until she could win favour by handing me over to Carlisle. Think about it. If she loved me, why did she leave me to burn in that fire? Why wasn't I with the rest of you? Because she couldn't care less if I burned to death like they did. She didn't need me anymore.'

Ellie looked stricken. Fresh tears sprung to her eyes. 'Stop it!'

'No! This has gone on long enough. You can't just keep believing whatever she tells you. You have to think for yourself! If she loved me, why did she wait so long to find me? If Selene and Carlisle were so wonderful, why did they torture people to keep them in line? What did they do to that poor woman who owned the manor? If Celeste was so perfect, why did she kidnap you from your real family?'

266

'To save me,' Ellie said, but I could hear the doubt in her voice. I was finally reaching her. I just had to keep going.

'To save you from a mother who loved you? Who is still looking for you after twenty years? They took you because it's easier to convince a child than an adult. Celeste wanted followers who wouldn't question her. Just do what she wanted.'

'No . . .' She shook her head. 'No . . . she saved me. Carlisle wasn't . . . the fire was an accident.'

'He set himself on fire trying to murder sleeping women and children. That's who he was. A coward and a liar trying to get a child to commit murder for him. And now Selene wants to use my child the same way she used me, for her own gain. None of this, none of it, is about freedom or faith or healing. It's about money and power. And that was all they ever wanted from you: for you to obey them and make them rich.'

Ellie covered her ears and let out a pained moan. It was guttural and animalistic – a wordless denial. I glanced over at Diana but her head was tipped back, snores growling in her throat. She wasn't waking up any time soon. Ellie, however, was. She was finally conscious of all the things that happened to us. I could see it in the way she twisted her body, as if trying to escape from the emotions running through her.

Watching her, I felt an enormous and startling wave of pity. I thought I hated Ellie for lying to me, for manipulating me, but I didn't. She wasn't like Lona, my mother or the others, who'd fallen willingly into Carlisle's madness. She was only a child when she was kidnapped and forced into Luna Vitae. How was any child meant to withstand brainwashing and indoctrination? She was a victim just like me. Were it not for the fire, for my random escape, I might have ended up just like her. She was like a dark reflection of me. What I might have been, had things been different.

'Ellie,' I said softly, wishing I could reach out and hug her. 'Ellie . . . you know this isn't right. You're not like them. You're not a bad person. I know that. You're a good friend. You want to help me. I know that too. You're just trying to help.'

But it seemed I pushed her too far. She looked up at me as if I trampled on her toys, ripping down the barriers that time and denial had put up. I could see it in her eyes. She blamed me for making her think and feel what she was going through – blamed me and hated me. She was too far in to admit it was all a lie. Just like the rest of them who wanted that golden age at the manor back via my child. She had to stay loyal or lose everything, including herself.

'You're wrong,' she spat, straightening and backing away from me. 'I don't believe you. And I won't listen anymore.'

'You do, though. You know it's true,' I said, unable to keep my mouth shut.

Ellie cast one more hateful, despairing look my way, then hurried out and locked the door behind her. Leaving me alone and utterly friendless.

Chapter Thirty-Three

The manor was burning. Even from far away, under the trees, the smell was terrible and the smoke stung my eyes. My throat felt raw and my feet, bare inside wet trainers, were frozen. I looked around me at the women who escaped with me through the passageway under the floor in Carlisle's office, through the room where Lucia had been chosen and up the ladder in the old well.

Lucia.

Where was she? I looked around but she wasn't with the other girls. I saw Selene standing in the shadow of a tall tree, watching the fire eat its way through the manor.

Where was Carlisle?

It wasn't just me thinking it. I heard the question go around the little groups of women shivering in the snow. Carlisle wasn't with us.

He was so full of energy yesterday when he told us the plan. We would gather for a special ritual in his secret room and then leave the manor, heading off to a new and special place. We were told not to drink the wine at dinner. It had special drops in it. A lot of them, so everyone who was too faithless for the new way would sleep until we were gone.

We weren't to tell anyone outside that room and we had to pack a small bag. Just a few things. These were already hidden in the cars up at the clearing. I'd helped Lona to carry them once it got dark and everyone else went to bed. I'd helped carry the big black leather case down to the car as well. The one Carlisle filled with piles of money, watches and credit cards from his safe.

But Carlisle wasn't with us.

Finally someone – I think it was Astrid – went up to Selene and asked what we were meant to do now. We were all freezing cold, tired, scared. What caused the fire? Where was Carlisle, and what about the others? I felt suddenly sick. They were sleeping. The manor was on fire and they were sleeping in it still.

'Carlisle . . . is dead,' Selene said, turning to look past Astrid at the rest of us.

Two women fell to their knees in the snow. More of them cried out. They hugged one another. The girls started to cry. I felt numb.

'Where's Lucia?' I tried to ask, but no one heard. I realised that if she wasn't with us, she had to be in the manor. She was in the fire, with Carlisle.

Lucia hadn't been my proper friend in a long time. We didn't play anymore because I was serving all day and she was busy hiding until she was chosen. Then she spent all her time in Carlisle's room, posed like a doll on a cushion in the corner, where he could watch over her. But still, after everything, she was my sister. I felt hot tears cut down my frozen cheeks. Lucia was gone.

'Enough!' Selene shouted and everyone went quiet. She looked around, surprised, like she didn't expect it to work. Then she straightened up, tall and strong with the shining necklace dangling over her dark coat.

'We will go to the cars and take them to the meeting point,

the campsite by the cliff. We will stick to our story: we are a domestic violence shelter, there was a leak, we are in temporary caravans whilst it is being fixed. No one must know who we are or where we have come from.'

'But Carlisle is—' It was Diana who spoke, and Selene turned on her.

'Going to prison will not bring him back! And I will not have everything he worked for be ruined by your blathering. I am his priestess, and it is up to me to follow his word. That has not changed.'

For a moment everyone was still and quiet. I felt a kind of power in the air. It was the feeling of people speaking without words. Looking at each other to know what to do next. Reaching a decision as one. A familiar feeling, one that the manor had run on.

'Now, go to the cars,' Selene said. 'Get your maps out and get going. We meet in five hours.'

The crowd split into groups and Lona grabbed my arm, dragging me along. I kept looking back, hoping to catch sight of either of them, Lucia or Carlisle. The two people I loved most. I thought I saw something, a blur by the well. But it was so far away and everything looked so strange in the creeping red and blue light – the fire and the emergency services tearing apart the darkness.

Chapter Thirty-Four

Stuck with only Lona and Diana's silent company, I had a lot of time to dwell on everything I said to Ellie. It all came out in a great rush of accusations and anger. I wasn't gentle. I didn't give her time. There wasn't time. I had one chance to bring her around to my side, to gain myself one ally, and I blew it.

With no way of contacting Selene, or of knowing if she'd even listen to what I had to say, I was out of options. Trapped in bed, filthy and ignored by everyone, I gave up even the slimmest hope of survival. My death loomed with every day and there was no way to prevent it. I was going to give birth and then be killed.

I thought of my daughter and wondered what would happen to her. Perhaps Ellie might develop a conscience, too late for me, and contact social services. Marshal might even find her, though I doubted it. There was no official record of my pregnancy. I didn't even see a doctor before being taken. Added to that, the idea of him getting hold of her when I had the suspicions I did filled me with dread.

No, unless Ellie helped her, my daughter was going to be

raised by the cult that brainwashed so many. There was nothing I could do to stop it.

In the dark of my cell, I glanced over and saw Diana asleep in her chair. If she noticed anything odd about the night Ellie had drugged her, she gave no sign of it. Ellie said she dosed Diana's vodka, and Diana did seem to sleep a lot when supposedly 'on watch'. So it was quite possible that she was regularly blackout drunk even without the pills mixed in. Ellie took quite the risk in doing that. A risk she'd taken just to see me, to talk to me. I wished more than anything that I'd been able to reach her, to convince her of the truth, that I was in danger and only she could help me. If I wasn't so hard on her I might have managed it. Even if she didn't believe me, I could have maybe gotten her to bring Selene to me. Now I stood no chance of her coming back at all.

As I went over what I said to Ellie, I remembered what she said to me. 'If you hadn't come out here, digging up the past, you wouldn't have been hurt. We'd be at the cottage, together like sisters.'

'If you hadn't come out *here* . . .'

Not 'if you hadn't gone out there' but 'here'. Even though I fucked up and lost Ellie's help, she at least gave me one piece of important information. I now knew where I was, exactly where I'd been before: at the manor.

It made sense. After all, I'd seen marks from the stocks on Lona. Though at the time I assumed it was the same punishment, not literally the same stocks. But where in the manor was I? I'd been in all the rooms and outbuildings and seen no sign of life. Besides, surely even with the hoardings up, there would be no hiding all the activity if they were running a business from the manor.

I remembered that Selene said the money from Nutrisoul helped them to build and expand. It created a place where no authority could find them. A hidden place that was somehow still near the manor, connected to it. I remembered the room Ellie had told me about, where the 'testing' took place. It was hidden underneath.

What had that room been for originally, before the manor became a commune? Perhaps some kind of bunker built in one of the world wars? Maybe a former priest hole or secret passage left behind from an early time? Either way, it was an underground space which ran under the manor and perhaps linked to the old well I'd fallen down.

I thought back to my doomed escape attempt. How far did I get whilst running from the footsteps overhead? It felt like hundreds of stairs on my injured leg, going so slowly. But surely it wasn't more than two flights of stairs down. Three? Down to the utility boxes and a manhole. Was it some kind of escape route? Or were they still building, expanding further down?

I recalled the heavy metal door where I was captured. Was that a door into the old underground room? It certainly looked secure enough to be on a bomb shelter. Was that what they did? Tunnelled down or used underground structures that already existed: cellars, servant's passages, sewage tunnels, places to store ice and wine?

They had twenty years to plan and amass the skills and supplies to do it. Even working slowly, without diggers and cement lorries, they had time to do it by hand. Judging by the number of people I saw at the Nutrisoul convention, they had the manpower for it if those women were all involved and not just ignorant shills. Even if they were just selling products, there had to be more women, more members, within the underground tunnels I saw.

They must have found a way to get supplies and tools to the manor without being seen. A second entrance somewhere else? Another way to escape? Even as I thought it I knew it wouldn't help me at all. I couldn't get to any escape route.

As the pieces fell into place, my nightmare made some kind of sense. When I fell into that pit, I was standing where I remembered being as the manor burned. Perhaps I hadn't walked there from the house through the snow, but climbed up the rungs that had caught my foot in the well. Was that how the 'faithful' escaped the fire? A secret exit from the manor's original underground room, which came out under the well?

In the moment of my discovery, I felt like I gained a tool to use against Selene. But a few moments later that triumph died and I was left with a new kind of despair. Knowing just how well I was hidden meant realising that however slim I thought my chances of rescue were, they were, in fact, even more remote. I was fucked.

Curled into myself on the bed, I wept. Everything piled up on me, making it hard for me to breathe. Fear of the birth, of my own death, of what they would do to my daughter. Fear of Marshal and self-loathing at how I let him strip my life down and reshape it to suit him. Under it all was the deep, dark pain I'd had ever since I could remember: the loss of a mother. Not my mother, but the one I might have had if only she changed, if only we had more time together. Only now it was coupled with the knowledge that she did not die before she could become the mother I needed, but had instead thrown me away, like a burned-up match.

When my sobbing had dried up to mere sniffling, I wiped my face against the pillow and looked over at Diana. She slept right through all the noise I was making. Clearly a heavy night for the vodka. I was just worrying about what would happen if I needed to use the bedpan when I heard a key in the lock.

Caught in a snare of memories and fear, I held my breath, hoping it would be Selene, coming to see me, coming back for me, for once. My heart was laid open and vulnerable in hope. Though I told myself she never cared, there was still part of me that longed to be wrong.

But it was not my mother. It was Ellie.

For a moment my heart lifted and I almost cried again in relief. Then she stepped into the room and the light from the tiny lamp glinted on the knife in her hand.

'Ellie . . .'

My own frightened whisper startled me. It came out as a rasp, completely alien in the dense silence of my room. She eased the door shut behind her and came towards me, sparing only a glance for Diana's limp form.

'I thought about what you said.' Her voice sounded numb, dreamlike. As if her mind was far away.

'I'm sorry, I didn't mean to upset you like that,' I said, panicking, knowing I'd pushed her too far, broken her, made her into an unpredictable danger.

'I thought about it,' she repeated, voice gaining strength.

When she brought the knife up I instinctively tried to shield myself, but the restraints held my arms back and kept me from curling up into a protective ball.

'You were right,' she whispered, and I found myself looking up into her eyes, which were wet and wild with tears. 'You were right,' she said again. Then I felt her hands on my leg and felt pressure on the filthy cast.

'Keep still,' she hissed, rasping at the discoloured plaster with the serrated blade.

I was too afraid to speak. Afraid the knife might slip, afraid that Ellie would lose her nerve and bolt. I watched as she sawed at the cast, prising pieces away. Underneath it my skin was dry and engrained with dirt. I saw her wrinkle her nose but she kept working.

'I remember before the fire,' she whispered frantically, sawing away. 'He told everyone . . . he told them to stay upstairs. No matter what. That's what he said. No matter what. And I thought afterwards that . . . it was an accident, or God's plan but . . . he knew. He knew the fire would happen. Because he planned it and I heard him.'

I had nothing to say to that. I knew she was grappling with her memories, just as I was, trying to make the jagged pieces fit together, to take what she was told and make it mesh with reality, with logic. Finding herself in a mess of contradictions.

It seemed to take hours, but eventually my cast lay in chunks on the bed and my leg was free. It felt strangely thin and light after being trapped in plaster for so long. With a glance at the still sleeping Diana, Ellie took my arm and began to unstrap my restraints.

'She should stay out for a few hours, at least until Lona comes to take over,' she whispered as she undid the final restraint. From her sweatshirt pocket, she produced a pair of flimsy slippers. 'Put these on.'

I did so, finally able to sit up straight for the first time in months. My belly was so large now that I could hardly reach my feet. But I managed to hook the slippers over my toes and pull them up around the heel. They were like socks with thin soles. At least they'd soften my footsteps.

'You have to follow me and not make a sound, just do what I say,' Ellie said. Looking at her more closely, I saw that her eyes were wild and she was trembling slightly. Fear was coming off of her in waves.

I wanted to hug her. She looked so small and afraid, and she was doing such a monumentally dangerous and self-sacrificing thing for me. She was betraying everything and everyone she knew. Her whole life had been a long lesson in doing as she was told, but here she was, with me. Helping.

Saving me. But I didn't dare reach out. I was afraid she might vanish like smoke if I went too close. She was barely clinging on. I saw that. This was costing her everything she had. And she was doing it for me.

It felt so strange to be off the bed, moving around. My legs were weak from spending so long lying down. Despite my attempts to exercise, I could still hardly walk. Standing instantly made my back ache and my bladder feel full to bursting as the baby's weight shifted. I could hardly waddle. Ellie had to help me, keeping me upright with an arm around my waist. It was a relief to leave the tiny room behind, I hoped for good. Ellie shut the door and locked it, stuffing the key in her pocket.

She led me left, not the way I had gone before, towards the other double doors. Was this the way that led up through the manor or were we going elsewhere? I had no idea. For a moment my steps faltered and I began to worry that she was leading me to some kind of trap. Perhaps a door would open and Lona would be there with a syringe full of labour-inducing drugs. But surely they wouldn't need a pretence for that? If Lona wanted to she was free to come to my room at any time. Unless . . . was this a plan carried out in spite of my mother, with Ellie as Lona's ally? Was I being kidnapped from my kidnappers?

'Come on!' Ellie hissed, dragging me forwards.

I staggered on but my skin crawled with unease. I didn't know anymore who I could trust and who my enemy was. It seemed that no matter who had me in their grasp, I was no safer. I told myself that I already knew I didn't want to be in that room, so anywhere else had to be better. Right?

The hallway was bright and stark with nowhere to hide. I kept looking back over my shoulder, terrified that someone would be there, coming towards us. Ellie seemed just as scared. I could feel her arm around me shaking. It was almost comforting. I could believe that she really was helping me to escape. She had the knife in her other hand still, but clutched it close like a teddy, instead of holding it like a weapon. I badly wanted to take it from her in case I needed to defend myself.

The double doors led into an identical corridor, but at the end of that was a staircase. This one was not raw concrete but floored in linoleum. It didn't smell damp either. Did that mean we were closer to the route to the surface?

'Where are you taking me?' I whispered, burning to know. I made Ellie jump. She flapped her hand at me for silence.

I just had to trust her and limp along with her support. If I was right, and we were in some kind of expanded bunker under the manor, I only hoped she wasn't taking me to the well exit. My legs were very shaky and I was weak, barely able to walk even with her help. There was no way I could climb up that metal ladder, even without my swollen belly in the way.

The staircase had no signs anywhere, but Ellie knew where she was going. We crept up the stairs slowly, with Ellie peering up the stairwell at every turn. We passed another floor and I glanced down blank, featureless corridors. The air smelled strange, like many herbs and spices mixing together. I thought of all the Nutrisoul products Ellie had shown me. Were they being made or stored here, in this secret place? Or was there a more sinister reason for those scents, a ritual or sacrifice in the works?

On the next floor up there was a sign on the door that said 'Executive Wing'. That door had an electric lock with a sensor. I wondered if that was where my mother was, sound asleep, untroubled by my fate. The idea that she and the rest of them would live underground by choice was insane to me. Squirrelled away from the sun, hiding always. How could they think that this was a good way to live? Surely they had to wonder sometimes if they were doing the right thing?

Or maybe after so long on this path, they couldn't bear to look back at all that wasted time: their youth, their lives, their families. All sacrificed for an insane dream.

I realised how scared Ellie must be, perhaps even more so than me. This was her whole world since she was a little girl. Breaking the rules of Luna Vitae went against everything she was raised to become.

I was panting hard, one hand supporting my belly, the other clinging to Ellie like she was a life raft. I wanted so desperately to be out, to get away, but with every step I felt my strength draining away. Ellie kept dragging me along, but it became harder and harder to propel myself.

Finally, just as I thought I might collapse, we reached the top of the stairs. A final shorter hallway ended in a set of double doors without a window. They were similar to the strange submarine-style door I'd seen before. Made of metal, with a hefty latch, designed to keep the world out. Beside the doors, on the wall, there was a security system panel and a fire alarm trigger.

At the door, Ellie seemed to sag in on herself. The tension seeped away, leaving exhaustion behind. She propped me against the wall and stepped away. In the bright lights of the corridor I could see the dark circles under her eyes and the way her face looked thinner. Her hair was lank and she looked like she'd been crying.

'Ellie . . . thank you, thank you so much for helping me . . . are you all right? Are you going to be all right?' I was worried she was about to pass out. She looked so drained and weak.

She shook her head, fresh tears forming in her eyes. She seemed unable to speak or even look me in the eye. She just went to the security panel and pulled a crumpled bit of paper from her pocket. She carefully input a code, then stuffed the paper into her pocket again. There was a soft chime and then she pulled hard on the metal latch. There was an unbearably loud grinding noise and then the door began to swing inwards. Fresh air rushed in and I was overcome with an animal relief. Outside. I could see outside.

We were in some woods and it was pitch black out there. There was snow on the ground and on the branches of the trees. Overhead, a bird cried out sharply and the wind rattled bare branches together. There was a little concrete overhang beyond the door and in its shelter I saw a winter coat and a pair of dirty walking boots.

'Take those,' Ellie said recovering her voice, though it sounded wet and feeble. 'Follow the path. There's a clearing. They had me move the car there. The key's in the coat pocket. I put everything you had on you that day in the boot of the car but your phone's dead.'

'Why did they keep the car?' I asked, confused and overwhelmed. I kicked the boots free of the coat and stuffed my feet into them, flimsy slippers and all. My knees shook and I had to cling onto the wall. A torch rolled out of the coat bundle. At least I wouldn't be in the dark.

'I don't know. I don't know anything,' Ellie said, voice cracking. 'Just that they had me get him to keep paying for it but then . . . the emails. He got suspicious and we had to hide it. I couldn't go back to the cottage anymore. He was looking for you.' As she spoke she backed away, back into the throat of the tunnel from which we'd emerged.

'Hey, what are you doing? We have to go,' I said, beckoning her. She cowered from me like a scared dog.

'I can't go,' she said, shaking her head. She hugged herself and bowed her head as if scared I was about to leap at her.

'Ellie, once they know I've gone they'll figure out it was you who helped me. It's not safe,' I said, reaching for her again, but she flinched away.

'I can't . . . I . . . I belong here,' she said.

I looked at her teary eyes and realised what she meant. This was all she knew. Obedience to Luna Vitae, to my mother. Just like Phoebe had said of her escape, Ellie owned nothing, had nothing. The cult was her only refuge.

'Trust me,' I said. 'I can help you.'

'Worry about yourself,' Ellie said. 'I'll be OK here. They . . . this is my family.'

'You know that's not true. If you believe me you know what they're capable of.'

'I know!' she hissed. 'I had to let you go or they'd have . . . or they'd kill you. I couldn't bear that. I love you, Luce. Please don't go thinking I don't.'

'So come with me.'

'I can't,' she insisted, beginning to cry. 'It's too late to go back. I belong here now.'

I thought of those old photos of missing children. I wanted to tell her she had a family out there somewhere, a real family. But the words stuck in my throat. I couldn't promise her she'd be safe out there, or that I'd be able to do anything to protect her. I didn't even know if I could protect myself, from Marshal, from the world.

Taking advantage of my indecision, Ellie braced herself against the weight of the door and pulled it closed. The metal hatch swung in as I reached for her, and I heard the latch screech closed. Then I was alone in the woods. Lost and, for the first time, free.

Chapter Thirty-Five

Freezing in my pyjamas, I picked up the coat. It was clearly Ellie's and smelled like her perfume. It was far too small with the bump, but it was warmer than nothing at all. Unable to do up the laces on the boots, I scooped up the torch and plodded away from the tunnel entrance on shaky legs. My frozen fingers found the car keys in the coat pocket. Ellie was telling the truth. She gave me everything she could. Now my life and my baby's were in my hands.

I wondered why they bothered to keep the car and got Marshal to continue paying for it, then just stole it outright. Was it just a ruse to keep him believing Ellie was visiting me in hospital, or part of their plan to dispose of my body? Perhaps they planned to knock me out and make it look like I gassed myself in the car. Or stage an accident. That was one way to stop Marshal looking for me. Or maybe they were scrambling, disorganised, not sure what to do.

I glanced back only once, hoping to see Ellie coming through the door. The tunnel entrance looked just like an old equipment shed built against a hill. Prefab concrete and metal, with the number thirteen sprayed on one side in white. The kind of place ancient lawnmowers or sports equipment might go to rot and be forgotten. Large enough to drive a car into, even a small van. The tracks on the ground said that this was their main entrance. I turned and began to shuffle away.

I struggled to find my way. Walking without Ellie's support was slow going. My legs were waking up more but still each step took a great effort. After going a while, I glanced back and couldn't see the tunnel entrance through the trees anymore. My tracks were clear in the snow. I could only hope no one realised I was missing in time to follow them to me. I had to reach the car, had to get away.

A little further on and I could no longer resist the burning need to pee. Standing upright was putting pressure on my bladder, which pained me more with every step. Unable to ignore it, I pulled my pyjama bottoms down a bit and stood with my legs apart, trying not to pee on my clothes. It was bitingly cold. When I was done I glanced down and saw brownish redness on the snow. I hugged myself, teeth rattling together. Was there something wrong? I felt weak and exhausted but I put that down to my long confinement. What if it was something worse?

I forced myself onwards. If I was ill or something was wrong with the baby, that was all the more reason to hurry to the car, to get away and find help. I'd drive somewhere with people and get someone to call an ambulance. If my phone was really in the car I could use the charger in the glove compartment and call for help myself. I just had to keep going. Just a bit further.

In truth I had no idea how far away the car was. Ellie said there was a clearing, but not how long it would take to get there. The place where I'd parked originally was a long way from the manor. A hike that exhausted me even back then. Now I was heavily pregnant, possibly ill and very weak. I told myself not to think about how far it was, or how far

I'd come. One foot in front of the other took all my focus. It helped me shut out my fear, my exhaustion, everything. Even the pain.

It had started as little twinges as I followed Ellie. I didn't even really notice. I brushed it off as pressure from the baby. As I walked through the wood, trying to keep to the almost invisible path, it grew stronger. No longer twinges but elastic twangs of tension – regular and unrelenting.

Keep going, I told myself. *Ignore it. Ignore everything but the path. Get to the car. It'll be OK if I can just reach the car.* It started to snow again. Fat, feathery flakes drifted into my face as I waddled onwards. I was moving so slowly, barely able to shuffle each foot a few inches through the snow with every step.

As I slid my boot forwards, I felt a shivery quavering inside me. A second later warm liquid soaked my pyjamas, turning icy cold within an instant. I looked down in uncomprehending terror, my tired brain trying to make sense of it. Then I realised and panic lit me on fire. My waters had broke. I was going into labour. Now.

I looked ahead. No sign of a clearing. No sign of anything but the wide white ground and the thick black trees. Was I still on the path? Was the car ahead somewhere? Over the next rise or fifteen miles away? I staggered off again, now half sobbing with every breath. I was terrified and alone and the entire world was my enemy.

The first true stabbing pain hit me as I passed a skinny sapling. I gasped out a cloud of white fog, grasping the thin tree trunk to keep myself upright. Another pain came, then another, as I stood there trying to get my breath back. I looked up at the unchanging snow and trees. I took one step, then two. The trees swam, blurring together, spinning away from me. I fell hard, my knees punching through the crust on the snow. I threw my hands down to brace myself but couldn't find the strength to lift my heavy body back up. I crawled a few feet and then dropped to the ground, exhausted.

Collapsed in the frozen slush, I let out a wail of frustration and fear. Halfway through it became a yell of pain. Sobbing into the snow I tried to find any reserve of strength left in me. Mothers could lift cars off their babies, or fight wolves for them. I could find the will to drag myself on, to reach the car. But I had nothing left. I wasn't a mother. I never felt like a mother, not in all the months of pregnancy. This was the final proof. I'd failed my daughter. I'd failed myself.

The pains became harsher and closer together now, so I barely had time to recover before the next. They seemed to blur together until there was just pain. No respite. I rolled onto my back and grunted through my teeth. But soon I couldn't help but yell. Either I cried out or bit my own tongue in half. Somewhere in the midst of my delirium, I wondered if I would have the baby right there, on the snow. Perhaps then I could carry her with me, still have time to get away.

But of course, they found me.

They came upon me from all sides. Four women dressed in warm coats and sturdy boots. Lona, Sita and two women I'd never seen before, a bony blonde with wide, watery eyes and a black woman with multitudes of gold ear piercings. Between them, they carried a stretcher. The plastic kind mounted on the wall in sports halls – man-shaped and bright orange.

'Put it down there, Artemis,' Lona ordered. She pulled a radio from her pocket and pressed a button. 'We've found her. Tell Selene it's time. She's in labour.' Indistinct radio chatter followed; I was too agonised to understand it.

The stretcher hit the snow and without preamble I was rolled onto it, like a dead pig. I didn't have the energy to fight them as they secured my limbs with nylon straps. Then between them, like pallbearers, they lifted me up.

'Do we have to carry her all the way back?' the blonde woman, Artemis, grunted.

'No. We're going to the manor. It's closer,' Lona said. 'Silly bitch almost circled around to it. They're setting it up for the delivery now.'

I closed my eyes and gritted my teeth against another cresting wave of pain. I'd lost my way. I walked too far and nearly circled back to the manor. I loathed myself for my own carelessness, my own inability to save myself, to save either of us.

'Mani, watch that root,' Sita said.

The stretcher lurched a little as the tall black woman stumbled then righted herself.

'Bloody woods,' she muttered. 'I hope they've brought heaters up. My feet are numb.'

They chatted amongst themselves as if they were out for a normal hike. Between them, I moaned and grunted in pain, tears rolling down my cheeks. Snowflakes melted on my sweating face. Soon the manor appeared, a deeper darkness against the black sky. I wouldn't live to see the sunrise, I told myself, and began to cry, for myself and for the baby whose life I was leaving in the hands of my unfeeling mother.

They carried me right up to the manor's front door and inside. As they toted me up the stairs I saw other women standing on the landing, watching me. Diana was there, bleary-eyed, with one cheek red and swollen as if she'd been struck. Carmen was a few steps up from Diana, her plaited hair shining in the candlelight, a look of triumph on her face. Other women were there too. People I'd never seen before, seven in total, wearing coats over pyjamas and carrying candles. Ellie was not amongst them.

It was like a procession. They fell in behind the stretcher

as I was borne along the landing. Looking up, I saw the light from their candles dance over the warped ceiling. There was rustling and murmuring ahead of us. Then a door opened and I was carried into a room. Carlisle's room.

They deposited the stretcher on something soft. A smell of damp rose up. It was Carlisle's bed, left to rot in the abandoned manor. From the crackling sound when I was set down, someone had thrown a plastic sheet and some clean blankets or sheets over it. Clearly things had been hurriedly set up.

Now lower down I was able to see the room. The women who carried me joined the rest, who assembled around me. The space was lit by their candles and several hurricane lanterns. A red glow came from several portable paraffin heaters, which choked out hot air, trying to bake the room dry. The bed I was on had been moved since I was last in the room. I was opposite the mural now, looking at the faceless girl in her white dress.

A bolt of lightning rippled across my belly and I screamed in pain. Around me I heard muttering, then one voice rose above everyone else as a twelfth woman joined the crowd.

'Kneel for the birth of the Sun King's heir.'

It was Selene. She appeared at the end of the bed. Unlike everyone else, who appeared to have scrambled from their beds, she was wearing a long black robe with a golden sun on one breast, a silver moon on the other. Her face was painted gold and her greying blonde hair was held back by a circlet of opals. The gold and ruby sun pendant winked at me in the candlelight. She had clearly been waiting for this moment, prepared to go at a moment's notice.

A general rustling told me that everyone did as she said and kneeled. I heard a familiar chant begin to rise from them. A soft, worshipful sigh.

'*In dolor, servitium. In servitium, voluptatem. In voluptatem, libero.*'

There was a new part to it, some new phrase they added. It made no difference. I cursed at them and swore between cries, but they only chanted on, ignoring me.

At my side, only Lona and Sita remained upright. My mother cast one last look at the assembled kneeling women, then nodded to Lona.

'Strip her.'

Lona's rough hands manhandled my wet clothes. Every time I twitched or spasmed in pain, she became rougher, as if punishing me for resisting her. When I was finally naked, Sita laid a blanket over me. I was past caring if I was cold or not. The pains were stronger now, my body wracked with them. I could feel a crisis coming, a peak to the madness going on inside me. The baby was coming. I had to push.

They did nothing as I laboured, screaming and sobbing out my pain. In the few lucid moments, I looked up to see my mother watching me with impatient greed, Lona's disgusted face, and Sita's breathless excitement. I saw her lips form the words of the chant, in English now: In pain, service. In service, pleasure. In pleasure, freedom.

Only my pain was not leading me to freedom. Only to death. Death which, in my agony, I wished for.

At last, with a final heaving that made my ears ring and my face swell with blood and a held-in scream, the baby slithered free. I collapsed, almost passing out. I was vaguely aware of Sita rushing forwards, a tug as the baby – still attached to me – was moved. A great cry of joy went up around the room as she was cut free and held up. I caught a glimpse of a ruddy, blood-covered face, and heard a thin cry.

Then a pillow was pressed over my face.

Chapter Thirty-Six

Exhausted as I was, I fought instinctively. With crooked fingers, I clawed at the arms that held the pillow down, grasping wildly for hair or eyes. The cotton against my face was taut, squashing my nose. With every breath, I sucked it into my mouth. My pulse pounded in my ears and it felt as though my skull would explode from the pressure.

Then it was gone.

I blinked away black spots and saw Selene warding Lona off with a fierce expression. Her arms were up. Lona's forearms were deeply scored and bleeding, a long scratch on her cheek from my nails. Behind them, I saw shocked faces, heard muttering. Their mouths were dark circles of surprise and dismay. The baby shrieked as if she was furious as well.

'How dare you!' Selene boomed, her voice no longer a low growl but sharp as lightning strikes.

'But . . .' Lona stammered, hate-filled eyes turning from me to Selene as her dense brows knitted in confusion. 'You . . .'

'Take her to the shed, with the other traitor. We'll deal with them later,' Selene announced, and several women came forwards, putting their hands on Lona's shoulders. She shook them off, bucking like a bull.

'You told me to!' she bellowed. 'This is a trick. You bitch! Don't you see?' She looked around at the other women for support, for agreement. 'Selene wants power for herself, she doesn't care about the child. She knows I am a true follower, so she must get rid of me, silence me. She ordered me to destroy the vessel once its job was done.'

'I ordered you to kill my own daughter? The one who Carlisle chose himself?' Selene laughed like falling ice. 'You are mad, Lona. Mad and old and desperate. Take her away to the shed!'

This time the women came forward as one, their grip on Lona sure and determined. I saw Diana emerge, gleeful. She jabbed at Lona and she fell like a tree struck by lightning. As she convulsed, Diana prodded her once more and I saw the stun gun in her hand. This had all been planned. My mother outmanoeuvred her enemy in one play. For what could anger a room full of women more than an attempt on the life of one of their own in childbed?

'Lucia,' Selene cooed, sitting beside me on the bed and stroking my hair. 'You have done so well. Look at her.'

Sita brought the baby over, now cleaned and wrapped in a shawl. Outside I could hear Lona being dragged across the landing, the thump as they hauled her down the stairs. To the shed, that's what Selene said. With the other traitor. Was that where they took Ellie for her part in my escape?

I looked at the bundled baby. Her face was damp and creased, livid red. Atop her head was a tuft of reddish hair. My genes had won over Marshal's. She'd probably be annoyed about that later in life. Though how would she know about him? According to my mother, Carlisle was her father. There was no one here who would argue with her on that score. They needed the lie to live on, so they had something to believe in. To justify their past crimes: the kidnapping, the blackmail, the murder.

'She's beautiful,' my mother sighed.

She leaned forward and whispered to me and me alone, 'My heir.'

I felt my insides clench. I looked at her and saw the coldness in her eyes. I saw how little she cared for me, for anyone other than herself. If she ever had even the tiniest bit of love or concern for me, it died a long time ago. She didn't care about the baby or the other women in the room. She would sacrifice anything and anyone to maintain control.

'She should pass the placenta soon,' Sita said.

'Tend to her. The others will return soon for the naming.'

With that my mother swept away, done with her performance as the doting matriarch. Sita crouched before me and I heard the rattle of instruments as she went about her work. I was still in a lot of pain and delivering the afterbirth was another drain on my weak body. I wanted to sleep but was too scared of what would happen if I closed my eyes. Where might I wake up? What might be done to me?

'Small pinch,' Sita said, almost to herself. I felt the sting of a needle and then a cool spreading wave of pain relief. Whilst she worked away, I looked up at the ceiling and almost wished Lona had smothered me. Yet I felt vicious satisfaction that she was being punished. Perhaps that would be the last joy I ever knew, the mean-spirited glee at her torment.

'I've done some stitches,' Sita said, appearing at my side with a goblet of wine for me to sip. I longed for water but anything would do to soothe my torn and parched throat. I gulped the bitter liquid. Too late, I worried about what they might have put in it.

'You've done very well,' she said in her usual cheery manner. As if we were in a sterile delivery suite and not a mouldering manor house. As if any of this was normal.

'Hurts,' I muttered thickly. There was definitely something

292

in the wine. Some other kind of painkiller perhaps or a sedative. I felt it soothing the exhaustion and pain from my limbs.

'I know it does,' Sita said, wiping my forehead with a damp cloth that smelled of patchouli. 'The first ones are the hardest. Your next will come easier.'

Cold horror spread through me faster than the drugs. The next. I pushed myself up on trembling elbows, looking at Sita aghast.

'The next?'

'Yes.' She looked confused, as if my horror made no sense to her. 'This is your purpose, Lucia. To bear his many children, to ensure his legacy.'

I couldn't speak; my tongue went numb in my head.

'It has been ordained that we shall recruit men to our cause. To be dedicated as priests of the Sun. To pledge themselves as guardians of the heir and as vessels of Carlisle's power. They will help you to produce His children and help us spread our message and enforce His laws.' She smiled down at me. 'You will be honoured and your daughters will carry on your legacy in time.'

Selene was recruiting men now. More people, more power for her to exploit. More salesmen for her snake oil. I remembered her scorn when she talked about the prostitution, how they manipulated powerful men. She was using the same scheme again. Offering sex on tap would bring in the worst and weakest. The deluded and the cruel. That was who she planned on passing my daughter around to once I outlived my usefulness. My daughters, plural.

I wished both of us had died, my daughter and I together, rather than face that future.

Outside came the creak of the stairs. The women were returning. Sita quickly tidied a covered bowl away. God only knew what they were going to do with the placenta. I felt giddy, unreal. Everything was too strange and surreal, my blood swimming with drugs.

As the women filed in, tiny pinpricks of light filled the room as they relit their tapers from the lanterns. The portable heaters churned out hot air, making the flames dance.

My mother returned once everyone else was still.

'Now we have rooted out the traitors in our midst,' Selene intoned, 'prepare to welcome Carlisle's heir, in his name!'

'In his name,' echoed the women.

Selene continued to speak, her words blurring through the air, which was once again heavy with incense. One of the women swung a thurible on thin gold chains, spreading the smoke as she watched my mother. The room seemed to breathe around me, the walls rippling. My mind got loose from my body and saw it all from far away. As I looked around, I saw that every eye was on my mother. No one was looking at me.

I fought to still my spinning thoughts. I was unbound and unobserved. This might be my only chance to stop what was happening. If I let them take me back into that bunker all would be lost. I would never get out again. They would make sure of that. My daughter would grow up not even realising the trap she was in. I had to stop it. Everything in me screamed that I had to act. Only my body was so drained, so full of numbing drugs, that I could hardly think.

But I had to fight.

The scream boiled up from the soles of my feet, taking every ounce of my terror with it. It burst out like a swarm of bats taking flight from my jaws. With one wild movement, I seized the lantern nearest to me and threw myself from the bed.

I staggered, the floor seeming to tilt beneath me. I felt as if the whole manor was shaking in the wind, about to come down. Wheeling around, I found that everyone was looking at me now. I held the lantern up high and the few women creeping towards me fell back as if the light burned them.

'Lucia.' My mother's voice cut through the air. 'Put that down.'

I turned to face her, my legs shaking as I fought to stay upright. I looked beyond her to where a bassinet sat in shadow. The baby was quiet. I was led to this. My world was shaped and manipulated to get me to where I stood now. Controlled. Every part of my life was touched by them, tainted by them, by Marshal. An illusion to allow me to imagine I had free will, when that was taken away the moment I was chosen.

'Lucia,' my mother said softly, inching towards me. 'There's nothing you can do. This is your fate, your purpose. It is his design. There is no choice.'

I looked into her calculating mad eyes, and I chose.

Chapter Thirty-Seven

The lantern exploded on the floor and flammable liquid burst onto the carpet. Great smoking flames bloomed and spread. The women screamed and my mother sprang back. The floor was draped in carpets and scarves to hide the damp mess it was underneath. They burned well. Sheets of flame shot out, reaching for the walls and the ceiling. I was entranced by it, watching the yellow fire move like water.

Then I heard my baby scream.

I looked up and saw Selene holding the bundle of embroidered blankets, running for the door. She vanished onto the landing. Around me, women were beating at the flames, screaming. Two of them tried to smother the fire with the bedsheets. They weren't even looking at me. Fear stripped away their mystique and obsession. They were only ordinary people dressed in idiotic costumes.

I left them and ran after my mother, following the baby's cries.

Naked and unsteady, I pursued them. Behind me I heard only screams and frantic shouting. It was as if two points in time came together: the past and the present. All of it breaking down around me as I staggered down the stairs, escaping a fire at the manor once again.

It was dark and so very cold on the lower level of the house. The floor was covered in debris. I ran over it, heedless of my bare feet. I knew where she went. She went where she had gone before and where I had followed, fleeing to her escape route like a rat into its burrow. Carlisle's study.

When I reached the doorway I saw her. She was crouched over, trying to lift the rusted trapdoor. I guessed that they had not used it in many years – that narrow, inconvenient passage into the original bunker. Easier to bring things in and out via the larger tunnel in the woods. She was struggling against rusted hinges and fallen plaster chunks. Behind her, on the rubbish-strewn floor, was the bundle of blankets. I swept forward and scooped it up. Inside, the warm body of my baby shifted. It was the first time I ever held her.

'You!' Selene, sensing my movement, whirled around. The smoke from the fire made her eyes stream, as it did mine. Her gold paint ran in rivulets and her hair was matted down with sweat.

'You've ruined everything,' she snapped. 'Again!'

I wanted to run, but turning my back on her felt like giving a poisonous snake its chance to strike. So I stood there and felt the force of her fury, whilst overhead the fire raged and screaming women rattled the floorboards with their panicked running.

'I should have never convinced myself to have you,' she spat. 'Every day, I wished I had you taken care of. Every. Day. Hanging like a rock around my ankle, dragging me back. You ruined my life!'

'And you ruined mine!' I shouted back, unable to keep the poisonous words inside me any longer. How long had they been there, festering underneath my soul? Since before I could remember. Since the first time she left me behind whilst she chased after Celeste, Carlisle, after anyone or anything that wasn't me. Despite the blood between us, I

297

knew we were never a family. Since the moment she knew about me, growing inside her, I was her enemy.

'But you are not going to ruin my daughter,' I hissed.

A great cracking sound made my heart flutter. Then came a crash, a sort of explosion. The groaning of timbers left to rot, now shaken with the force of fire and too many footsteps. I glanced up and saw the plaster webbed with cracks, yawning open with fire behind them. My mother didn't see; her eyes were fixed on me. In her open hatred she was more familiar to me than ever. This was who she was beneath the robes and paint, beneath the mask of my carefree, bohemian mother. The furious cheated woman covering her resentment and pain with pretty words and fake enlightenment.

'I never wanted to be your mother,' she said, her face thunderous. She plucked at her waist, where a dagger dangled on a silken cord, half hidden in the folds of black fabric. In moments the blade was in her hand and she was coiled, ready to spring.

'You never were,' I said, clutching the wriggling bundle close to my chest.

She leaped at me. I staggered back, and the ceiling came down in a shower of burning timber. Selene screamed, one terrible roar of rage and hate and fear. Then the sound was cut off in a rain of falling furniture and debris. Her body was broken within a moment.

Plaster, smoke, dust and flames filled the room. I scrambled for the door and flung myself into the corridor, clutching the baby to my chest. I did not stop until I felt the frozen ground under my feet. Only then did I turn to look back and saw the manor engulfed in flames.

The entire first storey was ablaze, the floor giving way. The paraffin heaters in Carlisle's room gave it all the fuel it needed, and decades of decay had weakened the manor already. I saw, backlit by its lurid glare, figures in the snow, some running, some staring like I was, watching it all come down. Whether everyone escaped or not I wasn't sure. I didn't care.

I did not stay to see what they would do, the survivors. I only wanted to get away, to be safe. The painkillers weren't enough to blot everything out and my body felt like tender meat. Naked, I stumbled through the snow towards the outbuildings. To Ellie.

Inside the stone prison, I found her. She was handcuffed to an iron ring in the back wall of the first stall. Forced to look up at the sun mural, she hung there limply but stirred when she heard me come in. She was beaten quite badly. Her face looked awful – black eyes, fat lips and grazed cheekbones. Still, she looked up at me in mingled horror and amazement. God only knew what I looked like – naked and smeared in blood and soot, hair wild and stumbling like the first woman to walk upright.

'Loo-ee?' Her bloodied mouth formed the word and I shushed her gently.

'I'll get you out,' I said, then started looking around for anything of use. If the keys to the cuffs were elsewhere, I didn't think I'd have the strength to try and batter them open. Fortunately there was a key hanging on a bent nail. It was left in Ellie's line of sight, presumably to torture her further. I snatched it. It took a moment to get the cuffs open but soon Ellie was straightening up. I saw her take in my trembling body, turning red and purple from the cold.

'Here.' She stripped off her sweatshirt and passed it to me, holding out her arms to receive the baby. The sweatshirt was still warm from her skin and I almost cried as I slipped it on over my own frigid body. Ellie passed the blanket bundle back to me and then looked further into the shadows.

'Wait here,' she muttered.

She vanished into the darkness. I heard rustling and grunting. She returned with a pair of sturdy boots and drawstring pyjama bottoms. I squinted at them in the dark. They were Lona's things. I guessed she was unconscious in one of the other stalls.

'We should let her go,' I said, surprising myself. 'We can't just leave her locked up. They won't come back for her.'

Ellie squinted at me from bruised lids. Then she sighed and took another key from its hook on the wall, vanishing again. I laid the baby on the ground and painfully manoeuvred myself into the bottoms and boots. As I raised my feet up to do so, I felt exhaustion press in on me from all sides. If I didn't rest soon, I would collapse. The pain almost overwhelmed the drugs now, coming for me in a great barrelling wave.

Ellie returned without the key. 'She's out cold. But it's open for when she wakes up.'

Of course, when she did, she wouldn't have shoes or trousers. But my mercy only went so far. She would have to fend for herself.

Together Ellie and I left the little outbuilding. She shivered in the night air. I looked over at the manor and saw that the shadowy figures had melted away, fled into the night like ghosts. I didn't care. Thoughts of the police and justice were pushed out by the animal instinct to avoid pain. I just wanted to rest.

'They took my coat,' I said, voice slurring with exhaustion. 'The car keys.'

'There's a van. Our van. For supplies,' Ellie said. 'It's in the woods. Spare key should be hidden in it.'

'I can't,' I sobbed, looking at the dark woods, knowing how far it had to be. Ellie didn't say anything. She just pulled my arm around her shoulder and began to walk. She half dragged, half carried me through the open gate and towards the treeline, onwards into the lessening dark.

I was barely conscious, clinging to the baby and trying to shuffle my feet as Ellie propelled me along through the snow. The stolen pyjamas were quickly soaked with slush around the ankles and the wetness only rose higher. Ellie stumbled often, wincing and breathing heavily. I had no idea how she was upright. She was clearly beaten from head to toe and the bruises only looked worse as the sun rose.

At last we stumbled into a small clearing and I saw a track leading off ahead. Two ruts for wheels. A road had to be nearby. Whilst I stood gaping at this sudden evidence of civilisation, Ellie crossed the clearing. The van was concealed with camo netting, branches and snow. Not invisible from up close but it was probably hidden from the road. After clearing it off she kneeled painfully and felt around in a snow-crusted wheel arch. I waited, willing her to stand up with the key in hand. But she only groaned and punched at the tyre in frustration.

'Gone!' she said, like it was a curse. The word hit me and I think I would have cried, had I been able to feel my face.

'Was it that wheel?' I said, shuffling over, wishing I could just lie down in the snow.

'Driver's side. Yeah.' She pulled herself to her feet. 'We'll . . . we'll have to walk it. Get to the road . . . hope someone comes.'

As if in answer, my legs gave way. I barely caught myself on the side of the bonnet. One hand still holding on to the bundle of blankets. Hanging on to the slick metal, I looked up at Ellie. It was obvious to both of us. I wasn't going to make it even one step further.

'Go,' I said. 'You have to. Take her.'

'No.' Ellie looked at me as though I just suggested she eat me to survive. 'No, I'm not leaving you here. The bloody key's got to be somewhere.' She plunged her hands into the snow on the ground, scattering clumps of it as she searched.

'Here! It fell! I've got it!'

She unlocked the van, then ran around to open my door and lift me as best she could. I tipped gracelessly into the passenger seat and she placed the baby in my lap before putting the belt around me and closing the door.

Sitting was an entirely new kind of pain. I couldn't decide if it was worse than walking or simply different. I wanted so badly to sleep, but we were still so far from safety.

Ellie tried the ignition and after some false starts and spluttering, it turned over. With red fingers she spun every dial to high and soon warm air came gushing from the vents. It grew hotter and hotter as she accelerated and we began to bump along the track. The rocking motion shifted the weight of the baby in my lap and I leaned against the hard seat cushions.

'Stay awake,' she said suddenly.

I realised I'd closed my eyes. It didn't seem to matter. Only when Ellie pinched my hand hard did I force them open again. I rolled my head to the side and found her looking at me, eyes round and scared.

'You're bleeding. Stay awake and I'll get us to a hospital.'

I looked down and saw that the pyjama bottoms were not just soaked with snowmelt, but with fresh blood. I saw as well that the baby was asleep. Asleep or unconscious. I couldn't tell. I couldn't feel my fingers either. Couldn't lift my hand to check her pulse.

'Hold on, Lucy,' Ellie said from very far away, as the van slalomed towards the distant road.

But I couldn't hold on and consciousness was snatched from me in a blink.

Chapter Thirty-Eight

I awoke to the sterile smell and bright lights of a hospital room and immediately panicked.

Struggling upright I felt tubes and wires pull taut on my arms. My insides ached as I shifted, but there was no piercing pain anymore. I felt muzzy and knew one of the tubes running into my hand contained painkillers. I didn't even realise I was screaming until two nurses rushed in. They looked down at me, shocked.

'Lucia,' one of them said softly, reaching for me. 'It's all right. You're at the hospital.'

Hearing that name on their lips only scared me more. I tried to lash out at her but the other nurse, a man, quickly grabbed my arm and held me back.

'Lucia, I need you to calm down for me,' the first nurse said, still in that soft voice. 'You'll hurt yourself going on like this. Just breathe for me, OK? Breathe and listen.'

She was trying to reach out to me, to get me to look into her eyes. I flinched away and found myself looking past her, at the doorway. They'd left the door open.

Past the door, with its plastic sign showing the number thirteen, I could see pictures on the wall, photographs of smiling doctors and nurses. A man and woman in white coats hurried past and I could hear the distant robotic announcement that a lift had reached the fourth floor.

I went silent, breathing heavily. 'This . . . I'm in hospital.'

'Yes, love. St Mary's Hospital.'

'A real hospital.'

She glanced at the other nurse, who shrugged helplessly.

'That's right . . . a real hospital. Do you remember how you got here?'

'Ellie,' I said, remembering the van, the snow and the cold. 'Ellie brought me.'

'Good,' the nurse said, nodding. 'Your sister brought you in. Do you know how we can reach her? She looked in a bad way herself.'

'My . . .' My mind was whirling. They thought Ellie was my sister? What else did she say? Did they know what happened to me, how I came to be there? I hoped not. Surely Ellie had some sense of self-preservation about her, enough to hide her involvement. Either way, she was gone. I was glad. I didn't want her to get in trouble.

I cleared my throat. 'Yes. She drove me. Am I . . . all right?'

'You're doing a lot better,' she soothed. To her colleague she said, 'Can you get hold of Doctor Grant and tell him Miss Andrews is awake?'

Lucia Andrews. That was the name Ellie had given them. Not my real name or even my unmarried one. I was extremely grateful for that, though I didn't want to think why. Not right then.

'Your baby's doing fine as well,' the nurse said, once her colleague left. 'She was a bit poorly from the cold and very hungry. But we've had her under observation and she's really come on well. I'll be able to bring her up to see you soon.'

I'd been worried in those final delirious moments that she

died in my arms. But she was alive and safe. She was a survivor.

Doctor Grant came, a stern-faced Indian man with contrastingly warm eyes. He spoke to me as if I were a semi-wild animal and he was worried I'd take flight. Or bite him.

'Good afternoon, Miss Andrews. I'm glad you're feeling a bit better today.'

I supposed that was one way to describe finally regaining consciousness. He went on to explain that I'd been dehydrated, suffering from exhaustion and had lost a lot of blood. I'd also developed an infection due to the conditions under which I'd given birth. He didn't attach any kind of judgement to those 'conditions'. Didn't even ask me what they were. I understood that he was deeply concerned for me. Concerned and curious, but not willing to push me.

'I have to tell you,' he finished by saying, 'we are under a duty to inform social services of any suggestion that a child may be in danger. And to contact the police if we believe someone has been the victim of an assault or serious abuse. It is not my intention to frighten you, or to ask how you came to arrive here in the condition you did. But now that you are well enough to answer questions, there are some people who would like to speak to you.'

'I understand,' I said. He nodded.

'I hope you continue to recover well, Miss Andrews,' he said. 'I will leave you in the capable hands of nurses Maxwell and Farley.'

He was right. There were people who wanted to ask me questions. They came the next day. First a pair of police officers, one man and a woman. Then a social worker on her own. The police wanted to know how I had come by the injuries documented on my arrival at hospital: the poorly healed broken ankle, restraint marks on my wrists and ankles and my unwashed and neglected state.

I had a choice to make in that moment. Tell them the truth and I would repeat the same cycle as before. My secrets would trickle through various offices and agencies, to be discovered and published, outing me to those who might still want to harm me. Those shadowy figures had melted into the night but they were not gone. I knew there were still members of Luna Vitae out there – Lona and the rest. Would they want to pick up where Selene had left off, and imprison me? Perhaps, like Lona, they would just want me dead.

I chose differently. Though I answered all their questions, I gave only a version of the truth. Yes, I was abused. Yes, I was held against my will. No, I would not say who did it or why.

It frustrated them, I saw. They thought I was stupid or deluded. I think they assumed it was a partner who did these things to me, that I was protecting him out of some kind of love. I couldn't explain that I was protecting myself and my baby. From scrutiny, from discovery, from my past.

I knew, of course, that sooner or later, they would search for my name and find no such person existed. Then they would return, less concerned, less conciliatory. More questions for 'Lucia Andrews'. I didn't yet know what I'd do then. I could only rest and wait and try to regain the strength I needed when that time came. The time to make choices I'd have to live with for the rest of my life.

The social worker was more direct with her enquiries. She was an older woman in a thick cardigan, a long corduroy skirt and glasses around her neck on a beaded string. She reminded me of old picture-book librarians – just missing the bun on her head and a finger to her lips. But she was kind. Despite her harsh exterior, I saw the worry buried in her eyes.

'I'm here to help you, Lucia. I want what's best for you and your baby. Have you thought of a name for her yet?'

306

I hadn't. To be honest, I hadn't tried. I couldn't explain it to her but it would have been like trying to name an invention that I didn't think of, a place I didn't discover. She wasn't mine to name. Even after everything we'd been through. I knew our time together was limited. Almost over.

I'd grown to love her – something I thought was impossible when I first found out I was pregnant. Then it was fear and panic that were whispering to me, convincing me that I was the last person who could be her mother because of my past, because of where I'd come from and who my own mother was.

Now I knew for sure what my history was and I knew that I was nothing like my mother. I wasn't a terrible person, or a mistake, or unfit to be a parent. I wasn't dangerous.

But that didn't mean I brought no danger with me. I knew that no matter what, that would always be the case. As long as I was in the baby's life, she would be in danger. Not just from the cult, wherever they were now, but from Marshal too.

Selene was wrong about a lot of things. She was deluded and power-mad. But she was right about him. He was controlling me and I'd known it for a while. It was underneath every conversation with Carmen, every thought I had. I just wasn't able to see it. I didn't want to see it. I could look back now and realise that part of my panic over the pregnancy was about him, about being trapped with him by a child we shared, trapped in that house where I could barely breathe.

For the first few days of my hospital stay, I was stuck trying to work out what to do about Marshal. About everything. I could see our whole marriage through new eyes now. All the ways he manipulated and changed me. I wanted to confront him but I was afraid that once he started talking, that old magic would pull me back in. The same tricks Carlisle used to bend the world into his version of the truth. I needed something, anything, to prove to myself that no matter what he said, I was right about him.

I found it in an unexpected place. One of the nurses was chatting to me and just mentioned that my things were in the bedside chest of drawers if I wanted them. Confused, I waited until she left and then looked. There wasn't much, but clearly Ellie had left me with my stuff from the car, including my handbag. I was glad no one had gone through it and found the bank cards and my driving licence, both of which had my real name on them. At least I had a hairbrush in there, some mints and my phone, even if it was dead and the charger was back in the car.

I was about to put the bag away when I felt something in the very bottom. I pulled it out. It was a sheet of my birth control pills. I took them at the same time every day, and sometimes that meant having them on me for early staff meetings at work. It was practical to carry them with me, or so I'd told myself. Really I kept them on me so Marshal wouldn't see me taking them and start asking me to stop again.

I ran my finger over the foil and wondered what would have happened to me if I'd never gotten pregnant. Maybe the cult would have left me alone, and I'd have stayed with Marshal, unwilling to see what he was like. The thought of it made me shiver.

It was then that I noticed the rough edge on the plastic. Turning it over, I saw that it wasn't the pill packet, but tiny beads of glue. Yellowish glue. The kind I'd taken from Marshal's office to repair that broken pot. Picking at it, I was able to lift up the corner of the foil covering, where there was more glue underneath. Someone had peeled it away then glued it back down. I closed my eyes. Not someone. Marshal. I could picture him doing it, carefully removing the foil with his sterling silver letter opener. Shaking the pills out with the same blank expression he had on when he threw my wine in the bin. Like he was just doing what needed to be done.

I knew what I had to do. It wouldn't be easy. A year ago it would have felt impossible. But now I knew just what I had the strength to get through. I knew I could do this and I had all the evidence I needed.

I asked Nurse Maxwell if she could take me to a payphone. She wheeled me down the hall to a little waiting area, where beige plastic payphones lined one wall, separated by smoked glass. I had some change from my purse, and carefully fed it into the machine.

Then I called Marshal.

It was, oddly, the thing I'd most been dreading, hearing his voice on the other end of the phone. I felt in that instant all that residual attachment to him. Not love, but what I'd thought was love. I didn't love him so much as felt that I needed him, that I owed him. A feeling he only strengthened every time he undermined my decisions or made his affection a reward for doing what he wanted.

'Marshal Townsend. Who's speaking, please?'

'It's me.'

There was a long silence and I could imagine him clearly. The shock of hearing from me hitting him. His pinkish public schoolboy face blanching. His hand running through his blonde hair. The sweat beginning to prickle under his designer button-down.

'Lucy?' he whispered, as if afraid he'd break some kind of spell by uttering my name. 'Where . . . I've been trying to find you. Where have you been? The police have been looking, I was on the news. When I got that email about your toy and realised it wasn't you writing to me, I was so scared. What happened? Why was someone else writing your messages? Why didn't you answer the phone?' As he spoke he got progressively more worked up. I could feel the concern curdling into blame, worry into accusation.

Normally I would have been falling over myself to reassure him, to apologise. But what did I do wrong? I didn't run away or hide from him. It wasn't my fault that I vanished. So I stayed quiet and waited to see what would happen if I didn't fill my usual role. After a while, he stopped talking, leaving a long, heavy silence. Even seeing it for what it was, a way to force me to beg forgiveness, I nearly caved. Instead I waited, and eventually he spoke again.

'Lucy, I have been going out of my mind with worry. I think you owe me an explanation.'

'I do,' I said. But not an apology. Not anymore. 'Ellie was the one emailing you. Pretending to be me. Because I was kidnapped. She was helping Luna Vitae and they took me and kept me somewhere because they wanted the baby. I only just got away.'

Another silence. This one far longer and filled with disbelief.

'Lucy, that's . . . that's insane. How could they have taken you? I don't believe this. Are you sure that's what actually happened or were you just off somewhere else, ignoring my calls to spite me? Because you didn't want to go to the cottage.'

'Am I sure that I was kidnapped? Yes,' I said, getting annoyed. That was good, I needed that anger as fuel. A way to keep me strong against him.

'Jesus, I told you not to go out of the cottage. Do you see why I was so worried? Where are you now? Where's the baby? Is it all right?'

'Can I ask you something?'

'What?' he blurted. 'You're not making sense. Tell me if my baby's OK. Tell me what's happened and where you are. I'll come and get you right now.'

I closed my eyes for a second. There wasn't a 'Are *you* all right?' but just a 'Is the baby all right?' It felt as if everyone, from Marshal to the hospital to the cult, only cared about the baby I was carrying. Not about me at all. Apart from Ellie, who saved me. I felt an overwhelming sense of gratitude for that. Not just for her rescue, but for the fact that she cared about me.

'Marshal, listen to me.'

He kept talking, asking questions, demanding I answer. I stayed silent and eventually his voice petered out until all I could hear was his breathing, harsh and furious. I slid a few more coins into the phone when it chimed, impatient for me to find the strength to continue. To say what I needed to get out.

'Why are you being like this?' he finally said. 'Is this some kind of breakdown?'

'No, I'm just waiting to ask a question.'

'There's no need to be bitchy with me,' he said. 'What is it then? What do you want to know before you'll talk to me like a normal person?'

'I wanted to ask why you did it. Why you got me pregnant even though I told you I wasn't ready?'

There was a long, dangerous pause.

'Lucy . . . tell me where you are,' Marshal said, and I heard the strain in his voice, the effort it was taking not to explode.

'I had a lot of time to think about it, when I was locked up. The cult really needed my baby. They were waiting for me to get pregnant. Only I was taking the pill and they didn't know that.'

'So your little friend probably sabotaged it.'

'Only I never left her alone with my bag. You're the only one who had access to it.'

'Lucy, don't blame me because you couldn't take your pill on time,' Marshal said. 'That's on you.'

'I did take it on time. Same time, every day. Religiously,' I said. 'Because I didn't want to get pregnant. Ever. Same time. Every day. I checked every medicine I took to see if it would interfere with it. I even took the dummy pills to make sure I started the new pack on time. So it's sort of one coincidence too far for me, that I accidentally got pregnant against all odds, right when the cult wanted my child. Against 99% odds that I wouldn't.'

'Lucy, I don't know what you're saying. You can't think they had some plot to get you pregnant, that I would be involved in that. That's just . . . incredibly hurtful, and paranoid.'

'I know it was you.'

'You cannot be serious—'

'You tampered with my pill, replaced the normal ones with dummy ones from another pack, or a different pill that looked the same. And you stuck it back together with the same glue I took from your office before you started locking the door to keep me out. Maybe so I wouldn't see you tampering with the next pack.'

Marshal said nothing.

'So, I wanted to ask . . .' I swallowed and felt a tear run down my face. 'Why you did it.'

'Did what? Lucy, this is mad—'

'Please don't lie to me,' I said, cutting him off. 'After everything you've done . . . everything I've been through. You owe me the truth. What did you do?'

'Lucy, darling.' I heard him measure every word, like spoonfuls of sugar. 'I did not do anything. It was an accident of probability. That's all. A happy accident.'

I let the words sit there for a second, resting my head against the cool glass of the phone screen.

'You were never a good liar,' I said finally. 'I could always tell. I just wish I could have seen everything else as easily.

All the tiny manipulations. I thought you were this open, genuine, sensitive guy . . . but that was you pushing me. Working me.'

'Lucy, please,' he said, sounding frantic. 'This isn't . . . you can't just accuse me of something like that without evidence. A bit of glue, for God's sake. No one will believe . . .' He stopped short and I felt the change between us in the crackling of the line, the weight of his silence. 'No one is going to believe this insanity. You are going to tell me where you and my child are right now, and I am going to come and fetch you.'

'No.'

'What do you mean, "no"?' he exploded. 'You are my wife and that is my child. I have rights! I can have you in court, you know. I can make sure you never see your baby again if you don't stop this right now, and come home where you belong.'

I let him rant for a while. It was odd, hearing so many threats that didn't hurt me at all. He had nothing I wanted and I had nothing he could take. I already knew I would never see my baby again after this, for her sake. At last, as I funnelled coins into the phone, he paused for breath.

'I'm not coming back, Marshal,' I said. 'I'm going to file for divorce and you are going to grant it. Because if not, I will have to tell people what you did.'

'I didn't—'

'You took away my choice. You used me.'

He was breathing hard, as if fighting against another diatribe.

'You cannot threaten to take away a child that, as far as the world knows, does not exist. I never had a doctor's appointment, never told anyone at work. Only you and your parents know. That doesn't prove anything. There is no birth certificate, yet, and when there is . . . you won't be on it. I

313

saved my daughter from one narcissist sociopath, I'm not giving her to another one.'

'You don't have anything without me,' he snarled. 'You think you'll get a penny in this bloody divorce you want so badly? You'll get nothing. I'll sue for custody and I'll get it too. I am on the council, my dad is an MP. Who are you? Some insane hippy's kid? And no matter what you say, you won't be able to walk away from our child. You'll have to stay. You will. It's your duty – you're her mother. She belongs with us, together. She belongs to me.'

I think that I doubted myself before he said that. Maybe somewhere inside, I wasn't yet set on what I knew I had to do. I wasn't sure I knew for certain what I wanted after all those months of hating the fact I was pregnant, worrying for her future, struggling to save her. Perhaps there was a part of me that thought I was changing, inside, and maybe I did change a little. Despite never wanting to be a mother, I had to be, at least for a while. I protected her and she saved me, in a way. But that time was almost over now. It had to be, for both our sakes.

I felt my response come as naturally as my waters had broken.

'I gave birth to her, but she doesn't belong to me. And she as sure as hell doesn't belong to you.'

He started to shout something but I hung up. My ears rang in the sudden silence.

I looked at the phone sitting there innocently, my sweaty palm print still on it. I set myself free with those words. I realised as I said them that they were true. Still true, after all I went through with her. I wasn't a mother. I never wanted to be one. As much as I cared for the little girl I brought into the world, she wasn't mine. Even if that wasn't the case, even if I wanted to take on that role, I knew it was impossible.

She would never be safe with me. From Marshal. From the cult. The only thing I could do for her was what my mother should have done for me years ago.

I had to let her go.

Chapter Thirty-Nine

The bag arrived a few days later.

I was lying in bed, trying to piece together a plan for myself. I had to leave the hospital before Marshal found me. Before the police came around asking questions. Before Lona or some other insane cult devotee stormed my room to slit my throat. But I couldn't leave before my baby was safe. Before I knew she was going to be protected from all of them. That would be my last job as her mother. The most important one. I had to make sure she would have a good, safe life. Without me.

It all felt hopeless. I had no money and nowhere to go. But I was determined not to go back to Bristol. Back to Marshal. I would sleep in an alley if that's what it took. If I went back there he'd never let me get away again.

As for my baby, the circumstances of my arrival at the hospital helped to set things in motion. I didn't have to work too hard to make the social worker understand that the baby would not be safe with her father. Not that Marshal deserved that title. He wasn't on the birth certificate and I would not give any of his information to the hospital.

The social worker tried to tell me about the help available. Places I could go, schemes that would support me. If I was able to keep my baby, it would have been helpful. But that wasn't to be. It wouldn't have been safe for her.

Nurse Maxwell interrupted my thoughts, bustling in with a familiar holdall in hand. It was my bag from all those months ago at the cottage. I stared at it, unable to imagine how it reached me. Surely Marshal didn't leave it at the cottage once he knew I was missing. That could only mean Ellie had taken it before the ruse had been discovered.

'This was dropped off with main reception. I think they were a bit annoyed about it,' she said, making a face. 'Sounds like it was your sister. Can you not call her and ask her to come in? From the sounds of it she still looks like she's been in the wars.'

I could imagine. Ellie's face was bad the last time I saw her, when the beating was fresh. Now there had been time for the bruising to reach its fullest and darkest. She brought my bag? Did that mean she was still in the area? Where and how was she surviving? What were her plans? I bit my lip, hoping she was all right and that I'd be able to find her, to help, once I was recovered.

'I expect you'll be glad to have some proper pyjamas,' Nurse Maxwell said, reaching as if to open the bag.

'Yes . . . If you don't mind, can I unpack by myself?' I asked, feeling a sudden certainty that whatever was in the bag, it was for my eyes only.

'Of course.' She smiled, albeit slightly uncertainly. 'Let me know if you need anything.'

Once she was gone I unzipped the bag and went through the contents. It did seem to be everything from the cottage: my clothes, toiletries and even the paperbacks I brought along to read. All of it packed neatly and with care. I paused when I turned up the little box that held my mother's pendant.

Just holding it made me shiver. At least I could sell it, as Phoebe intended to do all those years ago.

Underneath the first layer of clothes I found another little box containing the pink pearl necklace. If the gifts were from Marshal, he must have had them delivered to the cottage. I could imagine him ordering present after present, trying to make me forget that I'd been packed off against my will. Several other expensive presents were packed in the bag: a cashmere shawl, sheepskin slippers and a designer perfume. I handled them with an uneasy feeling. All those things were brought to me at the bunker. Did Ellie go back to fetch them? Why?

The answer came via a card about halfway down the bag's contents, on top of a carefully folded sweatshirt. It was made from the back cover of a Nutrisoul brochure and had my name on it in Ellie's handwriting.

I opened the card.

Dear Lucy,

I know you will never forgive me for my part in what happened. I would never ask you to, and even if you did, I will never forgive myself. I betrayed your trust and because of me you could have died. Even after all that, you still came to save me.

I hope this goes a little way to help prove to you that I want to do what's right. It's from the Nutrisoul conventions, everything I could find in the executive wing. I know it's not anywhere near enough to repay you, to make up for everything. But it's a start. I hope you can use it for something to make you happy.

You will not see me again. As soon as I leave this bag for you, I will be going to the police with everything I know and all the information I could find in Selene's office. There are still so many people out

*there like me who have been lied to. They deserve to
know the truth. The others, like Lona, deserve to
be punished for what they've done. I deserve to be
punished. I will keep your name out of it, but I suspect,
if I know you like I think I do, that you will be long
gone by the time they come looking. I'm glad. You
deserve a fresh start. I'm only sorry it took so long for
you to get one.*

*I hope that once I'm known to the police, they will
find my mum, if she's still alive, and let her know I am
safe. Thanks to you.*

*I want to see her again. To tell her it wasn't her fault,
that I missed her. Just like I will miss you.*

Thank you for being my sister.
Ellie

I held on to that card long after my eyes were too blurry to
see the words, the rest of the bag's contents forgotten. I could
only look at the words and feel that I was seen. For the first
time, I had a family.

After carefully folding it away, I looked back into the
holdall. I took out the sweatshirt, then froze.

Lining the bottom of the bag were rolls and rolls of bank
notes. Tens and twenties, but mostly fifties, all neatly rolled
and held with elastic bands. Just looking at it I could see that
the bag contained tens of thousands of pounds. The takings
from Nutrisoul, which Ellie had returned to the bunker to
steal. For me.

I wished I could tell her how brave she was – braver than
me – for going back there, for saving me. But I knew I'd
probably never see her again. I hoped she would find her
family and that the court would go easy on her. It would
be too dangerous for me to appear there, to speak in her
defence. But I could send some of the money. I could write.

She deserved her freedom. It took her entire life to get it. Perhaps I'd even see her again one day. I hoped so.

I got out of bed and stretched. They kept me in a little private room, I guess because I looked so awful I'd frighten the wits out of everyone on the ward. It had a little wet room. After peeling off my hospital gown I picked up some of the toiletries, zipped up the bag and went for a shower. My first one since being taken.

The mirror, screwed to the wall over the tiny sink, showed me a stranger. She was scrawny and soft in all the wrong places, at once malnourished and bloated. My skin was fish-belly pale from so long without sunlight. My wrists and ankles still bore the marks of restraints, and there were minute speckles of burn marks on my skin from the sparks that had flown as the ceiling collapsed at the manor. My hair, which had become thicker during the pregnancy, was shedding everywhere. I looked like a ghoul. But I felt better than I had in ages.

Still sore, I indulged in a long shower. The water was tinged with dried blood, but nothing bled anew. My long rest helped me to heal a bit. Though my ankle still twinged a little where it had been set without skill. My leg and back had never been broken. There were mere scratches on my hip from the fall, not surgery. Another lie to keep me under control.

I was done being lied to.

Once clean and dressed in clothes from the bag, I brushed out my hair. It had become overly long once again. It curled around my shoulders in reddish-brown ringlets, which would dry to their normal rusty colour. I had hated the look of it straight, all frizzy and dry. I would never have to wear it that way for Marshal again.

I looked normal enough when clothed. Most of the signs of what I'd been through were hidden away. I looked certain, controlled. In a way I never had before. I tried to remember the aphorisms I stuck up over my bathroom mirror in Bristol, but I found that I couldn't.

When Nurse Maxwell returned she saw me up and dressed and smiled.

'Looks like you're feeling more yourself.'

'I am. Thank you,' I said.

'That social worker, Charlotte, she's here to see you again.'

I nodded. 'Tell her to come up.'

'You're sure?'

'Yes,' I said, meeting her cautious gaze. 'I am.'

I asked to see her before I left.

The baby was curled up in a plastic cradle, brought into my room by Nurse Maxwell. A piece of paper taped to it said 'Baby Girl Andrews'. I stood looking down at her in her white babygrow, thrashing her mittened fists. Her face was less red and angry-looking now. It had smoothed out and cooled to a pale pink. Her hair had also lost its fire, turning reddish blonde. Perhaps it had been a trick of the blood that made it look like mine.

'Would you like to hold her?' the nurse asked.

She lifted the baby into my arms and then stood back and looked at me. It was as if she were expecting a kind of magical transformation. Like Cinderella's rags bursting into a wave of sparkles, turning into a gown. But it was just me, holding a baby. We remained separate, not transforming into that unit – mother and baby.

I looked down at her face and she looked up at me. Serious blue eyes squinting as if trying to place me. Nurse Maxwell closed the door gently, giving me some privacy.

I felt, bizarrely, as if I should say something. It seemed somehow rude to be leaving without so much as a 'hello'. I knew that she wouldn't remember me. She would likely never know I'd existed as anything other than a concept. I wasn't leaving anything for her, no letter or memento. She would be safer that way.

I think the social worker thought what I was doing was cruel. Maybe it was, a little. In the way a surgery is cruel. The radical removal of something that doesn't belong. But it was for the best and she would heal. If I had a gift to give, it wasn't a picture or a birthstone or a letter, just the freedom from a legacy of despair and misplaced devotion, freedom from my mother's followers and Marshal. She would be wholly herself, raised by parents who wanted her.

I would miss her. The way I would miss Ellie. The way I missed the idea of having a mother. I would think of her in a year, in five, in ten. I would always know she was out there. I knew that even when I was old and sitting in some care home somewhere, with all my life lived out, I would think of her and hope she was living a good life, a wonderful life. We shared something and, even if I wasn't going to be her mother, it made her someone very special to me, someone who would always own a piece of my heart.

I let her cling to my finger and smiled when she pulled. She was lovely. Looking at her I thought she deserved everything in the world, every kindness and opportunity, every choice. I hoped she would have them. I hoped she would know how lucky she was if she did.

When Nurse Maxwell returned I handed her over and watched as she was taken back to the nursery. Our time together was over. I had a new life to live now and so did she. Hopefully a better life, for both of us, than we would have had together.

No one stopped me on my way out of the hospital. I looked like a visitor or someone taking a bag of dirty clothes home. Dressed in my own things and toting the holdall I took the lift to the ground floor and walked into town. I felt light and free, blessed. I had my purse with me and my driving licence. I had looked up how to get a replacement passport. I wasn't going to wait on Marshal beginning divorce proceedings. He was never going to let that happen. So I was going to do the next best thing and vanish.

The newspapers I passed outside a tiny shop had new headlines, new scandals. Mine had finally withered and died. I knew it was only a short reprieve. Ellie's story would make it to the front page soon. I had no doubt about that. But by then I'd be gone.

On a whim I popped into a small art shop on a backstreet. I spent a pleasant half hour debating my choices. Lingering over them as if they were chocolates to be savoured. I walked away with a glossy bag containing a fat new sketchbook, pencils, watercolours and clean, new brushes. Anticipation coiled in me as ideas presented themselves. Images begging to be laid down on paper: dark woods, an evil queen in flowing robes, a baby girl in a basket woven by faerie fingers, a girl in white slaying a fiery dragon.

Walking through town looking for a place to stop for a while, I felt the weight of the pendant in my coat pocket. My mother's moon necklace tangled with the pink pearl Marshal had given me. I didn't want to take them with me. I didn't want to even look at them anymore. I looked across the market square and saw a church on the other side. It seemed as good a place as any to be rid of them forever.

Inside the church, I looked over the statues and plaques, enjoying the silence. The whole place was empty, cool and dry. The sound of my footsteps carried, echoing off the walls. At the far end of the church, in the shadows by a fire door, I saw a name that made me stop in my tracks, a laugh caught in my throat.

I left the necklaces on the shrine of St Lucy and walked away.

I stopped in at a café and waited by the counter. Whilst I stood there, I shifted the holdall from hand to hand. The bag wasn't heavy, yet it contained every possibility I could have ever wished for. I'd counted the money and there was a lot more than I first thought. Enough to travel on, for a while. I didn't care much about grand hotels and first-class flights. I just wanted to go, to see everything out there that had been waiting for me for so long.

I stepped up to the counter and ordered myself a coffee, double shot, with syrup. By the time it came, I'd made myself comfortable by the window. The barista set it down just as I sent an email enquiring about a campervan on sale. Not too big or luxurious, but capable of taking me to France and on to wherever I decided to venture after. A little dented, a bit cramped, but cosy enough for one.

Acknowledgements

Firstly, as always, a great big thank you to my family for being so supportive during this whole process. For listening to ideas you didn't understand for a plot you'd only been half informed of. For generally providing nods and 'I sees' until I disappeared back into my room. And for tea and coffee, which is always appreciated, if sometimes left to go cold by accident.

A huge thank you to my agent, Laura Williams, for her input on the story and encouragement. As well as to everyone at Greene and Heaton for their hard work, especially Kate Rizzo, for helping to navigate COVID-19 delays to paperwork and the vagaries of Royal Mail.

Thank you as well to my amazing editor Cara Chimirri for seeing my last novel into port whilst also tackling this one. I've felt in safe hands from day one and this book wouldn't be half the novel it is without your suggestions and queries pushing it further. Another big thanks to the Avon team for their amazing work on the cover and marketing.

I owe Rachel Faulkner-Willcocks for her advice on *The Thirteenth Girl* as well. It was a pleasure to work with you. All the best for the future.

A big thank you to Ware Library for the use of their study space, Wi-Fi and resources. You are an invaluable service that should not go unappreciated. (I am very sorry if you get a police visit because of that one time I googled 'best home tools for removing fingers'. I promise, it was work related.)

Lastly, I would like to thank everyone who read my debut novel and reviewed it or recommended it to others; book lovers, bloggers, new and old friends and especially those in my home village, who probably now own 80% of the signed copies worldwide. I really appreciate your help in spreading the word on *Stranded* and I hope you enjoyed this novel too!

Eight strangers. One island. A secret you'd kill to keep.

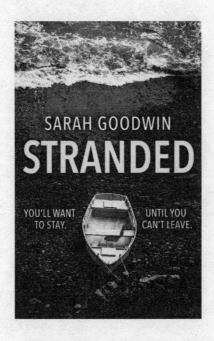

A gripping, twisty page-turner about secrets, lies and survival at all costs. Perfect for fans of *The Castaways*, *The Sanatorium* and *One by One*.